OUR ROGUE FATES

A Novel

SARAH GLENN MARSH

alcove press

For a complete list of content warnings, please see the author's website at www.sarahglennmarsh.com. Take care.

Books should be disposed of and recycled according to local requirements. All paper materials used are FSC compliant.

This is a work of fiction. All of the names, characters, organizations, places and events portrayed in this novel are either products of the author's imagination or are used fictitiously. Any resemblance to real or actual events, locales, or persons, living or dead, is entirely coincidental.

Published in the United States by Alcove Press, an imprint of The Quick Brown Fox & Company LLC.

Alcove Press and its logo are trademarks of The Quick Brown Fox & Company LLC.

Library of Congress Catalog-in-Publication data available upon request.

ISBN (hardcover): 979-8-89242-429-5
ISBN (paperback): 979-8-89242-430-1
ISBN (ebook): 979-8-89242-431-8

Cover design by Olivia Hintz

Printed in the United States.

www.alcovepress.com

Alcove Press
34 West 27th St., 10th Floor
New York, NY 10001

First Edition: April 2026

The authorized representative in the EU for product safety and compliance is eucomply OÜPärnu mnt 139b-14, 11317 Tallinn, Estonia, hello@eucompliancepartner.com, +33757690241

10 9 8 7 6 5 4 3 2 1

Praise for *Our Rogue Fates*

"I know a little something about finding treasure and maps of consequence . . . who knew that when Sam and Frodo came together, the skill would come in handy? *We Could Be Antiheroes* is such a treasure for you."

—Sean Astin, Samwise Gamgee

"An unusual take on Tolkien."

—John Rhys-Davies, Gimli

"Morally gray romance has a new queen! Sarah Glenn Marsh weaves a sweeping adventure set in a fantastic world with characters you won't know whether to root for or hide your gold from."

—Sara Raasch, *New York Times* and *USA Today* bestselling author of *The Nightmare Before Kissmas*

"A delicious second-chance epic romantasy, *Our Rogue Fates* is filled with loveable queer characters, a haunted swamp, and a quest for treasure that will keep you glued to the pages."

—Elayna R. Gallea, bestselling author of *Tethered*

"Sarah Glenn Marsh whisks you away to a new romantasy world with an immersive, enemies-to-lovers quest that'll have you holding your breath at every twist and turn, cheering for second chances, and fanning yourself from the heat—an epic story of love worth treasuring that'll stay in your heart long after the last page!"

—Matthew Hubbard, critically acclaimed author of *The Last Boyfriends Rules for Revenge*

"A heart-pounding adventure through the messy mire of family, friendship, and love. Sarah Glenn Marsh weaves a tale at once new and hauntingly familiar, where it's not the ghosts in the wood to fear, but the ones living in our hearts."

—Fiona Fenn, author of *The Crack at the Heart of Everything*

"Absolutely enchanting! *Our Rogue Fates* is a lush, romantic story with a diverse cast of characters, exquisite world-building, and a heart-pounding adventure that meant I couldn't turn the pages fast enough. I was hooked from the very first page."

—Jenna Wolfhart, author of *Forged by Magic*

"This enchanting, cunning, gorgeously romantic trek through the mire is equal parts addictive and dangerous. Guard your treasure and your heart."

—Amber Hart, author of *Wicked Charm*

"Monsters, a diverse cast of flawed but lovable characters, and a romance not even a swamp could dull the shine on. Sarah Glenn Marsh delivers an epic adventure along with a beautiful romance that left me finishing the book and wishing for another few hundred pages. I'm not sure I have the skills needed to survive in this world, but I would sure love the opportunity to try."

—J.J. Mulder, author of the Offsides and SCU Hockey Series

"*Our Rogue Fates* is a delightful read! The fantasy, the romance, the nods to Tolkien, this book has it all."

—Don Marshall, the Obscure Lord of the Rings Facts Guy and author of *J.R.R. Tolkien: The Father of Modern Fantasy*

"A sizzling queer romantasy that will send your heart on the quest of a lifetime. Sarah Glenn Marsh weaves atmospheric danger, morally gray characters, and achingly tender longing into an unforgettable tale. Griff and Mal's journey is messy, beautiful, and utterly unputdownable.

—TJ Rose, author of the *Killigrew Street Case Files*

"*Our Rogue Fates* is the book I've been waiting my whole life for. Epic, unapologetically queer and filled with characters I'll never forget – this book is both a sweeping adventure in a totally new world and a dangerously addictive romance. Fans of *The Lord of the Rings* and M/M Romance - get ready for your new obsession."

—Cale Dietrich, internationally bestselling author of *My Roommate from Hell* and co-author of *If This Gets Out*

"Sarah Glenn Marsh's romantic fantasy debut can be summed up in one word: fun! Her cast of flawed, funny characters made me want to round up my friends for a chaotic game of D&D… and then those same characters made me wince when their insecurities hit a little too close to home. Bursting with humor and heart, *Our Rogue Fates* is cozy, funny, spicy, and So Damn Real."

—S. M. Hallow, author of *The Halls of the Dead*

For those of us who carry on the story.

To Gnomish Lands
Thundering Woods
W
E
S
Farmland
Farmland
Goldenwood Gardens and Ranch
Widow Isabel's Land
To Dwarven Lands
Farmland
Barcombe
The Goatleafs Bakery
Linden
Mayfair
Appleby
Served With Love
The Wyvern and Wyrm
Charmed Creek
Strathmore
The Greatway
The Blue Depths
The Lonely Channel
Thrallkeld
The Fens
A World

Stormveil
Rook's Rest
Wolfwater township
Flaring hills
To Cardraine, Greatest Kingdom of Men
Wyvern's Covert
Old stone watchtower
Rotrose Mire
chest of silvers
Wyvern's nest
Troll cave
he Plains of Plenty
Rushing Rill
The Crooked Teeth
Emerald River
Mirror's Edge township
To Halfling Lands
Rogues

Chapter One
A Knife in the Dark

Griff Sayer had always known his family was going to be the death of him, though he didn't imagine it would happen quite so violently.

An early heart attack, perhaps, from the stress of his seemingly inseverable ties with thieves and extortionists and worse. An accident at work due to a distraction, maybe, like when he hammered his fingers last week upon hearing that his ex–best friend Mal was back in town again. A self-inflicted wound as he relived his worst, most painful moments, a slip of a knife that turned out to be too dull—well, he'd already been there. Even a covert poisoning wasn't out of the question, something untraceable slipped into a drink handed to him by a fan after a performance at the Maiden's Arms to silence him for knowing any number of things he shouldn't.

Being stabbed was, all things considered, fairly low on Griff's list of ways he'd thought he'd go out.

It also hurt a hell of a lot more than his adoptive mother had led him to believe over the years when she'd shown off her many grisly battle scars and lectured him on the most effective ways to survive torture.

But Wynnie wasn't there with him in the Wyrmwood on this brisk spring night among the trolls and orcs and other things that worshiped the shadows. She wasn't there to frown at the way he whimpered, so undignified, as he clutched the gushing wound off to the side of his abdomen with both hands and sank to his knees in a bed of leaves and bracken while the stars watched from on high. She might as soon have shouted at him to get up and chase after his masked assailants as smoothed his waves of dark hair back from his sweaty face with a tender hand and reassured him all would soon be well.

Lady Wraith, people called her in the city and far beyond. Famed for her obsidian eyes, her predator's stare, her mess of scars . . . and, most notably, her frequent victories against death. So many she didn't seem to belong to this world or to the shadow realm. It had always seemed to Griff like a fine line to walk, having one foot in each world; somehow, she made it look easy.

Dying outright was, he had to admit, surprisingly difficult; his stubborn heart was still pumping fast and strong, though that was spilling more of his innards into his shaking hands. He fell back against the forest floor as his head spun, still having enough presence of mind to keep holding pressure to the wound the way he'd been taught.

Wynnie would want details later, he knew, so she could take matters into her own hands. And he would give them to her, all except the part where the bandits had gotten the jump on him because, while he was supposed to be on watch, he had been drinking. About Mal.

Again.

Griff could have sworn he had seen him at the market the other day, a tall and slim figure just the same height, with hair a certain dark shade of gold—only it had turned out to be his own boyfriend, Liam, the one who was a dead ringer for Mal in the right light.

He raised his head a fraction and tried to count his assailants.

Three, four, five—oh, not five. Four. The fifth person clad in black was smaller than the rest. Her pale, angular face was unmasked, a gash welling on her cheek, strands of black hair ripped from the two neat knots on either side of her head where she usually kept it bound. She was fighting all four masked figures at once with her sword and staff, a whirlwind of devastation to anyone who found themselves within her reach as she stabbed and slashed and threw elbows.

He'd come here with Vic, his other childhood guardian. Wynnie's wife. She was soft where Wynnie was hard—which, growing up, had made one of them far easier to love, and was the reason he had agreed to this trip to help her check her hunting traps in the first place—but she was almost as fierce in battle. Even four to one, he knew in his bones that she wasn't outmatched.

The bandits quickly fled before her swift and silent rage, melting back into the shadows of the Wood. They must have gotten whatever they'd come for, perhaps not solely Griff's life after all—one of his packs was dangling from the hand of a fleeing figure.

The moment they turned and vanished, Vic dropped her sword and staff and bolted toward Griff, fear flashing in her gray eyes as she fell to the ground and pressed a small, warm hand to the side of his face.

Up close, he saw her tears.

Vic never cried, not that Griff had seen. Mostly, she was quiet, or else she teased and laughed in her soft, private way, only around those she trusted.

"Griff, stay with me," she pleaded, smoothing sweat-slicked curls back from his forehead. "No, no, no, no . . ."

The fear in her wide, whitish eyes was turning to outright panic, and Griff wondered if their masked attackers had done something to her that he hadn't witnessed on account of bleeding out and all.

Orcs had hurt her more than once before she fled her homeland, and she still flinched in proximity to most men, even human ones. Even now, unless she had a weapon in hand.

He tried to ask what had happened to her, but all that came from his throat was a wet gurgle. More blood.

Then darkness.

"It's all gone," Vic breathed. She had, in the brief moment Griff had apparently flirted with unconsciousness, dumped out what looked to be the contents of all the bags they had brought with them, most carefully packed by Griff himself. "Bastards took everything—all our bandages and salves. Our rations too."

That was inconvenient. He would have appreciated a bandage about now.

Seeming to have pushed through the worst of her shock, Vic gathered herself enough to start reaching for the things they still had at hand, like somebody's change of clothes. "We need to pack the wound, slow the bleeding," she muttered to herself, clearly thinking Griff was too far gone to hear.

He managed to slur a protest. "Fine."

Vic's gray eyes darted back to his; he knew she had heard that line from him often enough to be weary of it, and she had never once believed him. She shook her head. "This isn't fine. You're not fine. Nothing will ever be *fine* again if we don't get you some help . . ."

Griff didn't see what all the fuss was about; he could hardly feel the wound anymore. That had to be a good sign; perhaps the bleeding was slowing. Besides, they were deep in the Wyrmwood, at least a few days' march from Linden, their boot-scrape of a village on the outskirts of Mayfair. There was no way to reach help in the case of a near-fatal event, which was why Griff had so thoughtfully packed a full healer's kit.

"Not my son," Vic sobbed, tears and blood streaking her face. She rarely called him that.

Her finger pushed into Griff's neck, seeking a pulse, but while he felt the weight and chill of her touch, he didn't see her anymore.

He was in another part of the Wood altogether now, closer to home, and it was a riot of summer's green overgrowth. The air was like honey, thick with humidity and sweet. Birds were singing. The muddy ground was a confusion of centaur tracks and dogs' paw prints. Nearby, in the bracken just out of sight, one was barking.

"Griff, please." Someone interrupted the dog's fuss, perhaps somewhere behind him, their voice breaking.

He almost turned to see who it was.

But now, standing before him was Mal—not the twenty-six-year-old surly asshole he'd spent the last several years avoiding but the closest friend he'd ever had, a skinny boy of twelve or thirteen with tawny skin, messy blond hair, and an imp's wide grin—and Griff had missed him more than he could put into words.

"Are you two coming or what?" Alys called from just up ahead, out of sight. She was the third in their trio, the keeper of their secrets and the only other person who knew what it was like growing up in the immense and often unwelcoming shadow of heroes.

Mal reached out a beckoning hand, and that was all the invitation Griff needed to step off into a warm, sunlit afternoon with his best friends at his side, heading to their favorite swimming hole and making plans to race their little wooden boats. Just like old times.

Chapter Two
Too Bad

It was fine, really, that the Widow Isabel's house never smelled particularly good. Sometimes you couldn't wait for the stars to align—you just got on with it. Blood, sweat, tears, and momentum.

Mal Pryce knew that lesson like he knew the weight of his favorite knife in his hand; he was always doing what was necessary, though it rarely felt heroic. If he didn't, who would?

Leaning back in his chair at the widow's small kitchen table away from his mug of untouched tea, he tried his best not to breathe in that slightly floral, nauseating cocktail of soaps and faint decay that always seemed to permeate the dwelling of anyone very old and ill. The scent of looming death caught in his shoulder-length tangles of dark-gold hair would haunt him for the rest of the night.

It was nature. It was fated.

Life was short, fast, and brutal, and no one knew it better than he did.

One day, he was seventeen and thought he had the world: the loving two-parent household (even if Vic and Wynnie weren't his real mothers and Wynnie had a tendency to fight first and ask questions later). He had a promising line on a job (with people who had been his dead parents' enemies, but wasn't that just the way of things? Money was money, no matter whose pocket it came from). He had two loyal best friends—until Griff told him that he was nothing to him and left Mal breathless and shaking on the living room floor when he stormed out, the beginning of years of silence and bitterness between them, something too broken to mend.

And the next day, Alys was leaving too, their once-unshakable trio fully dissolved. She was off to carve out her own reputation and make her mother proud, and she said she needed to do it alone.

She had vowed to him that she would never leave Mayfair, but people said things all the time and rarely meant them. Griff and Alys had both promised him long ago that the three of them would always be together. That they would always keep Mal safe from the wider world.

Empty words.

They had been his world. Nothing was safe.

Blink again, and he was down in the lawless, ruined city of Thrallkeld, far south of Mayfair, attempting to make a name for himself that had nothing to do with his dead parents, his adoptive ones, or the best friends he had only thought he had.

Leaving home for a place where he trusted no one and no one trusted him made perfect sense. Down there, he was a half-starved, gold-sick boy in a thief's den, someone's hand always in his pocket while he was busy cutting their purse. He weathered betrayal after betrayal, because something about it had become warm and familiar after a while.

Blink, and he was under a thief-lord's knife, screaming with the worst pain he had ever known as the gangster carved up his chest for challenging him—no, that had been the second-worst pain. Worst of all was the certainty that no one was coming for him; the death of the tiny hope he'd been holding all along that Griff would come for him. He was utterly alone.

Blink. He was half alive in a witch's cottage, being spoon-fed bone broth while he tried not to inhale the pungent scent of the poultice packing the grisly wound on his chest and did his best to avoid looking at the shadowy figures skulking about on the lawn—the spirits he could now see after having brushed shoulders with death. A curse, as far as he was concerned: punishment from the gods for his unlikely survival.

Blink. He was back in Mayfair, a dog with its tail tucked between its legs, returning to the only home he had ever known because he couldn't think where else to go. He had failed in Thrallkeld. Failed at his dream of becoming king of the thieves. He was lucky his former employers still had a job for him—that all the skills he had honed in that ruined city made him more of an asset than ever.

Blink. Alys was home, carrying with her the weight of a reputation she hadn't truly earned and a highborn boyfriend who didn't truly fit her, and somehow they found their way back to friendship. Soon after, Griff was back from living with the elves—like he was so much better than other mere mortals—and they had nothing to say to each other with missing years in the way. But sometimes they came to blows, until Mal could hardly remember all the hurt that lay underneath. Those old feelings, the trust and tenderness and something bigger, something more than he had ever felt for another living soul—he'd taken them and buried them deep, shoved them underwater where there was no light or air so he didn't have to walk around in the worst pain he'd ever known every single day.

Blink again and he was in the Widow Isabel's house on a chilly spring evening, dropping around for tea after dinner as he did once a week these days. The old woman had put him on the deed to all the land north of Mayfair she wouldn't be using, and he wanted to keep it that way. He was a businessman, and that meant having leads on any number of potential sources of income at any time. His employers didn't need to know about any hustling he did on the side.

The widow's teacup rattled as she set it in her saucer, and Mal pretended to take a bite of a dusty lavender shortbread cookie as his keen gray eyes studied the crow's-feet at the corners of her washed-out blue ones.

He had never much cared for crows or ravens, the gossipy birds who skulked in dark, hidden places and served as spies for the Shadow Queen. Even if she was, technically speaking, his boss's boss. He had once had the fleeting and overly whimsical notion that the birds might keep him safe as long as he was working for her, but that illusion had shattered long ago. As far as he was concerned, he'd made it this far because he kept himself safe.

"You sure like my cookies, dear," Isabel observed in her reed-thin voice, giving Mal a strained smile. "Why don't I pack you a few for the road?"

Mal nodded, already growing restless. The moon was rising; it was nearly time for him to head in to work for the evening. His real job.

Accepting the cloth-wrapped bundle of dry cookies, he saw himself out and headed down the winding lane, a quiet shadow in the lamplit streets that led from Isabel's place to the green-and-white-striped cloth awning of a storefront that was, like all the shops around it, dark and closed up for the night.

Slipping a small key from his belt, he unlocked the door.

Fetching a silver flask from the breast pocket of his cloak—just as he'd done at the Widow Isabel's, where he'd poured a healthy splash into his tea in case he needed to take a sip for politeness' sake—he drank a few greedy gulps of whiskey. Licking a drop from his lip, he checked that the street was more or less empty before darting inside.

Served With Love was technically a tea shop, selling brews by the cup as well as bags of blended herbs, but the real business went on in the cellar beneath the cozy café. The shop was a front for a network of the Shadow Queen's agents, a place where they laundered their money and harbored stolen goods with the aim of helping the mysterious, power-hungry ruler secure a stronger foothold in the world. Mal didn't give a damn about their cause and whether they succeeded or failed, only that they paid better than most other places, and that as long as he got their goods safely to where they were supposed to be, they didn't ask him too many questions about his personal life. Such as it was.

Tonight, the shop was quieter than usual. Only Alanna—who preferred to go by her chosen name, Guts—was working down below, unpacking crates of contraband by the light of a single lantern. Her ruddy-blond hair fell over her shoulder in a tidy braid, and she was wearing a crisp blue dress with white embroidery on the sleeves, no doubt having worked a shift up front before the place officially "closed" for the day.

Mal had known her since his days in Thrallkeld. She had once run an underground club in the basement of a crumbling stone manor where people fought for prize money, though she seemed to prefer dressing up and playing shopkeeper these days, as if something about selling tea to Mayfair's citizens appealed to a girlish dream she'd had for her life.

As Mal descended into the cool, dim room, he called by way of greeting, "Think they killed that poor bastard yet?"

"Given that you had a hand in the planning, Mister Dangerous, he's probably feeding the worms as we speak," Guts answered, a little laugh in her voice as she pulled something heavy from one of the crates.

With training, Mal had won every fight he'd entered at her club, and when Guts moved up to Mayfair, she'd brought his old nickname with her.

"Well then, tomorrow we'll be celebrating over dinner," Mal remarked, a smirk on his lips as he recalled past dinners with his employers, no different at all than any other society gathering despite their dirtier hands. "Maybe you'll get to see how far I can throw a piece of Fern's dry chicken down May Hill." He snorted softly. "Bet it bounces."

Several of the shop's usual after-hours occupants were out on a mission tonight. They planned to take out someone who knew too much about what went on at the tea shop—probably a nosy Warden, one of those noble knights forever locked in a battle against the Shadow Queen's forces of darkness.

Bunch of moon-eyed idiots.

It was better, Mal had found, to simply accept the darkness rather than try to fight it and likely die in the process, as whoever his less-than-esteemed colleagues were murdering in the Wyrmwood tonight was finding out. In the dark, one could still live.

Too bad being a hero meant certain death; just look at the parents he had never known. Look at Rhun, the most storied Warden of all. He had been Wynnie's husband, the man who had helped raise him along with Griff and Alys until he disappeared.

Too bad nobody ever asked for Mal's opinions on these things. He knew quite a lot for his twenty-six years.

Too bad for whoever was bleeding out right now; Mal had plotted out the attack himself. As usual, he hadn't been given a name, but he didn't need one. He had the intended victim's dates of travel, their course (the Wyrmwood's best trapping grounds), and their number of companions (one), which was all he needed to make it look like a petty theft. It was one of those neat lessons he had picked up in Thrallkeld that made him so useful here.

Too bad they hadn't asked him to do the stabbing. Years into his service, yet he wasn't high enough in the ranks to carry out the job. And they had bigger, tougher thugs for that. Still, he was quick and efficient with his hunting knife and never hesitated. Just like Wynnie. Sure, she wasn't his real mother, but he had listened to her all these years as if she were—listened and taken her lessons to heart, even when he knew Griff and Alys weren't paying attention—and he had honed in himself a ruthlessness that made her proud.

Too bad for those on the mission, Mal and Guts would get first pick of everything in these crates. Even if it was all supposed to be loaded onto a caravan headed south toward the Shadow Queen's hidden stronghold once the contents were inventoried.

"Find anything good yet?" Mal asked Guts, bumping his shoulder against hers with comfortable familiarity before he took a seat on one of the unopened crates and sipped deeply from his flask. The whiskey stung his throat like irony.

"Couple nice bits of crockery. Assorted poisons. Coffee. Some crystal flowers," Guts listed off as she inspected some small packets of a shimmering, pale-blue powder. Her frown made it clear that she didn't consider the coffee or flowers much good at all, that she found them about as appealing as the packets of poison she now held in her hands. "They're dwarven make, though, the flowers. Probably fetch a small fortune from the right buyer. You going to help with any of this or just sit there looking pretty all night?"

Mal shrugged, pulling out one of Isabel's cookies and taking a stale bite. He laid the rest on the crate so Guts could help herself. "Where are the flowers? I'll take them if you don't," he said, starting to search around for them.

Guts flipped her braid over her shoulder, cut him a knowing look, and set the packets of poison aside. Then she pulled out a bundle wrapped in heavy muslin cloth from the crate and started to unwrap it with the air of presenting Mal with the spoils from another winning fight. A few of the amethyst petals had small chips and scratches, but most of the flowers were in excellent shape to his trained eye.

The part of him that loved shiny things wanted to tuck them into his tattered green jerkin alongside his flask, take them home to his shelf of other such glittering trophies nicked by his quick fingers here and there over the years. Amongst the flowers, there were even a few carved animals, the detailed grooves of their fur as realistic as only dwarven craft could be.

"How 'bout that," Guts said softly, plucking one of the small animals from the meadow of muslin and petals and holding it aloft. It was a griffin. "Just like the mark tonight: Griffin. Must be a sign you did something right."

She pressed the smooth crystal carving into Mal's hand, but his fingers didn't wrap around it like he meant them to. He couldn't make out what Guts was saying either—something about how he ought to take this home. How he'd earned it.

The statue slid from his slick palm and shattered on the floor, but rather than curse and grab a dustpan, Mal grabbed his flask and drained it, willing the whiskey to burn every last feeling out of him. "Kage told you his name, did he? The boss sharing insider secrets with you now?" Griffin wasn't exactly a common name, but still, he had to be sure before the nauseating wave of agony rising up inside him could completely devour him. "Griffin . . . Sayer, was it?"

It had been so long since he had spoken that name out loud to anyone.

"Dunno," Guts said, uncertainty slithering across her face as she took in the crumbs of glass on the floor in combination with Mal's shaking hands. "Some hero's son, he said. I was eavesdropping from inside the tea cupboard when they were gearing up to leave, so I didn't catch everything. Anyway, what's it matter? It's done. *You* don't have to fight him. I'm more worried about you damaging the merchandise."

He wasn't sure how much time passed before Guts prompted again, "Mal?" No nickname, which was unusual. He wondered if she could sense it in him, the crack that had just opened to let a little of the pain he'd been drowning in for so long scream into the world again.

She was right. He *was* Mister Dangerous, and there wasn't a damn thing to admire about it. He didn't want any of this, this sudden, crushing guilt that made it a battle just to breathe. He'd had no idea that Griff was the target of the attack, or he would have insisted on going with them. Insisted just so he could slit every single one of their throats before they had a chance to raise a blade against the man who had once been his best friend, who still mattered to him even though Mal had done everything he could to strip Griff's existence of any meaning in his life.

Griff and Alys were his world.

He couldn't just unmake his whole world.

He was seventeen and shaking on the living room floor again. Griff was ranting about how Mal had betrayed him. Let his dead parents down, disgraced them all by working for the Shadow Queen, some dark sorcerer who hid her decaying features behind a gilded mask. He *did* care that Griff was looking at him like he didn't know him. That he was telling Mal they were nothing to each other from now on, calling Mal a traitor, his eyes red and his voice full of a hurt Mal didn't recognize.

Griff's eyes had been red since the day before, when he'd walked in on Mal kissing some girl in his room at the cottage for the first time, trying new things.

But Mal didn't have time to wonder what that meant, or even time to defend himself more than by shouting a few curses and petty insults back at Griff before the person he trusted most in this life was gone. It had seemed so easy for Griff to leave him behind, like Mal had never really mattered to him at all, like he was worth nothing in the end. Like he was just a stain on Griff's boot.

Griff was so sure, even back then, that the Wardens were right to fight the Queen, that his purpose—and Alys's, and Mal's—should be to join the battle the way their parents had. Give up their precious life for it, like there couldn't be anything else worth living for.

When they made their way back to Mayfair six years ago, Griff had been quick to judge his new scars, his new swagger, his new sneer. Mal had wanted to fight him, had grown so used to fighting in Thrallkeld that he had found everything to insult about the other man. His clothes, his boyfriend of the week, the elves he cared more about than he ever had Mal. Over the site of their parents' graves, he had mocked and goaded Griff into breaking his nose, and he had given Griff his first black eye in return.

Every time his fist landed, every time his scathing words pierced Griff's armor like barbs, Mal somehow felt worse, until the whiskey helped him to feel nothing at all.

He had come to rely on Griff to let him down. But the whiskey wasn't helping this time.

Maybe because this time, *he* was the one who had let Griff down.

"Wait, are you seriously leaving me with this mess? Where are you going?" Guts called, her voice ringing with alarm and confusion as Mal raced back up the stairs to the main shop.

"Ate something bad for dinner," he lied without remorse. "Just gonna get some air."

With that, he took a seat on the long counter that faced the front door, skinny legs dangling, knife in hand and not enough whiskey in the world, to wait for his boss's return no matter how long it took. The Shadow Queen's agents had numbers on their side; he'd made sure of that. Which meant that Griff was already dead. And as far as Mal was concerned, that made Kage a walking corpse too, because Mal was going to avenge his fallen friend or die trying. He wouldn't hesitate. He owed Griff that much.

Too bad for his boss that unlike Griff, he was no one's hero. He didn't fight fair, whatever that meant. And he had figured out how to survive in the dark a long time ago. Alone.

Chapter Three
Rabbit Blood

Griff was unraveling, coming undone just like the threads of Mal's sweaters that had gotten stretched too thin at the shoulders from him secretly pulling them on over his own broader frame, back in the days of long ago when he still had hope that they might one day be something more.

He was a collection of songs, images, and feelings, twenty-eight years of them spilling out from between the fingers of those trying their best to hold him together, to prevent his fading away—but it was inevitable, wasn't it?

He could feel little pieces of himself steadily falling like husks of leaves from a dead tree as he sat on a golden shore in the Wood, racing boats with Mal while Alys perched in a tree above them and cheered, fully aware now that he shouldn't be there at all. He let the small boat in his much-larger hand go adrift in the current, whatever phantom Mal was saying to him blending with the rush of water as he tried to focus, to hold tighter to all the things he was before he lost them forever:

A foreman by trade, good with his hands.

A bard by hobby only, because talented musicians were a dime a dozen in Mayfair.

A Warden-in-training, hoping to fight the darkness like his parents before him.

Dog person.

Good cook.

Better lover.

Two years sober—well, until the bender that had landed him here, in the after. He'd never quite decided what he believed would happen beyond death, but then there was hardly a point in guessing when he was clearly about to find out.

Everything went white, quiet, and still.

There was no more phantom Mal. No golden shore.

Then came a babble of distant voices, all familiar, though he couldn't see anyone in the empty, almost-blinding brightness around him.

"Is he going to die?" Alys demanded tearfully, not laughing as she had been in the otherworldly Wood. "I should get Mal. He has to know too. I need to—"

"No!" This voice was deeper, firmer, leaving no room for argument: Liam. "Leave him out of this. He'll only be in the way."

"Infection . . . packed with something filthy . . . his fever . . ." A softer, smoother voice cut in and out, one Griff hadn't heard for a few years now. He couldn't quite place it, though he knew he should be able to.

"I did the best I could with what I had," an older woman relayed wearily. Vic. Where was Wynnie? "Those bandits took everything useful."

"Can you bring him back from the dead?" There was Alys again, sounding much clearer and nearer now, dancing on the edge of hysteria.

The panic in her voice touched some reluctant part of Griff. If he could have felt his fingers, if he could have reached for her, he would have done so for the first time in the achingly long years since their friendship abruptly ended with him fleeing their shared home for good. He would have rubbed her shoulder and pulled her against him like a best friend should, done his best to shield her from the hurt no matter what hurting had happened between them. He wished he could see her face again.

"Nobody's dead yet, so I wish you'd stop fucking saying that," Liam snapped, his voice rough with tears.

Griff could hear him coming undone too, and wanted to sing him one of their songs, something they'd written together on a late giddy night by the hearth shortly after he'd moved into the narrow little house with several locks on the front door. But from wherever he was, he could only listen to Liam's muffled sobs. He would miss Liam's face too, the sandy-blond hair that fell into eyes of light gray flecked with a blue so deep it was almost violet, the proud grin he wore whenever he solved any kind of puzzle, the way he was too humble to realize he was usually the smartest person in the room (except, maybe, when it came to Griff).

He would miss walking beside Vic in the Wood, making birdcalls to delight her, watching her point out flowers and herbs that caught her eye, marveling at the way one who had been raised in such tumult and violence as she had now took such genuine pleasure in simple things, regarding meadows and brooks and flocks of starlings with a childlike wonder.

He would even miss Wynnie. Much as he'd run from her when he was older, they were still connected, bound by years and memory and love for the same people. Chosen family, like his and Mal's and Alys's parents had been to each other—all Wardens but Wynnie, and the best of friends.

But if everyone around him was losing control, there wasn't any hope left for him.

"Griff, my dearest friend . . . come back to us. You're still needed here." The soft, smooth voice he'd heard earlier was now whispering louder inside his mind, and he was ashamed he hadn't been able to place it right away as her features flashed vividly to mind: ruby lips, soft brown skin, and leaf-shaped ears peeking through hair as white as snowdrop petals. It was Princess Rosemaris: only royal daughter of the elves' last stronghold and the person who had saved his life more than once.

Her words somehow dampened the sounds of the others, letting him better focus on finding his way out of this strange bright place and back to himself.

Yet it wasn't her voice but a scent that tugged him finally, unexpectedly, back into his body—that of lavender and lemon balm tea, a brew he'd sipped so many times when ill that he could already taste the floral mixture coating his tongue. And there was something else too, beneath the fragrant herbs: a certain musk mixed with leather, crushed grass, muddy boots, and the gut punch of cheap whiskey.

He'd know that combination anywhere, dead or alive.

"Mal?" Griff asked thickly, not yet opening his eyes in case this was some cruel trick of after-death.

"He's not here," Alys said, sounding less tearful and more exhausted now than when she'd been begging for someone to practice necromancy on his still-warm body.

It made sense, even to his drowsy mind, that he would smell Mal if she was near. Recently, he knew from the town gossip, she had moved back into Wynnie's cottage with her three children after Alys banished their father back to his hometown once she was through with him. And these days she often borrowed Mal's more practical clothes. As if Griff needed any more reminders that she had taken Mal's side in that stupid fight long ago, signaling the end of their friendship too.

Still, his earlier urge to embrace her hadn't fully gone away, and at last he opened his eyes to find he was in bed, propped up on pillows and thoroughly bandaged below the waist in the small one-story row house he shared with Liam Blackthorn, Linden's busiest locksmith and his boyfriend going on four years now.

The light streaming through the curtains had the hazy quality of late afternoon.

It painted Alys's ivory complexion and her lily-pale hair in shades of muted gold as her summer-blue eyes gazed into his, her head resting half on his pillow, so close their breathing was in sync. "Welcome back. How do you feel?" she asked, touching a few fingers to the side of his face like they hadn't just gone years without speaking. Like he'd been there for birthdays and Yules and to offer congratulations on the birth of her newest daughter—what would it have been, a year ago? Maybe two? And condolences (or perhaps more congratulations) on sending the children's father packing when she realized she wanted something else from life.

"I feel . . . numb, mostly, below the bandages," he answered finally, his voice gravelly with disuse. "Maybe that's a mercy." He could feel the contours of Liam's body pressed against his back but didn't turn away from Alys to check on him yet, fully captivated by the strangeness of seeing her here. "How long have I been out? Where's Vic?"

More than anything—more than lavender-lemon tea, a hug from Liam, or extra bandages—he needed to apologize to her for being a drunken fool when he was supposed to be the one on watch keeping them safe.

"Vic's home resting—she's not hurt, just worried. You've been out for just over a week," Alys murmured, pushing a few ringlets of raven hair back from his slightly damp brow; his curls were getting long enough to brush the tops of his shoulders, longer than they had been the last time they were this close. "According to the calendar, anyway. Feels more like a year. Don't move—Rosemaris said you're not supposed to put any strain on your stitches yet, and you won't be able to feel them with the numbing balm on there. I'll get you some water."

"Rosemaris?" Griff echoed roughly, reaching thoughtlessly to put a hand on Alys's forearm before she could pick up the glass on the bedside table. "Rose is here? She's actually *here*?"

For elven royalty to leave the sanctuary of Stormveil, it must have been a matter of life and death indeed.

"She was," Alys said, going still under his touch, staring at his hand on her arm as if something as unexpected as a baby dragon had landed there. Not that there were any dragons anymore. "But she left as soon as she knew you were out of the woods—to hear her tell it, she isn't exactly allowed to leave home."

That was an understatement. He wasn't sure she had ever left, or at least not in the time that he had known her. Few elves ever did.

When he was just nineteen, after fighting with Mal, he had gone to live with Rosemaris and the dwindling population of elves in their hidden sanctuary above the clouds. Stormveil. There were certain perks to having elven royalty for distant relatives—though having them in his bloodline hadn't granted him their incredibly long life, heightened senses, or subtle magics, they had treated him as one of their own, educating him on everything from the arts of healing and speaking their ancient language to why their people had retreated from the world with what remained of their light.

On his other side, Liam began to stir. Griff withdrew his hand from Alys and turned to look at his boyfriend.

The locksmith was curled up with his back to Griff, one arm wrapped snugly around their little red hound dog, Badger, who was still snoring away. Griff rubbed his work-worn fingertips down Liam's back just the way he liked, trying to gentle his rest.

"He hasn't left your side, not once," Alys confided quietly as Liam's eyelids fluttered. "Rosemaris had to give him something to help him sleep a while . . . even though he's not the one you've been asking for in any of your fever dreams."

Him asking for Mal wouldn't have surprised Liam, Griff thought with a guilty twist in his numbed gut. Mal was the reason they had started seeing each other casually in the first place. Liam looked just enough like his old friend that Griff could fuck him from behind in the dark while paying him a pretty price to call him by another name. Always *Right there, Mal* and *Harder, Mal, I need to feel you*. Always Mal.

Of course, Liam didn't have Mal's perpetual sneer curving his lip, and he was far kinder to Griff than Mal had been in many years. Somewhere along the way, Griff had started using Liam's actual name when they tangled together in the dark, and then in the light. Liam stopped taking Griff's money and emptied out a couple of drawers. Griff's late-night visits turned into morning pancakes and tea and kisses that lingered and coming home to each other to write songs by the hearth or go out with their friends. They got a small red dog, called Badger because he was relentless in getting people's attention. They shared their love of music and their histories. Behind the many locks on their front door—put there by Liam to keep out his father's fists—they had been busy building a fine and cozy life.

Pulling Griff back to the present before he could begin to think of how he would make things up to Liam, Alys continued thoughtfully, "Mal hasn't been here. He still doesn't know anything about the attack. I . . . we, rather," she amended, glancing at the restless Liam, "thought it best you decide for yourself what you want to tell him, once you could talk to us."

"I don't want him to know anything," Griff said firmly. He didn't even have to think about it. "He doesn't deserve it."

"*Deserve* is—" Alys started to argue, but after another look at Griff's face, she quickly changed course. "Okay. I understand. But between you and me, there's no denying that you think of him. Often. And he makes sure we hear your name plenty at home, even if perhaps not in ways you'd like. If you would just—"

"How did you know I was in trouble, anyway?" Griff interrupted, trying to get his pulse back under control before it could make him sick. "You, Liam, Rosemaris? Did Vic drag me all the way back here herself and come find you?"

"I dreamed it, actually," Alys admitted, picking at a loose thread on the quilt that covered Griff's legs. "I saw you in the Wood, in the dark, and you were drenched in blood. The shock woke me, and then I felt this pain here . . ." She touched a spot below her navel, just off to one side beneath the belt that held her sword and knives. "And I knew it was real. I found a horse, and Liam and I rode out to get you."

"You just *found* a horse?" Griff asked, the most trivial of questions somehow standing out as important.

Alys smiled sweetly. "Well. I suppose I stole it, if you want to get technical."

There was the Alys he knew. Always taking what she wanted from the world without apology and damn the consequences, just like her mother. She was Wynnie and Rhun's daughter by blood, though they had taken in Griff and Mal when their parents were killed, allowing the three children to grow up under one roof and become the best of friends.

Alys had made quite a name for herself as a mercenary in the past several years, one Griff couldn't escape even from a distance. The Warg of the West, he'd heard her called in every tavern from here to Mayfair proper, because rumor had it that if you happened to be unlucky enough to get closer than the end of her blade, she'd tear you up with her teeth and use her little knives like claws until you were begging for her to end it quickly.

Her mother must be so proud.

But however feral Alys was, however cunning and manipulative and selfish he'd known her to be over the years, she had apparently been certain that something was wrong with someone she loved and been determined to save him at any cost.

Griff was quiet for a moment, trying to let this all sink in. Then he started to protest: "But to come all that way when we haven't—"

"You'd have done the same for me," Alys insisted over him. "That's what friends do."

"Of course I would," he agreed without hesitation. "Whether we're friends or not. Because you're you."

Things grew quiet then, neither of them entirely sure what to do with that after so many years of silence.

Before Griff could figure out what to say that might get them talking again, the bedroom door swung open.

Badger woke at once and wriggled out from under Liam's arm, scampering to the foot of the bed to stare at the newcomer. He didn't bark, but he also didn't wag his tail in its usual frantic pinwheel of welcome.

"Oh, Griff. Finally," Liam's sleep-roughened voice said near his ear. "I missed you so much." Having awoken at last with the dog's sudden movement, Liam buried his face in Griff's hair without even glancing toward the door, and Griff's arm came up around his back at once, pulling him in tighter—stitches be damned.

But before they could really start getting reacquainted, Morwyn Kindrick-Mordecai commanded from the doorway, "Everybody out. Now." Her onyx eyes were unreadable as they settled on Griff's. "I need to speak with my son."

Kicking off her boots as the others departed, Wynnie settled on the bed in the spot Alys had vacated beside the tousled-haired, green-eyed, sharp-jawed man who didn't look a thing like her, though she had known him from birth and been his guardian since he was five.

"You could do a lot worse than Liam Blackthorn," she said, rather than asking how he was feeling. "Good lad. Keeps his nose out of other people's business, and that can't be easy, job like his. Oh, and that raspberry crumble cake he gets for breakfast from Bluebell's? It could win Mayfair's spring baking showdown if that woman was bright enough to fill out the entry form."

Griff stared at her as he cradled his water glass between his hands. How the fuck would Wynnie know Liam's breakfast preferences? It wasn't her business to know that. Bad things tended to happen to people Wynnie decided to know too much about.

And yet here she was, smiling at Griff with some semblance of motherly affection over the rim of his glass as he lifted it to wet his throat again.

It wasn't her small, calculated smile either, the one he had seen most often over the years. If he had to guess, he would have said this one was real. It softened the lines of her face in such a way that for a moment he could even imagine how on an evening long ago, her future husband Rhun had mistaken her for a goddess of mercy come to ease his suffering after a troll attack laid him out at an inn most often frequented by bandits and smugglers.

Of course, the warmth of that smile was utterly ruined when Griff noticed a fleck of crimson on her neck.

"Why are you here?" he asked bluntly, impatient to get back to Liam and apologize for calling out that other name in his fevered state.

"To check on you, love." She pushed some of her thick blond hair over her scarred shoulder, revealing the familiar hilts of the long knives strapped to her back. "Just like I've been doing every day since they brought you home."

"And whose blood is that on your neck?" he asked around another sip of water, as casually as if he were inquiring about the weather. "Have you dropped by to see how they're healing too?"

After all—Griff knew the story by heart at this point—Wynnie had approached Rhun on the night of the troll attack with the intention of slitting his throat and stealing his gold, not carrying him up to the heavens, but she'd seen something in him as she reached for him. And for a time, the quick-fingered, murderous thief had become what Rhun believed her to be. She'd never stopped sleeping with a knife under her pillow, but she had stopped thieving and killing and become a wife, mother, and neighbor who baked the best peach pies.

At least, until the world took Rhun away from her, putting her right back where she had started: on no one's side but her own, the most cutthroat of sell-swords. Having briefly worked for the Shadow Queen but somehow escaped her service, she was happiest serving only herself. But where Vic loathed the shadows and the Wardens in equal measure, Wynnie still counted a few among the knights as friends—or at least, not adversaries—dancing toward whatever allegiances suited her in the moment, or killing when that was more convenient.

"Oh, that's from a rabbit. Last night's supper wasn't going to skin itself," Wynnie answered smoothly, touching a few fingers to the spot she'd missed and blinking guilelessly. "Anyway, I wanted to see you so—"

"So my blood could end up on your neck too?" He had never made a secret of his disapproval of the way Wynnie handled her affairs. After all, Vic got by in life without hurting anyone, even if she was just as much on her own side in all things.

It required a practiced eye to note the way Wynnie flinched at the mere suggestion. Griff, having such well-trained vision, felt a small thrill of satisfaction at the damage he had just inflicted after all the times she had let him down over the years—times she had chosen murder and mayhem over being there for birthday parties. "Why were you researching what my boyfriend likes for breakfast, anyway?" he demanded while he had the advantage.

Wynnie took a breath, recovering herself with remarkable speed, true to the tales of all the blows she'd survived over the years. "Knowing who you're in bed with is part of keeping you safe, which you've clearly demonstrated you aren't capable of doing on your own."

Griff's eyes narrowed. "I don't remember asking for you to be my personal guard. And I know that's not rabbit blood on your neck, so cut the shit about my love life and tell me why you're really here, or get out so I can spend some time with the people who actually care rather than pretending."

"You want to talk pretend?" Wynnie invited, her nostrils flaring as she pressed a hand into the quilt between them. Little crescent moons from someone's nails crossed all over the back of her hand—that rabbit had put up a hell of a fight. "You think you've walked around so free and easy all these years since you left—writing lines in your love songs that clearly aren't about your precious boyfriend-of-the-moment, auditioning to join the ranks of those Wardens you call heroes when all they ever did was send your parents to their deaths—without a cost? You think you cut yourself off so thoroughly from the rest of us lowlifes that the gods deemed you Good and Righteous and gave you some special protection from ever having a target on your back?" Now her eyes narrowed, her voice growing dangerously soft. "You're free and safe to follow your whims because I do what you won't. I pay the price for you, and I'm here because it seems you're still in danger."

She paused for a moment, her eyes seeking his. "Maybe I am the monster you clearly believe me to be, but how can you be so sure when we don't even know each other anymore? I miss you, Griff. I wish you'd come home."

He stared into those dark and depthless eyes that asked so much of him, certain that without some kind of map, he was bound to get lost in them. Her gaze was a lightless, airless place, an ocean he could drown in. And wasn't he supposed to find some comfort there rather than lose himself?

"You're wrong," Griff said softly when he found his voice again. "I do know you, and I have a pretty good understanding of what particular flavor of monster you are."

Wynnie flashed a smile that was all teeth, not about to let him see her flinch again. "You're so much like your father. Always so judgmental. So certain that you know just how to be good, but what is that, anyway? Good isn't anything, darling. It doesn't exist."

She stood and started pulling on her boots. "Anyway. You might want to keep watching your back. And I'll watch it too, no matter how much you disapprove, no matter what you think of me, no matter how much that hurts. I won't ever stop trying to keep my family safe. It's a big world out there, and it's going more to the orcs with each passing day."

She leaned in and gently smoothed his wayward hair back from his face, then drew away.

He didn't speak again until her hand was on the door; something about her leaving so soon and the unsettled warmth of her fingers having passed through his hair made him say, "Wynnie."

She turned back at the sound of her name.

"What kind of blood was it, really?"

"Mix of things," she said, leveling with him at last. "Human, mostly. Hunting your attacker."

"Okay," he said on a heavy breath.

"I'll be back to check on you tomorrow," she told him, opening the door to reveal Alys, Liam, and Badger waiting in a huddle just on the other side, clearly having heard every word. "Vic too."

"See you then," he agreed, and she vanished quickly like smoke.

Chapter Four
Mister Dangerous

Mal gave the straps on his pack another once-over, decided he was as ready as he was going to get, and scratched the still-healing skin on his itchy right forearm. The first day of summer had come and gone, which meant it was officially time for him to leave town on his latest assignment—and he would, first thing in the morning. Right after he figured out how to tell Alys what he had to do. How he was going to right this very stupid wrong.

He had been trying to find the words for weeks now, ever since that spring night in the tea shop when he had waited until the pearly light of dawn for his boss's return.

Kage—which wasn't his real name, if Mal had to guess—hadn't seemed particularly surprised to find him sitting there with his hunting knife out in welcome. Hadn't, perhaps in a testament to what was until now a rather successful working relationship, even commented on the dried tracks of tears glistening on Mal's dirty cheeks. He had, however, shown off all of his pointed teeth as he snarled and easily dodged Mal's attack, his fingers closing painfully around the younger thief's wrist until the knife clattered to the floor and Mal was worried he had broken something.

"What's eating your insides?" Kage rumbled as he casually changed position to lock Mal in a proper chokehold with more strength than any man possessed. When he closed his mouth, he could mostly pass for human rather than the half-orc he was. The only other difference was his eyes, their pupils nearly serpentine, but one had to get as dangerously close as Mal was now to notice a thing like that.

"Griffin Sayer," Mal spat with what little air he was being afforded. "You killed him. *Murdered* him, you fucking half-wit, inbred, sorry excuse for a—"

"*We* murdered him," Kage interrupted calmly, the look he was giving Mal almost indulgent—as if he were doing him a favor by giving him more credit (and not letting him finish the insult). "Or rather, we should have. But my birds saw the wretched elf-princess calling at his home not an hour ago, and her guards all aflutter nearby in the wood with weapons the likes of which we couldn't hope to counter with anything here. I suspect we failed, but next time, we'll torch the body for added insurance."

Mal had intended to kill Kage right there in his own shop, to feed him to the worms. He needed someone to answer for what had happened to Griff. But if there was a chance he was still out there, still breathing, somehow miraculously clinging to life . . .

"I want to make a deal," Mal spluttered. Kage was crushing his windpipe, but if he knew one thing about his boss, it was that he couldn't resist an exchange of wits and wagers. "For Griff's life. For his safety. Whatever it takes to spare him—name your price."

Kage had eased up on his throat sometime during the talking. Releasing Mal at long last in favor of straightening his rumpled black shirt, he trapped the fallen knife under his boot and leveled a calculating gaze at him.

"And I want to buy out my contract—I'm done with this place. There's not enough money in the world that could make me want this anymore," Mal added, feeling bolder now that he could draw a full breath.

Kage's eyes narrowed. He studied Mal for an uncomfortably long moment, in which Mal resisted the urge to rub his throat. Finally, he commanded, "Wait here."

He disappeared into the cellar, leaving Mal alone with a spinning head and no place to steady himself, returning just a few minutes later with a yellowed piece of parchment in hand. Mal frowned at that; he had never signed an actual contract with Kage, yet part of him expected to see his own blood staining the paper as he joined his boss at the counter to study it.

A little piece of the corner crumbled into dust as he tried to flatten it. Kage turned to look at him again, but Mal stared determinedly at the counter.

At the map being presented to him.

A rather detailed map at that, leading from Mayfair out to the Rotrose Mire, the beast-riddled and supposedly rather haunted swamp that Rhun had been exploring with two of his old friends when he vanished for the final time while the others were sleeping.

According to them, Mal's childhood guardian had either killed himself or been dragged off, and the rest of the big, bad Wardens had come running home without their dear old friend. Some heroes.

They had, Mal recalled, been striking toward a lake when they last saw him. A lake that supposedly held ancient treasure that would aid in the fight against the Shadow Queen and finally turn the tide in the Wardens' favor, helping them lay all her dead creatures to rest. He remembered huddling behind a door with Griff, neither daring to breathe too loudly as they listened to

Rhun's friends speculate on what the treasure might be before they left.

Swords to fight spirits. Impenetrable armor. Coffers of gold and silver. The crowns and bones of long-dead kings of elves and men, imbued with remnants of their power even after all this time.

They promised Rhun the Mire held resources, weapons, and aid to give them hope.

At the time, Mal had assumed it was all nothing more than legend, something to entertain men deep in their cups at the end of the day. But he spotted the glitter of gold in Kage's eyes as his boss ordered, "Find the treasure on this map and bring it to me, and you can have Griffin Sayer *and* your freedom. You can have the whole fucking world, for all I care."

Follow a set path, bring back a fabled treasure, and get everything that mattered most to him? Nothing was ever that simple. But before Mal could demand to know the catch, Kage continued, "You're to leave the moment summer arrives, when the roads east are easily walkable. You'll have four weeks to get the treasure and bring it to the shop. The riches on this map belong to the dark lady, and she's been sorely missing them for far too long."

"Four *weeks*?" Mal repeated incredulously, because that didn't strike him as long enough at all to wade through a swamp filled with ghosts and monsters. A swamp that was apparently so deadly that neither the Shadow Queen nor any of her supposedly devoted servants were willing to brave it to reclaim this important treasure.

Kage nodded once, tersely. "Four weeks, Mister Dangerous. That's when I'll be heading south. I can deliver the goods to our Queen in person, and be rewarded handsomely for having put up with you and your mouth in the first place. Unless . . . you're not up to the task."

"I'm not saying that. Just—what if it takes me four weeks and a day?" Mal demanded, though he had already decided he was taking the deal. The dangers didn't matter to a man who was already as cursed as he was; what mattered was knowing Griff would be safe, and that he never had to see the inside of this fucking shop again or smell a cup of Guts's triple-berry brew once he returned triumphant.

Kage's smile was never warm, but it was especially cold when his sharp teeth glistened with spit. "Then every spirit and beast in the Mire—every loyal servant of the dark queen, near and far—will hunt you down and tear you to pieces. You'll still be free of your contract, but you won't have any say in what happens to the hero's son." When Mal didn't say anything for a moment, he added more thoughtfully, "Either way, I win too, because I'll be rid of you, whether you're dead or no longer one of my charges. Before you become too much like the hero's son you so clearly worship."

"I'll do it," Mal said quickly, getting it over with like swallowing bitter medicine. He didn't even bother commenting on his boss's wildly incorrect opinion of what he thought of Griff. "In four weeks. Less than. You'll see."

Kage's smile only grew, filling Mal with a quiet dread. "Roll up your sleeve, then," the half-orc said, rummaging for something behind the counter.

When Mal didn't rush to comply, Kage stopped searching and did it for him, roughly shoving his shirt up to his elbow and leaving the paler skin of his forearm exposed.

"What the fuck?" Mal growled, flinching away as Kage pulled out a needle and a small bowl of ash. He knew what the supplies were for, of course; he had seen Guts get a tattoo here when she first signed on. It also wasn't lost on him that Kage hadn't brought out any alcohol to clean the area first, or any for Mal to drink. Bastard.

"I'm going to mark you," Kage explained, dipping the needle into the bowl. "A magical symbol of our agreement that will let our queen and her servants keep track of your progress on this assignment. There are plenty of faithful undead in the Mire, should you require motivation, or any reminders of how much time you have to finish the task."

Apparently, some of the dark queen's servants were as expendable as he was against whatever made the swamp so deadly. Figured.

Mal stared down impassively at his bloody, stinging skin, watching as Kage forced ash beneath it. The pain was nothing compared to knowing he had brought Griff to the brink of death. If anything, the sting was a welcome distraction.

"The binding magic in these marks will be broken upon collection of the treasure—or upon your death, as I doubt my lady wants a spirit with a mouth like yours under her command for eternity," Kage informed him somewhat more cheerfully as the dark, swollen shapes of raven's feathers began cascading down Mal's forearm in the dim lantern light.

That was something, at least. Once he gave the Shadow Queen her gold, she wouldn't have a magical means of stalking him anymore. And Griff would be safe.

That alone was worth whatever it cost in the end.

There was a sameness to Mal's days in Linden that had always made him ready to leave again after just a few weeks. He was usually thankful for his work guarding the dark queen's caravans in and out of Mayfair, for another chance to put the drowsy town at his back and actually hear himself think. Because when he was at home, though the cottage held a certain charm with all its little spiderweb castles and the scent of Wynnie's baking forever permeating the walls, there was also . . . Mags. His constant shadow.

Her real name was Margred, and while they weren't actually related, she called him uncle anyway. And ever since Alys had broken up with the girl's father, Mags was forever seeking her Uncle Mal's attention.

She had even learned how to pick the lock on his bedroom door—not that she needed to; Mal knew she was always listening through the paper-thin wall to whatever the adults were discussing. So Mags had learned more than most kids her age already, and missed little when it came to the details of their busy household.

With his bags packed and nothing left to do but explain his impending absence, Mal had settled himself outside in the overgrown garden to try to read a passage from the dwarvish-language philosophy book that he carried with him wherever he went, trying not to think about where Alys was right now. And most importantly, trying not to think at all about who she was with.

As Mags approached, skipping every other step and humming under her breath, he put down the dog-eared chapter on solitude and sighed.

"Wynnie said Griff and Vic went hunting in the Wyrmwood, but they aren't allowed to do it again. Wynnie and Vic were arguing about it in the kitchen," Mags reported as she threw her arms around her uncle's neck and he gave her a tight squeeze. Her blue eyes—so much like Alys's—glinted with knowledge she had sensed was forbidden. "Did you and Mom go hunting with them too? Are you going again soon? Is that why you packed the good knives?"

"No," Mal said flatly, looking out over the creek and the distant trees beyond that led to the Wyrmwood. "We didn't go with them." He chose to ignore the question about where he was heading next entirely; the less Mags knew about that, the better.

"Why not?" the girl pressed, dropping down beside him and crossing her legs in a pose identical to his.

Mal sighed. "Because I could always stand to go a few more years without having my day ruined by Griff and his fucking mouth or getting punched just for existing, that's why."

"Why do you hate him so much? Is it the punching?" Mags asked, picking up Mal's book and thumbing through it as if she could read already. "Sometimes Rodric kicks me and says he's the best at kicking, even when I kick him back harder, and I still love him."

Mal was quiet for so long that Mags had started gathering weeds and flowers, nestling them in the paws of their unhappy-looking stone griffin statue, by the time he spoke again. "Someday you'll learn about people like him. You'll learn that most people need a fucking fairy tale to keep them warm at night."

Mags wrinkled her nose in distaste, patting the stone griffin on his cracked head before turning back to her uncle. But before she could ask him what was bound to be another prying question that he didn't want to answer, Alys appeared, wading through the weeds.

Her comings and goings had been different lately.

True, he didn't always tell her where he was going either—he preferred not to talk with the few people he cared for about anything that went on at Served With Love, so that in case he ever got in real trouble there, they wouldn't know anything they could get hurt over. But Alys usually told him everything. Like him, she didn't have many other friends, so when they'd both returned to Mayfair and picked up their friendship after years apart, he'd been the one to hear the ins and outs of her days.

Only not for a few weeks now.

He recalled her leaving earlier that morning; he had glimpsed her through the window, pale braid swishing at her back, a bouquet of flowers in hand. Curious, he had followed her for quite a way, though he wasn't proud of it. Long enough to watch her enter the row of houses he always avoided walking past on his way into town. She was going to Griff's, and he couldn't for the life of him understand why. It wasn't like Griff was particularly kind to her, even if the punches he'd thrown her way over the years were verbal, insults like the ones Mal was always making toward him. No doubt to punish her for her continued association with Mal—so what had changed?

"Mags, why don't you go check on your spider?" Mal suggested as Alys drew nearer. "I didn't see him crawling on the breakfast table this morning."

"Teacup's missing?" Mags gasped, her eyes shining with sudden worry.

"Yeah. Teacup. Grab your sister and have her help you look. Rodric, too, if he's not playing with those kids across the creek," Mal added, pleased with himself for coming up with this quick and easy distraction that would at least keep the children occupied long enough to let him talk with Alys uninterrupted.

He had put it off long enough, and now he was out of time.

He was on his feet before his old friend could climb the porch steps to the front door, making himself and his question unavoidable. "How's Griff?"

"What do you mean?" Alys asked, blinking innocently. She would, he knew, pretend to understand much less than she actually did if she thought feigning ignorance could get her out of a difficult situation. It was one of her many talents.

"How long have you been going over there?" Mal continued, keeping his voice quiet and controlled, even though in some way he felt like he'd been betrayed again. She was *his* friend, not some elf-boy wannabe's. They were the most alike of their little trio from back when, both willing to walk a darker path than Griff's polished boots would ever step down.

Remembering what Mags had overheard, he added, "You planning some kind of hunting trip with him? I should have known; you've always loved fairy tales."

Alys frowned as she studied him, then motioned for them both to take a seat on the bottom of the porch steps. "Did Wynnie tell you what happened to him?" she asked, twisting the end of her pale braid around her fingers like she always did when she was grappling with something. "Or Vic?"

Mal shook his head and scratched viciously at his right forearm. He probably should have put some kind of balm on his feathered tattoo to help with the healing, but part of him had hoped it would all flake off if he just kept scratching hard enough. Fucking ravens. Fucking Shadow Queen knowing that he was asleep in his bed, or walking the streets, or finally hitting the road to do her dirty work for her.

Alys's eyes clocked the frantic motion. Of course she had noticed the new ink, which was Mal's only tattoo. And of course she hadn't pressed when he told her it was something to do with work, thanks to the trust rebuilt between them. Only now, she pressed gently. "I know I should have told you about spending time with Griff again. Maybe especially about how it all started. But you . . ." Her gaze softened, and for a rare moment, he was the only thing reflected in her keen and caring eyes. "Whatever happened to no secrets between us?"

Damn it.

He pulled out his flask and chugged the whole thing, not bothering to even wipe his mouth with the back of his hand. Then he led her inside, down the hall to the first door on the right, into his childhood bedroom where his pack and the delicate old map were waiting.

Even though he hadn't held the knife, he still couldn't look at her while he explained his part in the attack on Griff. He knew how his face might betray him, and he had no words for why he was so stricken at the potential loss of a man he frequently claimed was nothing but a nuisance. More than that, he didn't want to see the way she was looking at him, not even when he started to explain how he was going to make things right and what his tattoo really meant. Didn't want to know how close this confession was bringing him to losing his only other friend in the world for a second time.

He could hear Guts back in the cellar, her voice ringing with soft laughter and admiration as she called him Mister Dangerous, not knowing it was the last thing he wanted to be. That name felt like nothing more than another curse now.

But when he finally chanced a look at Alys, her eyes weren't narrowed in accusation or disdain. Rather, they were slightly misty and focused on the map. "This is Papa's handwriting. Rhun's, I mean. It's so messy, I'd know it anywhere. The letters are just like the ones in his journals; look, there, see how he puts three dots over each of the *i*'s?"

With that, she hurried out of the room, presumably to present him with one of Rhun's old books as proof. He slumped down against his pack, wishing Wynnie were home right now to steady him with a look or a few words in the way that only she could.

Alys reappeared seconds later, out of breath and carrying a leather-bound journal in one hand and a cloth-wrapped bundle in the other. She pressed both into Mal's hands and knelt on the woven rug beside him, pulling away the wrappings to reveal a sword.

Or, at least, part of one. The tang was broken, and there were some unfamiliar runes carved into the much-abused scrap of metal. The flowing script made him think it was elvish.

"Papa's friends brought this back when they"—she usually couldn't finish the sentence, but this time she managed—"came home. You know, without him. They said he broke it when he . . . when he . . ."

"Fought a nasty troll that was guarding their path." Mal picked up the story for her when she faltered a second time. "That was the first time he almost died out there."

"Which is why you're not going alone," Alys declared, sounding much more sure of this than of her father's fate. "I won't lose you to that place too. And I want to help buy Griff's safety—because he matters so much to both of us."

"No. This is my mess to fix. It has nothing to do with you," Mal protested, though weakly. He would be glad to have someone he could trust out there, especially when he only had four weeks to cover a lot of distance and confront the however many unknown dangers that awaited him.

Alys was already wrapping up that broken sword again, her eyes on the doorway, as if she intended to start packing and making arrangements for the children immediately. "Then you fix your mess, and I'll be right beside you while you do it, watching your back while I finally get answers about what really happened to my father."

Mal had often wondered about Rhun's inevitable end too. A betrayal? A murder? Hell, maybe he had simply decided to walk away from everything he knew while he had the chance. Everyone else left Mal, after all. It would make a certain sense.

"I'll make sure we don't fail. We'll get that treasure. For Griff, and you, and . . . Papa," Alys pressed, her head held high, her eyes bright and determined.

Being perhaps the only person in the world privileged enough to have seen every side of her, Mal could guess what this was really about. More than just protecting those she loved, she wanted to see what she was capable of without her ex and his constant comments dragging her down. Without Wynnie in the way. To find out who she was on her own, to learn whether she could do what even her legendary father couldn't by putting her hands on that treasure.

Mal wasn't going to be the one to stop her; he had missed seeing that fight in her eyes ever since she'd moved back to the cottage. Besides, he would never tell her that she couldn't do something, having realized long ago that she was capable of more than she even knew.

"Then we leave at first light. Wouldn't want Her Dreadful Majesty getting impatient," he said darkly. "At least it's a chance to blow this stupid fucking town. I'll probably have to look for work elsewhere again once I'm no longer, uh, brewing tea, anyway. Linden was never big enough for anything I have planned. I'll have to find a castle for that."

And Griff would be safe and happy with his perfect little boyfriend, far away from the man who had nearly been the death of him, never knowing about the raven's feathers on Mal's arm or what that renewed sense of peace and protection had cost.

They hadn't spoken since their last fight some two years ago, and Mal would be content to go the rest of their lives without exchanging another bitter word or seeing who could hit hardest next time.

"Aren't you forgetting something?" Alys's eyes roamed his face with intense scrutiny. When he didn't answer, she impatiently supplied, "Griff. We all deserve the chance to find out what really happened to Rhun, if we can. You can't keep leaving him out of things. Papa—Rhun—took you both in without even thinking about it. He loved you both."

"I don't know about that," Mal argued when it came to Rhun's affection, pulling at a loose thread in the rug. He wasn't sure he had ever felt it. It had been so long ago. But there was one thing he was sure of. "Either way, Griff shouldn't be around me. You know that." He tasted bile in the back of his throat despite the whiskey. "Someone always gets hurt."

He had nearly been the death of Griff.

He didn't belong anywhere near him, no matter what answers the Mire held for them all.

"You should ask him to come with us anyway, and you know it. He's probably safer out there with us than he is here in the city with the people who almost murdered him," Alys urged in a familiar tone, one that invited no argument.

He had none to make this time, because she was probably right.

"We can't tell him why we really need the treasure, though," Mal said at last, after some careful thought. "If he knew it was going to end up in the hands of the Shadow Queen, he'd turn us in to the Wardens on the spot, even if he had to drag us through the mud himself. And you know how much he likes staying nice and dry up on that pretty moral high ground of his. We'll have to tell him something else. Like . . . we're after the treasure to get rich. So we can buy ourselves a real castle and finally get the fuck out of Mayfair."

Alys shot him an encouraging grin, and he knew those words coming from his mouth sounded entirely believable. He really wouldn't mind being king of something someday. "That's settled, then," she said cheerfully. "Sounds like all that's left is the asking."

Mal scrubbed a hand into his tangled hair and sighed.

He still hated Griff. All Griff ever did anymore was disappoint him, judge him, make him so angry that he couldn't bear to touch what lay beneath it all, the things he'd never had a chance to hold up to the light and never would.

Yet knowing Griff was out there, alive, unquestionably mattered to him, even if they had proven they were better off leagues apart. Knowing he was out there was part of what kept Mal going in the days of longest dark.

"Go to him," Alys insisted, a mother trying to convince her children to eat their greens.

But she didn't need to tell him again; he was already making his way to the door, fingers digging into the itchy skin of his forearm as he disappeared.

Chapter Five

Mayfair's Most Eligible

Some monsters were born, and some were made. Having grown up in a place like Mayfair, Griff was well aware of the difference. Mayfair was a sprawling metropolitan area with smaller villages like Linden, Appleby, and Strathmore clinging to the edges of its skirts, and its size—not to mention its unique position just outside the taxable jurisdiction of any ruling monarch—made it a favorite calling port and sometimes home to tradesmen, travelers, and anyone looking to make a name for themselves on either side of the law, whether by daring to fight the Shadow Queen or by joining one of her covert networks of smugglers and spies.

Mayfair was certainly the only place west of the Crooked Teeth, the vast and icy mountains teeming with trolls and giants and other foul beasts loyal to the dark queen, where one could find centaurs at the market, shopping for fine dwarven crystal alongside humans, and the occasional enterprising kobold or halfling, hawking wares from exotic candies to silks to wooden toys. There was a wizened old dwarf shaman who would read futures in the tiny imp's bones he threw (for a handsome fee), a gnomish cheesemonger who offered a fantastic wheel of sharp white, and a half-orc blacksmith enchanting blades that sang or whistled while they were doing what they loved best: cutting things. While the various species of the world were downright hostile to each other at times—except whenever they needed to band together to push the Shadow Queen back into the darkness again—in Mayfair, they lived and worked as neighbors, just as they had since the city's founding some thousand years ago.

The village of Linden was fairly quiet, but closer to the city was always a riot of noises, smells, and faces rushing past in a beautiful array of varying skin tones and features, and Griff loved it. So many people to meet and rhythms to learn.

He was moving slightly slower than usual as he made his way through the winding cobbled streets to his first day of work since the attack. Rosemaris might have saved him, but not even her magic or the elves' rarest healing potion had been strong enough to completely cure this particular wound; he was still stricken at times by sudden, sharp pain, and it wasn't the sort of hurt any balm or tea could touch. And since it was nothing more than an ugly scar on the surface and he was tired of sitting around the house all day, he had decided there wasn't going to be a better time to try seeing what his body could still do.

. . . Right after he paused for a little a break outside the Wyvern & Wyrm, the city's largest tavern, to watch the sun climb higher while breathing in the eye-opening aroma of coffee—a fairly new dwarven import from the far south that gave him the jitters with just a few sips.

He leaned against the base of the sturdy stair rail leading up the few steps to the pub's entrance, scrutinizing the wooden sign depicting two creatures tangled in a vicious battle. Freshly and clumsily hand-painted by the halfling who currently owned the place, it rocked steadily back and forth on its hanger above the door in a warm early-summer breeze.

It was still fairly early in the morning, but it was going to be the kind of day where Griff regretted wearing so much black all the time regardless of the season. He was already sweltering beneath a dark linen shirt that remained unbuttoned at the collar, but at least he no longer needed any bandages that would have added to the warmth.

He was about to make his way up the steps for a sip of coffee when a familiar figure left the pub and came bounding toward him.

"Griff!" Dove cried happily, stopping partway down the stairs. She was notably petite where he was tall, so a few stairs up was the perfect vantage point from which to throw her deep-brown arms around his neck.

He pulled her into a tight hug despite the way his wound protested. He had seen her a few days ago when she dropped by to spend the evening playing cards and laughing with him and Liam, and she had looked much the same then as she did now: bright-eyed no matter the hour, always in her muddy Warden's uniform and boots like she was either just returning from or about to disappear into the wilds to fight some rampaging beast again, a full quiver on her back and the tip of her scabbard dragging the ground.

"Good to see you out and about," she said, stepping into the shade of the tavern's roof so that the sunlight wouldn't beam so directly onto her long raven hair and roast her. "You working on the Goatleafs' place today, then?"

He grinned a little and nodded, touching a few fingers to his tool belt. This project was one of his own design, a new bakery in the north ward of the city on the way to Barcombe.

"How are you feeling?" she asked next, a question that put more focus behind her golden-brown eyes. As a Warden, she had some training in the healing arts as well as fighting, tracking, and foraging—training Griff would be plenty ready to start again if he could find a permanent solution to end the pain beneath his scar. It was a dark world outside the confines of Mayfair, and he wanted to do what he could to make it a little lighter for everyone. After all, it was what his father had done, the path already laid out bright and clear before him.

"Bit tired, and . . . you know. The pain comes and goes, like we talked about." He frowned, running a hand over the area where he now bore an inch-long scar that made him wince anytime he caught sight of it. Worse still were the nightmares that had plagued him since it happened.

"What, did Liam keep you up all night again?" Dove teased, sensing his frustration and trying to lighten the mood, at which Griff scrubbed an embarrassed hand over his face. That mouth of hers was going to get her in trouble someday, probably in the middle of territory negotiations between centaur herds or something equally dicey. "I saw him yesterday, by the way. He was running errands with that . . . Alys."

She scrunched up her nose, making no secret of her distaste for the other woman. Alys was, after all, wanted for several petty crimes no Warden could quite prove, right along with Mal, Vic, and Wynnie.

"Easy. She's my friend too," Griff protested gently, no longer so inclined to say or hear a harsh word against Alys now that they were making up for lost time. "It's actually been nice, having her around again."

Alys appeared on his doorstep surprisingly often these days, sometimes with flowers and an appetite for Liam's raspberry pancakes, sometimes with the intention of going for a picnic or a walk and telling stories from their childhood (though she spoke carefully around the glaring issue of Mal's existence in these old tales). Acting, for once, like the friend he had missed for a long time now. Reminding him why they had mattered to each other in the first place.

Dove shrugged, and Griff saw in the set of her face that he wasn't about to change her mind. "Anyway," she said, a gleam of interest returning to her warm brown gaze, "they looked like they were heading to the jeweler's—you know, the dwarven gent who makes the really nice rings?"

There was a too-long pause while Griff tried to work out who Alys might be marrying. Wouldn't she have told him if the children's father had come back into the picture? Last Griff had heard, just a few days ago, she had still sounded very done with him and his lofty expectations and un-asked-for judgments.

A gnome wheezed past, pushing a wheelbarrow laden with fresh floral bouquets, and Dove raised a hand in greeting. Rather than lifting his colorful cap and waving back, however, the busy farmer grunted and turned away, quickening his steps. Wardens weren't exactly popular in the city; they were trained more like knights than guards, but they tended to stick their noses into all sorts of matters where they weren't welcome. There were also some who thought they shouldn't idealize the elves like they did, preserving their history and lore, as if collective memory had forgotten in their absence that they were once the source of so much beauty and goodness, like the magic that had saved Griff's life. That it was their light and strength that had broken the Shadow Queen's grip on the world in the first place, their efforts that had pushed her back to her own realm, where she spun orcs and wraiths and all sorts of undead from her dark magic.

She plotted to smother the world in her darkness and supernatural horrors, then save it by uniting all peoples and creatures under one banner—her own. Murdering strategically so that someday she alone would possess magic and could use it to remain feared (or, in her twisted mind, adored) in her new Deathless Empire. It was the nightmare the earliest Wardens had stood against since they first formed into a band of mercenaries fighting for the light wherever they were needed. They had been appointed by the elves as they retreated to Stormveil, most Wardens having some elvish blood in their lineage in the hope that they would be the most inclined to protect the world the elves had loved for so long.

Most folks worried vaguely about the Shadow Queen's return, but only the Wardens worked tirelessly in secret to prevent the possibility of another full-scale war by any means necessary—which meant making everything their business, and hiding their true purpose as more than monster hunters from the general population.

"Maybe Alys was just . . . window shopping? Daydreaming?" he guessed, shaking off the malaise of his thoughts. Alys was more like Mal that way, always hoping and scheming.

"Maybe," Dove agreed, her full lips twitching into a smile before she added, "Or maybe somebody's thinking about finally taking Mayfair's Most Eligible off the market for good, if you get my drift."

Griff wasn't proud of that nickname, often heard throughout the city, though he knew Dove meant it fondly, in the way of acknowledging how many men admired him or wanted to be with him—not in the way of chastising him for having made a few too many conquests even for his own liking since returning from Stormveil. But so what if he'd dated more than his share of Wardens and often taken home whoever happened to have the nicest smile at the pub that night? He didn't owe anyone anything from before he started seeing only Liam. There was, admittedly, the time he got down on his knees, sloppily and against his better judgment, for an entire company of visiting knights from the kingdom of Kattan—all eight of them—but that had been after a stupid fight with Mal, and he had been trying to heal his black eye by soaking it in whiskey. A bit of field medicine learned from Wynnie, of course.

"You really think?" Griff asked Dove at last, her meaning finally starting to sink in. He'd had a foreman's steady hand in building the life he and Liam shared, and he planned to keep waking up to raspberry pancakes and going on walks with Badger for a long time to come. He didn't need to dream any bigger than that. Liam knew almost every detail of his past and accepted it all, the good with the ugly. Liam had taught him how to do some amazing things with his mouth. Liam was a better musician than him. And Liam loved him. "Huh. Griff Sayer-Blackthorn. I like the sound of that."

Dove's smile widened. "It does have a certain ring to it. Just don't tell him I dropped any hints or I'll never hear the end of it, yeah?"

Griff held up a hand, folding in a few fingers. "Warden-in-training's honor," he vowed, even though he wasn't exactly that anymore. That big dream of his own was out of reach unless he fully healed, and he wasn't sure what the path ahead looked like if he didn't—dark, and full of thorns. The grin quickly slid from his face and he added, lower, "Any other news?"

Dove—whose real name, of course, wasn't actually Dove; that was only adopted to protect her kin from any retaliation by the Shadow Queen's people—frowned and shook her head. She was one of several of his Warden friends trying to track down his attackers. But neither they nor Wynnie had made much progress yet.

They said their goodbyes and Griff continued on his way, his head too full of lovers past and present and a wedding in his future to remember that he had wanted a coffee.

He and Liam had something with the potential to last, and apparently, Liam saw it too. Something true, a growing love that Griff was often afraid he would somehow shatter if he didn't hold it carefully enough, and didn't quite know what to do with. He didn't know how to stay, did he? His parents hadn't stayed. Nor had Rhun. Nor even Wynnie, in her way. Still, what he had with Liam was the realest thing he had ever felt for a man in his bed.

And *Griff Sayer-Blackthorn* had such a nice ring to it.

He stopped only once more on his way to work, to help an elderly widow cross the cobbles at a busy intersection where horses and carts were speeding past. "Where are you headed today, Miss Isabel?" he asked her kindly, intending to help her all the way to her destination before moving on.

She pointed to a striped green-and-white awning above a darkened door with faded gold lettering painted directly on the glass, and Griff's shoulders tightened. Of course. Served With Love. Most locals knew to leave the unassuming tea shop well enough alone and looked the other way at who came and went, but there were some older folks like the widow who really appreciated the strong taste of what their shop girl put together—and none of it was poison, at the end of the day. That would be awfully bad for business.

"Have a good day. And be safe," Griff said, holding open the heavy glass door for her without once glancing into the dim interior.

Then he finally got to work.

It felt good, sweating in the summer sun again as he swung a hammer with his crew, to have a body that more or less did what he asked of it—aside from the occasional breathless stab of pain that made him drop a tool here or there. He had missed this. Though not, apparently, as much as his crew had missed him.

All but Wills, who the others said had been out sick for the past week or so.

"What's it like, boss?" Owin apparently couldn't help asking as he passed by, carrying an armload of heavy beams to be cut to size. He was a rosy-cheeked, curly-haired stout young halfling, as strong as any strapping man on the crew, though he didn't yet seem to have developed a sense for what kinds of questions might be too personal. "Almost dying and all that? Bad as they say?"

"Keep swinging those crossbeams around without looking at who you're about to hit, and you just might find out," Griff answered with a grin as he sharpened his wood-splitting maul. After so many weeks away, he had even missed the lad's constant chatter. "Cool me off after you put those down, would you?"

Owin tossed some water from his open canteen, spraying Griff and everyone around him.

Griff shook his wet hair like a dog drying off from a swim, and his crew scattered, swearing and laughing and slapping him on the back as they fled.

He was back to doing what he loved, and before he knew it, the sun was sinking behind the roofs of the nearby houses. Smoke rose steadily from their chimneys in thin streams, fragrant cedar, birch, and applewood carrying to Griff on a cooling breeze. The streets were quickly clearing—a dwarven couple returning home with an armload of groceries here, a few men and what looked like some distant elf-kin there, ducking into a nearby pub for dinner and drinks. Griff had someone waiting for him at home too. It was almost time to call it a day.

First, though, he had one last pile of wood he wanted to split to prep for tomorrow. He tugged off the inconvenience of his damp shirt, cast it aside, and grabbed his maul again, his calluses fitting comfortably against worn impressions in the handle.

As he got to work, a shadow fell across his path—a familiar shadow, one that made his blood run cold and his skin prickle with certain, present danger. He was sober again, since the attack; there was no way he was seeing things. But he decided to let that shadow be a phantom for as long as it liked, focusing on the job at hand rather than calling any attention to it.

Though it surely wanted his attention.

Chapter Six
Just a Job

Backlit by the fiery sky, his lanky silhouette etched in amber, Griff looked like something out of Mal's wildest dreams. He watched for a few self-indulgent moments as Griff swung his maul into the wood on the chopping block. Followed the drip of a bead of sweat from Griff's neck all the way down past his navel, pale skin gilded by the sunset. Touched his tongue to the corner of his mouth, thinking of all the times he had seen Griff do this when they were growing up, three best friends under one roof, every other night a party that called for a bonfire.

After Rhun's disappearance, Wynnie was always out, always covered in someone else's blood when she turned up again, but Mal never had to worry about being warm or where his next meal was coming from because Griff took care of the woodpile.

He took care of things. Birthday presents. Scrapes. Mending clothes. Even though Griff was only two years older, he thought of the little things while Mal's sights were forever on the horizon.

The dull, rhythmic thud of the maul in tandem with Griff's laboring breaths would always be a familiar tune, one from a time when Griff still knew how to stay.

Mal could never forget it. He'd tried.

Unaware that he was making any sound at all, a groan rose from the back of his throat as he watched Griff work that rather resembled the sound the family's old dog, Whiskey, made when someone scratched behind his ears. The hound was more gray than brown now, with fur like velvet and sagging jowls, a sagging stomach to match, and failing eyes that—much like Mal's did—glimpsed certain darting shadows and wispy figures that others simply couldn't. Poor old dog must be cursed too, though Mal couldn't imagine what *he* had done to piss off the gods. All dogs were good dogs, after all.

He took a deep breath in through his nostrils, steeling himself. Quickly sipped from his flask, that constant silver companion flashing in and out of the breast pocket of his jerkin in a span of seconds. And then, as fortified as he was going to get, he approached.

The clip of his boots against the cobbles didn't quite grab Griff's attention the way Mal had expected it would. Nor did his shadow falling across the current object of Griff's focus, or the dry clearing of his throat.

So between strikes of the maul, Mal let a few words fall from his lips: "Preparing for tomorrow when everyone else has already gone home? Whoever hired you should really raise your pay."

At that, Griff left the heavy tool embedded in the chopping block and pushed some dark hair out of his face with a scarred hand, blinking sweat from his eyes at the intrusion.

Mal rarely glanced in a mirror, but he still had some idea from Griff's startled expression of how he must look: like some kind of gray ghost with his woolen cloak around his shoulders. Still wearing the same style of patched and torn hunter-green jerkin over an equally mended shirt and brown cloth pants worn thin at the knee, because he had never taken great care of his things; cool gray eyes always running some calculation; the set of a jaw that was always braced for impact; crooked nose reset too many times to count; tawny skin already deepened by the start of summer, more like Wynnie's than Griff's eternally pale complexion; shaggy golden hair tied back in some semblance of a bun by a leather strap, full of so many knots that at this point he would have to cut most of it off just to run a comb through it.

He looked like death warmed over, and he felt like it too, having to stand here facing the man he'd almost put in an untimely grave. It was all he could do not to roll up his sleeve and rake his nails over the raven's feathers on his forearm until he bled.

Griff was silent for so long that Mal was about to ask if he needed some kind of help. When he finally spoke, he said dryly, tentatively, into the air between them, "Can I get that in writing? Addressed to my employer?"

Just before the light shifted, a hint of a grin slipped across Mal's face, echoing back across the years to a time when things were so much simpler. When it was the three of them, just them and Alys, invincible in their bond and existing in their own narrow world where they were certain that one day, they would be even greater heroes than their parents had been, writing their own legacy together.

Yet that had been nothing more than a dream, an empty promise. Mal could count on two hands the number of times he and Griff had spoken in nearly ten years.

"What are you doing here?" Griff asked bluntly, clearly unsettled by this breach in their unspoken agreement to stay the hell away from each other. "Is something wrong with Wynnie? Or Vic?" A brief pause followed in which he looked stricken, and then, "Is it . . . Alys?"

Mal glanced quickly toward the smoke curling from the nearest chimney just over Griff's shoulder, which was easier than looking at Griff himself, and shook his head. "Everyone's fine."

"Dove saw Alys in the jeweler's recently. The expensive one who makes the rings," the foreman offered curiously. "Any idea what that might have been about?"

Mal shrugged. "No more than I know why she's started hanging out with you again. But I doubt any man could win her over with a bit of jewelry or a stupid title. The last guy certainly couldn't, and they had three kids. That stuff is all just someone's moneymaking scheme, anyway, and calling each other special names is for the chronically insecure."

Griff hooked his fingers into the back of his waistband, glancing sideways at Mal like he feared one small misstep might provoke his temper, and simply nodded. Maybe he had lost his appetite for bloodshed since the attack.

Mal, meanwhile, tried not to stare too hard at Griff's still-bare chest, sweat glistening where it had dried on his cooling skin. Tried not to let his gaze wander lower, to the waistband of Griff's pants, unwilling to look upon evidence of the stabbing he had plotted even though he probably deserved to have to see it.

"Anyway," he continued, his voice heavy with the effort of what he knew he had to say next. He might as well get this over with before things could sour like they always did. Still, the words had to be dragged out of his throat from some unfathomable depth. "I'm actually here on business."

Maybe he should have chosen his words more carefully, given the way Griff blanched like he'd just chugged a bottle of the moonshine one of the barkeeps at the Maiden's Arms sold under the table to regulars. He was so delicate, so easy to rile. He must have folded immediately when they stabbed him. A perfect, pretty victim.

Mal's stomach churned. He almost regretted hitting the flask.

"Business?" Griff's shoulders were rigid with tension. Thanks to the foreman's lack of a shirt, it took little effort to notice, and Mal definitely wasn't trying to study the lines of muscle there for any other reason. "You've got funny ideas of what exactly business is, Mal. I'm pretty sure your version includes scams and intimidation and outright extortion."

Mal didn't bother correcting him. Griff was mostly right, to be fair. But it still stung, the way he always thought he was so smart, thought he could read Mal like one of his books, one where he had every chapter memorized. Arrogant bastard.

When Griff tilted his head a little at the lack of a scathing rebuttal, Mal huffed a breath and began like he had practiced in his head on the way here: "I have a lead on an exciting new prospect, a chance to strike it rich and get some answers about the past. And I'd like for you to come along . . . with Alys and me. To Rotrose Mire. As our official healer."

"You want to go to the Mire? On purpose?" Griff paced a few steps around the chopping block. "Of course you do. Even knowing the stories. Even after Rhun . . ."

Rotrose Mire lay to the east past the Wyrmwood, across the Plains of Plenty—so named because they were seemingly endless fields of tall grass, some ancient explorer's idea of humor—out where the friendliest faces they could hope to encounter were businessmen like Mal, roaming bandits, or even wargs, huge hairy dog-beasts of the Shadow Queen's with jaws like a steel trap. And then there was the Mire itself, full of orcs and trolls who worshiped the dark queen like some kind of deity, most destined to join the ranks of the undead under her command; carnivorous plants; poisonous berries that looked temptingly like common fruits; and sinister beings like revenants, walking corpses with souls inside created by the Shadow Queen to bolster her army. Her control over the dead was precisely what made some believe she had once been a human necromancer rather than, as others argued, an elf gone mad.

"That's far from here. A long journey, especially on foot. And dangerous as hell, besides," Griff pointed out after pacing a few more rounds.

"Which is why we'll need a healer," Mal said again, trying for patience. "In case the roads aren't as friendly as in a fairy tale."

"I'm hardly that," Griff protested, though Mal had it on good authority from Alys that he had learned something of the art from the elves.

Mal circled partway around the spot where Griff was pacing, leaning against one of the beams already secured to the bakery's foundation, the partial roof throwing him into shadow as the sun sank lower. "Then stay here," he said, voice and eyes flat as the road that led toward home; he could generally count on Griff to do the opposite of what he asked for, anyway. "Work your straight jobs and play hero like your dear old dad." His withering tone made it sound like such a bad thing, which was mostly habit at this point. He always made the things Griff did or wanted sound so small and stupid. It was the only defense he had when Griff acted so far above him, like he was a precious elf from Stormveil and Mal was some shambling corpse of the dark queen's, trying to bludgeon him to death. "Parade around town with your boring little boyfriends, and keep on telling yourself you're so much better than the rest of us. Alys and I will get rich and not have to share the extra coin with you."

Turning more fully toward Mal, Griff sank onto the chopping block, casting aside the maul to make space and then resting his chin in his hand. For a moment, it looked as though some true pain had crossed his face—was the wound still bothering him? That didn't seem normal. Too much time had passed.

"Alys put you up to this," he accused, distracting Mal from his concern. "This is all starting to make sense—she made you ask me along because she still thinks we can all be friends. You don't actually want me there."

Mal's gray eyes narrowed, his mouth becoming a thinner line. He hated that Griff really could read him still, after all this time. "So? Like I said, you don't have to come. It's just a job."

"Like cozying up to helpless old widows to get your name on the deed to their land is just a job? Like that scam you ran on the farmers outside Barcombe where you were a 'wolf hunter' was just a job?" Disdain dripped from Griff's voice. "What the hell is in the Mire that's worth risking life and limb for, anyway?"

Mal shrugged, trying to let Griff's sneering judgment bounce off his weathered cloak like rain. "Look, a job is just a job as far as I'm concerned—not good or bad, just work. Some jobs just happen to make more money than others, which is where I go, because I'm in it for me," he said coolly. "It's a hungry world out there, in case you haven't noticed, and all I'm trying to do is not end up on anyone else's plate."

Griff shook his head like he had heard this all before, which was probably true.

"I found myself in possession of a map recently," Mal continued while he still had Griff's attention. Normally, he had no problem walking away from Griff's unwelcome scrutiny, but he couldn't do that this time. Not when thoughts of Kage making a second attempt on Griff's life while Mal waded around in some swamp kept flashing vividly to mind.

"The writing on it is Rhun's, Alys thinks," he clarified, having saved this reveal in case Griff really needed convincing. "It looks like it leads to the stockpile of riches the Wardens were searching for when they went out there and came home without him. Ancient gold and weapons and armor from one of the first elven empires, all tucked into the barrows of their kings."

He paused there to let the words sink in, and sure enough, Griff's green eyes swiftly widened. He didn't need to spell out the significance—that the treasure, or the hunt for it, might tell them the truth about what had befallen Rhun in the end. He crossed his arms. "Anyway, I don't see the need to elaborate unless you've decided to come."

Mal was certain, by the time he finished, that he could see a spark of interest in Griff's eyes. It wasn't a yes, not yet, but it was at least a step toward taking him far away from the agents who would want to finish the job and might not care about Mal's treasure hunt.

"Say I was. Planning to come, I mean. For Rhun and Alys." Griff leaned forward on his elbows. "Could we actually travel together for several weeks and not come to blows? You think it would change things between us? You really think we can be anything but each other's demons?"

He shivered a little, no doubt becoming more aware of the chill working its way over the city, a rapid cooling now that the day was done.

Mal drummed his fingers against the side of his leg for a moment before answering, trying to get the hammering of his heart under control. "I don't expect a trip to change a damn thing, no. But you're hardly my worst demon." In stark contrast to the dusk, the temperature in his voice rose steadily as he added, "Just say you're not going already."

Griff rubbed his hands over his arms like he was trying not to shiver again, and leveled a look at Mal, one he held for a long moment as he asked, "If I go . . . is there any hope for us?"

There was a younger man's petulance in Mal's voice that he couldn't quite disguise as he demanded in return, "Hope? What the hell does that mean? That we're suddenly going to be friends again? That I'll come over and make nice with your boyfriend and eat his shitty cooking like Alys does?" The questions burned with frustration, like they came from a caged animal glancing at things beyond his power to reach for, to give.

Peeling away from the beam he was leaning against, he knelt before the spot where Griff sat, fixing him in his unflinching gaze. "When are you going to accept that this is who I am? You always ask me things even though you know you won't like the answers, and then no matter what I say, you judge me for it. I don't know who it is you want me to be, and frankly, I don't care anymore," he snarled, letting that animal out of its cage for a moment, stretching its weary limbs. "When am I going to be enough for you just as I am? Ever? Is there any hope of *that*?"

Griff reached for him. Two callused fingers slipped beneath Mal's chin, through the gold stubble growing there, and rose to rest against his cheek as Mal's eyes widened in surprise and he lapsed into dumbfounded silence.

Neither breathed for a moment, but Mal's pulse raced beneath Griff's fingers.

Neither moved.

Griff could surely smell the whiskey on his breath, they were so close. Cheap stuff, swill, though Mal could have afforded better. And beneath it—the lemon soap Vic had always scrubbed his clothes with.

Mal couldn't look away. Not because he had any fear that Griff might strike, but because he could smell sweat and rosemary shampoo and the kohl that often lined Griff's eyes, a distinct combination that set his face more firmly into his usual nettled expression; nothing good ever came of getting this close to him, though Mal could see why so many men did. Not that he was keeping track. Griff had the sort of classic, poetic beauty that belonged on a painted fresco dedicated to some god or another, and half the time he didn't seem to know it. He applied himself to things so earnestly. He loved to learn; he was such a hopeless dork—

Mal stopped himself there, before he could have another stupid, useless thought.

"I'll go," Griff breathed at last, and the tightness in Mal's chest eased just a little. "I'll go," he repeated, sounding more certain now, as Mal's pulse continued to flutter wildly under his touch. "And I'll tend the fire and clean your cuts and sleep at your back without judgment. And maybe you'll realize somewhere along the way that you've always been enough—you just haven't let me get close enough to show it, or to try to make anything right. Not since . . ."

Did Griff know his fingers were trembling against Mal's skin? He couldn't think what had possessed Griff to reach for him like this when nothing had really changed.

Soon enough, Griff lowered his shaking hand. And as he did, he said in a would-be casual tone, "Who knows? Out in the Mire, you might even find out whether I'd die for you."

As Griff's hand fell away, a spell was broken. A breath of relief at gaining some distance escaped Mal's lips as he rose to his feet, steady and lithe as ever—as if that touch hadn't made him weak at the knees.

It had also, inexplicably, made his tattoo burn. Or perhaps that was just the result of too much vicious scratching.

Griff, on the other hand, didn't move. He seemed to have every intention of sitting on his chopping block a while longer before retrieving his shirt.

But behind him, something did shift away—a shadow, taller than Griff's, unfurling itself to its full imposing height as it separated from the fabric of night. Mal blinked hard, but still the thing remained. Even Griff shivered at the chill radiating from it, though Mal was certain he couldn't see it; he had only been able to see ghosts himself since he'd died for a few seconds in Thrallkeld. They never spoke to him, at least not in any language he could hear, but seeing them was punishment enough for having cheated death. Though usually they showed their faces, unlike this figure of solid darkness.

Maybe that explained why his tattoo was suddenly searing. After all, this thing had to be some servant of the Shadow Queen.

"It's just a job," Mal repeated brusquely to Griff, as if nothing at all were amiss, as he adjusted his cloak against the coming night, not remotely because the absence of Griff's hand against his cheek had left him colder than before. "And nobody's going to die. I'll make sure of that."

It was the least he could do.

Mal's feet were itching to hit the road again; he'd had his fill of Griff's questions for now, and this had been their longest conversation in years. Most of all, he wanted to get away from that strange shadow—though when he glanced at it again, it had already vanished, absorbed back into the night. Often, these things appeared just for a little shock; this one, he decided with more conviction now, had appeared to speed him on his journey, or else to check out the man who had just agreed to join the expedition.

"When do we leave?" Griff asked, rubbing his hands along his arms as if to warm them. He drew in a breath, then said quickly, gruffly, almost like he didn't know how, "I've missed you, you absolute shit."

While a flash of discomfort crossed Mal's face at such genuine emotion offered so casually, the crude nickname made the sentiment a little more palatable. A soft, appreciative snort issued from his nostrils as he set his feet on the path to home.

"Don't get all sappy now, you sentimental fuck, or this trip really will be a hazard to everyone's health," Mal said with a half-roll of his eyes, feeling a little more like himself now that the shadow had gone and his tattoo wasn't burning so much.

But something uncertain washed over his face just after, something that made him turn hastily away from Griff before the foreman could read whatever showed there as he wondered if he could trust what the other man had said: that he had missed him.

After everything.

The emotion in his voice had sounded real enough, as real as the darting shadow or the wood-splitting maul resting on the stump. But all the insults he had fired back at Mal over the years—those had been real too.

Mal had no more idea of what to do with that than he did the large shipment of dwarven crystal glasses for which he still hadn't been paid, which were currently sitting packed in large wooden crates in a hidden glade in the Wyrmwood.

"Oh, and we leave in the morning. First light, so you'd better try to get some rest while you can," he added briskly over his shoulder before breaking back toward the road, and the far more reliable warmth of a yet-distant fire.

Chapter Seven
Trustfall

In hindsight, Griff had probably gone overboard by baking Liam's favorite cake just to cushion the blow before telling him about the trip.

It was no one's birthday or anniversary, yet there he was, wearing nothing but his underwear and the really cute apron with the daises on it that never failed to make Liam smile. He was counting on that smile before he spilled the news of what he had agreed to tonight, what he'd been thinking about constantly ever since, so it was a good thing he had somehow managed to make it home before his boyfriend.

Of course he was going. Because while he knew better than to trust everything Mal said, he was familiar with at least a few of the treasures in that legendary pile sunk deep in the Mire—the benefits of his education in Stormveil. There were crowns that supposedly still carried the might and will of their rulers. A lyre strung with the hairs of some long-extinct beast that played the purest notes. And, more importantly, a pair of gleaming silver vambraces, crafted by elven healers more powerful than any left alive today, that could cure any effects of magical poisons. Which, he suspected, was exactly why he hadn't fully healed in the first place. If he could find those vambraces, he could finally be free of this staggering pain—if not the nightmares—and join the ranks of his friends as the Warden he was born to be.

Besides, Mal had come to him. Mal had asked for him, no matter whose idea it was to begin with. And while Mal might be a liar and a crook, Mal was also Mal, and Griff would follow him anywhere and keep him safe. It was what he did. He could never bear the thought of a world without Mal, demons and all.

Because while the Mal who had returned from Thrallkeld was a bully (if there had been a competition for Meanest Mouth in Mayfair, Mal certainly would have won) and his favorite activity was picking on everything about Griff, he had also glimpsed something of the old Mal tonight. The old Mal, who didn't hate him. Who wasn't full of insults and stinging indifference. Mal who was endlessly curious, Mal who had the highest hopes for this life of anyone Griff had ever met, self-possessed and confident in a way Griff had always admired. Mal who included Griff in his big dreams and held out his hand to call him to another adventure, forever seeking. Mal, whose loyal heart never wavered, a heart he showed to few.

Mal, who Griff had called a traitor for where he worked, when what he hadn't been brave enough to say was that he only felt betrayed by Mal kissing some girl instead of him. He had really screwed that one up, and Mal had never received a single one of the letters he'd sent from Stormveil trying to make it right. Words he hadn't wanted to hear by the time they both found their way back home. Not that saying sorry ever fixed anything.

Maybe Griff had been the Meanest Mouth in Mayfair back then.

The front door swung open, pulling Griff away from thoughts of glittering coins and dark-gold hair more precious than any metal.

Liam barely cracked a smile when he trudged in late from work to the cozy sight of his boyfriend in the kitchen, bringing in a light chill and the smoke of other fires that clung to his clothes and hair.

Instead, caution mingled with curiosity on the locksmith's face as he hung up his cloak and made his way into the kitchen, where he watched Griff pop the cake tins in the oven before sliding his arms around the foreman and growling hopefully into the almost-elfin curve of his ear: "Could you please explain what exactly we're celebrating, babe?"

"You," Griff answered immediately, turning to catch Liam's lips hard with his own. Against them, he added, "Us."

It was a good answer, good enough apparently to inspire Liam to kiss Griff's neck until Griff was sure he would be sporting some marks in the shape of his mouth there come morning. Unable to ignore the guilt writhing in his gut any longer, he cleared his throat. After all, he didn't have much time to explain. He would be leaving in just a few hours, and Liam was bound to see the pack sitting at the foot of their bed soon enough.

Liam's gray eyes, the same shape as Mal's but sprinkled with violet, peered worriedly into Griff's. "Really, though. Did I miss an important date or something?"

"No, it's not that. You never do. It's—I saw Mal tonight," he began. Gods, why was it so hard to find the words even though he'd been practicing? When Liam pulled out of his embrace, Griff didn't fight to keep him there, giving him the space he clearly wanted. His arms dropped to his sides. "I mean, he came to see me."

"Fuck," Liam said passionately, and not in the usual way.

Even with the warmth given off by the stove, their hearth blazing, and the kisses they had just shared, the locksmith gave a little shiver, as if the chill of the night had snuck in and found him again. "Explain," he urged as Griff fidgeted with a fraying thread on the bottom of the daisy apron, desperate to do something with his empty hands.

"Right." Griff swallowed audibly. "Well, he's going on a trip. A business trip. He said it shouldn't take more than four weeks at most, and . . . he's asked me to come with him—in an official capacity, of course. As a healer." He gazed steadily, if warily, at Liam as he explained, willing him to understand. "We leave at first light."

"No," the locksmith said simply, firmly, as if that settled the matter. "You're not going."

"Alys will be there too. All three of us," Griff continued, determined to get through all he had to say, as if he hadn't heard Liam's outright denial so soon into the telling. "You like her. You know her. She wouldn't let him hurt—"

"Hurt you? You think he's going to hurt you? What, like Alys is going to have to draw her blade to save you from tripping and falling right onto his dick?" Liam abruptly strode out of the kitchen, apparently seeking more distance and startling a dozing Badger into opening a hopeful eye in search of crumbs.

"I don't trust anything about Mal, and you know that," the locksmith continued hotly from the living room. "And now, after several really good months of not having to hear about him, you're bringing that fucking name into our house again when you're not half asleep."

As Liam rattled around in a drawer somewhere, Griff walked slowly, sheepishly, out of the kitchen. Still, he gave his boyfriend the space he sought, stopping to lean against the kitchen entryway and going no farther.

He blinked when he realized Liam had a pair of scissors in hand, his heart giving an unpleasant lurch as the locksmith held them up to his bright-gold locks just beneath his ear. "What if I cut my hair? It won't be the same length as Mal's anymore. Will you still love me then? What else of mine is the same length as Mal's? Well?"

The cake had been a mistake, clearly. This was going worse than Griff could possibly have imagined. Still, he held fast to his calm in the face of Liam's anger. He had plenty of practice at that, thanks to Mal.

"It's not going to be like that," he assured his sweet boyfriend, who had a remarkably sour look on his face, scissors still held aloft. "Not at all. Not ever. For one, as far as I know, Mal only likes women. He had some on-again, off-again girlfriend for years. Sage or Saffron or something. More importantly, Mal hates me, remember? He only asked me because Alys insisted. He doesn't really want me there."

Which was more or less true. Griff had said it, and Mal hadn't denied it, anyway.

"Good! So listen to him, then, if you won't listen to me, and don't fucking go," Liam pleaded lowly. "It isn't going to end well, for anyone."

Under the table where he had been napping, Badger once again raised his head and sniffed, this time as if searching for a threat. His coppery gaze landed on something near the window behind Griff and stayed there. He wagged his tail uncertainly.

Hardly noticing what had caught the dog's attention in the heat of the moment, his voice growing quieter with regret, Griff insisted, "I have to, though. He asked. And I couldn't live with myself if he got hurt. Please, Liam, don't you see?"

"I don't, no," Liam said flatly in a terrific imitation of Mal. "And I don't see who exactly is going to heal *you* if you're in trouble. Certainly not some fucking scammer who preys on old women. You know how much trouble Rose is in for coming down here, you read her letter—there's no way she can save you a second time."

"Still. Even if it's dangerous, I have to go." Griff took a cautious step toward him, then another, and pried the scissors from Liam's reluctant fingers. Finally able to take a deep breath, he held those familiar gray eyes he loved so well and explained, "He found a map that belonged to Rhun. We think it must be the route he was taking with his friends when he disappeared—this is a chance to get some answers about what really happened to him. I mean, it's been years, but it feels like we owe it to him—and to Alys, and Wynnie—to find out what we can. My dad was Rhun's best friend; he'd want me to go too."

Liam stepped around Griff, returning to the kitchen table to pull out one of the chairs, where he sat down heavily. His expression was calmer now, if still wary. He knew what Rhun had been to Griff; he hadn't had much of a father himself, only a drunkard who was the reason Liam was so good with his fists.

Griff took the chance to add softly, "And . . . there might be something out there, an artifact in the treasure Mal's after, that was designed to combat the effects of magical poisons. It's got healing powers beyond even Rosemaris's, beyond the strongest elven potion."

He didn't need to say more. Liam would understand what that meant for him too.

Swallowing a few times, the locksmith finally said in a more controlled voice, "Your mom came by this morning after you left for work. I meant to tell you."

"Which one?" Griff asked.

He hadn't seen Wynnie in over a week, but he'd seen Vic just yesterday, when he had visited the cottage porch to deliver some of that strong elven healing potion for their dog, Whiskey. It was provided to him in a series of secretive handoffs from the Wardens courtesy of Rose, a vial of cherry-scented, ruby liquid that was nearly priceless these days. When magical poisons weren't involved, it could stall a man's death for a day or two, give a body a fighting chance, and it was all that kept the old dog alive anymore. But no one aside from Griff and Vic, who drizzled the vial over the dog's evening meal once a month, needed to know the reason behind their old friend hanging on for so long.

"Wynnie," Liam said finally, seeming to have come back to himself a little more. "She found the guy who stabbed you—one of them, at least. Your *friend* Wills, from your construction crew."

Griff sure could have used a chair to sink into himself as he heard that name, but he didn't want to crowd Liam just yet. "Oh," he breathed, willing his scar not to twinge. "Okay."

No wonder Wills was still out sick, if Wynnie had gotten hold of him. She wouldn't have been able to kill him, not without bringing far too much unwanted attention on herself—not in Mayfair, with all its Wardens—but she could have given him any number of lasting wounds to rival Griff's. Not that he minded at this point. His fingers mapped the area of his scar over his apron, feeling it ache with only a phantom of the usual pain.

"Wynnie said Wills was working for the Shadow Queen. And that she *took care of it* and expected you wouldn't want the gory details." Liam paused there, exchanging a knowing look with Griff. To her credit, his former guardian did understand at least this one thing about him: his distaste for violence. "She also said—and I agree—that you trust far too easily, and it's going to be the death of you," the locksmith added pointedly, frowning as he watched Griff trace the injury that had nearly ended him.

Pushing Wynnie's sense of justice and his own shortcomings on choosing friends to the back of his mind for now, Griff took a tentative step toward the table, keeping his voice soft as he tried again to broach the subject of his departure. "Look, I have to go. I have to find answers about Rhun, if I can. And if I find that artifact in Mal's pile of gold, so much the better. The only thing that's going to come back from this trip with any bruises on it is my ego after Mal has his fill of insulting me all day long, and that's a—"

"No. Don't," Liam interrupted, and loudly. "Don't you dare. Don't you promise me anything right now." He held up a hand, bidding for silence, and Griff complied, not attempting another step forward into the tense space between them.

Hadn't Liam known from the start, from the first coin dropped on his nightstand, that Griff wasn't very good at staying?

"What kind of business is it that little creep usually does anyway?" Liam asked eventually.

"I don't exactly know," Griff admitted. "I think . . . he does a little of everything. Real estate. Shipping. Protection. He just seems to go wherever opportunity arises." Perhaps that was all a generous way of putting it, but he wasn't seeking to upset Liam any further. Just the opposite, yet the look on his face had Griff wondering if the sweet-natured locksmith was currently contemplating murder.

"It's just a job," he said hastily, recalling Mal's earlier words to him. This time, when he closed the distance between himself and Liam, the locksmith rose from his chair and met him with an outstretched arm, pulled him back into the warmth of his embrace, his heartbeat still rapid against Griff's chest but his breathing, at least, starting to slow. "Just a job," he pretended he was telling Liam, rather than himself. "Extra coin for us—from the sound of it, enough for us to buy a bigger house. Enough for us to get another friend for Badger, and maybe a horse. A chance for me to finally heal this wound all the way. And possibly a chance for some closure about Rhun."

Liam's arms tightened around him. He slid his hands under the apron, into the comfort of familiar skin, offering plenty of wordless understanding.

Mal's skin had been so warm, too, the feel of his cheek beneath Griff's fingers achingly familiar and yet completely new. Mal wasn't asking Griff to die for him, and yet he would, if it came to that. He and Mal had sat together and talked without coming to blows, and that was more than they had had in long time, that was more than enough—how could Mal ever think he wasn't enough for him, how could he not see that a simple touch was enough to still be keeping Griff warm, even now? Was he thinking about it too? That moment when neither of them had dared to so much as breathe? No doubt Mal had already put it out of his mind, if he'd thought of it at all. And so should Griff, because he could never tell Mal how he felt. He didn't think he would ever be able to get warm again after hearing the laughter that would surely follow.

"Just a job," Griff repeated at last, once again telling himself as well. "A job. For us."

Eventually, he hoped, saying it enough times would make it true. He ran his hands up into Liam's sandy-blond hair and kissed him until he drew some soft noises of wanting from the other man, as if a shared moment of pleasure would somehow make this *enough*.

"I've still got a few hours before I have to hit the road. We might as well make the most of them . . ." Griff murmured.

Liam pulled back, looking for a long moment into his eyes before they ventured further.

But while Griff smiled back at him, he couldn't help that his gaze was already somewhere else again, following the wisp of a ratty gray cloak into the deepening night in his mind's eye as he relived those moments with Mal.

"Will he hold you through your nightmares like I do?" Liam asked softly.

Griff wasn't sure what to say to that. He shook his head, a denial of sorts. He couldn't imagine Mal ever doing anything so tender, not even for Alys, and she was his best friend. Mal had come back from Thrallkeld with a permanent chip on his shoulder, and Griff wasn't convinced the thief knew what gentle was anymore, if he ever had.

"Well, perhaps you'd better remember who does that, then," Liam suggested, raising one hand to cup the side of Griff's face, softly feeling into his hair. "I do, because I love you so much." He took a bracing breath. "But if you go on that trip, if you walk out that door in the morning, you're fucking dead to me. Leave here with them, and we're done. If Mal wants to find out what happened to Rhun so badly, he can risk his own neck and come back to tell you about it. I need you here. I don't care if that means I never get to retire—fuck the money."

Liam leaned in and nuzzled Griff's cheek before adding, his voice never rising, "If you go, any of your shit that gets left behind is going out on the lawn for the neighbors to pick through. And that includes your everyday lute, your favorite lute from the elves, and your entire collection of pants that hug that fine ass of yours just right."

In the end, the combination of his favorite strawberry cake and Griff in just that apron proved too much for Liam to resist, though Griff made no promises about staying or going with the dawn. He managed to convince the locksmith to come to bed to share the cake, to snuggle and get their sheets dirty in all their favorite ways.

And if later, in the sweaty, bewildering dark, Griff couldn't tell whether it was Mal's or Liam's hand wrapped around him just right, well—that was between Griff and the pillows, and they weren't about to start talking.

It was just a hand, after all. Just a job. Just a man.

He had someone to hold him through his nightmares already, someone he trusted. He would be a fool to risk that over answers about a man long gone, an artifact that might or might not still exist, and a shadow of the boy whose carefree grin and reckless ambition did funny things to his heart. A boy who certainly didn't exist anymore.

Griff Sayer-Blackthorn had such a nice ring to it.

Chapter Eight
Spiders

It was fine, really, that Griff hadn't shown up to depart from the cottage with them as the sun peeked over the horizon. Mal didn't care one way or another what the man did. At least he was consistent in being a letdown. That was one thing Griff could apparently commit to.

He would simply have to take his chances with Kage and Wills and the others who had failed to kill him before, and Mal and Alys would go risk their necks to buy his safety in the meantime. And maybe learn something about where Rhun had really gone all those years ago. Mal's money was on desertion rather than death, though he had packed enough whiskey—two large bottles, one in each of their packs—to keep his flask refilled no matter the outcome.

Surely that would be enough to sustain him for four weeks. Less. Now that he had Alys with him, he would make it back with the treasure so fast Kage's head would be spinning as he watched Mal walk out the tea shop door for the final time.

Maybe they could even keep a little of what they found for themselves, just enough to persuade the Wardens to forgive some of the stupid things they suspected Mal of before he split town again. Assuming they could be bought.

He walked briskly in step with Alys through the unseasonably cold, cloudy morning, making good progress down the road with it being just the two of them. How it should have been in the first place. Alys was unusually quiet, and Mal gave a rare smile in her direction—grateful she wasn't berating him for not trying harder to make sure Griff came along, because he had done his best. Even if his best was never enough for Griff.

They were on the outskirts of Linden when footsteps approached rapidly from behind, and Mal's heart gave a sudden kick as he recognized the cadence of the panted breaths that accompanied them. "You're late," he said by way of greeting, not bothering to turn and look at the other man. "I think you've already forfeited your share of the profits."

"Fine by me. I don't need a big pile of gold just to feel something," Griff huffed between breaths, the redness in his cheeks making it clear how hard he had worked to catch up. "Ran into a little delay with packing—as in half my shit was still on the front lawn when I left. So you'll understand why it took me a minute to catch up." His pack was straining against its ties and the kohl around his eyes was smudged as if he'd been crying, but Mal wasn't about to pry for personal details he didn't really want to hear, and apparently, neither was Alys.

They simply slowed their pace until Griff fell into step with them more or less without issue. And for the first time in nearly a decade, they strode along the road leading east as a trio.

All three were tall and spindly. Alys, breaking from the others to wander closer to the sagebrush and colorful fireweed that lined this section of road where houses and trees were growing increasingly sparse, easily had the palest hair, while Mal's was more a burnished gold, and Griff's was inky dark. All were armed—Alys with her father's old sword and her collection of knives, Mal with his daggers and fists, and Griff with a humble-looking sword that must have been a Warden's hand-me-down and his wood-splitting maul.

Mal was surprised he had brought it, but even more surprised by the calm he felt upon seeing it. Maybe he had underestimated Griff as just a helpless victim.

Alys smiled and sang something under her breath as they walked, as if she were completely unaware (or otherwise deeply pleased) that the three of them coming together again like this was rarer than an eclipse. She struck him now, as she did some days when she wandered into the cottage with a handful of flowers that she hadn't checked for bugs and their eggs, as a stark callback to her elven ancestors. One foot in this world and one in some magical otherplace that only she could see or access. Sometimes he wondered about all the things she saw that no one else did.

Griff, meanwhile, seemed to keep his eyes mostly trained on the horizon, though they occasionally turned skyward, as if questioning all the gods and spirits that had ever been described to him as to the nature of his purpose here.

Not that Mal was paying him much attention.

The rank mist lingering slightly to their north took up most of his focus. The foul weather inspired him to dig out a scarf and wrap it around his neck before pulling his cloak hood back up and adjusting the toggles. The cloth was knobbly and black, a humble homespun affair, but Mal suspected Griff might recognize it.

The scarf had been his once. But somehow, in the years before they both left home, Mal's red one had made its way into Griff's laundry pile, and the black one had found its way to Mal. And was still keeping him warm today.

Scarves weren't cheap; it would have been a waste to just burn it.

Further east, the way was even less inviting, to Mal's keen eyes, with the breeze becoming a howling wind that shook the dark treetops. This far north, mornings and evenings still carried a bite sometimes even in early summer. Yet this was something more. It had the look of an unnatural storm, a few snowflakes even swirling on the gray horizon in the distance where the clouds crouched in thicker, closer to the earth.

A spell gone awry, perhaps—magic in the wrong hands. Mal wouldn't have been surprised. Wardens saw things like that sometimes, being out here. Enough for him to have heard plenty of their stories circulating in the taverns where he drank back in Mayfair. Wardens really couldn't shut up about themselves.

"Be right back, you two," Alys announced suddenly, cheerily, putting any such stories far out of Mal's mind. She turned and let the tall brush swallow her lithe form, grass whisking against her canvas pants as she strode away from them.

"Where are you going?" Griff called after her. It was clear from a quick look at his face that he didn't want to be alone with Mal.

"I have to pee!" Alys's playful voice drifted back in a light gust of mist. "Give me a minute. If you're both good, maybe I'll even bring you back a treat."

Mal had no idea what kind of treat Alys might find on the outskirts of Linden, though he knew it was bound to be something that excited only her. He decided to take the pause as a chance to study the map, pulling the hopelessly wrinkled old parchment out and attempting to unfurl it, its torn edges fluttering in the rising wind. Maybe four weeks there and back was, as it seemed on paper, an impossible task. Another unforeseen complication of living a cursed existence. But he had done things that felt impossible before, and this would be no different.

"What's our course?" Griff asked haltingly, as if against his better judgment.

Mal arched a blond brow but didn't glance up. "Well," he said evenly, "right now we're heading east. At some point we have to turn north, but there's no footpath that close to the Mire. I think it's likely we'll have to carve our own way forward, following what's outlined on this map, until we see the lake."

"And the treasure? The armor, the swords, the barrows of the old elven kings—they're just floating out there?" Griff asked, edging closer for a better look at the map.

"Yeah, and since you were late, you get to fish it all out, gem by gem and coin by coin," Mal said, unable to keep a touch of sarcasm from his voice as he pointed to the little island marked in the middle of the lake.

With that, he rolled up the map and stowed it, slipping some mittens (another of Vic's whimsical and fleeting attempts at domesticity, much like the old black scarf) over his hands as he added, "We should press on through the night and make camp tomorrow evening instead. Cover more of the plains. I don't like how open it is out here. This place could be crawling with Wardens at any time, and it'll be easier going unnoticed by dark."

It would also help them get some more distance under their feet early, which he hoped would satisfy Kage and his queen and whoever else she had set to watch their progress.

Griff, who didn't seem to have packed any mittens, rubbed his hands together for warmth as they waited. There were little scars all over them that Mal couldn't recall seeing the last time they'd fought. But then, he hadn't been looking. "These are the things you think about, then?" the foreman muttered between blowing on his chilled fingers. "Keeping your distance from those who keep us safe?"

Mal's shoulders tightened a fraction. There was that un-asked-for judgment again. It was going to be the longest trip of his life if Griff kept that up, especially when he was only out here risking his neck to protect this ungrateful man in the first place.

Rather than indulging a question he knew was meant to sting, he took a sip from his flask and asked one of his own instead. "What happened there?"

Griff followed Mal's gaze to the backs of his hands, where the scars were faded mostly to white, and drew himself a little deeper into his cloak as he sighed and said, "Work accident. Accidents. One of the risks of doing physical labor for a living."

It was an answer that invited no further questions.

As Mal reached for his flask again, a spark of silver darting in and out of his cloak's breast pocket at not half past ten in the morning, Griff glanced pointedly at the dark lines of ink that trailed down his wrist, the start of the design of falling raven's feathers that now ran the length of his forearm. "Who gave you that? And why's it so red?"

Mal trailed a hand over his sleeve that concealed most of the flaky, itchy image within, a gesture that was becoming habit. He was silent for a long moment, resentful at having been asked something in return, and when he finally spoke, it was in a tone as unwelcoming of questions as Griff's had been moments earlier. "My boss. It was just business."

"I don't know—a tattoo seems pretty personal to me. Seems like the kind of story you might want to tell when someone asks."

Mal turned to study Griff's face more closely, not sure what he was going to find there. More judgment, probably, if history was any indication. Or maybe . . . was Griff really curious about him? About the stories he could tell? Not that he would be explaining the real reason for their treasure hunt when they had barely left Linden.

When their eyes met, Griff immediately glanced off in the direction Alys had disappeared as another rush of wind flattened the tops of the pink-red fireweed, and Mal dismissed the notion altogether. Of course Griff didn't want to hear about his life. If he did, he would have asked a long time ago.

Mal was relieved to see Alys's white-blond head bobbing back toward them at top speed a few moments later. As she got closer, he noted something clutched in her fists, the dark-purple flesh of berries peeking from between gaps in her fingers.

"Anyone else feeling peckish?" she asked with a gleam in her cornflower-blue eyes as she distributed handfuls of berries to Mal, then to Griff, saving plenty for herself as well. "Vic taught me some about foraging this year," she added proudly. Mal suspected she was trying to impress Griff.

"Thanks, Alys," he said with more enthusiasm than he felt, flashing her an indulgent smile to match. The berries were exceptionally bitter, which made not grimacing a challenge. "They're really . . . fresh."

"Vic taught me some about foraging too," Griff told them as he tried a berry, not bothering to hide his wince as the taste hit. "Not sure I know about these, though."

They pressed on into the mist, following the edge of the road for now, the day growing oddly bright though they were still heading toward that dark horizon.

Mal, who had initially set a grueling pace to try to impress his employers, began to lag slightly, and when Griff eventually caught up to him, Mal noticed a sheen of sweat slicking the other man's face, more than just mist dripping from the curly ends of his raven hair.

He dropped his own hood as well, too warm to continue on otherwise.

"As your hired healer, I feel a certain obligation to tell you that you don't look so good," Griff confided lowly to him, just out of earshot of Alys, who was walking on the opposite side of the road and seemed to be whispering to the occasional nodding flowerhead.

That's when Mal realized his heartbeat had picked up an unusual cadence. A hand pressed to his forehead came away slick, too, though the mist had let up in the past hour or so. He stopped in his tracks, blinking as if the world's colors had just shifted from rose to gray, and let out a familiar grumble. "Alys . . . what did you say those berries were again?"

She turned, her eyes suspiciously bright, and said, "I didn't. I don't know the name. One of Vic's favorites, though. At least, I think. I was . . . sort of . . . already high when I picked them. It's possible I got the wrong ones." A flush darkened her cheeks as she admitted, "I ate a couple of those dried mushrooms you brought me from work before we set out this morning."

Now Mal knew why Alys had seemed so at ease with the three of them back together again when there was so much still unsaid. She'd been too out of it to think about all the bad times, the things Mal couldn't even drink away.

Beside him, Griff had started frantically scratching at a spot just beneath his shirt collar as if it itched worse than Mal's tattoo. Quickly the foreman's hands moved down over his torso, all the way down to his pant leg, which he pulled up as if expecting to see something there. He swiped a hand across his back, into one of those hard-to-reach-places, his eyes growing wider and more panicked by the second.

Mal's lips quirked, amused, as Griff started unbuttoning his dark linen shirt. "No one's paying you to put on *that* kind of show," he commented dryly, but he wasn't sure Griff even heard him.

The other man was too busy muttering, "Get them off me. Just need to get them off."

"Get *what* off?" Mal asked, a bite of impatience in the words. "I don't see anything." And he, of course, was used to seeing things others couldn't.

"Firespiders," Griff breathed, his voice hushed, as if he thought talking loudly might upset the dime-sized, bright-red creatures that, as far as Mal could tell, weren't even there. Clawing at his shirt, he added, "I can't remember how many bites before the venom paralyzes someone my size . . ."

Far be it from Mal to pretend he knew the first thing about healing. Still, he leaned a little closer to Griff to observe with some urgency in his tone, "You're about the same color as the curdled milk I threw out last week. How many of those berries did you eat?"

Alys giggled as Griff tried and failed to wriggle out of his shirt with his pack still slung over his shoulders and his cloak still fastened.

But Mal wasn't finding much humor in the situation himself, even if perhaps he ordinarily would have; narrowing his eyes against the sun's glare, he realized there was a shadow behind Griff that wasn't his own. A taller, darker shade that was puppeting his every movement but not quite getting them right, copying the frantic itching and the way Griff was now running off the road and into the grassy field that flanked their left.

It looked a lot like the solid shadow he had seen behind Griff last night. But why was the Shadow Queen already sending emissaries to spook him? To hound him into picking up the pace? He was already going after the treasure as fast as his two legs could possibly carry him. And why wouldn't this thing just show its face like every other spirit he had encountered? Glare at him or something?

Of course, just then he couldn't even be certain whether what he was seeing was real or a result of eating all those berries.

The way his tattoo was suddenly burning like the day he'd received it as he took a step toward Griff decided for him. Whatever it was, it was real enough. Dead enough, and dangerous enough.

And he was going to get it off of Griff, because the whole reason he had brought him out here was to keep him safe. He had, after all, worked several stints in Protection when the coin was good. With a growl, he raced after Griff—apparently still more possessed of his faculties than the other man, even if his breath was now coming in rapid gasps—catching up with him easily and colliding with him, knocking a gust of breath from Griff's chest as he wrestled the slightly larger man to the ground in a tangle of packs and clothes and smashing foreheads.

"What the hell?" Griff spluttered as he shoved an elbow into Mal's face. Another connected with his ribs. "Get. Off!"

No longer seeing the extra shadow, Mal growled back as he dodged a quick elbow, "Didn't want to be here in the first place," rolling off Griff with a few muttered curses. Then he lay on his back in the tall grass, staring up at the strange-hued sky and wondering if the loud pattering he heard was each drop of his own sweat hitting the ground.

No, he decided a few moments later as Alys's legs came into view. It must have just been her footsteps as she wandered over. She should really learn not to walk so loud when they were out where anyone might discover them.

Griff, just a few feet farther into the grass, also managed to roll onto his back, taking some gulping mouthfuls of fresh air that reassured Mal he was still very much alive.

There was a large, flattish rock nearby breaking up the field, and Mal watched as Alys climbed onto it, riffling through her pack until she came across one of her many sketchbooks and a pack of charcoals. Settling herself cross-legged, the pad in her lap, she started to draw something—much the way she had done since they were little, to the delight and wonder of other children and adults alike.

"Did you get all the spiders off, at least, when you tackled me?" Griff asked hoarsely, drawing Mal's attention back to him.

"There were never any spiders," Mal said firmly, in a tone he hoped left no room to question the matter further. He was much more concerned about the shadow without a face that had now appeared twice, both times behind Griff, though there was no sense in alarming anyone about it while they were in this state.

Griff sighed. "Is Alys going to be like this the whole time we're out here?"

Mal shrugged. "I'm not her boss. It's called business *partners*." He glanced back at Alys, who continued humming and drawing, her pupils blown wide, her smile relaxed. She was often like this at the cottage, too, as if there were something about being "elsewhere" she found easier. Floating just outside herself, as if she couldn't bear to spend too long in her own skin.

This was the legacy their parents had fought so hard to protect: an artist who loved her drugs, an enterprising but often-maligned businessman, and a foreman with commitment issues. The heroes who killed the Shadow Queen's last living dragon at the steep cost of their own lives, the ones who ended the last great war with their sacrifice, who were lauded by all the bards from here to the far south where dwarven empires dominated and coffee plants grew, had surely had greater ambitions for their children than this.

Their legacy, wrestling each other to the ground, sweating hallucinogenic berries out of their pores, and unable to follow a simple map for a full day.

Fucking fantastic.

"Wonder what the kids are doing right now," Alys said thoughtfully after a while—Mal couldn't guess how long it had been since he and Griff had collapsed on their backs and agreed without speaking that they weren't going to move until the worst of this had passed. "Hope they're staying out of the creek and minding Vic."

Beside him, Griff started shaking with quiet laughter.

"What's so funny?" Mal grumbled, not sure he wanted to hear the answer. He rarely did with Griff.

"Just—it makes sense that Vic's the one watching Alys's kids," the foreman explained between bouts of laughter that shook his shoulders. "Wynnie thinks a dagger is a good birthday present for a six-year-old." Scooting closer to Mal, he added with a glint in his eyes, as if they were sharing a delightful secret, "Bet Vic still does everyone's laundry too."

Mal really wished the berries had made Griff quiet rather than chatty. He had already had his fill of hearing that low, musical voice for the day.

"What are you drawing, Alys?" he called over to the rock, determined to just ignore the man beside him until he sobered up.

"Little Mal, at the moment," she answered sweetly, not taking her eyes from the paper.

At another giggle from beside him, Mal groaned and gathered some clumps of grass between his fingers so he wouldn't be tempted to curl them into fists.

"Is that . . . is that what the ladies call your . . . ?" Griff choked out, making a vague gesture between his own legs even as Mal narrowed his eyes at him in a clear indication that he should shut up before someone got seriously hurt.

Was he really that much of a joke to Griff? And why did he care anymore?

"It's a cat. I hate that wretched thing," Mal explained with an air of long-suffering. He had always harbored a dislike for cats in general, so much so that as children they often idly speculated that he must have orcish blood somewhere in his family line.

"No, really," Mal insisted as Griff's laughter died down. "This one is worse than most. It only comes inside to eat the dog's food or attack someone—with claws, teeth, you name it. That beast has a taste for blood and a serious attitude problem. I have no idea why Alys named it after me, of all people."

The clouds scudding past broke apart, reforming into a dozen mesmerizing shapes that soon drew Griff's attention, much to Mal's relief. He'd had enough of Griff picking at his personal life for one day.

"Look!" The foreman grinned, flinging his arm wide above Mal's head.

Mal suspected he had meant to nudge him in the side and missed.

Griff pointed with his other hand this time, indicating two large scraps of fluffy cloud overhead that had collided to form the clumsy shape of a pouncing cat. "It's Little Mal."

"Shut up," Mal ordered, though thanks to the berries, without his usual ire.

Griff pointed to a different one. "And there's Whiskey, the dog."

They used to play this game on golden afternoons after they'd had their fill of swimming or sheep tipping, a sacred outing on which Alys never joined them (on account of it being mean to the sheep, she said, though they had never actually invited her, either). As far as they were concerned, the sheep needed a little excitement now and then and never came away sporting so much as a bruise. They had even made a little game of trying to catch the sheep's bell collar, which generally ended with bruises on their own knees and unchecked amounts of laughter, after which they would practice their cloud spotting while trying to catch a breath. For a few glorious years, they were the menace of several local farmers.

"I think that one's a turtle," Mal offered groggily a few minutes later, trying to pretend this was normal, that they could still share anything without the fear of Griff ruining it. "See?" He arced his body a little closer to Griff's and pointed at a domed shape above them from which wisps of cloud protruded like a head and a tiny tail.

Griff smiled, if somewhat hesitantly.

At that, Alys finally looked up from her drawing to survey the pair of them fondly. "Isn't this great?" she asked, her dilated eyes shimmering with sincerity. "The three of us, finally together again?"

Mal turned hastily away and retched in the grass.

Chapter Nine

Knights and Robbers

Once they had recovered enough to drink some water and Griff remembered how to put one foot in front of the other, they did exactly what Mal had planned. They hiked through the fields that bordered the road, using the tall grass as a screen to keep them from view, and persisted through the crisp, star-flecked night with the wind whispering secrets in their ears until sunup.

By the time they were ready to finally make camp the following night, though Griff glanced back a time or two, no cheerful chimney smoke from the houses in Linden could be seen on the horizon. In fact, there were no dwellings in this vast swath of the Plains of Plenty, only grass and the occasional rocky outcropping, some stray boulders and palm-sized stones.

. . . And one large ruined fortress, its roof long ago scalped by whoever had felt it would stroke his ego to conquer this unimpressive place between the Mire and Mayfair. It was to this hunched and weathered stone outcropping that Mal was leading them now, following a line of recent boot prints in the earth as darkness fell around them.

It was cold, and the constant wind stung their cheeks. Griff's feet ached from the punishing pace; Alys and Mal might go on "business trips" like this with some frequency, but he wasn't used to covering so much distance without a proper break, especially with a wound he could still feel much too often. No one seemed to feel much like talking, so the silence was broken only by the calls of hawks and killdeer, though Griff had noticed Alys watching him with some concern, as if there were something she wanted or needed to say.

"Are you really okay?" she finally asked him as Mal lengthened his stride and cut ahead, scrabbling up the hillside on which the old fortress crouched. The faint clunk of his scabbard against the walls could be heard as he started inspecting the place for signs of other recent visitors, like the boot prints they had been tracking.

Griff observed his movements, however faintly. Most of his attention was on Alys, on her hands twisting the end of her long braid, on her wide eyes fixed on his face with a touch more presence than what he was coming to realize was her normal state—a few mushrooms each day. Had she noticed how much his wound still pained him despite being half out of it all the time? They hadn't really talked about it back in Linden; he didn't want anyone thinking he was weak, or weaker than they did already after he had barely survived the attack.

"I mean," she continued, apparently sensing the need for clarity, "do you want to go home? Do you need to? I feel like . . . it's my fault you're out here, and so far it isn't going how I thought it would."

Griff exhaled slowly, holding up a hand to signal that he needed a minute to think. It was a heavy question on next to no rest.

Alys nodded, glancing away from him and up toward the half-moon that watched over them with a ghostly light, barely gilding the fortress and the grass barrens to the east with silver.

Small dells and tall brush dominated the west and north, eventually coalescing into the thick tangle of the Mire, which remained out of sight even as they began to climb the hill behind Mal.

"I'm no worse for the wear than I was already. Not in any way a hot bath and a long night's sleep in a real bed couldn't cure," Griff said finally, scrubbing a hand over the two days of stubble darkening his jaw. "But I still don't really understand why you asked me out here in the first place. Or had Mal do it. I'd like to know," he offered softly.

Alys scrambled up a patch of gravel to gain the level ground of the fortress, extending a hand to pull Griff up. He didn't need the help, but he took it all the same.

"Maybe one day soon, you will," she answered, infuriatingly cryptic, turning away so that her face was unreadable. "Maybe being out here—you'll start to see what I see."

"I see that you have charcoal on your mouth," Griff called after her as she slipped fluidly between a gap in the stones.

She giggled as she flashed out of sight.

He didn't follow as quickly this time. Rather, head spinning and tight from lack of sleep, he dropped onto half of a well-weathered large rock hewn open and took a moment alone. Somewhere in the distance, the yowl of coyotes rose from the Mire. The sound was clearer here, where even the half-rock walls still standing provided some shelter from the unchecked winds that whipped across the plains.

Griff imagined Liam had a fire going in the hearth. It was late, but they liked staying up when the rest of the world was quiet and still. He could almost hear echoes of Liam reading a bedtime story to Badger, one of the children's adventure books that the locksmith loved picking up from the market secondhand. Griff had been known to listen in too, adding oil to the lamp so they could get in just one more chapter before his eyes closed.

He had left behind a good relationship, and for what? A phantom of a boy he'd loved and the ghost of a man who had been a father figure for a few years? Maybe he had made a mistake, chasing shadows when he wasn't even a Warden yet and might never be now, a thought that made him ache with emptiness as if he'd lost something vital, an organ rather than a limb.

Then a hand thrust through the gap in the stones near where Alys had disappeared, warm and real, the dark, slightly crusty lines of raven's feathers stark on the inside of that tawny wrist where they escaped from the cuff of the sleeve.

"Planning to join us sometime tonight?" Mal asked him—not unkindly, Griff thought—as the thief made his way fully back through the gap.

Slowly, Griff clasped that cold hand, now bereft of its mitten, and kept his face carefully blank as he rose. Or, at least, he tried to. But he couldn't stop his eyes from roaming over Mal's gold-stubbled face with a glimmer of that barely concealed hope he had spoken about back when Mal appeared at his work.

Hand in hand, they passed through the open wall and into the relative shelter of the roofless old stones that had endured after all this time.

Griff swayed slightly with tiredness as he picked his way among the debris and over to where the others had already dropped their packs against the most intact of the inner walls. Mal's fingers tightened around his in answer, as if to steady him, brushing over some of the scars he'd asked about not long ago.

Mal paused for a moment, feeling over those rough little places again as his eyes moved from the hand in his to Griff's face. But if he wanted to ask about the scars again, this time he didn't give the question breath.

Before Griff could get his brain working to do anything—say, squeeze Mal's fingers in answer, or unstick his tongue from the roof of his mouth—Mal was moving on, dropping Griff's hand and saying with his usual confidence as the leader of their small, strange expedition, "We can lay out our bedrolls here, but we're going to need to set a watch now that we're out in the open like this. I'll take the first."

Griff settled into his bedroll and tried his best to get comfortable even with a few pebbles poking him in the side. Still, he was the sort of tired where sleep reclaimed him almost instantly despite the cold, despite the aches, despite the lingering question of why he was really here and the deepening concern that he wasn't going to get answers anytime soon.

He awoke with a start to hazy indigo twilight, the moon hanging at half height, wondering what had disturbed his rest. Looking around, he found Mal fully out of their shelter and still on watch. He was gazing down the hillside with his usual distaste, like a king surveying an utterly disappointing piece of his tithe, his eyes almost as silver as his flask.

Beside him, Alys was sleeping on just her cloak, her blade within reach, as if she wanted to be ready to stab someone the instant she woke.

Turning and catching Griff's eye, Mal crooked a beckoning finger.

Adrenaline quickly had him on his feet, grabbing his cloak—and on second thought, his sword—and joining his old friend outside the fortress.

Mal turned quickly at the sound of his approach, eyeing him up and down, his gaze glinting with some fresh light as the ends of his thick black scarf, once Griff's, danced on their own in the breeze. "You really do look like your father sometimes," he observed quietly, without inflection. "Maybe it's the sword."

The great Seimon Sayer, the Warden who'd ridden against the last living dragon on his beloved stallion Griffon and dealt the killing stroke even as the beast struck him down too. He might not have been in Griff's life enough for him to truly remember the man, but he cast a long shadow that Griff hadn't yet figured how to step out of, though he'd tried—making himself bigger or smaller didn't seem to do a thing when they shared the same height, the same features, the same breadth of their shoulders.

"You know how to use that thing, right?" Mal asked, eyes narrowed in assessment.

Griff didn't answer but managed not to roll his eyes. He'd spent years training with the elves, and if a centuries-old general couldn't teach him a thing or two, it was probably hopeless.

Now he followed Mal's gaze down the hillside, watching a small orange glow in the distance. Faint noises wafted up with the wind: a clatter of iron, a few muttered words becoming a cascade of laughter, and a soft whinny.

The firelight reflected in Mal's eyes as he spoke in hushed tones. "There's four of them. And they have a packhorse." He pointed at a black speck moving away from the fire toward a pocket of shadow.

"So?" Griff asked, uncertain how any of this spelled trouble for them.

Digging into his pocket, Mal pulled out a length of twine and began to tie back his unruly, knotted hair. "You feel alert enough to make some bad decisions?" he asked Griff casually as he did so. His smile wasn't warm; the glint in his eye made it something else entirely.

Griff studied the unhurried motions of that black speck a few moments more before observing softly, "You've always wanted a horse, haven't you?"

Mal started unraveling the scarf around his neck as he answered. Wrapping it differently, covering his face with it so that only his eyes were visible, before he pulled up his cloak hood and adjusted the toggles. "It's not about that," he insisted, as though Griff had offended him. "When we grab that treasure"—he gestured vaguely in the direction of the Mire—"we're going to need a way to carry it all back. Although," he added, a crinkling around his eyes suggesting that he was grinning beneath the scarf, "I also want one just so I can name it Griff."

With that, he put a foot down onto the rocky incline that made up this side of the hill, casually beginning his descent like he hadn't just goaded Griff, knowing full well that he had always resented being named after his father's stallion.

"Shouldn't we wake Alys?" Griff called softly after him, choosing to ignore the slight.

Something sailed toward him, and he caught it instinctively: a crimson scarf, the one that had been Mal's when the black one had been his.

"Wrap your face with this," Mal instructed. "It'll be just like sheep tipping. But better, because you're doing it with the best in the business. The king of the thieves—well, one day."

Griff had his answer, then. And he couldn't resist being part of Mal's scheme, not when it included him.

He picked his way quietly down the rocky hillside behind the other man, careful with where he was placing his feet so as not to send any stones falling ahead of them to announce their presence.

Partway down, Mal met him with a steadying hand that gripped his arm. "Careful on the job," he said, slightly muffled by his scarf.

Confusion flitted through Griff's eyes, the only part of his face visible beneath the crimson wool. He'd very much had the impression that Mal would only laugh if he did something like trip over one of these rocks—but then, there was a horse at stake. Something Mal wanted, something of value.

"Let's go get that horse," Griff muttered, taking a few more steps down the hillside and out of reach. "So I can listen to you argue with some other creature named Griff for a change."

"'Griffon was a really good horse,'" Mal quoted as he descended the final few steps back onto level ground, something Wynnie had told Griff often over the years when he complained about his name, even after he ultimately shortened it.

There was no more talking after that.

Crouching in the brush for cover, they drew nearer to the fire and the sounds of the four men making an early breakfast around it.

"This is my year, lads," one was boasting over the clatter of a pan on the coals and the packhorse's soft snorts. "I'm going to win it all."

More of that laughter they had heard earlier on the wind followed this claim.

"What?" the man insisted, sounding slightly hurt. "We come from a whole city of bards; we have an advantage here."

Griff realized they must be headed to the big music competition held across the mountains in Cardraine every summer; these were hardly bandits, and they had no idea that they were about to be less one horse simply for being in the wrong place at the wrong time.

He turned to ask Mal whether they shouldn't reconsider when Mal drew something from his cloak, a flash of silver gleaming where it caught the firelight: his flask. He motioned as if to press it into Griff's hands—a first, in all the times he'd seen the item so far, and clearly an offering of some significance—but Griff shook his head, and Mal shrugged before taking a sip himself and stashing it away again.

Mal didn't know he was sober these days, Griff realized on a heavy exhale. There was so much he didn't know. So much still unsaid.

Evidently suitably fortified, Mal now pointed toward the object of their mission tied up several yards away. Not a packhorse at all, Griff saw as he took in the beast's smaller profile, its large, almost comical ears. A mule.

Mal pointed next to Griff, as if to indicate he should be the one to seize the creature. Then he pointed to himself, motioning toward a traveler's pack on the ground just outside the warm circle of firelight. One of the men had just pulled something from it—a wooden bow that he seemed intent on polishing, given the soft cloth in his hand.

Griff was just trying to work up the courage to step out of the shadows without feeling like a total lowlife when Mal's eyes squinted like he was fighting back a yawn.

Mal stepped back hardly an inch as the shudder of exhaustion ran through him, but it was enough for his heel to crack a twig.

The mule snorted a steamy breath into the dark morning, and the laughter around the fire stopped. The man holding the bow had been smiling, but now that smile was gone. "You all don't suppose . . . ?" he began softly, no need to finish the thought. Traveling the road east was a well-known way to be swiftly relieved of all a person owned.

Mal certainly looked awake now.

In fact, he was looking to Griff, as if, for once, he didn't have a map and a plan. Of course, Griff didn't either. He thought quickly of what his father might do if he'd decided to steal a horse—never mind that Seimon would never lower himself to such an act. He thought of his father's long unbreakable stride, the way he moved with purpose, always impressing someone when he walked by.

He wanted, more than anything in that moment, to impress Mal, to see those silver eyes spark with admiration rather than mocking.

And like a hawk having sighted its prey, Griff shot from their place of concealment and swooped toward the mule.

Chapter Ten

The Warg of the West

"Bandits!" one of the men cried. His shout rang in Mal's ears as the mule snorted and stamped. It jerked at its tether as its eyes flashed on the sight of the crimson-clad figure running toward it with a sword raised, intent on cutting its ties.

At the corner of his gaze, Mal noticed the man with the bow reaching for his quiver, a sight that chilled him worse than any shadow.

Another traveler, the quickest to his feet, started after Griff but tripped over the handle of his cast-iron pan, sending up a shower of sparks that sprayed into the nearby brush.

Embers danced along the sleeve of Mal's cloak, drawing a grunt of surprise and startling him from the shadows before he had time to think how he was going to get himself and Griff out of this with all limbs intact and no arrow wounds, never mind the mule now.

Arrows. The archer. Shit.

He was slotting an arrow, aiming at Griff in the dark as the foreman, oblivious, quickly cut the mule's rope.

Mal set himself on a collision course with the man, drawing a hunting knife swiftly from his belt as he ran, shouting, "This is hardly being careful on the job!" to Griff as he closed in on the archer and swung his fist to ensure that arrow misfired. Then, "Go, I've got this!"

Taking the mule's lead, Griff started urging the creature back toward the hill and Alys, making frantic gestures like there was an owlbear on their heels.

He didn't get far.

The arrow didn't fly true, but rather than landing in Griff's back, it sank into his right calf just above the ankle. He managed to take a few stumbling steps forward with the creature—momentarily filling Mal with a wild, false hope—but then he crumpled to the ground.

Still, he was amazed Griff didn't let go of that mule's lead. If anything, he seemed to cling tighter to the rope as the mule began to drag him forward.

The archer swore as Mal hit him again, though he managed to hold on to his bow. The two were locked in a struggle of elbows and fists and muffled grunts and the knock of the wooden bow against various body parts. A sharp twang echoed as Mal managed to use his knife to sever the bowstring, feeling a grin of victory coming on as he gripped the archer in a tight headlock, squeezing the air from the man's throat—but just then, the cook who had tripped over his own pan threw a rock that struck Mal in the neck.

Another rock opened a gash just below his eye, and he swore.

Blinking through the pain, he saw the third man stride bravely toward the place where they struggled, brandishing a short sword.

Listening to Griff's faint groans, the direction of which he couldn't even fully discern in the darkness, he wasn't sure he had this handled anymore.

But then, finally, with another firm squeeze, the archer went limp in his hold.

He let the man drop into the dirt as he held his hunting knife aloft, fending off that short sword and a barrage of rocks alike as he tried to make a hasty retreat while also figuring out where exactly Griff and the mule were now.

But the men were advancing, and he had to keep his eyes on them. They were forcing him deeper into the brush where he'd hidden earlier, backing him effectively against a wall.

The fourth man, who had evidently abandoned his breakfast to try to chase down the mule and its unlawful new owner, was having a time keeping up with the pace of the nervous beast, even while it was dragging a body.

The man and Mal both stared for a moment as the rose-gold light of day finally began to seep over the edge of the eastern horizon, illuminating the animal's frantic beeline toward the hill and the man with an arrow in his leg trailing behind it, face concealed by a scarf as red as his bloody pants, hitting every rock along the way.

Mal was so obviously cursed, but he rarely felt it as keenly as he did now.

"Fuck," he whispered like a lover in the throes of passion.

And he was certainly feeling passionate as he gazed around at the chaos of the camp: the upturned pan, the smoldering remnants of little fires in the grass, the unconscious archer, the cruel shaft of the arrow protruding from his old friend's leg.

Four weeks wasn't going to be nearly time enough to get the treasure. Not with a wound like that. Not on top of Griff's old wound from the attack still clearly bothering him, no matter how he tried to hide it.

Griff was going to be so bad for business.

All the commotion had apparently woken Alys at last.

Relief broke over Mal's scarf-wrapped features at the sight of her bounding down the hill, rocks flying away from her feet as she skidded to the bottom with her sword already brandished—Rhun's old sword from the war, a heavy relic, glistening wetly with the reds and golds of the early sun like a warning, or a promise.

By the time she reached the place where Mal was barely holding his ground with the hunting knife, her cheeks were pink with exertion. Still, her eyes were alert, flashing with dislike as she dodged a rock and held her sword above her head, striking a pose for the three men who were still conscious.

"Morning, boys." She grinned lazily around a yawn. "Who's ready for the big, bad warg?"

She sprang at the rock thrower first, laughing as she sliced her blade this way and that to force him to dance.

Mal had always loved watching her work. There had been a few years when Theo, the man she almost married, tried to pressure her into domesticity, into things like needlework and brewing a perfect cup of tea for his perfectly boring houseguests. When Alys finally sent him packing, Mal had been almost as relieved as she was to see the back of him.

He had missed having a business partner—a friend—who could truly hold her own, someone he could count on.

With a renewed gleam in his eye, he charged the man brandishing the short sword. No longer backed into the brush like some cowed creature being hunted, he feinted, dodged the man's blade as it breezed by, then whisked his knife across the man's throat.

There came a gasp, then a gurgle.

The man took one more swing at Mal as he began to fall, slicing into his ankle before he finally met his fate.

The cook, still seemingly torn between pursuing Griff and the mule and aiding his fellows, took one look at his fallen companions—one bleeding out into the dirt, one perhaps merely unconscious—and decided, after it all, to run.

Which left only the rock thrower.

Alys's idea of a dance and her wild smile were ordinarily enough to unsettle most men into fleeing or handing over their purses, whatever was the order of the day, but this one seemed to be made of stronger stuff than most.

As the cook fled, the rock thrower glanced briefly in that direction, giving Alys an opening to drop her sword and try to grab him in a headlock. She was probably hoping to render him unconscious like his friend by the fire, a move Mal knew well from their past experiences on the road together. But as she threw her arm out, a knife flashed from somewhere, a hunter's blade gripped in the man's large and steady hand. Angled right toward her ribs.

Mal cried out a warning.

Alys was half a second quicker than the man as she covered his hand with her own, and just a touch stronger as she gritted her teeth and redirected the blade, sinking it deep into the man's stomach.

He dropped to his knees. Blood began to trickle from his mouth.

And beside him, Alys fell to hers. "Oh no," she whispered. She stared at the man. "Oh, oh, no. I—I'm sorry, I—"

"He was going to kill you," Mal said firmly, though he tried to keep his voice gentle. "I saw the whole thing, and you had no choice." He sighed, and the noise came out closer to sympathy than impatience, which was a relief. Sympathy didn't come easy for him. "Look, Alys, I know how you feel about killing, but . . . it was bound to happen one day, our line of work." After checking to make sure the man with the knife really wasn't breathing, he rubbed a hand across Alys's back for a few moments and then said, "Will you be okay right here? I need to go get Griff."

She nodded resolutely.

But Mal had gone only a few paces toward the darting mule with his old friend attached when Alys gagged and threw up beside the body.

Mal winced but kept going, because Griff needed him more, making steady progress across the plain toward the mule. It seemed the beast wasn't used to dragging the weight of a grown man and it was finally tiring, perhaps even calming in the absence of so much noise and swearing and clashing blades.

At some point, Griff's scarf had come loose. Mal picked it up, draping it over his shoulder on his way over to the exhausted mule.

He grabbed the creature's lead rope, working it gently from Griff's stiff hand.

The other man answered him with a groan.

"Is this what you thought I meant by making bad decisions?" Mal asked, letting the worry in his gaze shine undisguised as he pulled off his scarf at last and crouched where Griff lay prone in the grass, dirt and scratches streaked across his pale, sweaty face. "Or is it that you just don't give a damn about yourself?"

"I—" Griff panted and seemed to fumble for words, which was understandable, given how short of breath he was.

Mal's stomach churned unpleasantly. He hated seeing Griff like this. Hated Griff for being such an idiot, for nearly getting himself killed and making him watch. He had asked him on this trip to keep him safe, but here he was, nearly finding a means to die anyway and complicating whatever hope they had of securing the treasure in time.

He shouldn't care like this.

Griff had made it clear, on a long-ago day when he was just seventeen, that they were nothing to each other anymore.

It shouldn't matter if Griff lived or died, especially if Mal didn't have a hand in it.

But it did.

Griff's eyes shone clearer as he gazed at something past Mal's shoulder, lifting his head a little. "What's wrong with Alys?"

Mal turned. She was making her way toward them at a shambling gait, her face almost as pale as Griff's, a bit of spit clinging to her lower lip.

"She just killed someone. One of the travelers, the guy with the rocks," Mal explained to Griff, who now looked confused in addition to weak and dizzy. Maybe he didn't know yet, despite his renewed friendship with Alys, that her reputation was only for show.

Mal was used to walking away from the bodies he'd put down without a second glance. Someone had to do the dirty work, and it had been years since his first kill. Like all things, it got easier with practice. It was a harsh world. He'd been a victim himself many times before he'd learned how to fight and make something of himself, and if he lost sleep over every enemy who would have stabbed him first if given half a chance, he wouldn't have made it very far in this life. But Alys was different. She had always tried to avoid killing, even if she wasn't bothered by him and Wynnie doing what had to be done.

"The Warg of the West," Griff rasped, pushing himself up onto his elbows to get a better look at Alys. He definitely didn't know, if he was using that name when no one was around to hear but the three of them. "That's what they call you. There are songs about—"

"I know," Alys said softly as she knelt beside them, her eyes glistening as she thrust a hand out as if to feel what warmth remained in Griff's cheek. "Please don't tell Wynnie. Promise me, Griff. I'm so sorry. It's my fault you're hurt—I didn't wake up until there was already so much shouting—the mushrooms, you know, they can help me sleep through anything."

Even Mal's brows lifted slightly at that. Alys wasn't in the habit of making apologies, so she must really mean this one. Her first kill had put an uncertainty in her gaze he rarely glimpsed there, a raw vulnerability she must work hard to keep concealed most days.

Griff put his hand over hers. "Doesn't hurt that much," he insisted with a wan smile. "Not like it's going to hurt when you and Mal have to take out that arrow. But I don't understand—don't tell Wynnie *what*?"

Alys withdrew her hand and wiped at the tracks of tears on her cheeks. "That that was my first. My first . . . murder."

"She can fight, though," Mal added, his tone firm as he let his admiration show on his face. "She's a technical genius with that sword, and she can take a hit as well as I can. She's bloodied plenty of people. That's not a lie."

Alys finally wiped her mouth with the back of her hand and nodded, seeming not to trust herself to speak just yet.

"So the Warg of the West? All the stories and songs?" Griff asked, plainly still lost.

As Mal looked back at her, Alys dropped her gaze to the mule's hooves. It tapped a restless foot. "I paid a bard to write those songs. And later, Mal paid some people to say that stuff about who I'd killed and how. As a favor to me, because he's a good friend," she added to Griff before casting a small smile in Mal's direction. "I got busy with the kids, and I didn't want Wynnie to think that meant I'd slacked on my training or that I didn't have half her nerve. It was just easier this way."

"I won't tell a soul," Griff vowed solemnly, his gaze softening as he studied her. "Far as I'm concerned, you killed all these men yourself. I could even write a new song for you sometime. Keep up the legend—"

"You're stalling," Mal cut in, his eyes still on Griff's and glinting with understanding. "You're going to have to tell us how to get that arrow out without permanently damaging your leg." He waited for Griff's resigned nod (and accompanying grimace) before asking Alys, "Help me get him up on the mule? We might as well warm up by the fire while we do this. I want their packs too—smelled like they had good food."

"I could make us breakfast if they have eggs and bacon," Griff panted, still clearly stalling as he swept an appraising gaze over Mal from head to toe. "I've seen you hit that flask more often than I've seen you touch hardtack or jerky or any of the rations since we left home. Do you even know about the joys of being adequately hydrated? You—"

"You're delusional from the pain, you fuck," Mal snapped. He hoped the threat was clear: He would only let the comments slide so far, no matter how much Griff was hurting, before he added to the pain.

Not that he really would. He couldn't imagine ever laying a hand on Griff again, not since the stabbing in the woods. He knew sorry couldn't fix a damn thing, but he was going to be sorry for the rest of his life regardless—even if his life was doomed to be remarkably short if he didn't get to that treasure soon enough. Even if Griff was still a hopeless dork with questionable loyalties.

"Oh, I hope they have cake," Alys murmured as she helped Mal carefully haul Griff onto the mule's back. "I think dessert might be just what we all need."

Mal stifled another yawn as he stuck his still-bloody hunting knife back in its sheath at last and began to lead the mule toward the now-abandoned camp, where the fire still crackled and offered warmth to the three bodies sprawled on the ground: the archer Mal had strangled, the man he had stabbed, and the one Alys had been forced to kill. The cook was nowhere in sight. He was probably halfway to the festival in Cardraine by now, screaming to the hills about bandits.

Maybe Alys was right and some sugar would do him good too. He needed to wake up, needed to get that arrow out of Griff's leg. He was going to make sure it healed better than whatever the elves had done for his stab wound, which clearly wasn't enough.

"If you need a little something before we do this," Alys murmured to Griff from the other side of the mule, where she walked with a hand on his back, making sure he stayed propped up as the pain steadily increased, "I have mushrooms, and a few of those berries left."

Griff, who seemed to be just clinging to consciousness with the same stubbornness with which he'd held on to the fleeing mule's lead, barely managed to shake his head.

As they neared the fire, the strangled archer groaned, then coughed softly.

Out came Mal's bloody knife again. And once again, he yawned, bone-tired. His work was never done, even with two business partners along for the ride. "Look away, Alys," he cautioned before he quickened his steps and knelt by the man who had only been playing at being dead.

"Tell me about your kids, then," Griff said a little loudly, apparently more alert now and hoping to distract her. Mal hadn't expected the help, but it was welcome. "There's—the boy is Rodric, is that right? And then Margred? And . . . ?"

"Your nephew turned six this year," Alys answered him, her voice wavering only slightly. Mal nearly glanced over, surprised. As far as he knew, Griff hadn't even met the children. She must have really missed him, too, to be using such terms already.

"And be sure you don't call him Rod," Alys added thoughtfully. "Leo Raintree did that last month, and Rodric scattered a box of pins all over the floor of his carpentry shop so he would step on them."

Griff laughed, and even Mal snorted appreciatively at the story as he finally cleaned some of the gore off his knife. "Leo probably deserved it anyway," Griff said of their childhood antagonist, and Mal's chest warmed for the first time since he'd seen the arrow pierce Griff's leg. It seemed they still had a few enemies in common who weren't each other.

"Next is Margred, you're right, but she goes by Mags," Alys continued, a smile in her voice that Mal knew well. She was proud of her brood, in her way. "She's been asking me for a dagger for her fifth birthday if she learns to spell her full name. And she'll talk your ear off if you give her half a chance, and probably even if you don't. She wants to be just like Mal when she grows up."

Mal smiled to himself a little at the thought of the girl as he searched through the seriously dead archer's pockets, though he was bracing himself for some cutting comment from Griff. When one didn't come, he had no idea what to do with his hands but touch the flask in his jerkin pocket for reassurance.

"And then there's Deryn. My Derry-bird," Alys said fondly. "She's two. She talks to all sorts of things. Spiders. Her doll. Shadows."

This had struck Mal as vaguely concerning for some time—he wondered if the littlest girl also had the ability to see things most couldn't, but it wasn't like he was going to ask a toddler about her experiences with the shadow world.

"They sound great. I can't wait to get to know them," Griff said, though his voice was hoarse with pain. "Although I don't think I'll be walking barefoot over any floors in rooms where Rodric has been. Never knew you wanted to be a mother, Alys."

She tilted her head to the side, like he had just struck a chord she'd never heard before or whispered a bit of elvish. "Neither did I," she said plainly. "I thought it was just . . . something I was supposed to do. It's in almost every story and song. But I'm really glad I get to be their mom, and it's much easier raising them with Wynnie and Vic than it was with Theo—their father." Dropping her voice, she growled, "He wanted me to be a *lady*."

"Sounds like he didn't really know you, then," Griff remarked softly, earning an appreciative noise from her. "But it must be nice, having the children around. I'm not planning on any myself, of course, but—sometimes I think about what it might be like to have a couple kids to dress and send off to school. Playing on the weekends. They must keep you busy."

Mal glanced over again at that. "Makes sense you'd like kids," he remarked in what he thought was an offhand tone. "You're just a big kid yourself, aren't you." Because who else but a child would bolt after a mule like that, completely forgoing any semblance of stealth? That was how he meant it. He hadn't intended for so much warmth bordering on fondness to creep into his voice, but Griff gave him a small, slightly bewildered smile in answer.

A hint of color washed over Alys's cheeks too as she considered Griff's words. "Sometimes they're my whole day, when I'm not on a business trip like this one or foraging in the Wood. But sometimes I don't see them as much as I think I ought to—or maybe not as much as I'd like to. I'm not sure which it is," she confessed softly as she balled a cloak behind the foreman's head like a pillow. "Hey, Griff?" she whispered as she settled in near his head, holding tight to his shoulder as Mal prepared to snap the arrow shaft. "You're sure you don't want one?"

Mal stayed focused on their quiet conversation, trying not be sick with the knowledge that he was going to cause Griff even more pain in a few moments. When he glanced up, he saw that Alys held a dark berry in her free hand, slightly squished from being in her pocket.

"You know what—why the hell not," Griff agreed, sounding unusually grateful.

Mal tried his best to be gentle, even though he didn't know how.

But no amount of careful hands or funny shapes in the clouds could keep Griff from screaming in the end.

Chapter Eleven

Daggers

Progress was slower for the next few days with the lower part of Griff's right leg now packed in salve and wrapped in a heavy layer of bandages that barely fit in his boot. His limp was greatly pronounced as he held the mule's lead and dragged himself along at its side. At least the creature had taken to his change in ownership as placidly as if this were routine, but no amount of small things going in their favor seemed able to raise Mal's spirits. He kept snapping at everyone about how little time they had left out here, like he had another business venture lined up the moment they got home and he needed to hurry back.

Finally, there was a smear of blue-green on the horizon—the Mire—and a pocket of warm air enveloping them as they traveled just out of sight of the road. Still, Mal and Griff kept their scarves wound around the lower halves of their faces, as each gust of wind was now something of a game of chance: Would it bring the cooler, dry air of the plains, or a whiff of the warm and fetid stench of the Mire?

"I'd let a rotrose spray me if it meant we were out of this damned wind already," Mal muttered as he limped—though nowhere near as badly as Griff did—near the mule's other flank.

Alys, having wandered a good deal ahead of them again, paused and turned back to watch them catch up. A hint of a smirk at her lips, she suggested to the worse off of her limping friends, "You could always just ride Little Griff."

Griff's leg radiated pain with every step, but he was about to summon some sort of protest—the last thing he wanted was to look weaker than he felt, riding the pack animal already burdened with the extra food they'd taken from the travelers—when Mal grinned and said, "Actually, Alys, I think the mule might be Big Griff, if we want to be accurate."

That sealed it. Griff wasn't getting on that beast—it was insulting on so many levels—but he still wasn't going to give Mal the satisfaction of knowing his goading was having any effect. He limped determinedly forward, his mouth set in a firm line.

But Mal, putting a hand on the mule's lead as well, tugged the beast to a stop.

Griff turned back to him, a question in his gaze.

"Look, we really need to reach the edge of the Mire by dusk," Mal said with his usual impatience. "Unless you're feeling poor enough that we need to make camp here . . . ?" Pausing just long enough for Griff to shake his head, Mal patted the mule's empty saddle. "Up you go, then. Else we'll have another ghost leering around the cottage, and I'll never hear the end of it from Wynnie."

Griff's mind turned over the more baffling part of that statement. "There's a ghost in the cottage? Since when? How do you know?"

Mal nodded, and before Griff could properly ask, he said brusquely, "I know because I can see them. And yes, they're horrible. This one has been around since about the time Alys moved in with us. She has a broken arm and a torn throat, some kind of mauling victim, and she's a stage-five clinger." That was new, at least to Griff, and it brought up several more questions—since when had Mal developed such a rare ability? Were there any spirits around them now?—but Mal's tone and his pointed look made it clear he wasn't interested in seeing anything right now but Griff on the back of that mule.

And with a grunt of effort, up he went.

The mule skittered sideways in protest, trying to balance this new load (a skill no doubt learned over the years) while Griff gripped the base of its mane and Mal held tighter to its lead until creature and rider alike settled in.

"Okay up there?" Mal asked on a panted breath.

"Why? Worried about me?" Griff returned softly as he patted the mule's neck.

Mal snorted, glancing up sharply. "Maybe in your dreams. We're just each other's least favorite afterthought, remember?"

Griff nodded and looked away, out across the great grass sea, as Mal tossed the mule's lead up to him and beckoned Alys to join them.

"I have something for you, by the way," Mal said, and Griff didn't look back, assuming he meant a gift for Alys. But unshouldering his pack, Mal dug out a long object awkwardly wrapped in cloth and used both hands to pass it up to Griff.

Maybe Mal had become more generous in recent years. Though the last time he'd really known the bright-haired thief, Griff had been the one taking all sorts of odd jobs around town to make sure he had enough money to get Mal a really nice cake and one of those dwarven crystal statues he had long admired on his birthday.

Pulling away the trappings, Griff saw he had just been handed a blade—or part of one. The tang was gone, leaving only metal with no sure place to grip. There were ancient runes engraved into the steel near the base in another language, one Griff had studied well.

"This was Rhun's. Apparently he broke it out here. He ever teach you any languages?" Mal asked, the words unceremoniously dropping them into the no-man's-land of a topic they had both long avoided: the father figure they had shared for a few years until he was gone.

"No, but I can read this anyway," Griff said—to Mal's back, the other man conveniently having turned and pulled up the hood of his cloak so that Griff couldn't read his face. Still, his rigid posture suggested he was listening carefully to every word. "It's elvish. But the writing on the blade doesn't tell us much—it's just a proper name, like Griff or Alys or Mallow."

Not even the use of Mal's full name, the elvish one he had always loathed, provoked him into turning around, though the line of his shoulders sharpened.

"It says *Amaranth*. Perhaps that's who owned the sword, or maybe whoever forged it gave it a special name," Griff continued, a growing suspicion gnawing at him the longer he inspected the blade. "The elves are awfully protective of their weapons. An old piece with markings like this probably has some enchantment on it. Do either of you know who gave it to Rhun in the first place? Something that could give us a clue about what it can do?"

Mal turned back to him, a hand disappearing into his cloak and reemerging with his flask. He took a sip. Then he shrugged and said, "All I know is his friends brought it back from the Mire like it was the last piece of him. A troll smashed it, or so they said. Maybe we'll find the rest of it while we're in there. Putting it together might tell us more."

With that, he pulled something else from his cloak. It was a rolled parchment neatly tied with string, which he tucked under the edge of the mule's saddle.

"You're putting me in charge of navigation?" Griff asked curiously.

Mal took another sip from his flask. "Sure. Why not?" Lower, he muttered, "Be a shame to break the chain of chaos you've already set in motion."

Griff wasn't sure whether this was meant for him or for Mal himself.

They rode and walked on throughout the warm, windy day, watching the line of once-distant trees grow taller on the horizon, the stench of the Mire growing with each step. As the last of the light bid them farewell, Mal signaled for them all to come to a stop at the edge of the trees, through which there was no marked path—the dense tangle through which they would have to break their way.

It had been over a week of hard travel, but the Mire was finally in their sights. They had made good time, all things considered. Even if Mal kept muttering otherwise.

"We'll make camp here," he announced with an air of generosity, putting a hand on the mule's lead again, much to Griff's relief. There was something restless about the shadows surrounding them with the light failing, and Griff had no desire to greet any curious, hungry creatures lurking at the edge of the Mire.

He rolled up the map, which he had been studying as he rode, raising his green eyes to the deeper emerald of the tree line. "You know," he began gently, "our map doesn't really show the topography of the Mire, but I'm afraid it's going to be hell getting as deep in there as this X would suggest we need to be to reach that treasure, even with two working legs. Not to mention the part where we'll need to cross a lake. And I know you'd like to do it all in less than three weeks' time, as you keep reminding us, if that's even possible."

He had been feeling the strain of his injury all day, even while astride the mule, and he couldn't imagine dragging his aching leg over tree roots and through stinking pools of standing water, let alone trailing blood and herbs where interested creatures could smell it. "I'm going to turn back. Let you two go on. I'd only slow you down worse in there."

This would be his last night with Mal and Alys. And maybe that was a good thing—leaving now, before any worse injuries occurred, as they so often did when he and Mal were in close proximity. Maybe Liam would undo all the locks on the door when he knocked. Maybe, despite assuring Griff that it was over for good as he picked his way through the mess of his things on the lawn, Liam would be feeling differently by then. He had always had plenty of room for Griff and all his baggage in his heart before, anyway.

Griff started to dismount, his hand seeking support in the air where he was slightly off-balance and landing firmly in Mal's.

Mal flinched at the contact even though he had held his hand up, but quickly seemed to recover himself.

He took up some of Griff's weight so he could slide to the ground without putting pressure on that bandaged leg, waiting until Griff was standing again before asking lowly, "Why did you have to charge the mule like that? We could've waited longer, done the job undetected and unscathed—like ghosts, but with better timing." But it seemed he didn't expect an answer, as he just as quickly went on, "But forget leaving. I'm not abandoning you on the edge of the Mire. We'll all camp here for as long as we have to, even if we really can't spare the time. I'll figure it out. Unless you really don't want to stay . . . ?"

His eyes skimmed Griff's face, which Griff knew from catching a glimpse of himself in a puddle earlier was still paler than usual, as he waited for an answer. Strangely, there was hope in those gray eyes even Mal's surly expression couldn't quite disguise, as if he actually wanted to keep Griff around.

Maybe it was just wishful thinking on his part. But the pressure of Mal's hand, the way those fingers had given the slightest squeeze as they wrapped around his own—that had been real enough for him to trust.

Mal wanted to be near him. Finally. After all those wasted years. That settled it.

"I'm staying," he declared, hoping he sounded more confident than he felt.

"Good," Mal said, though he still didn't look entirely pleased. His tone invited no room for argument as he grumbled darkly, "You're not dying on my watch. I have too many debts already. And dead means done, so I don't want to see your ghost hanging around, either, you sentimental fuck."

His voice must have been too thick with emotion for his own liking. Out came the flask again, something Griff was coming to associate with Mal's discomfort.

"Wouldn't dare disturb your wildest dreams with my presence, or spend my afterlife on your bedroom ceiling, you miserable shit," Griff said with more warmth in his words than the wind carried, limping his way to the closest tree so he could tether the mule.

Nearby, Alys was already building their evening cookfire, off in her own world or otherwise quietly listening to all that was happening around her.

As he tied the mule's rope, Griff studied her for a moment, the Warg of the West. Wynnie had always pushed Alys hardest, putting her through her paces in seemingly endless lessons, trying to train her up into some more beastly younger version of herself. Griff had assumed for years she'd been incredibly successful, as she was in most of her endeavors. Had assumed she was lucky in both business and love, yet all he could picture now was Alys with tears in her eyes and mushrooms in her pocket, knowing where to cut to bleed a man dry but wanting nothing more than to draw pictures and let the reputation she and Mal had carefully crafted keep her from having to feel the dagger strike of her mother's utter disappointment.

He should have seen it. He should have been kinder to Alys all these years rather than turning his back on her simply because she and Mal were fast friends again by the time he returned to

Linden, signaling whose side she had chosen. Maybe there were no sides and he had been looking at more than one thing all wrong.

Mal was digging for something in his pack with a deep scowl on his face by the time Griff limped his way back over. Apparently, Griff promising not to haunt the enterprising thief had inspired him to dig out not just his flask this time, but a large bottle of whiskey that was mostly full. In his other hand was a roll of something wrinkled and white—bandages. "Better have a look at your leg, make sure we can keep up a good pace first thing in the morning," Mal declared, his tone all business.

Picking the driest patch of grass, Griff lowered himself carefully to the ground before eyeing that amber bottle again. "I'm not thirsty—not for that," he said quickly.

Mal shrugged. "Good. Because it's for the wound. And the pain will have you regretting your life choices, unless you've got a better idea."

"Some herbs will do, just as they have been—we'll make a poultice. Best if they're picked fresh," Griff said quickly as Mal rolled up the cloth of his pant leg with an unusual amount of care—a lingering effect, perhaps, of the way their hands had touched earlier.

"Describe them for me, and I'll go look," Mal agreed, leaving Griff with the roll of bandages for now as he rose once more. A dark grin played across his lips as he added, "You're much better off having me search than Alys, anyway. Who knows what berries she'd bring back this time."

Griff glanced skyward as Mal slunk off toward the brambles. A few stars had pierced the dusk; the first tendrils of smoke were just rising into the air from Alys's fire as well. He inhaled deeply. He wouldn't be alone tonight after all, even if he still wasn't quite sure how to stay.

"Mal," he called quickly after the other man. His dark silhouette paused partway to the tree line. "When you come back, maybe you'll tell me more about your ghosts?"

Perhaps Mal had trouble finding the few herbs Griff had named; some of them did look a lot like other plants. Or perhaps he was simply seizing the opportunity for some solitude. Either way, by the time he reappeared at the fireside, night had truly descended, the mysterious cries of night birds had replaced the howling wind of the plains, and Griff had made a simple potato-and-leek soup that he and Alys were sipping out of tin travel cups.

Mal swatted at a mosquito too close to his neck, then dropped down between her and Griff before handing him the herbs for inspection.

While Griff was checking them over, Mal began right where they had left off. "I've seen ghosts since Thrallkeld. Not the way most people who claim that sort of thing do—not in dreams, or funny little whispers or feelings. I really see them, as plainly as I see you and Alys here."

Griff had never been one to dwell on things like spirits—there were some ghosts who roamed free, merely souls with someone or something still tethering them to this world, but nearly all things undead fell under the command of the Shadow Queen, and those were vile creatures he wanted nothing to do with. It wasn't at all because he was afraid of things he couldn't see. No way.

"I can't hear them, though. I mean, not that the one at Wynnie's could possibly talk much with her throat so fucked up," Mal continued, rubbing his neck. "But they can hear me. I know the one in the cottage can, at least."

Out came the flask. He screwed and unscrewed the cap, ultimately leaving it open as he looked over its top at Griff. "And then there's this shadow that's been following us. I've spotted it three times now, though it doesn't want me to look right at it. When I try, it just moves around on me, kind of like when you get one of those floaters in your eye." He took a long sip from the flask. "The first time I saw it, it was behind you, Griff, the night I asked you to come with us. The second time it was behind you again, the day Alys gave us those berries. And I saw it just a few minutes ago, while I was coming back from collecting these herbs. I guess it wants me to know it's not going anywhere, just like everyone else who wants something from me. I wasn't even going to mention it—what's the point, when it's just one more problem on a growing list?—but I can't seem to figure it out on my own, and I'm tired of trying."

Griff wasn't entirely sure what to make of the tale. The Shadow Queen had spies and assassins in the form of enslaved spirits, which in his opinion gave weight to the theory of her being a necromancer of some sort, but they didn't usually hound one person for days or weeks without just killing them.

"It doesn't really feel like a person," Mal went on. "More like . . . a great, big empty. Like it's hungry. Like it could feast on me or any of us and still not be satisfied," he explained, hitting the flask again. "Tonight it was behind you, Alys."

"I could have gone the rest of my life without knowing that," she said, too loudly in the otherwise quiet night.

Griff half wondered if this shadow had been trying to warn him off his recent life choices. "Sounds like some kind of omen," he considered out loud, leaning closer to the fire. As he filled up a soup mug and set it in front of Mal, he thought of the few people he knew who had passed. There was only one shadow that really linked the three of them. "Could it be . . . him? Rhun, but in disguise somehow?"

He, too, darted a glance at Alys. Her other hand, he noted, had reached for one of the knives on her belt. It flashed in the firelight as she moved slightly, pointed out into the night as if to serve a warning to anything unseen that might think of approaching.

"What?" Mal blinked. "The shadow—Rhun? No. I don't think he'd want to hide; he'd want us to witness him in all his knightly glory."

Alys frowned but didn't say anything.

"Then it must belong to *her*. To the Shadow Queen," Griff concluded.

"What the hell would she want with a couple nobodies like us?" Mal said quickly, exchanging a glance with Alys that Griff couldn't begin to interpret. "Besides, if it *was* one of her lackeys, I'm pretty sure it would have no problem showing me exactly what it thought of me. Whatever this is, it hasn't announced its demands yet."

Griff nudged Mal's mug a little closer to him, concerned by the way his eyes were starting to swim behind the glaze of all that whiskey. Without a word, the thief fell onto his back in the grass, staring up at the cosmic soup above rather than the one in his untouched cup. The flask fell from his hand and rolled toward Alys, and he started rubbing his tattooed forearm.

"Well, since you can't hear it, have you considered offering it a quill and ink?" Griff asked, mostly teasing.

But Mal must not have heard him right, because he answered with, "Of course I want you alive. It's why I stay away, though you haunt me like this too."

It didn't even make much sense. But it must have to Mal, who went on slurring as his eyes fell closed, "I'm gonna . . . gonna die, one day soon. Real soon. And then you all can . . . live free and easy . . . no more danger, no more shadows, no more big empty." The words were like an exhale of relief.

Griff looked over at Alys, who didn't seem remotely alarmed. Mal getting himself into this state couldn't be an infrequent occurrence. But something he had said—probably the part about Rhun, who she still missed dearly—had cut a deep line of thought into her brow, and she was staring into the fire, hugging her knees to her chest.

Wishing for a sip of that flask himself, Griff swallowed some water from a canteen instead and then pulled an extra blanket from the travelers' pack. Mal stirred as Griff covered him, blinking his silver eyes open to slits narrowed against the firelight, just enough to make out Griff's face.

Griff had to work not to ask whether the shadow was behind him right then as he smoothed some of Mal's hair back so it wouldn't end up in his mouth as he slept.

"You should take better care of yourself if you want to make it home, you clumsy fuck," Mal murmured a touch more coherently, though his eyes were closing again already. "Be more careful, or all of this will have been for nothing."

The sour stench of the drink turned Griff's stomach right along with the words he didn't quite understand. "Sure, if you'll eat some breakfast with me tomorrow, you whiskey-soaked shit. You drink too much."

He wasn't certain if Mal's answering groan was a yes, and would have to try again in the morning. Still, he adjusted the edges of the blanket, lingering beside the other man long enough to confess, "All this time, I thought you left me alone because you hated me. And I understood—I'd hate me for what I said back then too."

"I . . . do hate you. So much. All the time. It's bad," Mal mumbled—to Griff, to the darkness, or perhaps to both; Mal didn't seem to know himself. His breathing grew heavier and his eyelids fluttered once or twice, but he didn't open them again.

Griff rose heavily on his good leg and stumbled back to the fireside, where Alys now had the flask in hand, his mind turning over the strange day and the even stranger things Mal had seen, and said. Mal stayed away because he wanted Griff to live. It made a certain sense, the longer he thought about it. No one attracted danger quite like Mal.

But rather than staying lost in his own musings, he looked at Alys and, deciding she probably also needed some present company tonight, reached out with one arm to pull her into a tight hug. She leaned in harder, and so did he. He'd needed this as much as she had.

"I had to choose him back then, you know," she confessed to his shoulder. He stilled his breath, listening carefully. They hadn't really talked about it since they'd rekindled their friendship, and he'd started to think they never would. "Mal had no one to look out for him. You did, though. You were always going to be okay. And I hoped, coming out here, that both of you might finally look at each other and see how things could be better than okay . . ."

When he started to draw back for a better look at her, he found her eyes overly bright with a tempest of emotions yet hazy with the influence of whiskey. She went on in the quiet. "I've been wondering—what happened the day we left town? Is Liam waiting for you at home, or . . . ?"

Griff heard his answering laugh distantly ring hollow. "Waiting to say 'I told you so' at my funeral, more like. We broke up," he explained, his old friend's presence easing the recounting of painful details, like the way his favorite lute had gotten mangled as Liam did some impromptu summer cleaning. "And a part of me doesn't want it to really be over, but the part that wants to keep following Mal is still so much louder, so I couldn't stay." After another moment's thought, he added firmly, "Speaking of Mal—he doesn't need to know any of this."

Alys's eyes narrowed, Griff still fixed at their center. "Then how will he ever see what you gave up to be here? I do, you know. I was there at the beginning. I saw what was between you two back then, and had to watch as it all fell apart. And now I see how all the jagged edges could still fit together just so."

Griff wasn't entirely sure what she was getting at, but he was certain of at least one thing. "Come on, Alys, he's never really seen me. It's time I made my peace with it."

"Fairy tales. Princesses and frogs," she muttered on a gust of breath tinged with whiskey. Leaning forward slightly, she asked with the spark of an idea burning bright, "Can I kiss your cheek? Just in case it does the trick and breaks a curse, though we both know I'm no princess and you're certainly no frog."

Which made absolutely no sense, but then, this was Alys. He nodded, pulling her in closer with the arm he had draped around her shoulders.

And then her lips brushed soft and dry over his cheek near the corner of his mouth, full of gentle affection, though all Griff could think in the moment was how unfair it was that Mal could enjoy kissing women when he had tried but never could, that he would never be just the right shape for the one he wanted most to want him too.

"So, am I supposed to turn into a prince now?" Griff teased as they both drew back. "I don't feel any different yet."

But Alys didn't answer. She was staring, startled, at something across the fire.

Mal's eyes were open again.

Mal, who came striding silently toward them, one hand on the hilt of his dagger like he had murder on his mind.

Chapter Twelve
Survival

Mal stalked closer, too blinded by rage at first to realize that he wasn't actually gripping his dagger by the hilt. In his whiskey-induced stupor, he had the blade by . . . the blade, sharp edges cutting into his palms where he clutched it with both hands.

Maybe he liked that, actually, he decided as he stalked toward Griff. He could strike Griff or Alys with the hilt while also effectively cutting himself, letting him feel something other than the agony of yet another betrayal.

No one ever chose him. No one put him first. There was always betrayal.

He expected nothing from Griff but the letdown.

So why didn't any of that make it hurt any less?

Somewhere out of sight, a raven cawed some low commentary, and Mal snarled. The birds would have their chance to gloat over his downfall soon enough. They would probably pick at his corpse when he collapsed here after the pain of Griff and Alys having so little regard for his feelings that they would make out beside his unconscious body just ended him. Sure, Alys had just kissed Griff on the cheek, but that was awfully close to his lips, and there was no telling where things would have led if Mal hadn't interrupted.

"You," Mal seethed, rounding on Alys first when he reached them. "You're never fucking satisfied, are you? It wasn't enough to have him back as a friend? You wanted to, what, marry him and take his side and forget all about me?"

She recoiled as if stung, eyes welling, and strode off toward the mule without a word.

Next, Mal took a staggering step toward Griff, raising the dagger a little higher; Griff winced, though apparently not out of fear of being struck, as he murmured, "Mal, your hands . . ."

"And *you*," he rasped, spitting somewhere near Griff's feet, his face dark with anger as he stared into the other man's. "Talk about a pathetic repayment for all those years of friendship—did you come out here just so you could fuck her and fuck me over at the same time? Two-for-one special where you steal my only friend? Is that what this is to you, some kind of game? Do you have any idea what it's cost to keep—to keep from hurting you all the time?"

That was too close.

Still, even though Griff was the one killing him right now, he couldn't bear to turn the knife on him.

Mal dropped the dagger from his shaking hands, grabbing a bloody fistful of Griff's shirt to taunt the larger man into wrestling him to the ground, bad leg and all. This dance, at least, was familiar.

But the words Griff shouted in his face down in the damp grass were not.

"What friendship?" Griff demanded hoarsely. "We're not—you can't possibly—you don't know the first thing about me!" He broke off for a breath, and twisted away as Mal tried to shove his face into the dirt to prevent being shouted at any more. "You certainly don't know my heart, or you'd know exactly who I wanted to be kissing just now, and you'd know that it's always been you, you craven piece of shit! I love you. I've been in love with you since before I left—it's *why* I left that day, after that fight—and I've never been able to stop, completely to my own detriment."

Mal heard the words as if from a distance over the rush of blood in his ears, and suddenly, he stopped fighting Griff altogether and collapsed in the grass.

"I . . . I didn't mean . . ." Griff gasped.

Mal had to be dreaming. All of this had to be the whiskey talking. It would make more sense than any of the alternatives. "Didn't mean any of it?" Mal tried to finish for him, the words slow and dazed. Of course he didn't mean it. Griff was always spouting nonsense, which was surely a by-product of having lived with the elves, who were so out of touch with reality.

If he meant it, Mal would have to rearrange his entire worldview, which seemed like an awful lot of work right now when he was on a damn deadline.

"Didn't mean to *say it*. Because what's the point?" Griff answered just as slowly, clearing his throat in the quiet. "I know it would never work anyway. You're a drunkard and a thief and a con man with the meanest mouth. And you *hate* me."

Mal said nothing, his head spinning sickeningly from the whiskey. Stewing in silence, he curled his bloody fists until a bit of red ooze leaked out the sides, but he didn't raise either hand as if to strike again.

He did hate Griff. So much. He meant that. And he also wanted him to keep talking.

Eventually, seeming to have had enough of the tense silence broken only by the odd pop and crack of the flames, Griff murmured hesitantly, voice a little rough from shouting, "I should take a look at your hands. Get them wrapped. We have plenty of bandages."

"I can do it myself," Mal said almost automatically, without looking up from toying with the ends of his black scarf. Why had he really kept the ratty old thing all these years? Why did he care so much about a kiss on the cheek that he had been willing to spill blood over it? "I'm fine." For one who had seen ghosts for so many years, the words now echoing in his ears haunted him worse than any dead girl with a torn throat. "Griff," he added suddenly, unable to swallow the words that came bubbling out. "If you meant those things you said . . . tell me again tomorrow. Say them again in the daylight. Because right now, I just can't believe a word."

The edges of his vision burning and blurring, he staggered quickly to his feet and hurried closer to the firelight, but he realized bitterly that he wasn't quite fast enough to prevent Griff from seeing the rush of tears that streaked his face.

He made his way toward Alys, who had returned to crouch at the edge of the blaze she'd made. She watched him approach with a hand pressed to her mouth, her face drawn and wary.

He took a breath, and for a moment he was confident he would hold it all together, hold it in. But the recipe of anger and hurt and helplessness rushing through him proved too much, and he darted his foot out to kick one of the soup mugs into oblivion. It crashed somewhere nearby in the bracken, sounding like it might have shattered on a rock or dead branch.

It was at least enough of a release to put him in motion again, if nothing else. He took a few brisk steps toward the bramble where he had hunted for herbs, then turned back to the fireside and Alys, sinking down next to her and putting an arm around her shoulders, the only comfort he had ever known.

She let him lean against her despite his earlier heated words, asking for nothing in return. Almost like she knew exactly how the sight of a gesture between friends had swiftly cut to something at the heart of him that he hadn't touched in years.

Griff's parents might be as long gone as Mal's own, but at least Griff had the elves. Alys had had Wynnie and Rhun, her own family, for longer than either of the boys did. But all Mal had ever had—his one constant for as far back as he could recall, even after Griff left—was Alys, who was as good as a sister to him.

"I didn't mean to upset you," Alys began tentatively, trying to work her mouth around some sort of apology. "I just thought—"

"It's fine," Mal said firmly, cutting her off, but he leaned against her a little more in a show of wordless forgiveness. "Me and Griff," he muttered, shaking his head. "What a joke. That judgmental fuck has probably slept with half of Linden—half of Stormveil, too, for all we know. He can't commit to anything, probably not even himself. And no, a guy he paid to sleep with doesn't count. I've heard enough about how they got together." He attempted to snort derisively, though it held none of his usual conviction as he stared into the flames. He didn't really know what Griff was capable of, it turned out, because he'd never even known how the other man felt. There was so much he didn't know.

"Him and his straight jobs and his stupid boyfriends," Mal went on, because at least this rant was familiar. "And he wants to be the hero like his daddy, for what? So he can die young and have his name in a bunch of songs while everyone who ever cared about him picks up the pieces? No thanks."

"I heard he sucked off twelve visiting knights from Kattan in a single evening once," Alys murmured unhelpfully, a little drunk or high, or both. "Or was it eight?"

Looking away from her, outside the circle of their fire, he didn't even recognize this world anymore—one in which Griff loved him. Didn't know how to tell if it was real.

But the part of him that had kept that scarf all these years wanted him to figure it out, and it was getting louder, more demanding.

Mal reached for the whiskey bottle Griff hadn't wanted to use on his leg and took a few gulps. He needed just enough to put himself back on the ground and into the welcome relief of darkness, where he was alone. Where he could count on himself to do what needed to be done. To survive.

Chapter Thirteen
Dark Signs

Griff wasn't sure Mal remembered the deal they had struck about actually eating some breakfast, but while he didn't touch any of their rations, he also didn't pull out his flask upon waking—not even when Griff sat down by the dwindling remains of their fire to take a look at the cuts on his hands and properly wrap them while Alys ate her own breakfast in a rare moment of quiet contemplation.

"Turn your hands over for me," Griff instructed, eyes down, waiting patiently until he was afforded a view of Mal's livid-looking palms just across from him in the golden light of early morning. "We're going to need to wrap these after I put some balm on them. And maybe we'll put your mittens over the bandages to keep them extra dry."

"That bad, huh?" Mal said without emotion as he, too, studied his bloody hands.

"Bad enough that I'm sure you're wishing you'd stabbed me instead," Griff admitted as he began to dig in his pack for the salve he'd brought. "Or maybe you wish you'd stabbed me a long time ago and been done with it. That might have been easier for me, too, because then I wouldn't be out here, spilling blood and feelings all over you."

He had finally let it out. Finally told Mal everything he had kept inside for too long, and the world hadn't ended. Part of him was surprised to wake up and find how little had changed—but then, maybe the changing had started back in Mayfair, when Mal approached him that night. Or maybe Mal really couldn't love anything as much as he loved gold.

Mal sighed, a hint of discomfort flitting over his face as Griff applied a dab of the balm and tried to smear the strong-smelling herbal mixture along the lines bisecting his palms with the lightest strokes possible. Still, he didn't make any of the foul remarks Griff expected.

"A lot of things would be easier if we could change history," Mal agreed on an exhale. "But we can't. And I don't want you dead, believe me. Far from it." He tried to flex one of his swollen, crusty palms a little and blanched, immediately relaxing it again. "You've killed me in so many ways over the years, and then I saw what looked like . . . well, a lot more than it was, for a second, and hurting you back felt like the natural next act in the tragedy you started."

Griff's eyes rose to Mal's, wondering what had bothered him so much about seeing him kiss anyone. He paused, another dab of salve on his fingers, not yet applying it. "You know I'm gay, right?" he said matter-of-factly. "Just so we're clear. Alys knows too, and it'll never be like that between us." That part was easy. What was harder was admitting, "Back when you first got with your girlfriend at the time—Sage? Saffron? Sorrel? Sorry, I've tried really hard to forget her name. Anyway, I was crazy jealous because—because of how I felt about you. I couldn't stomach seeing you kiss her. I overreacted." He somehow resisted the urge to point out *much like you did last night*. "I said some stupid shit I didn't mean, and then I went to live in Stormveil."

Okay, so perhaps he still had Mal beat for overreaction of the century.

Mal regarded him back steadily, coolly, his voice lowering as if he were about to impart some terrible secret the world shouldn't know. "You were my closest friend. And then you weren't. When you left, I evolved." Holding up those bloodied hands, palms still turned to Griff, he added, "This is it. This is me now, or what's left of me. I don't know whether I could love you. I've never even been with a man. I guess . . . I've never really thought about it much. But you should stay out here with us if you want to. I just need time. And when it comes to you and me, know that I can't promise you a thing."

Griff thought then, as he had on their several nights out on the plains, of how warm the hearth would be with Badger curled in front of it. He thought of a door opening, of arms that readily reached for him, and knew there was a chance he could still ride back and make amends with Liam. He thought of easy kisses and effortless laughter, pancakes and flowers on the table.

But there were flowers out here. Wild ones, strong and untamed, dancing in the wind.

If he had wanted easy, deep down, he never would have put his boots on that morning. He would still be in Linden.

He put his own hands on his knees, palms down, inviting Mal's gaze there. "Work accidents," he said, as he had the first time he'd been asked about those scars. "Because sometimes when I should be paying attention to whatever tool is in my hand, I'm thinking about me and you and how I let it all get so bad."

Mal sat silently, seeming to take it all in. Then he offered his upturned palms to Griff's salve again, his face more relaxed this time as Griff spread balm over the cuts.

"Bandages and mittens. Between my hands and your leg, we're going to look like quite a set," Mal finally said, a grin briefly tugging at his lips. But just as quickly, he was frowning again.

"I'm afraid you'll lose that leg if you don't take good care of it. You'll need to ride Little Griff for as long as the Mire permits, stay off it. And I can get you more herbs. We can still make good time without putting you in more pain."

Beyond the repeated annoyance of the mule's name, there was something more to Mal's offer. Griff wasn't sure exactly what, but he found himself smiling a little as he said, "Okay. You can get more herbs—thank you."

Still, Mal continued to frown as Griff unwound a clean roll of bandages. It was a good thing he had packed so many, along with two precious vials of the cherry-red elven medicine he hoped they wouldn't need.

"I always thought you loved it in Linden. Or at least in Stormveil, up above everything. I thought you hated all this." Mal swatted at a mosquito near his ear, then swept his hand in a grander gesture to indicate the waiting dark trees of the Mire and the plains behind them. "But if you actually like being out here, I have it on good authority that there are treasures out in all this wilderness like you wouldn't believe, not just the one we're after . . ."

Griff had seen the particular gleam that lit Mal's eyes as he mentioned treasure a few times before, when he spoke of how well certain jobs paid. It was a look that contained both passion and ambition, a dragon's hunger for a hoard of gold and shiny things.

"Actually, the place I feel most at home is out in the Wood," he said as he started wrapping Mal's left hand. It was a tribute to this shaky new peace between them that he didn't add *when I'm not getting stabbed in the middle of the night*.

"Where we used to race the dogs and try to grab the bell off the sheep's collar?" Mal asked, looking up from his hands again and narrowing his eyes, not in anger or derision this time but as if studying something new: a face that had been present for so much of his life.

Griff nodded as he started to wrap bandages over Mal's other hand. Those hands had done some damage to him over the years, but he was just as guilty. "Back when we didn't fight." He glanced up, cautiously, to the other man's face. "I don't want to fight with you anymore. That's not who I want to be to you. I want . . ." With Mal returning that gaze, he couldn't quite bring himself to say more than, ". . . so much, with you. But most of all, whether you can love me that way or not, I want you to know that you can count on me again."

Mal pulled his newly bandaged hands back. Griff thought he might grab his mittens himself and rise. Instead, he demanded of Griff, or the Mire, or perhaps the odd shadow he kept seeing, "Who the hell am I supposed to fight, then, if not you?"

His eyes moved back to Griff's, and something in Mal seemed to coil and shift, a serpent picking a new direction to strike. He reached out and grabbed a handful of Griff's black shirt as if he needed something to steady himself even while on the ground. "I'm not sure I know how to stop throwing punches at any of us," he admitted on a bitter breath. "But I do know that my world changes whenever you come and go from it. If you don't stay . . ."

Caught by the front of his shirt, his heart picking up speed, Griff leaned closer. Just like the night before, blood was pounding in his ears, but he was still sure of what he had just heard from how closely he was watching Mal's lips. "I want to stay—for good, this time."

And while there was no further tug on his shirt, Griff kept leaning in until his lips were just brushing over the curve of Mal's ear as he spoke—words for him alone. "I want this. You. Your problems, your cold, your foul mouth, your warmth. I'm sick of living in my head. I wasted years wishing things were different, but I've made my choice. I made it even before I told you the truth, when I agreed to come. Even if it's to my own peril and you do kill me. At least I'll have died on my own terms. Maybe even died happy, and how many can say that?"

Mal didn't offer him the reassurance of any words in return, but his bandaged hand shook slightly where it gripped Griff's shirt. And as Griff's lips grazed over his ear with steady words about wanting and staying, a low groan slipped from Mal's throat.

Griff wondered if the Meanest Mouth in Mayfair was as soft and pliant as it looked.

"Gods, why now?" Mal hissed suddenly, releasing Griff's shirt. He started fumbling at his belt with a bandaged hand, trying to grab his hunting knife while glaring at something over Griff's shoulder and demanding, "What do you want? Just show your face or fuck off already!"

But when Griff turned, heart lodged in his throat, all he saw was the breeze stirring the grass, the morning shadows of the bramble and dell, and the waiting Mire. And Alys, clutching something small and pointed that gleamed dully in her hands like steel hidden beneath a solid layer of caked-on dirt.

"What is it?" she called as she strode quickly over to them, her gaze darting every which way and—like Griff—apparently finding nothing of note.

Her eyes eventually settled on Griff's, the worry in them for once undisguised as Mal answered, "It was the shadow again. Right with you, Alys, while you were grabbing whatever the hell that is."

Griff's back stiffened with a chill despite the heat given off by the dying embers of their fire. He believed Mal, even without proof.

"But it's gone now?" Alys asked, her voice sharpened by nerves.

"Yeah," Mal said, still struggling to draw his knife with his bandaged hands. "It disappeared when you started walking over here."

"You mentioned that stabbing the ghost in the cottage hadn't done much good—you think whatever this is can be killed or frightened off with a blade?" Griff was able to find words much more easily knowing the thing was no longer around. For now.

"I hope so," Alys said passionately. "I'll even do it, as I won't have to see it."

Mal sighed and stopped trying to draw his knife. "I don't think a blade will work, no. But—I'm also not just going to sit here and let it hurt you, either of you. Maybe it hasn't even made up its mind what it wants to do, but it's going to have to get in line behind some much-bigger problems if it wants a piece of me." With a frustrated breath, he gave a dark look to the mud on his boots. "You two could turn around here. I can handle this myself. In fact—that's what I should be doing."

"It's just some shadow. It can't be that scary if it doesn't even have a face," Griff insisted—he wasn't ready to go home yet, to abandon Mal and his bandaged hands that could hardly grip a knife out where wargs and trolls and orcs hunted. He actually wanted to stay. "Whatever it wants, Mal, it hasn't hurt any of us yet, so perhaps it can't, or perhaps it doesn't even want to."

Mal didn't look convinced by the sudden show of bravado. "Seems like shadows cling to me these days. A wiser man might consider seeking sunnier climes."

A grin flickered across Griff's face. "Good thing no one ever said I was wise, then. You saw the way I ran down that mule."

"I'm sorry I missed it," Alys said, but despite the teasing in her voice, she didn't quite smile. Instead, she held out the item she was cradling. "You two should look at this. I found it just over there—kicked it, or I might not have seen it."

She pointed to a patch of earth that was more mud than grass as Mal peered over her shoulder at the dirt-crusted dagger. "Found yourself a bit of . . . bit of treasure . . . already?"

His voice faltered as he took in the shape of the dagger in Alys's hands, and Griff quickly saw why. The weapon was muddy and worse for having been out in what was surely years' worth of weather, but there was no mistaking the silver raven etched atop the hilt. The three of them had only ever seen one other piece like it—one that belonged to Rhun. It was also, according to Wynnie's inventory, one of the weapons he'd had on him when he and his friends departed for the Mire. And now here it was again, looking as if it had been lying in wait for quite some time before Alys's boot trampled over it. Waiting for them to find it—unless something or someone had wanted them to?

"Huh. Maybe our extra shadow actually *is* Rhun," Mal muttered, though Alys was stubbornly shaking her head, like she wasn't even willing to consider the possibility that her father had been reduced to nothing more than a faceless phantom. "Guess it would make sense that he's trying to stick so close to us, maybe look out for us."

Griff half wished he could see the spirit too, if only to say a more final goodbye. To thank him for the dagger, which was perhaps his way of offering them some closure. But then he thought of Vic's bait traps that she set in the Wyrmwood to hunt, a little morsel inside to encourage some creature or other to come closer. He wasn't normally given to such flights of fancy, but he couldn't entirely shake the thought as he watched Mal wipe away enough of the mud to read the initials etched faintly just below the bird's talons: *R.K.M.*

"What do you think happened out here?" Alys asked haltingly, cradling the dagger to her chest as if it might bring her some comfort. "Do you think his friends were lying and they killed him—or someone did—before he ever set foot in the Mire?" She only had Griff and Mal to ask, after all. Rhun's friends had passed away some years back, and Wynnie had never been interested in looking for answers. She had been more focused on bloodying any of his enemies in Mayfair she could get her hands on.

"The knife probably fell off his belt, and by the time he realized it—if he ever did—he was already on the road to start a new life when he met with some misfortune," Mal muttered darkly. "Guy always was a little . . ." He twirled a finger in the air. "You know, not all there."

Alys shot him a scowl.

Griff didn't offer any ideas of his own, though he knew the full story better than either of them because he was the one who'd questioned Wynnie about it the most: Four friends rode off to war to kill a dragon—Seimon and Aurora Sayer, his parents; Garth Pryce, Mal's father, whose wife had died fighting a giant when Mal was still a baby; and Rhun Kindrick-Mordecai, arguably the most skilled warrior among them. Wynnie had taken care of all three children while they were on that journey—and, at some point in that uncertain time when Rhun was presumed dead, met Vic—and realized she would be keeping them for a long time to come when only Rhun returned, declaring the boys his own in honor of his fallen friends.

But Rhun had come back changed. Startling at loud noises, prone to fits, sometimes unable to speak above a whisper for days at a time. Missing a couple of fingers from one hand.

The war had long been over by the time he resurfaced. He had been held captive somewhere, tortured for information about the Wardens' plans to round up scattered bands of the dark queen's forces, and escaped only after managing to kill one of his keepers. They patched him up in Stormveil, but not even the elves' best healers with their centuries of knowledge could fully restore his mind.

And then, a few years into raising Griff and Mal alongside his daughter, he disappeared on this treasure-hunting trip with a couple of friends who had also survived the war—this time for good. Griff knew that Alys needed to believe he died a hero, stalked in the Mire by servants of the dark queen and dragged off to be quietly murdered by old enemies while his friends were sleeping. He also knew that Mal had already observed enough leaving in his brief lifetime to decide that's just what Rhun had done in the end, meeting his demise in the midst of deserting his family.

The truth, Griff suspected, lay somewhere between Alys's and Mal's versions of things. Rhun had probably been having one of his bad spells when he left the company of his friends unexpectedly in the middle of the night. Might have been somewhere else in his mind altogether when he did something like stumble into the lake and accidentally drown.

His friends, by their account, had searched the area for well over a day before something startled them so badly that they were forced to flee, even though they were closing in on the fabled treasure. They refused to discuss it, even with Wynnie.

Griff thought it likely that they knew what had really happened to him and simply didn't want to cause any further pain by recounting his last moments.

Perhaps Griff and his companions were about to come close to reliving those moments as they followed Rhun's map.

Chapter Fourteen

Stupid Mistakes

Back in Linden, Mal's mornings were generally uneventful. He would often greet the sun with a groan as it streamed in through the window of his childhood bedroom right at eye level and roll over to press his face deeper into his pillow, claiming a moment of peace before the patter of little feet began or a clamor rose from the kitchen as Vic attempted to cook breakfast.

Inevitably, Mags would burst into the room, making a flying leap onto the mattress to rouse her uncle and then leading him by the hand toward the kitchen—allowing him no time to pull on a shirt, though the mess of scars across his chest and back had mostly faded over the years and no longer earned so many questions from the girl. Meanwhile, he would half listen as a stream of words flowed past his ears from Rodric about some game or other he had been playing with the neighbor boy across the creek. Mal wouldn't even attempt a response until he was at least on his second cup of tea, a splash from his flask sometimes added on a listless morning.

He would kiss Derry's favorite doll good morning as she held it up to him. Ruffle Mags's pale hair or Rodric's golden head, whichever he could reach as they orbited the adults in the cottage, and rub his eyes with his other hand as he contemplated how best to spend the day. Fishing at the creek, perhaps, or better yet, waylaying a wagon brimming with silkweed that was bound for Mayfair proper. He didn't smoke the stuff himself, but there was good money to be had from shipments like those. Later, he would consider a call for tea at the Widow Isabel's that would surely drag on longer than he'd like.

In sleepy Linden, there were no moments of gut-wrenching fear, no glittering promises of riches and the protection they could provide. To some, such days might hold a sense of understated luxury compared to their current demanding circumstances—swapping well-tended hearths for restless campfires, favorite hand-thrown mugs for battered tin cups, quiet strolls along neatly kept village paths for the drudgery of splashing through stagnant water.

Yet Mal was more awake out here, more alive breathing in the humid air and sweating it out in this unfamiliar territory than he ever had been in a cozy town too small to contain his ambitions. Even if they might be traveling in step with Rhun's ghost, the man as much a mystery to Mal in death as he had been in life.

At least this morning was, if nothing else, filled with purpose. They were finally gaining ground again—Little Griff's hooves leaving deep impressions in the softening earth—toward ancient barrows brimming with riches, even if they wouldn't get to keep what they found. Mal kept unfolding the map, turning it this way and that as if doing so might give him a better sense of direction toward Rhun's elusive X deep in the heart of the Mire.

The edges of this swamp weren't so different from the Wyrmwood closer to home. Mal even recognized a few of the birds making calls to one another. Sometimes Griff whistled cheerfully back at them in imitation of their unique sounds, and Mal caught his eye, impressed. Bards and their party tricks.

They had already seen two or three rotroses, the luminous scarlet-red flowers that shunned the sunlight and whispered seductively to passersby to entice them down to their level so they could consume flesh with their acid. The trio gave the bloody blossoms a wide berth, and Mal hummed softly under his breath to help drown out anything he didn't want to hear as they passed, occasionally rubbing the mule's neck to reassure him too.

He also spotted a handful of the dark queen's actual servants at a distance, phantoms whose eyes glowed green—something he now recognized as the mark of her enchantment, her command over a creature or spirit. They leered at him, all ephemeral bony limbs and silently screaming blackened lips. Each time he happened to catch a glowing eye, the spirits mouthed something at him and held up their fingers—or what was left of them—counting down the time he had remaining to reach the treasure. It didn't rile him, much, beyond the uncomfortable prickling of the feathers on his arm. He knew the terms, he knew the time, and this was the sort of behavior he expected from dead things—unlike the shadow that continued to follow them, whose eye color he couldn't begin to guess.

For now, however, the most curious sight afforded to him was Griff, who pulled off his dark, sweaty shirt when they stopped for a moment by a clear-enough-looking pool to give the mule some water and rest. Last time he saw the other man like this, Mal's eyes had been entranced by the way Griff's muscles contracted as he raised his splitting maul to hew another piece of wooden beam. This time he noticed other things too, like the thin dark line of a recent scar that started below Griff's navel and disappeared past the waistband of his pants.

The scar he was responsible for.

Griff was close enough that he could have run a finger along the uneven surface of the mostly healed wound. But he wasn't naïve enough to think that a simple touch, even one that meant everything, could erase his part in what had happened there or ease his own guilt.

He deserved to feel guilty about that forever.

Griff loved him, and he had nearly been the death of him. Still might be. The Mire wasn't exactly the kind of place anyone went for a relaxing vacation. Or went at all.

Mal was just about to glance away when Griff caught him staring, and their eyes locked. "I got stabbed in the Wyrmwood," Griff said, running a hand down his stomach, "by not-bandits. Wynnie handled it."

Mal wanted to drop to his knees and beg forgiveness. He wanted to tell Griff what he had done and how much he hated himself for it. How he never would have imagined that Griff would be a target, or else he would have fought to secure protection for him long ago. Not that he was exactly high up enough to demand that much of Kage. This life-or-death hunt in the Mire was the best he could negotiate.

But with those green eyes looking so warmly into his, he could barely make a sound. Even Griff seemed to find the prolonged silence strange after a time, so when Mal got his tongue working again, he said lightly, teasingly, "How about that. You and Wynnie finally have something in common."

Their former guardian had a scar in about the same place. Hers was from an orc attack that had left her with her guts spilling out between her fingers, and still she had stayed on her feet until the fight was won. She had beaten the infection that followed, too, and returned to the world no worse for wear except for a new mark on her already thoroughly decorated skin.

Griff shook his head, turning to the mule as it twitched its ears to swat away a cloud of hovering midges, and gave the creature an affectionate scratch on its hindquarters. "Figures if I got something from her, it wouldn't be her sword skills or the stare that can frighten off anyone who crosses within a mile of her."

Mal chuckled darkly, though he didn't really feel like laughing. He slapped a mosquito whining too close to his ear with extra vigor, but that did nothing to ease his misery.

"Hey, Griff," Alys cut in as she tied her damp, sweaty hair into two topknots on either side of her head in Vic's usual style. "Speaking of scars, I've been thinking: I want you to train with me. I want to teach you some proper sword work."

Mal thought it was an excellent suggestion. He was, of course, trying to keep Griff safe, but maybe Griff himself could help more in the effort. Especially if Mal failed and didn't make it back with the others.

Griff, however, seemed to take offense. "I've trained with Wynnie and Vic, same as both of you," he protested, sounding more confused than hurt. "And I trained in Stormveil too. And with the Wardens. Just because I don't like hurting people doesn't mean I can't, if the occasion arises."

Mal had never thought much of the elves. Why care about a race of beings who thought they were too good to even live among everyone else and let the world go to shit while they watched from on high? He glanced at Griff and said matter-of-factly, "Clearly you need her help. You almost got gutted in the Wood. And we all know how you handled that mule heist."

"You want to stay with Mal, don't you?" Alys pressed, as if she had overheard at least some of their private exchange, or guessed at Griff's feelings more easily than Mal had. "There are things out here worse than what's in the Wood, so I need to know you'll have our backs if we find ourselves in over our heads—which means fighting dirty, like the elves and Wardens never would have taught you." Softer, her eyes glinting with meaning, she added, "The last thing I want is to lose you again, least of all to a stupid mistake."

"Fine," Griff sighed, clearly outmatched, and likely lacking the energy to argue after several hours of riding and ducking to avoid low branches. "I'll train with you, Alys."

He didn't suggest that Mal join in, and Mal didn't offer. The last thing they needed was to raise blades against each other, even in a practice setting, after all those years of swinging fists. It would feel too real.

"Good, then." Alys smiled at her protégé. "You'll be a regular legend in no time." Finished with her hair, she started unbuttoning her shirt—an old work shirt, patched at the elbows, one she had borrowed from Mal's pile as usual—letting the uncovered skin breathe without a hint of bashfulness.

Things like this had been such a common occurrence growing up that even Griff didn't bat an eye. Alys had always preferred men's clothes. But when Mal shrugged and decided to part with his shirt too, he caught Griff openly staring.

Mal was covered in scars. Little ones, mostly. Knife marks, or sword. Slashes, drag marks, a few that looked like stab wounds. He had plenty of bruises, too, from fighting for sport. But where Griff's gaze seemed to stick was on the garish, inches-long mark carved over the left side of Mal's chest where it looked like someone had tried—and mostly succeeded—at completely and roughly opening him up, hewing into muscle and bone.

Returning Griff's stare, Mal ran a finger lightly up over the mark and said without emotion, "Rough crowd down in Thrallkeld. Didn't make a lot of friends. The leader of the thieves' guild there, Renaud, tried to cut out my heart when I challenged his authority. Damn near succeeded, as you can see. I made some stupid mistakes back then too."

"What stopped him?" Griff asked, his gaze troubled as he continued to study the scar that, all these years later, was still gruesome, even if its color had faded with time.

"An accidental fire," Mal said simply, his eyes sliding away from Griff and toward the denser trees ahead of them, making clear he was done talking about it. He wasn't sure he was ready to let Griff into that part of his world just yet. How many other men had done the same, only to get burned by Mayfair's Most Eligible in the end? Griff had left a boyfriend back in Linden just to be here, after all. "We should go. Get this shit show on the road—time's wasting again, and we've already done too much of that. Two days too much, by my reckoning. Mule's had enough water anyway."

"You want to ride for a while, since you're in such a hurry?" Griff offered Mal the lead with a meaningful glance at the thief's own bandaged ankle, where one of the travelers had slashed him with a knife. "My leg feels some better today, so I can walk. Must be all those herbs you brought me."

The comment slowed Mal's steps for a moment, brought him a little closer to Griff and the pack beast. "I—told you no one was dying on my watch," he said earnestly, finding himself trailing into silence as he returned the other man's steady gaze. But he didn't stay there long, unable to be too distracted from the matter at hand. "That arrow wound still needs rest, though. Mount up."

As they resumed their slog, Alys drew a knife from her belt while Mal pulled out the map again. Selecting a sapling, she put a distinct angular cut into a green twig and left it to dangle just out of casual sight. "I'm going to make us a trail, to get back to civilization as quick as we came," she told them, slapping a mosquito as it landed on her slick stomach.

"Good thinking," he agreed.

Much better thinking than whatever had possessed her last night. Still, he didn't want to dwell too long on that, or on why it bothered him so much—Griff kissed people all the time. Of course, he didn't usually have to watch. He had certainly kissed his share of girls from Mayfair to Thrallkeld, moving from one to the next without ever settling. Because he'd never found the right taste in the warm and willing mouth against his. Never the right shape of the thigh beneath his hand. They were all beautiful in their way, and they certainly made him feel things, even if they weren't quite right for him in the end—but Griff was beautiful too. Plenty of men were, and he felt the same sorts of things about that. He supposed he was attracted to all kinds of people, now that he considered it, but when it came to who made him feel the most—who occupied his thoughts far more than the rest—it was unquestionably Griff. And now, more specifically, thoughts of *him* being the one to kiss Griff, which were definitely new.

What the hell was he supposed to do with that? If Griff stuck around long enough, maybe they would both have a chance to find out.

The sky, or what they could glimpse of it through patches in the trees, began to change toward afternoon. As the sun slipped lower, it became a muted glow, clouds gathering more thickly with each passing moment. Dark birds descended quickly from lofty heights into the thick canopy overhead, and just a few minutes later the patter of raindrops began to disturb the puddles at their feet, drumming lightly against the greenery that surrounded them and quickly growing heavier.

As Mal hastily stashed away the fragile map, lightning flashed and thunder rolled, shaking the treetops. "Let's find someplace to wait this out," he suggested, glaring balefully at the ravens who would no doubt be reporting on his progress just like the green-eyed ghosts. "I'd rather we keep your leg as dry as . . ."

His voice trailed away and his heart plummeted at the sight of the empty, rain-soaked road. While he was lost in thought and Alys was busy marking their trail, Griff and the mule had vanished.

"What happened? Did you see which way they went?" Mal demanded.

But Alys only shook her head, wide-eyed, sapling knife still in hand.

"Griff!" Mal shouted into the trees.

All he got were a few annoyed answers from the birds there. When no voice called back, he kicked a rock into the puddle ahead of them before reversing their course to follow the mule's hoofprints. Of course, those were rapidly being washed out by the driving rain.

"Fuck!"

After catching his breath, he tried again: "Griff!" The word rang out into the greenery, thoroughly irritated, though a close listener could note there was a touch of desolation to his cries beneath the anger as he added, "Come back!"

He was going to be the death of Griff. Or Griff was going to be the death of himself, and Mal was going to have to watch—he'd been sure he could keep him safer out here than he could in Mayfair, and so far he had never been so wrong about anything in his life. Except, apparently, how that infuriating moron felt about him.

Leave it to that unserious hero's son who couldn't quite commit to the title himself, let alone commit to anyone else, to disappear on them in what was shaping up to be a nasty storm.

If he died out here from his own stupidity, it would serve him right.

Yet to Alys, who was already starting on her own frantic search of the trees, Mal pleaded, "Help me look for him. Look for tracks, drag marks, anything. We have to find him."

He couldn't quite bring himself to call it luck that they had an assortment of dark feathers mingled with the most visible of the mule's prints to guide their way.

Chapter Fifteen
A Murder

Griff was too distracted to answer the faint calling of his name right away. He was following something that had caught his eye just off the path, a bit of shiny that had quickly rolled away from him as though he'd accidentally kicked it rather hard with his boot. Yet he was almost certain he hadn't.

One of the ravens that had descended during the storm's approach clocked him with a beady eye as he drew closer to the object that had finally rolled to a stop: a man's heavy signet ring set with a garnet stone, the band one of dulled gold, the red gem at its center carved with a distinct family crest.

Rhun's family crest.

First his dagger, and now his ring. It seemed the shadow that might be Rhun had wanted him to come this way for some reason; and although he was curious enough to follow, Griff also thought warily, once again, of Vic's bait traps.

He hadn't called out to the others because it had happened so quickly, and because he wasn't going to follow any bauble or sign very far out here. He didn't want to vanish like Rhun, to become nothing more than bits of steel and jewelry scattered in muddy water.

Dismounting from the mule, he finally picked up the ring and looked around. He had wandered into an area where the trees and shrubbery muted the worst of the storm's effects, though it was unpleasantly full of more of the birds Mal hated.

Water ran heavily from branches that twisted down toward the earth like weary arms, providing patches of cover. In those branches, a flock of ravens perched, wings rustling, beaks moving softly with conversations tapering to a halt, as if Griff had just interrupted some sort of covert meeting.

One of the birds dropped in a swift flutter and took a couple of skittering, three-toed hops toward the base of the biggest tree, the one in which most of its companions were roosting. Regarding Griff with an unreadable, reptilian stare, it opened its beak slowly, almost as if intending to speak.

He knew there were some birds in the Mire that could mimic human speech—not for any good purpose, as they were another of the dark queen's creations—but this bird only gave a throaty caw.

Raking at the earth for a few moments with determined swipes of its talons, the raven glanced back again at Griff, as if waiting for the human to catch on and start scrubbing through the mud much like the bird was doing now.

Its black claws scratched frantically, resuming the task as Griff strode closer, one hand on his maul just in case. Water flowed in where mud was cleared, and soon enough came the sound of those talons scraping against what sounded like—and looked like—a piece of wood.

Kneeling in the mud near the bird, Griff reluctantly tucked his maul back into his belt. There were, he realized as he scrutinized the damp ground, a few glints of silver in the mud here and there: old coins, tarnished and stamped with a starry design that the elves hadn't used since back before they founded Stormveil. He had seen the like only in history books.

There were probably more beneath the wood, he guessed. With the bird looking on, he too began to dig, and with the help of the storm, it didn't take long to reveal a rotting wooden chest in the grip of mud and roots at the base of the tree, its lid still held in place by rusty iron latches. He guessed they would give way with any amount of pressure, frail as they were with age and weather.

It was like the shadow had wanted them to find this treasure. Not *the* treasure—they weren't nearly far enough into the Mire after a day's slow march to have reached Rhun's X on that map—but this old chest, these old coins. Why? Was Rhun perhaps feeling helpful and fatherly from beyond the grave?

The raven finally stopped digging, gave Griff another mysterious beady-eyed stare, then darted into the branches to sit among its fellows and watch the proceedings imperiously.

Maybe, Griff half hoped but mostly doubted, whatever was within this chest would be enough to satisfy Mal's thirst for riches. As such, it didn't feel right to open it without the others here.

"Mal!" he shouted over the rain, only to be rewarded with a jolt of pain from his scar that left him gasping for air. There were other reasons they needed to keep going too. When he had caught his breath, he tried again. "Alys! Over here—I found something! I found some treasure!"

Mal stalked toward the sound of Griff's voice with a sour look on his face.

"Griff, what the *fuck*? I can't believe you're joking about the treasure right now when we should all be looking for shelter," the thief growled as he ducked beneath the low branches with Alys in tow, raising the collar of her shirt over her head to act as a shield from the rain. "Wait—what's this?" The scowl on his face wavered and he stopped in his tracks as he took in the sight of Griff and his bandaged leg sprawled in the mud beside a wooden chest.

As his friends crowded around, he polished the ring on his shirt and showed it to them. Alys took it right away and tried to put it on, but it was much too big for any of her fingers. They would have to find her a chain if she wanted to wear it.

"I don't like this," Mal said, backlit by another flash of lightning. "Any spirit—even Rhun's—giving us stuff. Nobody gives things away for free."

"It's not him, though," Alys countered steadily, frowning. "I would feel him. I've never forgotten what it was like to be around him, even just his presence in the next room while I was trying to fall asleep. Big and warm and steady."

"And then there's the birds—those fucking birds! Nothing good ever happens when they're around," Mal went on rather than arguing with her, dropping to his knees beside Griff. He must have seen something of the lingering effects of the pain from his scar etched into his face, as he asked, "Are you sure you're all right?" When Griff nodded, he admitted, "I thought you were teasing me when you shouted about treasure."

"If I wanted to do that, I have years' worth of ammunition saved up," Griff said quietly. "Fake treasure isn't even on the list of how I'd do it, and besides—I don't have a death wish, remember?"

Mal frowned. "Tempting, but I've still got the scars from that old routine." Then he added, a dark edge to his tone that still wasn't quite teasing, "Though if you ask me, you'd be getting the better end of the deal. You'd be a happy phantom rather than a sad elf, and I'd be the one having to face Wynnie's wrath when I told her you'd gone and done it all on my account."

Griff surprised even himself with the grin that flickered over his face.

The next crash of thunder sounded a little farther off than the last. As the sound softened, the ravens in the trees chattered to each other as if discussing the new arrivals.

"I wonder if Papa planned to take these coins home to Wynnie when he left the Mire," Alys murmured as she stashed the ring in her pocket, perhaps reconsidering the shadow's identity after all. "They look really old," she added, plucking a loose silver from the mud and rubbing it clean with her shirt to study. "We could always melt them down for the metal. I doubt they're in circulation anymore."

"Definitely not," Griff agreed, blinking rain from his eyes to take a better look at her on his left, then at Mal on his right. "Anyway, I think we ought to open this thing together. Unless you'd rather do it yourself, Mal, as group leader . . . ?"

"This is a strange place," Alys murmured, no answer at all, her voice small and full of foreboding. "Maybe Papa wanted us to have this treasure instead of the one we're looking for. Maybe he wants us to take this and turn around here, because he knows something we don't . . ."

A raven overhead cawed in answer.

Mal hardly seemed to be surveying the glittering coins or listening to Alys's uncertainty. Instead, he was still holding Griff's gaze. "You know, I seem to recall you not that long ago promising you wouldn't do anything as stupid as going off and dying on us, and I intend to hold you to it."

"Have you considered why it matters so much to you?" Griff asked softly, his eyes searching Mal's. He had made it clear how he felt. It was up to Mal to figure out the same.

But the temptation of the chest seemed to prove too great for Mal at last, finally claiming his focus. Nudging at the splintered wood to test its strength, he answered Griff's first question instead of his last: "The three of us should open it together, I think."

The ravens seemed to approve. As Griff and his companions each put a hand on the chest, the birds began leaping back and forth from branch to branch, their chatter a near-constant hum that was building to something more, craning and elongating their necks as they peered down from the heights.

Mal scowled upward.

"You think they're going to let us take anything we find out of here without a fight?" Alys whispered.

"Screw them. We can carry a hell of a lot more, and we're not walking away empty-handed, not after we've come this far," Mal vowed as, together, they popped open the old iron latches.

The wooden lid practically came apart in Griff's hands, and the force of the impact rocked them all back onto their heels in the muddy water.

Inside was a large and decorated brass goblet, a couple of blue glass bottles, and a glittering heap of the same star-adorned silver coins mixed with mud. There was a wide hole in the side of the chest, which explained how dirt had gotten in and some of the coins had slid into the surrounding earth, even if it explained nothing about the shadow's true purpose in guiding them here.

The ravens grew even more enthusiastic at the sight that had just been revealed. A few began to dive into a patch of slimy moss on the opposite side of the chest, perhaps having spotted something to eat, tearing up the turf with their beaks and claws.

"These coins are of an old elven design," Griff said above the din, running his fingers over a few of them. "And those bottles—that's elven wine, the good stuff. Rhun would have tried it when they treated him in Stormveil after the war."

"This stuff is probably cursed," Mal said darkly, picking up a handful of coins and, despite his words, looking pleased at the sound they made as they slipped through his fingers and clinked back into the pile. "If anyone wanted us to find it, that's why. But joke's on them. I'm already cursed anyway. Doomed to suffer until I die. But this still makes us rich at the end of the day," he concluded with cheerful spite, abandoning the coins in favor of rubbing his shirtsleeve where it covered his tattoo.

Griff was no expert, but he didn't think tattoos were supposed to trouble a person that often. It hadn't looked infected when he'd gotten a glimpse, merely irritated from the frequent scratching, but it was still strange. He also didn't think they should be taking any of this stuff if Mal really suspected it was cursed—just like he wasn't convinced that the man himself had been cursed—but before they argued about any of that, he wanted to get out of the rain and away from the birds. Find shelter, as Mal had suggested.

Eyes dancing in the low light as she showered herself in a handful of coins, some of her good humor clearly restored, Alys asked, "What are you going to buy first, Mal?"

"A bed fit for a king, the biggest bed this side of the Teeth," Mal answered like he'd thought about this before. "And for you, Alys, the most expensive paints," he said fondly. His gaze then shifted to Griff, and he leaned a little closer. "And for you—what would you like? Another lute? Or how about a horse?" A grin tugged at his mouth as he added, "One that you can name."

Up close, Griff realized that Mal had mud splattered on his face from not wearing his hood. He reached slowly toward a spot above the other man's eyebrow to wipe some away before it could fall right into his eye, saying warmly as he did so, "Sure, Mal. I'd love a horse."

Mal's grin widened in answer, wild and full of teeth, as it always did when he was excited. But the look softened into something more like curiosity or wonder as he took in the length of Griff's sodden hair trailing down over his shoulder.

Mal wasn't the only one who hadn't bothered with his hood this afternoon.

The thief reached out and ran his fingers through that river of darkness, following the path of a curl to its end. "Your hair's gotten longer," he observed on a breath that gusted over Griff's lips. "Pretty. I like it like this."

Griff's heart was lodged so firmly in his throat that he found he couldn't speak around it, and all he could do was nod dumbly as he practically tasted Mal. And if his eyes fluttered as Mal stroked those fingers experimentally through his hair, well, some things couldn't be helped.

Gray eyes widening and narrowing as he continued his scrutiny of Griff's face up close, Mal went on in the same sort of low exhale, "For all everyone says it, even me, you don't actually look much like the portraits of your father. You look just like . . . your own. Like Griff."

"Is that a good thing?" Griff managed to ask, sharing a little of his breath in return.

Mal gave a nod, slight but firm. He leaned closer still, a fire in his eyes Griff had never seen there before, one that had nothing to do with riches or giant beds or adventures. Well, maybe a giant bed could be involved.

"Mal," Alys said urgently, interrupting as she reached for the bird-topped dagger that had been Rhun's. "I—I think we should get going . . ."

They both turned, heeding the call before their lips met, though Griff's heart was beating as though they had, clamoring inside his chest so hard it was making him dizzy. Maybe this was how he might go out after all—a heart attack, here and now, from the shock of one of his fantasies coming to life. If he was going to stay, he needed the lust and adoration that had been sparking in Mal's eyes to be real, not just something painted from his wildest dreams.

Mal rubbed his tattoo again and swore under his breath, startling Griff from his thoughts.

While they were occupied, the entire flock had descended from the trees at the sight of that chest bursting open, like they had been waiting for this moment. Anticipating it.

Now the ravens were growing increasingly frantic in their digging near the chest. They seemed to have found some treasure of their own, beaks ravenously tearing at the earth to reveal more of whatever they were after: gray slime and bits of decayed cloth at first, and then slivers of red and white as strips of flesh were torn away from an unfortunate limb to offer glimpses of muscle and bone beneath. And at the end of that limb, almost touching the wooden lid of the chest that had fallen apart, the distinctly elongated shapes of finger bones began to appear amid the ravens' frenzy.

The finger bones twitched.

Or, at least, Griff thought they had, though he hoped it was his imagination.

"Did you see—those bones, did they just—?" He wasn't doing a very good job at voicing his suspicions, not with one of those damned ravens staring at him. A slippery piece of tendon dangled from its beak, and it kept on staring as it gulped down its meal.

"Either it's the mushrooms I ate earlier, or those bones are twitchy," Alys confirmed breathily.

In his periphery, he saw Mal moving quickly, grabbing the fancy goblet and the blue bottles before he started shoving as many coins as he could reach into his pockets despite his clumsy, bandaged hands.

"Help me, quick," Mal urged the others as another bird hopped closer, now eyeing Griff's bandaged leg with open curiosity, clicking its beak. Before Griff had time to react, Mal shooed the thing away with a forceful swing of his boot, roaring, "Fuck off!" as it took to the sky, cawing a reproach.

Griff was busy shoving coins into the pockets of his pants and cloak when he saw the finger bones start pulling themselves up out of the mud, revealing more of a skeletal arm. He nudged Mal and nodded in the hand's direction.

There were several types of undead at the Shadow Queen's command, and only some were named and known. The ghosts she managed to enslave were simply unlucky wandering souls; they could do little more than unsettle the living through the power of suggestion. Wraiths were stronger spirits, and thus more dangerous, able to move objects and grasp at clothing, even tear skin or crush bone. Revenants were more like living people, able to shamble around in their rotting or bony bodies and retain something of their personalities and ability to think for themselves. Ghouls were much the same, but feral, like wild animals always on the prowl, lacking a revenant's sense of judgment or self-control.

Griff suspected the twitching hand belonged to one of the latter two creatures, but he didn't want to stick around long enough to find out.

"Guys." Alys pointed shakily at a puddle several feet beyond the chest. "There's more."

Griff glanced over sharply to see what she meant: more bony hands hastily clawing their way out of the earth. The birds had led them to a field of walking corpses that would tear them limb from limb if given half the chance; he had a gnawing suspicion, as he watched them attack the dirt with their beaks, that they were trying to dig the bones up faster.

Mal was already on his feet, coins spilling from his pockets, wincing at the pain in his hands as he grabbed hold of Griff and worked to get him upright too. "Money can buy a lot of things," he panted, "but I'd rather not finance our funerals."

The mule snorted and stamped its feet, clearly as eager to leave as the rest of them now that it had spotted the scrabbling hands.

Alys started to help Griff onto the restless beast's back while a raven tugged at the loose end of his bandages.

Mal kicked it away, snarling with clear distaste at the feathers that littered the muddy ground even as his heavy pockets clinked with promise. "Come on," he urged, "we need to get back to the path before whatever the hell is down there digs itself . . . out . . ."

But Griff was too slow to mount the mule. His hands were shaking too much to get a good grip for hauling himself over, even with Alys's help. The mud was sucking too much at everyone's feet, forcing them to stand their ground.

And now there were five revenants—five shambling, withered gray corpses of orcs with a greenish cast to their snakelike eyes—strung out in a line, reddish mud still crusted into every crack and crevice on their wrinkled, snarling faces, their teeth as sharp in death as they had been in life, even if a few were broken or altogether missing.

The mule whinnied and skittered backward, dragging Griff with it.

Alys drew her father's sword.

Mal gave Griff and the beast a shove and shouted, "Run! Go, this—it's my fault. I'll handle it!" He nodded to Alys, who joined him in forming a barricade of sorts in front of Griff. Then he drew his hunting knife just as the undead orcs sprang after them with impressive speed for things long buried.

Chapter Sixteen

Stay

Running certainly wasn't Mal's worst idea ever, but Griff couldn't bring himself to do it. Not when Alys was fighting three on one, every orc taller and broader than she was, their surprisingly strong fists capably blocking each swing of her blade.

One orc soon had its decaying fingers tangled in her hair, jerking her head back roughly to expose her milky throat for its companions.

Griff didn't have time to think as he grabbed his maul from his belt, ignoring the way his scar throbbed in a painful protest, and cleaved through the torso of one of the hungry revenants that hadn't even bothered to glance his way. It was a bloodless blow, for which he was glad. But his relief that the creature couldn't bite into Alys's throat from on the ground was swiftly replaced by stunned horror as he realized both pieces of the body were writhing around in the mud and fallen coins, trying to piece themselves back together.

They were going to have to hack these things into little pieces to make them stop.

Alys flashed him a quick, startled look of thanks, adjusted her stance, and jabbed at the orc still tangled in her hair while kicking out at its companion who stood there leering at her and licking its cracked lips. Or at least, she tried to—half of the orc on the ground was clinging fiercely to her legs.

Griff swung with his maul again, not so different from chopping wood. He laughed, dry and humorless, at his own absurd observation as he discovered that severing the undead orc's head from its neck stopped all the parts from moving. He hadn't gotten to battling revenants in his Warden's training yet.

"Go for the heads! Cut off the heads!" he shouted, and as soon as Alys had cut through the neck of one orc and was finally able to deal with the one tearing at her hair, he reasoned she could manage on her own and turned to look for Mal.

The other two orcs had him pinned to the ground. One was gnawing on his boot while the other drooled in his face, growling something too soft to make out, claws stabbing through his much-abused jerkin as the orc trapped his arms in place, rendering his hunting knife useless.

Griff had no idea what Mal had meant about this attack being his fault. But he couldn't dwell on it now, not when Mal needed him.

He swung his maul again, and as the head of the orc pinning Mal flew clean off and landed somewhere near Alys, their eyes met over the stump of its neck. Mal's were shining, coin bright, with a mix of fear and gratitude. Looking at Griff like he was more than something to be protected and worried over. Looking at him like he was a hero.

Griff smiled for a breathless second. And then, so did Mal.

Yet there was still the matter of the revenant trying to swallow Mal's foot, boot and all. As the creature clamped its jaws down again with renewed ferocity, apparently upset at the loss of its companion, Mal grabbed his fallen knife a little clumsily in a bandaged hand and growled, "Let me have this one."

He had gotten a good start on hewing through layers of old, leathery muscle and sinew, hacking his way toward the creature's spinal cord with extra viciousness—as if the thing had insulted him on a more personal level than simply hungering for his living flesh—when Alys called softly, "Guys, look at this!"

Griff clutched his maul tighter and whirled around to face her. Yet all three orc corpses surrounding her were missing their heads, their remaining body parts unmoving. No more twitching fingers scratched at the earth. Alys herself looked unscathed beyond a few claw marks on her cheek slowly oozing beads of red and the tangle at the back of her head where one of the revenants had pulled out a bit of hair.

But if she was at all distressed or hurt, she didn't show it. She had picked up the orc's head Griff had sent flying, and now that Mal had dispatched the last revenant, she was busy admiring its features up close. When she realized her friends were staring, she grinned tiredly at them and held the head aloft.

"Darling, isn't it?" she said of the withered head with scraps of shriveled flesh still filling the hollows of its gray cheeks. Deprived of its second life, its glassy eyes stared out dispassionately at the rainy afternoon as the wind stirred what few tufts of wiry hair still clung to its scalp. When no one agreed with her, she added, "Just needs a bit of love. A spike, maybe, for mounting, and a comb run through his hair."

Griff was still too shaken to form words, and his scar was throbbing in a way that demanded most of his focus, but he shook his head at her over the sound of Mal pointlessly stabbing the torso of the revenant he had already decapitated.

"For the record, this is *not* motivating," the thief snarled at the corpse.

Griff blinked a question at Alys, but she only grinned and bopped what remained of the orc's nose.

"He looks a bit like Leo Raintree, that asshole," she declared, and suddenly, all three of them were laughing as the features of their old playground bully flashed to mind. "That settles it—I'm keeping it, and I'm calling it Leo. My very own treasure."

That's when Griff's knees finally buckled, a pulsing pain from beneath his scar demanding that he put down the maul and stop playing hero.

†

The following day dawned clear of rain, a touch of morning mist burning off as they pushed deeper into the Mire while nursing new scrapes and bruises, deeper into places where mosquitoes and dragonflies were plentiful and where covering their heads to get through clouds of midges was a common occurrence. Where the path to either side was lit by the occasional glow of rotroses, by glossy blue clusters of poisonous berries on pretty purple bushes and lurid yellow vines that wrapped and strangled the trunks of trees with increasing frequency.

They didn't talk much, and Griff guessed they were each still working through the events of the day before in their own way. He kept pace on the mule, who, if anything, seemed appreciative of their strange surroundings as a sort of vacation from the usual dull scenery of the roadside rather than flinching from any odd cries or rustlings in the bushes.

When they happened upon a swath of relatively dry ground, a gentle slope dotted with trees that climbed high enough to rise out of the muck, they made camp early, just before sunset. The discovery of something of value out here had spurred Mal to set an even more grueling pace today, but now Griff thought even he looked ready for a chance to catch his breath.

And count their riches. Naturally. They had all been too exhausted and shaken to do so the night before, and Mal had pushed them onward until they nearly collapsed. But tonight, after a quick supper from their rations, each of them emptied their pockets until they had a large pile of star-stamped silver coins sitting in front of them.

"Wait just a minute," Mal said, pulling out the large goblet he had taken from among the coins and filling it with amber liquid from his flask. "There. That's better."

Alys frowned at the cup, at its scratched gems and what looked like rust on the stem. "That thing could be poisoned, for all we know."

"Worth the risk," Mal declared as he knocked back a sip, toasting his companions and then toasting the coin piles, his eyes full of the metal stars but never once glancing up at the ones glimmering overhead.

"You'll have a hard time using these anywhere near Mayfair," Griff pointed out. "The few who recognize them will know you came by them through unusual means, and no one else will know what to do with them."

Mal scooted a little closer to him and cracked a sharp-toothed grin, setting Griff's pulse racing at the unexpected closeness. "All very good points. Which begs the question: How do you feel about counterfeiting? Going to turn us in to your Warden pals, or will you look the other way if we restamp these to look like Maysilvers?"

Griff didn't even have time to think of a reply before Mal cut a look over to Alys and added, "You're in charge of design—that is, if you're interested in lending your artistic talents to such a worthy cause?"

She leaned toward the pile of coins, scattering a few bits of silver as she grinned and ran her fingers over the treasure spread before them. "Of course I'll do it. I'd love to." She turned to Griff expectantly, eyes wide and hopeful. "Well? Will you help us too?"

She seemed to think there was a chance. Seemed to think Griff was one of them again.

But Mal looked bleak and withdrawn as he watched Griff and sipped from his goblet, his body rigid with tension, the same posture he held when they fought and he was waiting for a blow to fall. Griff's chest ached at the sight.

"I think," he said slowly, because he was too deep in this swamp now to map himself a way out, and if he hadn't wanted that, if he didn't still want Mal after everything, he would have turned back well before this, "that we're going to need to make some really big purchases to get our supply circulating in the local market, so you'd better jot down all the things you want to buy for your kids, Alys."

Mal lowered his goblet to reveal a slowly forming grin, a hint of mirth warming his eyes that banished some of the tightness in Griff's chest. "And you'd better start thinking of horse names."

Alys, who had climbed to her feet and was starting to put her sword belt back on, smiled at them for a long moment and said, "I'll work on that list while I'm out there, then."

Mal frowned. "Wait. Out where?"

"I'd like to hunt around the area for a while, get a feel for the land, and see if there's anything else of Papa's we might have missed. You'd be surprised how well I can see at night." Alys grabbed the shriveled orc's head now mounted on a stocky dead branch and bobbed it in their direction, then grinned again like this had been her intention all along. "I'll take Leo with me, so I won't be alone. I've got my sword, and I've got the broken one too, in case I come across the rest of it. Besides, who ever heard of a warg that's afraid of the dark?"

She quickly disappeared into the blackness between the trees, leaving Griff worrying and asking, "Shouldn't one of us go with her, at least?"

Part of him wondered if Alys was just trying to give them a moment alone together after they had nearly kissed yesterday, though he didn't voice it out loud. He still didn't know how Mal would feel about spending time together on purpose or about kissing another man.

Gazing thoughtfully the way Alys had gone, Mal said, "She might have only killed the one living man, but she can take care of herself, as you saw yesterday. Even if we hadn't been there, she would have figured out the trick with the heads." Softer, he added, "And I think . . . there are some things she's just got to do for herself."

"Should I be offended that you don't speak of my sword skills quite the same way?" Griff asked, trying to keep his voice light.

"Probably," Mal admitted in his usual blunt manner. He went over to the saddlebags near the tethered, dozing mule and pulled out one of the blue bottles. "But I hope your knickers aren't in too much of a bunch to try this with me."

Settling on the ground just beside Griff with the goblet and the bottle, close enough that their knees were touching, he didn't make any attempt at the cork with his bandaged hands just yet. Instead, he cut an unreadable look across at Griff and said, "You might as well go ahead and take a look at these cuts too. I lost my mittens when we were fighting those damned revenants, so the bandages probably need changing. I'm in the mood to curse, anyway."

Griff could have said something about being sober, but he didn't. Instead, he quickly dumped out the remaining whiskey in the goblet and hoped Mal wouldn't notice, then started working at the old cork in the dusty blue bottle with a tool on his belt. Elf-wine had many incredible qualities, not least of which was that it didn't form a habit the way human or dwarven wine did. It tasted like bottled starlight, and its effects were closer to something like Alys's mushrooms, if anything. A gentle, temporary high.

As he fought the cork, he glanced up at Mal and said, "You want my professional opinion as a healer? Worst case, you're going to have a scar on your right hand to rival that impressive one on your chest."

Mal reached for the empty goblet, holding it clumsily between his hands for Griff to fill. "Hope it doesn't bother me for the rest of my life the way your scar is hounding you."

Griff poured a little too much wine, nearly to the goblet's rim, so he wouldn't have to meet Mal's eyes. "You've noticed, huh."

"Mmm," Mal murmured, and Griff thought that might be the end of the conversation. But then he said, "Certain poisons derived by magical means will do that."

"I know." Griff set the bottle down and raised his eyes to Mal's, surprised that he had guessed this much. "But there's something in that treasure—or there might be—that was enchanted to cure such things. A pair of silver vambraces made by elven healers. I was hoping to wear them for a little while before you sell them to the highest bidder or whatever, as long as it doesn't interfere with your plans."

"Of course not," Mal said. "That's all the more reason we need to press on as soon as we can." He took a long drink from the heavy goblet, the fingers of his other hand tracing a line down his chest. "My scar wasn't made by any kind of poison," he added. Then, with another look at Griff, "Alys doesn't like me talking about my time in Thrallkeld."

"I'm not her," Griff answered evenly, and Mal held his gaze.

"No, you're not." Mal took a breath, seeming to steel himself for whatever he was about to say. "I . . . left my dignity on the living room floor that day. When you and I fought that first time." He swiftly glanced down, hiding whatever emotion flashed through his eyes. "I went to Thrallkeld to try to get it back."

The air was growing cold as the night around them deepened. Griff set the bottle he had been holding gently in his lap, drawing his cloak tighter around him as he listened, afraid that if he spoke now, the moment would be over too soon.

"It started out okay. I met a girl, Ella—we were friends. We worked together to get by, running schemes and picking pockets," Mal explained, his face darkening as he continued. "Renaud ran things down there—several things, but namely, the thieves' guild. He had a big house, fine clothes, and pockets full of gold, and I wanted it. All of it. I wanted to conquer the city like Wynnie used to dream of doing before she met Rhun, give her something to really be proud of. So I challenged Renaud when I thought I was ready, but—he still had the upper hand, as you've seen." Mal's smile was as black as the look in his eyes. "For a while, I managed to avoid capture. I hid in a ruin and ate through my rations, and then I resorted to eating rats. But once those were gone too, I was forced to move, and Renaud's people found me. He said he was going to . . . make an example of me."

"Maybe he made an example of a seventeen-year-old boy, but I'd like to meet him now and see what *I* could make of *him*," Griff growled. The thought of that scar, what had clearly been a grisly wound on Mal's chest, had some protective beast rearing up inside him. Had him abandoning his usually gentle nature in favor of Wynnie's bloodlust. "I could go after him for you, settle the score once we're out of here and my wounds are healed."

Rats.

Alone and afraid and desperate to prove himself, Mal had resorted to eating rats to survive. No wonder he was so thin.

Mal had been starving, hiding and running for his life like a hunted animal, while Griff was above it all in Stormveil, debating whether he should have one or two sugar cubes in his hand-painted porcelain teacup and cracking jokes to make Princess Rosemaris laugh.

That awful scar was his fault.

Maybe no one could have talked Mal out of going, but Griff could have been there. Fought beside him. Bled with him.

He took out his feelings on the blue bottle in his lap, pouring another generous serving into the goblet and toasting to Mal before taking a much-needed sip.

"You can't—Griff, you really can't go after someone like Renaud," Mal said seriously, sitting taller, his eyes gleaming with sudden alertness even as he took the goblet to have a taste for himself. "Much as I'd love to see you take a swing at him with that maul, you don't have a chance against someone like him. Most people don't. He's got so many men loyal to him all over that city, you could kill him but still end up dead."

He shook his head, silent a moment as he gazed off someplace Griff couldn't follow. "I asked Wynnie to do it. I think she might be the only one who can. But you—I need you alive. Because I need you to look at my hands before I get some kind of infection and die in one of the stupid ways I told you not to." He thrust his hands out, upturned palms coming to rest on Griff's thighs.

"Then I'm at your service," Griff said, a telltale warmth creeping up the back of his neck that made him grateful for the cover of darkness. Conditions were still too damp for a fire, which also meant he had to use the faint starlight for guidance as he unwrapped Mal's soggy bandages.

"One of Renaud's men knocked over a lantern in the tent where they were holding me," Mal finally continued in a low voice as his tender hands were exposed to the air, being turned this way and that for Griff's inspection. "I wasn't in any shape to move on my own, but Tansy—Ella's girlfriend—pulled me out of there and got my heart beating again. She's some kind of witch. Usually avoids people because she can't stand the noise of cities and the things we build over her rivers. But she healed me for months in her cottage, in a swamp not so different from this one, and talked me through suddenly being able to see ghosts." He sighed, his eyes roaming warily over Griff's face before he went on. "She said dying for a minute is what changed me."

Griff took another sip from the goblet, passing it back toward Mal and studying the unwrapped wounds along the other man's palms as closely as he could in the dimness, taking both Mal's hands in his again. "These aren't as bad as they first looked. You should let them get some air tonight, and they might be even better by morning. Probably no scars, either."

With his healer's judgment delivered, no need to dig out salve or other bandages, Griff knew he could let go of Mal's hands then. But he didn't. He was very much aware that he was still holding on to them both, aware of every place they touched, the heat of fingers and palms, and just as aware that Mal wasn't pulling them back.

"Mal," he said, his voice steady despite a sudden dampness in his eyes. "What I did to you back then . . . the things I said . . . I hurt you so much worse than anything you faced in Thrallkeld. I was a coward, running off like that. Just because of feelings I was too scared to even admit. I'm sure it doesn't matter now, but—I'm so fucking sorry."

Mal's hands were heavy in his, and Griff gladly took their weight. "Renaud may have tried to cut out my heart," he murmured, "but someone else beat him to it." He exhaled slowly, his eyes silver in the starlight as they roamed over Griff's face. "Plenty of others have tried to claim my heart, but they never understood that what doesn't stay never really belonged to them."

"I almost came for you," Griff admitted, though he could feel his throat tightening. "So many times. When I found out you'd gone to Thrallkeld, I wrote you every day. Every damn day. Letter after letter, begging to reconcile, telling you how I really felt. When you didn't answer, I almost went down there anyway. Apparently, Lord Valerian was burning all those letters. They never even got sent. Rosemaris told me, much later, when she found out. Her father thought it better that I stay in Stormveil."

It was, Griff knew, a poor excuse for not just leaving anyway. He hadn't been the elves' prisoner. He had just been scared—scared of what Mal would think of him, scared Mal wouldn't want him back, scared he couldn't be what Mal needed. He still was. He didn't have treasure or castles or plans for a life far grander than the one he had already built, all the things that seemed to put an extra spark in Mal's eyes.

But tonight, with the wine giving him courage, he was determined to try. To stay.

Chapter Seventeen

Uncharted Territory

Mal's eyes widened at the admission, then narrowed, and quickly slid away from Griff's. There was a certain bile rising in his throat, one he hated more than the taste of rats. Emotion, a well of it threatening to escape him all at once. But there were still things he wasn't ready to say, and he needed a familiar place to shelter. "It's fine. I mean, I'm fine now. I didn't need any stupid letters, anyway. It doesn't matter."

The words stuck in his throat, much the way a bit of extra moisture stuck hatefully in the corners of his eyes—but if Griff noticed, he didn't call attention to it.

"Fucking elves," Mal added with a bit of extra venom. He glanced at the nearly empty goblet. They had already demolished a good portion of what was in the bottle. "Sitting in a tower singing sad songs and having tea parties seems like a waste of several centuries to me. You ought to spend less time around folk like that."

"Good thing I'm down here to stay, then, isn't it?" Griff was trying to tease, to lighten the air between them again.

But Mal was utterly serious as he curled the fingers of his left hand around Griff's and murmured, "It is. Good. You should stay. With me." He raised his other hand, an explorer mapping the edges of some new land as he used it to push a lock of Griff's unruly hair out of his eyes, his thumb then trailing over the curve of Griff's cheek.

The tingling in his fingertips had to be some side effect of the elves' wine. Mal really had to give it to them—that was one thing they had gotten right, even if they apparently tore apart families and friends by burning mail that didn't belong to them.

Mal tightened his fingers around Griff's, gently tugging the other man toward him.

Choosing what he wanted, if not what he deserved. He didn't deserve Griff after what he had done, but he was a thief and he had a taste for the finer things that wouldn't ever be satisfied with less. He was Mister Dangerous, and from now on, as long as he drew breath, all that meant for Griff was that he would be safe in Mal's company.

At the tug, Griff tipped forward ungracefully, as if his whole world had just been knocked off its axis, catching himself with a hand at the top of Mal's thigh and bringing them nose to nose. He seemed unable to look anywhere but into Mal's eyes. Right where Mal wanted him.

Maybe Griff knew something about staying after all.

Mal gazed back, finding Griff framed in a halo of light at the center of his focus. If there were any shadows or green-eyed ghosts lingering beyond the edges of this golden glow, beyond this face that was somehow new to him, he couldn't see them right now. Didn't need any more reminders of what was at stake when it was gently breathing over his lips.

"What a lightweight," he observed, his voice offhand and distracted as his eyes continued their survey of Griff's face in this fresh light, "tipping over before the toasting is done."

"What the fuck are we doing?" Griff whispered. With his free hand, he brushed his thumb across Mal's lower lip, asking a different question altogether. It was a request and a prayer and too tenuous yet to be given breath.

That thumb moving across Mal's lower lip was all the encouragement he needed to cross the border into a rich expanse of uncharted territory. Silent questions were answered in the way Mal closed that last sliver of distance between them, breath warm with an aroma of sweet wine and sultry whiskey. "We're doing whatever the fuck we want," he boasted quietly, stealing a brush with Griff's lips, as if such thievery were inherent to the path they were stepping down together. "That's how it's done in my world. So stay."

Running his tingling fingers up into the soft and welcoming texture of Griff's hair more freely now, he let his hands offer a hint of guiding pressure, an invitation for a deeper, longer kiss.

"A pack of wargs couldn't keep me away," Griff assured him in the narrow space between their lips just before they met again. He ran the heat of his palm down Mal's thigh, like he needed the feel of fabric and solid flesh there to let him know this was real and not some daydream conjured by the elf-wine.

The kiss took Mal's breath away, their lips and tongues sharing honey and fire and a hint of bottled summer sunshine; in a world of spirits and liars and things that were never quite what they seemed, Griff's kiss was the realest thing Mal had ever known.

And the taste was just right. The shape of the thigh beneath his hand and the stubbled cheek scratching against his own seemed to have been pulled right from his own quiet, unvoiced desires, an answer he badly needed.

Hands that had once traded blows with this very body now roamed over it with reverence, Griff's fingers delving gently into the gold tangles of Mal's hair, then lowering to frame the sides of Mal's face like he wanted to remember how he looked in this moment forever.

"I think I like it here, doing whatever-the-fuck with you," Griff murmured against his mouth before kissing him harder still. He grazed his teeth along the curve of Mal's ear as he added, "I mean it. I'm staying."

Mal was only vaguely aware of the words spoken close to his ear, too distracted by the way his pulse was ringing in his head, by so much light coursing through his veins. Heavy breaths against Griff's neck were his only attempt to answer.

As they traded more kisses, Griff's hands made their way under Mal's shirt, feeling out the contours of his chest, the tight flesh of that grim scar. Mal's own heartbeat quickened in answer, strong and very much alive beneath those stroking fingers.

Griff's lips moved lower, exploring along Mal's jaw, then down his neck, sucking a mark into that tawny skin while Mal pressed an encouraging kiss into Griff's hair.

Shirt hanging half loose as Griff kept on exploring with his hands and lips, Mal let his own hands wander under Griff's collar, admiring the muscles in the other man's shoulders and upper back, the ones that tensed up when he swung that maul; the ones that once had been used to swing fists in his direction. Only now there was something welcoming about them, something tame and pliable and willing.

Bunching up a handful of Griff's shirt, Mal delivered his appraisal of all his new discoveries with an eloquent "Mmm." Any pain in his hands was hardly felt, dulled by the heady cocktail of elf-wine and emotion as he grew more opinionated on the course of their evening, catching Griff's lower lip between his teeth and pulling gently, a further invitation to leap into the dazzling unknown.

Layers fell away.

Boots, scarves, belts; Mal cast them aside with the same regard he showed for keeping his things neat back at the cottage—none. Shirts were hastily discarded too, a few buttons popping and rolling away unseen. Then Mal impatiently tugged off Griff's pants, though he took extra time and care with the bandages over Griff's right leg, and kept his eyes carefully away from the dark line of a scar he knew sat just below the other man's waistline.

What Mal withheld in conversation, he made up for in generosity with his hands, with his mouth on Griff's neck, his tongue darting more than once along a swath of skin there to absorb this marvel that was as curious, in a way, as the chest of silver coins: the taste of someone new.

When Mal urged him to lay back with some gentle pressure on his chest and then knelt between his thighs, Griff hardly seemed able to draw a breath as Mal's gaze swept over him, unflinching in the pale starlight. Griff was dripping before Mal had even touched him, already aching for Mal's hand that slowly reached out to feel him, and for Mal's hot breath that gusted over his most sensitive skin.

His mouth was usually so full of boasts, but now it was full of Griff instead, and he found he rather liked the taste. Griff put some new tangles in Mal's messy hair where he threaded his hands through it, urging him forward, deeper, more, until after just a few minutes of this he was warning, "Mal, if—if you don't stop—"

Mal grinned, pulling off just long enough to urge Griff farther down onto the cloak they had spread over the ground. "Bet I can make you forget your own name," he murmured. "But you're always going to remember mine." With that, he swallowed Griff again not quite to the root, but as close as he could manage without gagging. Not bad for his first time with another man, he guessed, because Griff was babbling in some other language and his foot was twitching against the ground.

He caught a few words here and there: *King. Lord. Beloved.*

But when he came, it was with Mal's name on his lips.

And while he floated off someplace else in the moments after, Mal's fingers ventured lower than where they had been, teasing

Griff's thighs, stroking lightly between his cheeks in a careful new exploration before retreating.

When Griff came back to himself, he took one look at Mal and arched a dark brow. "You going to keep these on all night?" he teased, hooking his fingers into the waistband of the pants Mal was very obviously straining against.

He groaned as Griff put on a little show, popping off the buttons one by one with his teeth. Mal provided plenty of encouragement with the searing heat of his gaze as he watched Griff work those pants down off his hips until they, too, were cast off into the night.

The skills Griff had apparently learned with his hands and mouth over the years were ones Mal could only describe as somewhere north of masterful. What good sense the foreman lacked in matters of thievery, he made up for with the instinctual way he opened his throat to fit Mal all the way down the back of it, welcoming him in as far as he was willing to go.

"What—?" Mal gasped, his eyes blinking open at the unexpected sensation, his breath catching. "The fuck?" he demanded, trying and failing to even raise his head to get a good look at Griff, marveling at this display of magic. He pressed his head back against the grass instead, very aware of a faint trembling in one of his legs and the heat building between them.

If there were stars or a bright moon or even the dark queen's servants ogling them from the thickets, Mal didn't see any of it. Everything that wasn't the mercifully tight clench of Griff's throat was utterly lost to him for a time.

He eventually regained some breath and enough composure to realize that he was stroking Griff's hair, had Griff's head cradled against his chest. They were both flushed and hot and sticky, and yet Mal was fully uninterested in untangling himself after so long apart.

He was tired. He could feel it in the weight of his limbs, and in Griff's too, but what he wanted more than sleep was to be inside of him. So when Griff took their joined hands and sucked Mal's fingers into his mouth, coating them with plenty of spit in the absence of the oil Mal was sure he had read about somewhere, he found a second wind, let Griff guide his fingers and guessed the rest with the other man's increasingly ragged breathing telling him he was on the right path again as he stroked him gently open.

When Mal finally pushed inside him, he did so with the same brash determination with which he'd entered the Mire. Pursued another high for them both with one hand wrapped around Griff, his mouth on Griff's claiming every kiss offered to him there, and the same lust with which he chased after the elusive treasure.

They moved as one, fluid motions of Mal's hips rolling through them both until they cried out again and again, no longer a collision of opposing forces.

Later still, the moon having made over half of its journey across the sky, they drifted toward sleep together wrapped up in one of their cloaks and nothing else. Griff's arm was draped over Mal's waist, cradling the other man against his chest.

"It wasn't fine," Griff whispered into the crook of Mal's neck, soft enough that if Mal was already asleep, it wouldn't wake him.

But Mal was still up, hardly breathing, silently taking in every word. Daring to hope for something for once: that this night on which his life had irreversibly changed was real, that this version of Griff who loved him was real and not some elf-wine fever dream.

"When I didn't come to Thrallkeld, when you didn't get my letters—nothing about what happened was fine. You weren't fine, and hell, I wasn't fine. Far from it. I tried to drink myself to death. And when that didn't work, I tried finding other ways to drown." Griff's arm tightened around him a fraction, his fingers gently brushing over the bits of scarred skin he could reach there, keeping Mal warmer than he had been in years. “It damn near destroyed me, missing you.”

Mal still said nothing, though the grass became a little damper as he listened.

A few moments later, he snuggled deeper into the sanctuary of Griff’s embrace and let himself be held.

Chapter Eighteen

The Boyfriend Special

Mal woke to the smoke of a cookfire wafting over him, carrying the scent of breakfast and the distinct sound of something sizzling away in a pan. He smelled bacon and sausages, and before he cracked open a wary eye, he half wondered if he was home and the memory of dark hair, green eyes, warm hands, and faintly muttered dares and curses had all been a strange dream.

He needed to know.

Opening his eyes, he was greeted by a Mire awash in morning sun and rich new colors, hues of green and brown having deepened in the absence of mist and rain. Sitting up at last, hair sticking out at every angle, Mal let the cloak bunched in his fist fall away, baring his tattoo and scars without a hint of shame, like this were any other morning at the cottage in Linden where he had grown up.

By the fire, Griff and Alys were preparing some sort of meal.

Her bedroll was laid out near the spot where the two men had slept, wrapped in nothing but Griff's cloak. She must have returned sometime late in the night. Leo the Orc Head had a wilting rotrose tucked behind one of his batlike ears and was watching over the breakfast proceedings from atop his pike with a listless expression.

His friends were busy cracking eggs, but there were no chickens out here. They needed to be packing and heading out immediately if they didn't want another visit from a bunch of ghouls or revenants trying to speed them on their way, like what had happened back at that chest of silvers. Griff's injured leg had already slowed their progress more than he had been accounting for, and the orc who'd had him pinned down earlier confirmed his fears as he snarled a raspy message from the queen: They needed to pick up the pace and stop being so easily distracted by shiny things—her words—or she would keep finding creative ways to motivate him. Like having her birds unearth those revenants. Maybe Rhun's spirit had accompanied them there to try to warn them of the hidden danger, if the shadow really was him.

"What in the five hells?" Mal muttered, not bothering to pull on a single scrap of yesterday's clothes as he ambled over to the fireside just a few feet away.

Alys, her hair freshly braided in a style reminiscent of the braid in the mule's mane—which had to be Griff's handiwork—looked no worse for wear after her nighttime explorations as she smiled at him and said an easy, "Morning."

At the collar of her blouse was a tarnished silver pin. A Warden's cloak pin. Mal knew immediately who it must have belonged to even before Alys noticed him staring at the relic and said, "I found this last night, maybe half a mile north of here. His initials are on the back, just like the dagger. It was right next to a nest of some kind of eggs. Griff's cooking them up for us."

That settled it, at least in Mal's mind. The shadow was Rhun, helping them along in their task, making sure they ate and tried to stay out of trouble—perhaps because his spirit was eager to see Mal free of the dark queen's influence. Or perhaps simply so they could live long enough to recover his body.

"I know that look," Alys remarked lightly.

"What look?"

"The one where you look like you just got voted mayor of Mayfair. Because you were right about the shadow," she explained, pressing her palm to the heavy pin. "Papa must have remembered how much I loved his scrambled eggs. I'm glad we have someone on our side out here, even if it means he's . . . well. You know."

"I know," Mal said gently, giving her shoulder a squeeze. Then in his usual brusque manner, he went on, "He could be making himself a lot more useful, though, if you ask me. Figure out how to keep the ravens away or something." He sat down between his companions and reached for the water canteen someone had left within reach. Griff was back in last night's pants but still shirtless, flipping something in one of the two pans heating over the fire. Having the travelers' extra pan had clearly inspired him, or else he really loved to play kitchen. Given the ball of dough he'd spotted waiting for a turn in the spare pan, Mal suspected the latter.

"Alys, I know a hot meal would be nice, especially eggs, but we need to leave. Time's wasting," Mal warned lowly, worried that the kindness of their guardian shadow was lulling her into a false sense of safety.

"You're the one who's going to waste away if you don't eat some breakfast for a change. It's just one morning; we can make up the time this afternoon."

Sliding whatever he was fixing from pan to plate, Griff turned and handed it to Mal. There was a thick slice of fried toast with an egg at its center. "Egg-in-a-hole, double yolk. Still your favorite?" Griff asked with a private sort of grin.

"Yeah," Mal said slowly, his groggy brain not having quite caught up to this turn of events, the part where last night was real. Still, he lifted the toast and attacked it with more enthusiasm than he had shown for anything but the flask. Alys had a point: They could push themselves in just a few hours, and if any more revenants surprised them, they were at least slightly more ready now that they knew how to handle them.

"'S good, Griff," he added thickly around a mouthful. "Thanks."

Alys held up her doughy hands and said eagerly, "Wait till you try Griff's cinnamon buns."

Griff watched him demolish the toast with a touch of pride, undoubtedly the only man this side of the Teeth who ever carried small portions of flour, sugar, shortening, and cinnamon on such a dangerous expedition. At least that explained why his pack was so damn heavy—the better to exercise those beautiful shoulder muscles, at least. "From now on," he murmured as Mal tore into another piece, "I'm going to bring you every delicacy from here to the southlands. When we get home, I'll fix you coffee and cocoa and pasta with truffle sauce. You'll love truffles. They're expensive."

Mal snorted at that. "Seems like you're catching on to a few things here."

"We'll call this the Boyfriend Special," Griff declared as he prepared another piece of double-yolk toast in the pan. When he had finished, he slid his arms around Mal's back to pull him in for a kiss.

Mal let it happen, but as soon as Griff had drawn back, he quickly reached for a piece of bacon and shoved the whole strip in his mouth. He needed a moment to *think* about how everything had changed. Feeling entirely out of his depth for once, more than he did around stalking shadows or shambling corpses or sharp-toothed bosses, he finally swallowed and said, "Griff—we need to talk."

About how they were going to explore this new thing around their old friend, who seemed so lost lately. About what had happened in the Wood and his part in the attack, before he didn't have the nerve to say it at all. He could own up to that much without telling Griff where the treasure was going to end up, at least for now.

"I've heard that line before. Said it enough times too," Griff told Mal, frowning. "You regret last night," he added, softer, not a question, rising to his feet. "Well, I don't. And I meant what I said after. Nothing that happened when I went away was fine. If missing you could have killed me, I wouldn't even be here."

Griff put a bracing hand on the nearest tree, the one to which the mule was tethered. Little Griff flicked his tail in a small show of sympathy, or perhaps judgment.

"Griff, slow down," Mal pleaded, his sleep-slowed brain struggling to think of where to start or what he had said to make this go so wrong already. "Just—"

"I can't be here right now," Griff insisted. "I—I'm going to go find somewhere to wash up." He started to reach out, making as if to put a hand on Mal's shoulder, but dropped his fingers to his side at the last minute instead.

"What are you talking about? Griff!" Mal pushed against the grogginess and reached for the hand coming toward him, but found the swing of his fingers missing Griff's as they drew away again.

He scrambled to his feet, far from a graceful thing, wincing against a growing headache. "Fuck!" Cursing to himself as Griff's tall form retreated into the greenery, he started scanning their surroundings for his cast-off pants to ward against the morning chill.

Deep in a pocket of shade, a green-eyed ghost missing a few rib bones held up its hands and mouthed silently at him, pointing toward the waiting path. Scowling at it as he yanked his pants on, he then slumped down beside Alys, watching her rescue some blackened toast from the pan before she started arranging lumps of dough in another.

"He remembered you like cinnamon," she remarked softly.

"I didn't mean to hurt him," Mal said lowly, poking at one of the buns until a bit of cinnamon oozed out the side. "Not like I did so many times before." He grabbed the bun just to have something to do with his hands. "I didn't know back then—how he felt. I had no idea."

"But now you do," she countered steadily. "And you both deserve the happiness you're finding in each other, even if you hit a few bumps in the road along the way."

He squeezed the bun. Just like kicking the teakettle, it felt like some kind of release. "You deserve to be happy too, Alys. If not with Theo, then—somebody new."

"Who says I'm not already? Happy, that is," Alys said lightly, making a neat ring of cinnamon buns inside the pan and leaving a hole in the center for Mal's squished one. "The three of us are back together, and that's all I've ever wanted. Well, besides being the one my babies tell all their secrets to instead of Vic. But I understand why it's her." She paused to swat a mosquito that landed on her cheek. "Of course, this isn't my first pick of destinations, but Griff's safety and your freedom matter most. And look, I know we're taking a risk staying put this morning, but I'll fight whatever comes our way. We're still making good time, even if Her Dreadful Majesty is already getting antsy."

Maybe they could rest their feet here just a little longer without consequence, but when it came to Alys's happiness, Mal still wasn't convinced. Ever since they had entered the Mire, there were new shadows gathering at the corners of her eyes and mouth. Maybe the swamp was wearing on her. Or maybe it was years of other people's expectations—the man she almost but never married who wanted her to be a society lady, the mother who wanted her to be a warrior, when neither of those things was really her. Maybe she had more to learn about herself than their breakneck journey was allowing.

"Look," he tried again. "This thing Griff and I are doing—if we're still doing it," he added, glancing off the way Griff had gone, "it can wait. We have the whole rest of our lives to explore that once we're home. We don't need to figure it out in front of you when we should all be focused on getting to the treasure."

"Why wait?" Alys asked earnestly, no longer fussing with breakfast but really looking at him. "You two can kiss in front of me. I thought that might happen out here. Hoped it would, even. I've known how you feel about each other for a while now, even if neither of you has ever wanted to listen to anything I had to say on the matter. I suspect you could have figured it out for yourself if you'd paid even the slightest attention to the lines of his songs." Her face softened as she added, "He makes you laugh, Mal, like I haven't heard since we were kids. That's its own kind of music."

It took a few minutes for Mal to dredge up more words of his own as he digested this. In the quiet, Alys continued, "You expect everything of Griff. Have you ever thought about that? There's no one alive—not even me—who could ever disappoint you the same way he does, because he's your world, your guiding star, the one you've always looked to even when you could hardly stand it."

"Alys, if you knew all that already . . ." He was starting to put a few things together, like her fairy-tale bullshit from the other night. "Going off on your own—were you really hoping to find more of Rhun's things, or were you trying to give us time alone?"

"Both," she answered without hesitation, touching her new-old cloak pin.

"And convincing me to ask Griff along on this trip like it's somehow safer than him staying in town?" Mal asked, though once again he knew the answer.

"It can be hard to hear yourself think in Mayfair sometimes," Alys said by way of admission. "Maybe that's why you're both such terrible listeners. And I just thought—after what happened to Griff, and what you had already agreed to do—this trip might be a chance for you two. I was tired of seeing you both miserable, and I hoped if the three of us could spend some time together, maybe you and Griff would finally see what's been clear to me for so long," she concluded, a plea in her gaze for him to understand. "I love you both, and I thought maybe, if you realized how you feel about each other . . . we could all stay like this after we bring back the treasure. That we could all be as close as we used to be."

"Alys," Mal muttered, wishing he had the right words on the tip of his tongue. As Griff would soon learn, he hadn't had a lot of practice at saying how he felt. "I love you too. Always will," he finally managed. She should have let him and Griff figure things out in their own time, whenever that would have been, but she meant well. "And for the record, if you put this much energy into solving your own problems, I think you could rule the world someday."

A frantic crashing in the bracken drew her attention then, and Mal reached for his knife as Alys grabbed her sword. The Shadow Queen's impatience had him even more on edge than usual.

But it was Griff running toward them like a startled hare trying to escape a hound, the ends of his hair dripping as if he had found someplace to splash water on his face and scrub the cooking grease from his hands.

Mal's tattoo prickled with extra ferocity, and he groaned.

Griff stumbled and nearly lost his balance as something shook the ground like an earthquake. In the distance, a few trees swayed before cracking and falling. "Run!" Griff gasped as he approached. "Fuck the map, fuck the treasure, just—untie the mule and let's go!"

But neither Mal nor Alys moved. Instead, they glared a challenge in the direction of the fallen trees. After all, they had both graduated from Wynnie's school of never turning their backs on a fight. Was the queen so pissed that Mal had taken the time for breakfast that she had sent another lackey to try to eat him?

She should really be grateful he was sweating his ass off in this miserable swamp in the first place when she wasn't willing to come get the gold and baubles herself.

Frowning as the ground shook again, Mal adjusted his stance and drew a second knife. Alys grabbed the pike that held Leo's head with her free hand, as if the sight of it were going to scare off more than mosquitoes. Well—maybe the stench of it could.

Griff might have been upset with Mal when he left, but now he didn't hesitate to grab his arm the moment he reached him, trying to tug him toward the trees as their terrified mule brayed and bellowed at the end of its tether.

"It's a whole fucking—troll! It came to get a drink at the creek and it saw me, and we just—" He tugged again, harder, but Mal resisted. "Need to—" There was no outrunning something of that size, even if Wynnie's training would have allowed him to consider it. Already he could see the looming shadow of the heavy creature with skin the color of sun-washed stone and a head like a mossy boulder growing worryingly taller as it bounded toward them. "Go," Griff concluded on a panted breath of defeat.

He drew his maul, and Mal made sure to catch his eye and nod his approval.

Griff stood a little taller after that, those strong arms holding the maul aloft, bracing for the impact of the creature's arrival as it tore a blackberry bush out of the earth, thorns and all, and burst into their camp.

Even Leo the Head looked a little more wilted and pitiful on his pike when the troll rolled its massive shoulders, stretched up to its full height, and roared.

Mal winced and rubbed a bit of spittle off his cheek. "Fucking fish breath," he muttered as his tattoo throbbed, trying to cover up the fact that he knew his knives weren't going to be much use against this thing. They would likely be more of an annoyance, and the last thing they needed was to make this creature madder.

"Hurry up already!" the troll bellowed in a voice hoarse with disuse. The rough shape of a raven on the thick skin of its shoulder marked the creature as a thrall of the Shadow Queen's in a manner too similar to how Mal had been branded for him to look at it for long.

Mal didn't dare look at Griff, though the words could be explained away easily enough—trolls weren't known for their cleverness, only their strength. He tried to arrange his features into a mask of calm and polite confusion as he took in the broken piece of tree trunk the troll was wielding like a club, the smattering of fish scales clinging to one corner of its pale mouth, and the unmistakable deep scars surrounding a gaping hole in its forearm that must have been made by a blade that had shattered.

"I have no idea what you're talking about, you blabbering inconvenience," Mal said firmly to the creature, keeping his eyes trained on that club—much as he really wanted to make sure Griff wasn't about to pass out.

The troll didn't seem to care about his insults, nor did it seem interested in having a conversation. It swiped at him with its club, the motion clumsy thanks to whatever tendons Rhun had managed to sever in its wrist before it shattered his elven blade years ago.

Mal dodged the first strike easily. The second, however, came close enough to blow the hair back from his face and would have easily shattered his nose if he hadn't been quick enough to duck. It seemed to be focusing most of its attention on him despite Alys repeatedly striking it with her sword, which suited Mal just fine—this was still his mess—but in the process of backing him up against a wide tree hemmed in on either side by thorny brush, it also knocked Griff off his feet while lumbering past.

The sound of Griff's maul glancing off its arm was like metal scraping stone.

They were so fucked.

Or at least, he was, because he had nowhere to go but up the tree at his back, and the troll would have no problem plucking him out of the branches. It also seemed to have forgotten any instructions it had been given about not actually *killing* him while he was still within the bounds of the deal he'd made with Kage.

"Gonna grind your slow bones to pulp!" It gnashed its teeth, confirming Mal's fears as he got his footing on a low branch. He quickly started hauling himself up, scrabbling at the bark like a rat on the run again until he was several feet off the ground.

As a gray hand roughly the size of his head reached toward him, Mal edged back behind the tree trunk as best he could, nearly losing his footing. Down below, he was amazed to see Griff back on his feet already, maul in hand. He managed to catch the other man's eye for a second, nodding subtly at the branch beneath him and hoping Griff understood.

Strong fingers gripped the folds of his ratty cloak, struggling to get better purchase as Mal frantically tried to jerk free at the same time—while lacking anywhere to go. As he cursed and stabbed at the hands, the branch beneath him finally gave way.

He was falling, suddenly free of the troll's grasp, his torn cloak fluttering around him as he plummeted several feet toward the ground and into Griff's waiting arms.

Just in time. As Alys shouted something to regain the troll's attention, Griff flashed a brief, shaky grin at Mal and cradled him against his chest.

Mal was still alive. Safe in the arms of someone he was starting to count on.

Wrapping his own arms around Griff's neck, he licked his dry lips and finally panted, "This easier than chopping wood, you fuck? You're unbelievable."

"Just another feature of the Boyfriend Special. I could do this all day if you let me."

"You get that line from a library book or something?"

A hint of color returned to Griff's face. "Only original poetry here. You inspire me."

Mal couldn't help but laugh.

Griff's grin widened for a moment, but whatever he was about to say became a worried murmur. "Alys! What the hell does she think she's doing?"

The ground had finally stopped shaking. At first, Mal thought Alys must have cut the troll somewhere vital, as it was now sitting by their fire with its back to them, its club resting against its knee. There didn't seem to be any blood whatsoever, and Alys wasn't even holding her sword anymore—it had been discarded several feet away. But rather than trying to get back to it, she was sitting calmly across from the foul creature, holding up her orc's head.

Bewildered, Mal crept closer once he was on his feet, keeping a hand on Griff's arm as they crept toward the troll's back together, maul and knives at the ready again.

"And then, if you can believe it, Bluebell told me I couldn't have any more pie until I paid for the ones I'd tasted, when *I* was the one doing *her* a favor by making sure they were good enough to sell in the first place!" Alys was saying conspiratorially to Leo and the troll.

"Not fair!" the troll whined in response, making Mal's teeth rattle.

"Exactly!" Alys said indulgently, her eyes wide and her smile gentle. "Say, Gossamer, I have an idea."

The icing on top of Mal's chaos cake had a name? One that Alys was speaking like they were old friends, no less.

"Would you like to hear my son's favorite song? Maybe Leo and I could sing it for you while we take a little walk back to your cave, where it's not so bright . . . ?"

Mal exchanged a stunned glance with Griff, who looked equally confused and somewhat awestruck.

The troll wasn't climbing back to its feet. But it still seemed to be listening to Alys, considering her words, much to Mal's amazement.

"You know, my son gets mad sometimes too. Sometimes he gets so mad that he thinks about running away from home. Feelings are confusing, aren't they? They can get your stomach all knotted up, like eating a bad fish. Especially when you've got someone telling you to do things you know deep down aren't very nice. That really doesn't feel good," Alys continued, slowly and carefully rising and extending her much-smaller hand toward the troll.

When the creature reached for it, she didn't flinch, her smile still in place. "That's it, Gossamer. Let's take that walk and learn a fun song, and I bet you'll feel better," she said again patiently. "And I'll make sure I'm back by noon," she added over her shoulder as she started to urge the troll back down the path of destruction it had created. "Ready to double the pace and make up for lost time."

"That," Griff breathed quietly beside him as they watched Alys lead the troll away, its club forgotten by the fireside, "was some damn good parenting."

"That," Mal agreed, knowing full well he would never understand how Alys had the instincts to handle a situation like that without her sword when it was all she had ever been taught, "showed so much more skill than Rhun in any battle he ever fought. Guaranteed."

Chapter Nineteen

Who Wants Easy?

Finding themselves alone again and somehow still alive after their brush with what had to be another of the Shadow Queen's creatures, all Griff could see as he looked at Mal was the night before playing over in his mind. He had seen fireworks. Years of them, ones they'd missed seeing together every Yule, great bursts of color exploding above the treetops or perhaps behind his closed eyelids because he was kissing Mal, and Mal was kissing him back.

The ways they had touched each other in this very place still nearly stole his breath when he thought about it—even if their surroundings had changed, now strewn with broken branches and debris in which they knelt, facing each other.

"Told you I'd come back," he murmured. "Always will, from now on, even if it hurts. Though hopefully next time I won't have a troll on my ass."

"Good," Mal said lowly, meeting Griff's eyes. "Because I want you to stay, like I told you. I don't regret last night either." There was heat in his voice, a flare of his usual temper, but it sputtered and died as they continued to regard each other. "I wanted to talk to you, but I should have said it better. I'm not trying to push you away again. I'm trying to . . . give the mule a new name. Let's call it Prancer from now on, okay?"

He glanced at the poor pack beast at the far edge of the clearing, who was just starting to calm enough to examine a bite of grass. Then he extended a hand to Griff that was still slightly greasy from breakfast.

Cautiously, Griff reached out to lace his fingers through Mal's, and the thief slowly curled his own against Griff's as if he meant to keep them there.

"You make damn good eggs, by the way," Mal murmured, staring at their hands.

Griff smiled, though briefly, with so much on his mind to work through. "So," he began, "no regrets—you're certain?" He searched Mal's eyes as he gave their joined hands a pull toward himself, much as Mal had done the night before. "You didn't want to kiss me this morning." He dropped his voice a touch lower, just in case Alys and the troll were still within earshot as he added, "Which was a surprise, considering you didn't mind any of the other places I was putting my mouth last night."

Mal followed the summons of that hand, though he didn't fall into Griff's lap or against his lips so readily as Griff himself had done the night before. "No regrets," he repeated easily. "In fact, I"—his lips parted with surprise, as if Griff's last words were just beginning to register—"didn't mind that at all, no."

"Then what is it you wanted to talk to me about that couldn't wait until after cinnamon buns?" Griff asked, with half a mind to put them over the fire now so they might be ready for Alys's return. Whatever surprises she might bring back this time—hopefully, no trolls or extra orc heads—would be softened by the sugar.

Mal followed his gaze. "We probably shouldn't keep having fires like this, at least not once we leave this camp. Not all the orcs out here are as dead or as cute as the one Alys has on that branch, and they'll be drawn to the flames. We've had enough company the past few days as it is, and I'm sure we'll have more before this is finished." He leaned back on one hand, the other still joined with Griff's and resting against his leg. "Anyway, I wanted to tell you why that kiss felt so strange. I haven't had my whole life to think about you and me—I didn't even know it was possible—and now I'm trying to let my mind and heart catch up."

Griff slid his thumb across the back of Mal's hand, encouraging him to keep talking. This was the Mal he remembered, the one he could share anything with.

Mal glanced down at their hands again, and though he seemed to want to say more, he simply concluded, "I wanted you to understand where I'm at. That's all."

Griff gave their hands a squeeze. "It's quite the opposite for me. I thought about you every day, even in Stormveil. When I went to the ever-blooming meadows, you were there, collecting berries to throw at passersby. When I went to the high lakes, you whispered to me about how the water was cleaner even in Linden. When I walked through the autumn canopies of their woods, you said their colors were dull and faded. The waterfalls were too small, or too noisy. The gardens were overpowering. And the things you said about the castle itself were . . . memorable. I wasted so much time with phantoms, missing the real you."

"Elf gardens," Mal said disdainfully. Griff caught the undercurrent of anger there and knew why without asking: the letters his well-meaning distant cousin had burned. "What did I ever do to those elves, anyway? Bet their flowers smell like the lilac soap from that stall in Linden Market that always made me sick."

"Oh, that woman uses way too much perfume in those soaps," Griff laughed, recalling the very scent Mal was describing. "But she makes a decent blueberry pie—remember stealing them off her windowsill while they were cooling? Alys sure charmed the troll with that old story." He shook his head, mouth turned up in a slight grin. "We had plenty of fun back then, didn't we? The three of us and Whiskey, of course."

Mal hummed thoughtfully. "Sometimes it feels like we've had him since we were just pups ourselves, doesn't it?" Frowning at his own observation, he added, "Actually—now that I think about it—he was there before either of us moved into the cottage, right? He was only a year or two old then, but still, that would make him . . . uh . . ."

"Twenty-five, if I've got the math right. We've still got a few years on him between us," Griff said with a knowing look.

"But that's not . . . I mean he's just a regular . . . *how*?" Mal demanded.

"It should be impossible for an ordinary hound like Whiskey," Griff explained gently. "But he has the elves' special healing draft. I have a contact—well, a series of contacts—who make sure it gets to me without attracting any notice. I've been giving vials of it to Vic to pour over Whiskey's evening meals once a month since I returned from Stormveil. Shame it doesn't work on magical poisons," he couldn't help adding.

Mal's fingers tightened around his. "So he'd die without it? He'd already be gone."

Griff ran his other hand slowly down Mal's back, able to guess at least some of what was going through his head. "Yes, but that's not going to happen. That potion isn't going anywhere, nor am I. Nor is Whiskey. Nobody's leaving you."

Some of the tension left Mal's posture at that. "So all this time, even when we weren't talking, you were helping him—for me?"

"For both of us," Griff confirmed. His throat tightened as he added, "I didn't want you to lose your other best friend too. I packed two vials of the stuff for this trip too—just in case. More than we should need, but a great defense against most causes of death."

"Wish you'd tried this hard to look out for me *before* you cut me out of your life and disappeared," Mal muttered, his features hardening as he pulled his hand away from Griff's.

Just like that, the easy mood growing between them was whisked away on the breeze. "Maybe you didn't have everything you wanted back then, but you were still my closest, oldest friend. Until you weren't." There was a steady current of heat running through his voice again. "Some best fucking friendship."

Griff swallowed and forced himself to look at Mal even as the other man gazed determinedly at a spot over his shoulder. "I know. I fucked up. I was jealous and insecure, and you have no idea how sorry I am. I have to live with what I did for the rest of my life. Every time I see your scars, I know they're my fault because I should have been there."

Mal glanced back sharply at that. He seemed to want to say something, his lips slightly parted, but even after a long pause in which Griff pinched the bridge of his nose between his fingers to try to regain some composure, the blond didn't breathe a word.

So Griff went on, steadier again, "I would have apologized before now, but you've been so distant since you came home from Thrallkeld. I didn't think you wanted to hear it. And then last night . . . I thought you finally saw me. I thought you loved me too. But now, once again, I'm not entirely sure what to think."

When Mal spoke, there was some heat still burning in his voice. "First of all, I don't care about my scars. They're not your fault, anyway. But you didn't just break my heart, you left it smoldering in the wreckage of my life, and I did what I could to survive that. I thought—that day, what you said, what you called me—I thought you didn't want me any kind of way, let alone love me. I didn't know what you felt, and perhaps I should have, but you could have told me too. Anytime, you could have told me."

The glimmer of unshed tears in Griff's eyes must have been too much for Mal, as he averted his gaze again to stare hard at the grass. "I don't want you to leave anymore. I've told you so many times—I want you to stay. I'm telling you now, I fucking love you," Mal choked out. "But you weren't my friend or my enemy or anything when we were apart. You were just . . . gone, and I couldn't tell you anything then."

With that, he tipped his head back toward the morning sky, eyes narrowing balefully against the brightness as if he were admonishing the sun for its very nature.

Slowly, carefully, Griff shifted closer, putting his arms around Mal and drawing him into a warm embrace. Last night, with the help of the wine, he had understood how to be what Mal needed, but he didn't think he needed the wine for that anymore. He could just be here. That seemed to be enough.

"I love you too, and you can tell me anything now," he insisted gently. "So go on, Mal. Go ahead and tell me how mad you were back then. How mad you are. Tell me all the ways I've completely fucked up. But since I'm here to stay, at least let me hold you through it. Let me be the one to hold you through everything from now on." Softer, he added, "And when you're done telling me why I'm the worst, please tell me you love me again."

Mal brought his arms up around the ones that held him and buried his face in the dark hair near Griff's cheek, though Griff still caught a glimmer of tears before his face was hidden. "You're the worst friend I've ever had," Mal confided hoarsely. "You chose fancy elf parties and singing their sad songs over me." A frustrated exhale gusted over Griff's cheek before he continued, "I used to think about you sometimes in Thrallkeld. About our hunting trips with the hounds, and swimming together in the Wood—and every time I did, I wanted to hurl myself in the river because I knew you were somewhere else hating my very existence. But I just couldn't give you the satisfaction."

Griff held Mal a little tighter, and those wiry arms drew him in closer in return.

"You acted like you were so much better than me, with your nice shiny boyfriends and your stupid straight jobs, and I would have punched every tooth out of your mouth if Wynnie would have let me," Mal declared with fiery certainty. "I truly hated you." His fingers curled upward, tangling in Griff's hair, damp eyes finally meeting his again as he finished. "And I loved you, even then. I love you now. I wouldn't have minded if you'd come for me, to Thrallkeld, even when it was too late."

It felt to Griff like someone had knocked the wind from him as one of his longest-held fears and deepest regrets was confirmed. "I won't make any of those mistakes again," he vowed quietly, taking his time so his voice wouldn't crack. "I should have told you how I felt a long time ago, no matter what I feared would happen. I should have listened to myself and ridden to Thrallkeld anyway. You're worth it—you and your big plans, your foul mouth and worse temper." At last, Griff smiled despite his long-held anguish still simmering near the surface. "I want all of it. Even when you didn't know it, you were everything to me. You still are."

"You are so getting a horse when we get back to Linden," Mal murmured into Griff's hair, the assessment of his temper and other qualities bringing a half grin back to his lips. He ran a hand along Griff's thigh, stopping above the bandages there. "You're probably going to need it, with a busted leg like this."

Griff's smile widened. "I love you too. Enough to write a really sad elf-song about it. But I'd rather hold you, and . . ." Gently, he kissed along Mal's jaw, eventually making his way to the other man's lips. "By the way, this wouldn't be nearly as pleasant if you'd punched out all my teeth."

Mal snorted against his lips. "Not for you, anyway," he muttered, teasing in his own way before deepening the kiss, like he was trying to make up for the one he had all but rejected earlier. "And don't you dare sing any sad elf-songs about me."

"Right," Griff murmured into their slow kisses as Mal delivered that command. "Only dirty ones, and heroic ballads. Challenge accepted. Who wants easy, anyway?"

"Not me," Mal said emphatically before catching Griff's lower lip between his teeth.

"You must know what it does to me, the way you run your mouth," Griff murmured, his bitten lips forming a smile against Mal's. "Maybe I'll write a song about that."

"So that's what you really mean, every time you call me an absolute shit," Mal mused, running his tongue along Griff's bottom lip to soothe any sting there. "You clearly learned your flowery way with words in the elves' library."

Last night, there had been a certain haste in Griff's movements inspired by too many years of wanting. This morning, it was tempered by his finally having had Mal in his arms for many hours already. Although he hungrily returned each kiss, he took his time with each one too, savoring the taste, encouraging Mal to focus on him rather than his need to get back on the road as if that treasure were suddenly going somewhere. His fingers were in no hurry either as they ruffled Mal's hair until it was even more unruly than it had been when they woke.

Mal responded to that exploration of his hair with the shut-eyed groan of an animal being stroked just the right way, his tongue melting in the heat of each slow kiss, his hand at the base of Griff's neck urging him closer, his other hand inviting Griff's fingers to roam freely over his bare, toned chest.

It was a thoughtless moan from Griff's own throat that eventually spurred him back into action, disentangling himself from Mal just enough to guide him gently down to the ground on top of his own discarded shirt. He trailed his lips softly down Mal's stomach while his fingers hooked into the waist of Mal's trousers and gave an impatient tug, the buttons having mostly been lost the night before and the remaining few giving easily at the touch.

"Hmm," he said, darting a grin up at Mal as he sucked a kiss over one of his now-bare hips, "And here I thought you liked things with teeth . . ." He grazed them gently over the skin beneath him as he moved lower still, causing Mal's lips to part in anticipation. "So which is it?"

"I was wrong and you were right," Mal breathed for perhaps the first time in his life, his eyes fluttering and his words running together. "I do like your teeth right where they are after all. Nice teeth. Good teeth." He wove his fingers through Griff's hair, not pushing him lower with any impatience but making his own explorations in the meantime—first of those dark curls again, and then down along Griff's shoulders.

"Ooh," Griff growled over Mal's inner thigh. "I like it when you tell me I'm right. I aim to impress. Now let me wake you up the way I should have done in the first place."

As he started to run his tongue along the length of him, teasing the sensitive head with little licks and plenty of kisses, he gently squeezed Mal's ass with both hands. And when he was rewarded with a groan and a shimmy of the thief's hips, he took a few inches of Mal into his mouth while trailing a slow, gentle finger into his cleft, caressing and teasing just like he was doing with his tongue. Feeling Mal start to tense slightly, he immediately withdrew his hand, pulling off of him to pant, "Is this okay?"

"I . . . um. I've only done it the other way. And I . . . I think it's my turn to impress you this morning," Mal declared with a low growl of effort, drawing Griff back up into his arms and away from his spit-soaked hardness still in need of attention.

"Okay," Griff reassured him softly, understanding more than what was being spoken. This was too new, and Mal had never been touched like that before. Never trusted like that before, or let himself be so vulnerable. Griff wouldn't bring it up again; he would wait until Mal was ready, and he would be there if or when that time came, because he planned on staying.

Eager to find out exactly what Mal had in mind instead, he settled into the warmth of the other man and watched as his lover spit into his hand, then took hold of them together in his tight, slick fist and gave a few slow, delicious strokes. "Learned a thing or two about this while I was alone in Thrallkeld. Trust me." Lips seeking Griff's neck, he muttered against the skin there as he started up a slow rhythm between them, "Let me know when you're starting to feel . . . impressed."

And Griff did, when he found his voice again amid the wonder of all the tricks that hand knew, of the thrill of his own heat right up against Mal's and the toe-curling friction they were creating together.

A little of last night's urgency returned as the rhythm grew faster. Slicker, too, with both of them aching and dripping into the clench of Mal's hand.

"I like it in your world, living by your rules," Griff panted as he covered Mal's neck and collarbone in little bites and kisses from nice, good teeth. "Think I'm moving in."

Mal's lips clung to his in answer—as if those kisses were a ladder leading out of the shadows of the past, promising someplace brighter.

†

Later—two rounds later, as Griff lay in Mal's arms with no desire to get up and back in the saddle for a sore day's ride—Mal was stroking his hair when he suddenly scooped up some fallen leaves. He scattered the handful over Griff's tousled curls, a grin slowly forming as he took in the sight. "There, now you look like the elf you are. Have I told you how much I like your hair?"

"Maybe once or twice," Griff admitted, "but I'll never tire of hearing it." He didn't even bother to shake the leaves off, only laughed, probably looking like he'd just left a party with confetti all over him in the late morning light.

Mal's grin widened at the sound of that laughter, growing until it was toothy and devious, just how Griff liked it. It was the kind of grin that made the nearest stagnant puddles glitter, as if Mal's happiness somehow suffused this place with magic.

The thief held up his hands, index fingers and thumbs lightly touching at the tips to form a picture frame of sorts through which he glanced as if memorizing the sight of Griff from this new angle, his flushed face saying more than words.

"You know, when we get back with all those coins, I think I ought to buy you a bigger stove than whatever you've been using," Mal declared warmly. "Something with lots of pipes and burners, since you like cooking so much. Yeah?"

Griff loved the sound of that—just like he loved the way Mal's fingers were stroking along his thigh like he was thinking about another round. "A new stove. A whole bunch of burners and . . . bigger, longer pipes and . . . that'll be good, I think." His hot breath gusted over Mal's lips, his mind not remotely on cooking. "Maybe some bigger pots to go on it too. All kinds of bells and whistles. The biggest stove this side of the Teeth, right?"

"To go with the biggest bed anyone's ever had, and the best pillows in Mayfair, which I've already—" Mal stopped suddenly, and Griff's pulse picked up speed as he saw the way his lover's eyes had widened just a touch at something in the trees.

"Shadow?" he mouthed as Mal disentangled himself swiftly and pulled on his pants. "But I thought—it's Rhun, isn't it? Even Alys seems pretty convinced now."

Nodding, the blond man strode over to what, to Griff's eyes, looked no different than any other pocket of shade. But it must have looked like something else to Mal, who called back to Griff over his shoulder, "That's right, but apparently he needs a reminder about healthy boundaries, because he is not welcome to watch anything that's been going on between us this morning! Or last night, for that matter. Not okay."

The way his voice kept rising made it clear he was addressing Rhun's shadow too, and Griff couldn't help but smile at the way Mal was trying to put a ghost in its place.

Running a hand over his red, flaky tattoo, Mal scowled, though the expression took on a touch of thoughtfulness as he turned away from that faceless version of Rhun. "I wonder . . ." he said, striding back to Griff's side as if suddenly on alert. "Maybe he's trying to warn us about something."

He reached for his hunting knife, putting his other arm around Griff's waist as he cast his most scathing glower into the surrounding trees and pockets of shade.

Overhead, a few ravens rustled their feathers and clicked their beaks as they settled into the borders of the trio's camp, and Mal glared at them next before refocusing on Griff. "Keeping you safe seems to be a full-time job. Good thing I'm a businessman and not afraid of hard work," he declared, kissing some color back into Griff's face that had been leached away by the suggestion of more danger.

"Who wants easy," he said shakily against his lover's lips. Except that he did, right now, rather than being hunted by more revenants and wading around in a swamp full of the dark queen's creatures.

"We should pack," Mal said, almost reluctantly for a change, once Griff's shaking had mostly subsided. "So we're ready to go the minute Alys gets back. Double the pace this afternoon, remember? Though I really hope Rhun is wrong about the danger, or I'm wrong about why I keep seeing him. Maybe he's trying to lead us to better treasure."

Chapter Twenty Animals

Griff was sealing up the last of their packs and securing it to Prancer the renamed mule when Alys returned to camp just before noon as promised, frustrated from combing through weeds and puddles and finding nothing of interest. She still had the orc's head with her, which was unfortunate, but thankfully the troll was back where it belonged, taking a nap in its cave after being sung more than a few lullabies.

"You're a good mom, Alys," Griff told her as she handed him a full water canteen to pack. She must have revisited the creek in her wanderings.

She blushed and shook her head, but she was smiling.

"A better knight than Rhun too," Mal said firmly, which wiped away the traces of that smile, replacing it with something more thoughtful. "Don't be so hard on yourself about the search," he added as he pulled out his flask. "Maybe he ran out of personal effects to give you. At least he's looking out for us."

Griff wished he could do something that would help Mal reach for that thing less, but he had already guessed the reason why he'd just done so. He was searching for whatever he suspected Rhun had appeared to warn them about, and there was nothing Mal hated more than a threat he couldn't see coming.

"Wonder if Rhun and his friends fought more than just the troll out here too." Mal chased the words with a sip. "They should have marked the rest of that shit on the map for us, if so." Raising the flask, he glanced at his companions and said, "Still, here's to Rhun, the man of the hour, for bringing us all back together."

"To Rhun," Griff echoed. He had to use his maul out here more often than he would have liked, but he would do anything for the memory of the man who'd raised them. He hoped Rhun's spirit was lingering nearby for the toast, being reminded of their enduring love.

"To Papa," Alys joined in, taking the flask when Mal offered.

Leaving it with her for a moment, Mal strode over to Griff and pulled the black scarf from around his neck. He didn't say a word as he wrapped it around Griff's shoulders instead despite the afternoon's warmth, kissing his cheek and flooding him with a different heat as he did so, the old scarf once again passing between them like a promise.

Then they were off again, pressing deeper into the Mire, where there were fewer patches of sunlight breaking through and more ominously glowing flowers thriving in the gloom. All that remained of the camp where everything had changed was an empty blue glass bottle, the troll's heavy club, and an uprooted blackberry bush.

Griff tried to settle his nerves by answering various birdcalls as they picked up the path at a vicious pace, but the longer they marched, the less sure he was what sort of animals were making the sounds that seemed to echo from the bracken. He had heard rumors of the Shadow Queen keeping giant spiders out here, large as dogs and twice as motivated to hunt. After he fell quiet, the loudest sound any of them made was the slush of the mule's hooves as the beast trudged through puddles of muddy water alongside him, Griff having insisted on testing his leg while the daylight held.

Every so often, he stopped to pull a small knife from his belt and cut some herbs to use in their next hot meal, whenever that might be. He found comfrey for his healing kit. Wild onions for flavoring and a few withered morels.

He took mental stock of the supplies in their packs and the mule's saddlebags rather than thinking too long on the unanswerable questions spinning in the back of his mind, ones he was too nervous to ask Mal yet, like where he was going to put the biggest bed this side of the Teeth, or that new stove. Were they moving in together? Where? What were they going to tell people back in Linden they were—together? Mal didn't seem to care much for titles, from what he had told Griff back in Mayfair, and Griff knew better than to push him. On anything. Which was why he also wasn't going to ask again about Mal's punishing timeline to reach the treasure that seemed completely self-imposed.

A few brisk steps ahead, the blond man paused to pull out his flask as he gazed into the shadows that only seemed to be growing longer, pressing closer from all sides. The warm kiss of whiskey was apparently all Mal needed on his lips right now, and Griff left him to it, though he was itching to throw that flask far off into the Mire. He knew how hard it was to want to get sober, let alone stay that way.

Mal was apparently so unsettled even with the aid of the whiskey that when a raven shot out of the bracken, he grabbed one of his knives from his belt and flung it into the trunk of a gnarled, leafless tree some yards ahead of them with a wordless snarl.

Griff winced, not at the loudness of Mal's frustration but at a certain unwelcome pain from his scar as he stared at the knife protruding from that tree. As the burning intensified, he resisted the urge to make sure the wound was still closed while the others might see. Barely.

"Your knife skills could use improvement. You missed that bird by a mile," Alys teased Mal, trying to snap him out of his mood as she took Prancer's lead from Griff.

Something off the path had caught Griff's eye, and he wanted to get a closer look. Kneeling, he examined a cluster of wilted white flowers for usefulness while attempting to calm his racing heart. Yet he startled when a rabbit darted from beneath a nearby bush, scampering to its next hidey-hole as if being pursued by unseen forces.

He couldn't shake the sense that they were caged animals in here themselves, allowed to go about their errands only while the dark queen's servants toyed with them like predators playing with an easy supper, even if they had made fairly quick work of the revenants and tamed a damn troll. Their luck would run out at some point, and he could hardly blame Mal for wanting to get in and out of here as quickly as possible when he thought about it that way.

Off to his right, the man in question took another swig of whiskey before he finally retrieved his knife and started rummaging in the mule's saddlebags in search of something.

Apparently, the mule didn't like Mal's attitude much either. The beast's ears perked forward as if sensing danger, and he took a single step back that narrowly missed smashing Mal's toes.

"Ever heard of personal space?" Griff heard him grumble to the beast as something deeper off in the semidark caught his eye—truffles. The thing he was certain Mal would love if he made them into a rich, velvety sauce. Maybe the delicacy would earn a smile the next time Mal deemed it safe enough to have a fire going. Another true smile, the kind that made the swamp water glisten as if each shallow pool held gold dust.

Griff made his way carefully between the trees toward the low cluster of mushrooms half hidden by grass, his boot print falling neatly into the enormous muddy claw marks left by the passing of another creature. Still, that was nothing unusual. There were tracks running all through this place. "Found us something tasty," he called to the others over the mule's continued noises of distress. "Something that won't give anyone any strange visions—I'll be right back!"

"Shit," Mal called from behind him. "Wait, Griff—let's go together!"

Griff intended to stop there, to turn around and pause for the others to catch up.

But before he could turn away, ahead in the dense tangle of vegetation he saw a tall, broad silhouette of a man with shoulder-length hair, straight but jagged at the ends. He couldn't make out any of his features, but even his solid shadow was familiar despite Griff not having seen him since he was maybe twelve.

Rhun.

Finally, he was showing himself—and not to Mal or Alys, but to *him*. Rhun must have something to show him, some message to share, wisdom to impart. Griff quickened his pace as best he could on his hobbled leg, but where he should have caught up to the man and found him standing over some plump mushrooms that looked rather like porous potatoes, he met a pair of strange violet eyes a few feet away instead. Eyes that narrowed as they watched him while an unseen mouth hissed.

A wyvern, Griff realized in the heartbeat before she broke from her cover. Female, judging by the color of her eyes and the higher pitch of her vocalization.

Griff had half a second to wonder if it was her nest from which Alys had gotten the strange blue-shelled eggs they'd fixed for breakfast before the sleek, scaled creature lunged forward with a soft patter of claws against earth, branches cracking beneath its weight as it leapt from its place of concealment, dark as a shadow and larger than a direwolf.

"Mal, over here!" he managed to shout just before he was thrashed by a whiplike tail, knocked off-balance by a beast with claws that might as well have been daggers, before he even had a chance to draw his sword.

Chapter Twenty-One
Drug Mule

The snapping of branches quickened Mal's pace. So did the scream that followed, the way it stopped short being of particular concern.

He bolted through the dense tangle of green, branches whipping him in the face as his heart gave a sickening lurch. That must have been what it sounded like when Griff was stabbed in the Wood.

He couldn't keep Griff safe, in the wilds or in a city, no matter what kind of wagers or bargains he made. He understood that now.

Still, he ran faster.

The scene that greeted him as he broke through the trees wasn't nearly as lovely as any of Alys's charcoal drawings. The muscular black wyvern was sinking her claws into the equally black-clad Griff, a whirl of limbs and sharp points as they struggled—Griff, by some miracle, still conscious despite the abrupt way his scream had ended—making it difficult to tell where one ended and the other began.

In the thicket where the wyvern must have been hiding, something stirred. The shadow slipped out of sight, Rhun's spirit apparently not sticking around for the bloodbath, just turning his back on the sight of Griff in distress.

But Mal didn't have time to dwell on whatever part he might have played here, because the wyvern was holding Griff in place so that she could unhinge her jaw, venomous teeth sinking deep into Griff's shoulder and tearing something that made a terrible sound as she thrashed her prey in a display of dominance.

This proved to be too much for Griff. His eyes rolled back as he slipped free of the pain.

The wyvern was already backing away, attempting to drag her catch farther from whatever might threaten her meal as Mal recovered from the shock of it all long enough to draw his sword and shout, "Alys! Help me!"

The still-healing cuts on his hands twinged in protest as Mal gripped his blade and charged. He didn't care about the wetness that signaled his dominant palm splitting open again; he simply shifted the blade to his other hand and continued to rush the wyvern. At least these things didn't breathe fire like their larger, recently extinct cousins.

He didn't have a plan. Not unless he counted needling the beast like a bard who knew only one off-key tune. He loved this Griff who looked at him like he was something special, and he didn't ever want that to end. He had a dragon's heart, with his love of shiny things like the twin emeralds of Griff's eyes, and he guarded his own treasures with his life. This beast was in for a fight.

As his blade slipped from his bloody grip and hit the grass, he swore and aimed an irate kick at the wyvern's side, the dragon in him roaring up madder than ever. Desperate to do anything he could to save Griff.

He lashed out at the wyvern with his bloody fists as panic threatened to draw him deep into its blackened, unending maw.

He wanted to be someone Griff could count on too.

"Mal!" Alys screamed as she took in the scene from somewhere behind him—he wasn't sure when she had gotten here, though she must have started running the second she heard his call. "Your sword! Why the hell did you drop your sword?"

He didn't answer. He was breathless from continuing to beat and kick the creature's scaly body, doing little more than making it as livid and panicked as he was.

The wyvern hissed and slashed at him with her claws, managing to land a few deep scratches before Alys finally charged forward with her blade raised.

She plunged Rhun's sword in deep while Mal had the beast distracted. There came some telltale wet sounds as she pushed the blade down through scale and into the resistance of thick cords of muscle.

Her roar was louder than the wyvern's as the creature rounded on her and bared its dripping teeth, glistening with Griff's blood.

Mal, meanwhile, wasted little time in diving away from the next slash of Alys's blade, his face flushed with exertion and his palm bleeding freely.

Alys jabbed her sword into the wyvern's soft underbelly, earning a wrathful screech and a loosening of its jaws. Released from the creature's grasp, Griff lay on the ground, limp as one of his nieces' beloved rag dolls.

Seeming to realize she was outnumbered, the wyvern slunk away from Alys's blade that bit deeper than venomous teeth—though it still showed off its own as it retreated, an effect made no less chilling by the crimson rivulets running down the creature's flank and belly.

Mal grabbed his blade again, holding it up with both hands as the wyvern's violet eyes narrowed. The arrogant creature still seemed to be assessing whether there might be some better angle from which to snatch up her quarry.

Rushing at the beast with a growl and a flash of steel, Mal finally convinced the creature to try her luck elsewhere. She slithered into the dappled late afternoon shadows with another hiss, painting a scarlet trail as she went.

Mal tossed his blade aside again and quickly knelt beside Griff, fingers and eyes searching for signs of life as Alys dropped down next to him and started to do the same.

"Griff? Griffin Sayer. Look at me," she demanded of the bloodied, unconscious man as tears slid down her cheeks. "Open your eyes and look at me. I am not watching you die twice in the same year when I don't know any necromancy, do you understand?"

Mal had managed to escape the wyvern's claws with only a few slashes through his much-abused cloak, which was now stained a dark red. The cuts were burning and oozing, but he knew they were nothing compared to the punctures Griff had suffered in his shoulder, dangerously close to his neck.

Ignoring Alys's quiet sobs, he leaned in close to Griff, listening for breath and finding, to his immense relief, a thready pulse.

He whisked off his tattered cloak, pressing it against Griff's shoulder with the force of both hands as he said to Alys, "Where are our packs? We've got to stop this bleeding. Griff has—he has bandages, and whatever else healers use." He was usually so calm in bloody situations. What the hell was wrong with him? Griff needed him to think.

Griff needed him.

He had let him down that night in the Wyrmwood, not being there to stop the attack or to help, but he wouldn't fail him now. Griff could still count on him.

"He's got some kind of special elf medicine, something in a vial, he gives it to the dog—I think his pack is with Prancer," he managed finally.

The cloak was already turning scarlet beneath his hands, the color spreading.

"I love you. Please don't die," Alys whispered to Griff before grabbing her sword and disappearing back the way she had come.

Mal didn't know how long she was gone.

Holding a dying Griff in his arms was his worst nightmare. Worse than failing to get the treasure in time and being torn apart by a host of revenants or having to work for Kage forever. Every second of it was torturously slow, but also not nearly long enough when it might be the last they ever got to spend together.

"Mal—" Alys panted upon returning. "Mal, I—"

"I'm *fine*!" he snapped, though he was aware he wore the wild-eyed look of someone who was anything but. He scooted his knees under Griff's shoulders, remembering something about elevating the wounded area from a lesson of Wynnie's long ago.

Gazing down to where Griff's head lolled peacefully against his thigh, Mal whispered darkly, "If you die on me now after all that talk about how you wouldn't, I'm never fucking forgiving you. I'd take you as a sad elf over a happy phantom any day."

He closed his eyes for a minute, pushing that cloak harder against the hot dampness of fresh blood seeping through its many folds, and when he opened them, he found Alys white faced and offering out a bunch of shirts to him.

"Thanks," Mal muttered as he swapped his cloak for the shirts and tried not to think about how much blood Griff had already lost. "Alys, I need you to check his other wounds, and if any of them are bleeding, hold pressure with those shirts, okay?"

If he didn't keep his composure, if he didn't drink his flask to the bottom to steady his hands, it was all over for Griff.

"Okay," Alys agreed, kneeling again and starting to inspect Griff's other, shallower scratches. "But Mal, I was trying to tell you—the mule's gone. All we've got is my pack."

Mal's voice was a quiet scrape of chisel on bone as he stared at his hands and the bloody stain once again spreading beneath them. "What do you mean?"

"I fed him a few mushrooms when you followed Griff, so he wouldn't be so nervous," Alys answered breathlessly, pressing a balled-up shirt to a gash on Griff's thigh.

Mal's curse shot birds from the trees, and Griff's eyes fluttered open.

The dark-haired man seemed unable to speak, likely disoriented by the proximity of the ground, the position of the sky, and the terrible pain that was surely radiating from somewhere near his neck. He even tried to close his eyes again, probably hoping to fall back into a dream, but he wasn't so lucky this time.

He groaned softly as Alys pushed the shirt harder against one of his wounds. Then, blinking up at Mal, he said weakly, "The shadow tried to kill me, didn't it? It brought me here. Looked like . . . like Rhun."

Mal stared at the pale face beneath his and shook his head. "I don't know. I saw it, for a second, but it looked like a shadow, same as always. It was a wyvern that attacked you, and too damn bad for them both, because you aren't allowed to leave me yet." He used his bloody palm to sweep Griff's hair back from his face, then let his hand fall onto Griff's good shoulder. "You're probably poisoned. Not the magical kind. We're going to need you to tell us what to do. And the mule ran off with your kit."

Griff smiled wanly, coughed, and said, "Not all of it. I split our healing supplies across my pack and the others—figured someone might try to take some of our stuff at some point. Bandits, you know." Finally, his bleary eyes seemed to take in the gashes on Mal's side, the deepest one still bleeding freely. "You saved me, didn't you?" he asked and, without giving him time to answer, added, "You have absolutely no sense of self-preservation, you shit. You're going to need stitches. Lucky for you, I've done it a hundred times."

Alys and Mal exchanged a worried look over Griff's head. He had no concept of how bad off he was.

"I just . . . need a quick nap first . . ." Griff continued, his eyes fluttering closed again. "Five minutes . . ." His lips formed an easier smile. "Love you, Mal . . . luckiest man on either side of the Teeth . . . So much wasted time . . . Always been you, for me . . ."

Mal's adrenaline was still coursing through him, preventing him from feeling the worst of his own injuries. Leaning down, he rested his sweaty forehead lightly against Griff's and murmured, "Make it to tomorrow, and then you can play healer, you sentimental fuck." As those green eyes softly closed, Mal gave his good shoulder a firm shake, but Griff was once again drifting past his reach.

Mal knew he would be hearing echoes of everything Griff had muttered all night for many nights to come, whether Griff made it or not. "Tell me all those pretty words tomorrow too. Stay with me, no matter how much it hurts," he pleaded with the drowsing man.

Even though Griff was already unconscious once again, Mal leaned down to give him one of the things he claimed to like most in the world, a reminder of what was worth staying for: a brush of his lips against the other's, the mouth Griff was always going on about. He was past caring whether they had an audience or not, and sure now of what they were.

Then he was left to stare down at the shirts beneath his hands, watching the seep of crimson slow at last while Alys dug through her pack and let out a victory cry.

"What is it?" Mal glanced up, ignoring how the world had blurred at the edges.

"Elven medicine," Alys said triumphantly, eyes gleaming as she held up a tin with strange characters printed in Griff's neat handwriting on the lid.

"No, no, we need—" Mal started to say. This wasn't what Griff had described.

Tossing the tin aside, Alys pulled out a vial of cherry-colored liquid, and Mal's heart slowed enough for him to get a real breath. The other vial must be with one of the packs on Prancer, but at least they had this. They had a chance.

"We need to get this in him," he told Alys with all the air in his lungs.

"How much?" she asked.

"The whole thing," Mal guessed, because it wasn't labeled and Griff hadn't given him any instructions. If it could keep their dog alive this long, it had to be able to buy Griff some time, too, while his body worked to replace some of the blood he'd lost. He propped up Griff's head while Alys gently and slowly coaxed the ruby liquid down his throat.

"It smells good, at least," Alys remarked as she took a moment to wipe Griff's mouth with her sleeve. "Should we use what's in the tin too?"

"I guess," Mal said, eyeing the writing on the lid warily as he picked an irritating bit of dirt from the gash in his side. "I can't read what it says on the top, but hopefully it's some kind of disinfectant."

While Alys opened the tin to give it a sniff, Mal carefully raised Griff's shirt and used a water canteen to rinse every injury he saw.

"I'm putting this stuff on *you* next," Alys told Mal in a tone that left no room for argument as she approached with the tin in hand. It smelled strongly of herbs gone soft with mildew after not being properly hung to dry.

He knew she hated to think about anything happening to him, losing him like she'd lost Rhun, but that was life: over too soon, and never gentle on the way out. Griff's ashen face, his limp body lying in the garish, blood-spattered grass, was a stark reminder of that.

"The shadow was here," Mal said tersely, his mind reeling, trying to find the next direction in which to strike back at their enemies. "When Griff got attacked. Then it slipped away. Doesn't seem very Rhun-like to me, no matter what face it showed to Griff."

"No, he would never leave us at a time like this," Alys agreed quietly, lips pressed together in thought. "So either Griff wasn't supposed to follow him, misunderstood somehow, or it's not Papa after all." As she dipped her fingers into the salve and applied it to the first of Griff's many cuts and gouges, she glanced at Mal a few times before finally saying, "I wonder if the shadow made the wyvern attack. If it can do that. I mean—why else would a wyvern charge someone like that, in the daytime, when they usually wake at dusk?"

"Hunger. Or those could have been her eggs you took," Mal pointed out, anything to keep from thinking about whose blood was soaking his hands. "Of course, the shadow led you to those eggs in the first place, didn't it, with the cloak pin? And for Griff to be in just the right place at the right time . . . I don't know." Mal glanced down at his tattoo, thinking back to how it had prickled during the times he had seen the shadow—it only burned when one of Her Dreadful Majesty's servants was close, but that was practically all the time out here. "It's probably not Rhun, with our luck." Much as it pained him to admit being wrong, he added, "And I'd bet a lot of Maysilvers that thing is leading us *to* danger when it appears, not warning us."

Alys's gaze met his for a moment, and he glimpsed fear mingled with hurt there as she took this in. "That would explain why it doesn't really feel like Papa. Maybe the shadow wants the treasure too," she suggested, frowning into the tin of balm. "But . . . if it's not Rhun, if it's some ghostly thief who took his things, where does that leave us?"

"With too many enemies on our trail, and more to come once Her Royal Awfulness realizes we're going to stay put for at least a day or two with these injuries while our shadow competition is free to scout ahead," Mal concluded bitterly.

All he knew was that the strange entity, which might not be Rhun despite having Rhun's stuff, had to be his own fault somehow. Like everything else. His to handle, whether it was part of the deal he had struck with his soon-to-be-former employers or not.

While Alys finished putting the salve on Griff, Mal slid out from under him—stacking up a few more clean shirts to provide some cushion for his head—and finally examined his own wounds. Griff had been right that the one in his side would need stitches. But for now, cleaning it was a start. Mal dribbled some water into the wound, hardly wincing, then opened his flask and hissed a long breath through his teeth as whiskey burned into his raw flesh.

"What are you doing?" Alys asked, darting a worried look at him.

"I'm not using that elf balm, or anything else of theirs, unless we absolutely have to," Mal gritted out. He would consider forgiving the elves for those lost letters only if Griff woke up again. "If it actually worked, Griff wouldn't have been searching for other herbs. I don't even know if we should have helped him drink that red stuff . . ."

His voice trailed away as Alys curled over on herself, vomiting her breakfast in the grass beside Griff after tending the worst wound at his shoulder.

Mal ambled over to her, slow and stiff from the heat of the whiskey cleansing his side—he'd have to thank Wynnie for that healing lesson again—and put a hand on her back, rubbing in gentle circles. "You did really well. Better than any elven healer."

After she stopped heaving, Mal lay down beside Griff on his good side with a grunt of pain, all the better to listen for the cadence of his breathing that would tell him whether their triage efforts and the vial of rare medicine had been in vain.

Griff stirred a little at the renewed warmth, shifting closer to Mal. He didn't open his eyes again, but he did trail his fingers across the ground until they found Mal's hand. His was stiff with cold, but the force of his grip said he wasn't going anywhere just yet. Letting out another deep exhale, Mal curled his hand tightly around Griff's.

"You two should sleep," Alys said, coming over with the balm.

Mal didn't protest again when she started dabbing it into his wound.

"I'll keep a watch. With all this blood on the ground, there's no telling what might come hunting or trying to hurry us along," Alys continued steadily. "And I'll check back on the spot where we left the mule in a little while. Maybe he'll miss the grain enough to come sniffing around."

She could look all she liked, but Mal had his doubts. Prancer was no war steed and clearly had no training for battle. The beast probably felt no remorse whatsoever in trotting off at a brisk pace, silver coins they could have kept for themselves clinking in its loaded saddlebags as it carried their small fortune and their other vial of medicine away to parts unknown.

"Alys—" Mal said as she applied the balm to his side, an intense look of focus on her delicate features. He was glad she was here, grateful for her presence and her attempts to help, even if she had royally messed up with the mule. "You—"

"This stuff isn't going to turn you into an elf, and it'll help with the pain, you stubborn creature," Alys chastised him before he could say more. Her sticky fingers, finished with their task, came to rest under his chin. "You're not invincible, Mal. For all you like to say you're cursed, that the gods are mad you came back from the dead, you sure don't lift a finger to change the course of that fate. And I love you. Griff loves you. Bet he wishes you'd love yourself enough to put away the flask and put down the knives . . . For all that you worry he won't be here tomorrow, you ought to consider that he feels the same about you." Pressing her trembling lips together, she waited a moment and then said more calmly, "What did you want to tell me?"

Mal tilted his head, studying her in the leaf-filtered light of a fading afternoon gone so far south that he didn't know where they were anymore. "Just . . . I was thinking how your version of handling things is nothing like Wynnie's. Or Rhun's. I like your way better."

Mal took her sticky hand in one of his, the other still clinging to Griff's.

"Mmm," was all she said, her eyes glistening, holding his bloody hand tighter as she gazed down at the pale, slumbering Griff. "I don't know why people are always so quick to compare him to his father either. Griff's the better man by far. Don't let go of him, all right?"

She stood and released his hand.

"Are you sure you're up to the watch?" Mal asked her, curling himself a little more around Griff, who was concerningly chilled. Shouldn't that stupid elf medicine have done something already? "I can stay awake too. I'm not dead yet, as you said, and whatever troll comes out of its cave next is my responsibility, anyway."

"Rest," Alys insisted, drawing her blade again. "Wynnie taught me a lot of things I never knew I'd need. Maybe being like her isn't the terrible fate I always thought it was. Because whatever nasty things come our way, I know I can handle them." She shifted her blade higher, letting it rest against her shoulder as she added, "Alone."

It struck him, even through the haze of pain and panic and the worst of his exhaustion, that Alys was just as lonely as he had been before he found Griff again.

He wished he could take that loneliness from her. But he could barely even keep his head up.

Finding a comfortable place to rest his cheek in the soft texture of Griff's hair, Mal muttered to the sleeping man in his arms, "If the shadow did this somehow, I'm going to burn it right off the face of the earth with the brightest light I can find. I'm going to figure out what it loves and steal it all from right under its nose, assuming it has one—just so it knows what it's like to feel helpless while everything that's ever mattered to it gets ripped away."

Chapter Twenty-Two
The Night Belongs to Us

Five days after the attack, Griff was alert enough to know that he had entirely lost his taste for truffles. He would have to impress Mal with some other delicacy when they got home.

He had managed to stay awake ever since Alys convinced Mal that a fire was just what they all needed tonight despite the risks of attracting certain creatures: a bit of hot stew and a chance to warm their hands over the flames as nightfall crept into their camp, which they had been forced to make not far from the place where they had last seen Prancer and the shattered remains of their only other vial of elven medicine, now absorbed into the Mire after being trampled by a panicked hoof.

They hadn't wanted to risk moving Griff until he started showing real improvement, and it was only today that he had finally regained a little of his color. By dusk, he was sitting with his back against the sturdy brace of a tree, a sling fashioned for his shoulder and salve packed into his other gashes, the lingering taste of cherries still faintly present every time he swallowed.

Night wasn't so different from day this far into the Mire, he decided as he observed his surroundings, save perhaps for some change in singers in the chorus of constant background noise. There was an owl now talking itself into alertness, the far-off hunting cry of a pack of coyotes, a few less midges buzzing around his ears.

He listened hopefully for the jingling of a mule whose saddlebags were weighted down with heaps of silver coins, but so far it seemed that Prancer had truly decided their company wasn't worth the trail of treats Alys had laid out, or else he'd met his end with the hungry wyvern. The only sign of Prancer they had found was a second of their packs not far from where they had last seen him, mostly full of clothes and a few of Griff's supplies that hadn't fallen out with the lost medicine.

He also hadn't seen any more glimpses of a phantom Rhun—not that he would follow or trust anything he saw in the Mire again.

Near the fire, Alys was pacing, unraveling in the face of all that was troubling them: the shadow that might not really be her father giving them his old things—perhaps going after the treasure too. Griff's near death, and her part in losing the mule and the last of their lifesaving medicine in one swift and stupid move. He had been filled in on a great many things in his waking hours, none of it good.

Alys kept one hand on her sword hilt, the other clutching the neck of a familiar amber bottle—a jug of whiskey like the one from which Mal regularly refilled his flask. She took a long gulp from it every so often as she peered out into the night with a defiant scowl, not her usual dreamy stare that would suggest she was only half anchored in this world.

When Griff called out to her, his good arm ready to embrace her, she merely shook her head, her lip quivering—she was fighting her own battle, he realized, something Wynnie had taught them all was best accomplished alone. The guilt of losing much-needed supplies when they might have an unseen adversary was eating her alive. Their most powerful tool against death out here, the medicine he affectionately called Cherry Pie, was gone because of her. She was also probably grieving the belief that she had found her father again, and she didn't know how to sit with any of it.

"Hard to talk to her when she's like this—trust me," Mal commented softly. "Guilt's not exactly a lesson Wynnie taught; not sure she's ever felt it." He had settled against the same tree as Griff, his leather-bound book held open to the flickering firelight with one hand while his other, heavily bandaged hand rested in his lap. Every so often, he peeked over the top of the book and glared balefully out at something in the surrounding night. Griff supposed Mal was searching for the shadow that had tried to kill him, and he didn't want to think about that now that he had much worse pains than the ones from his old stab wound.

From his moments of wakefulness over the past several days, Griff knew Mal had spent his time tossing and turning on a bedroll beside him, unable to find a position that didn't irritate one injury or another—especially after Griff stayed awake long enough to stitch up the biggest of Mal's gashes. The elven salve seemed to have had some effect after all, and the wounds were more or less healing nicely, save for a bit of yellow ooze seeping from the stitches.

Griff leaned around the tree to watch as Mal listlessly turned another page, his gray eyes following Alys's silhouette as she paced, concern etched deep into his brow. That same worried look lingered as he turned to Griff.

"Need me to look at your bandages again?" he asked.

Griff glanced down at his shoulder in its crude sling. Just a few hours ago, the latest bandage change had revealed only a hint of pink, the greatest improvement yet. Having kept down a fair amount of Alys's attempt at supper, he was feeling more like himself than he had since The Incident, as he had taken to calling it in his head.

"No," he answered softly, worried that raising his voice might disturb Alys. Reaching out with his good arm, he invited Mal to draw closer, up against his side. "But it's tomorrow. And yesterday, you said—or was it the day before that?" He interrupted himself, a hint of embarrassment creeping in at the thought that he had mistaken the day. "Anyway, right after I got hurt, you said I should tell you some things tomorrow. Which is now. Or as close enough as I can tell after losing all that blood."

"You're at least three days late," Mal said as he let the cover of his book fall back over the pages and followed the summons of that arm into the warmth of Griff's side. "But just this once, I'm not holding any grudges, even if we're going to have to run the rest of the way to reach that treasure now." Settling in hip to hip, Mal studied the pallor of Griff's face before meeting his eyes. "All right, talk pretty to me."

Griff brought his good arm up around Mal's shoulders, and from there ran his fingers through snarls of gold hair.

Mal's brows drew together slightly as he took in the sight of a gesture Griff hadn't made toward him in many years—but as Griff's fingers worked their way into his hair, he relaxed against him.

"Actually, I want to ask you about something I've heard you say a few times," Griff said, tightening his arm around those narrow shoulders. As if his fragile skin that had nearly been shredded to ribbons could somehow act as a shield against the threads of fate. "You think you're cursed for some reason?" When Mal nodded, he continued softly, "Well then, I'd like to understand. To listen. No judgment."

Out past the circle of firelight, Alys's pacing paused.

She sighed and took another gulp of whiskey. Maybe she was feeling cursed, too, having trusted the shadow and now questioning her judgment.

"I do need to let you know about that," Mal admitted softly, only frowning briefly at Alys. "I don't exactly understand it all myself, but something happened when I died for a minute back in Thrallkeld. I feel like . . . the gods have it out for me. Like I have bigger debts than the ones I can count. I don't know how, and I don't know when, but I've got to live while I can, get rich while I can, because soon I'm afraid it'll all be over for me."

"Yet I take it going home now is out of the question?" Griff asked with open eagerness. "Because I'd really, really like that." He could live with the random attacks of pain from his scar even if it meant never becoming the Warden he had always felt destined to be, maybe find some other antidote even if it took years. But if they stayed in this swamp much longer, he wasn't sure he'd come back alive.

Home. What he wanted to build with Mal. Rooms upon rooms that they could fill together, where the hearth was already blazing with the fire of all his feelings for this man, old and new, freshly fueled and going steady. They didn't need any treasure for that.

"If we leave now, the Mire wins. The *shadow* wins, and—put it this way, we'll have both suffered for nothing. We can't do that," Mal insisted, and Griff had to admit there was something about the spark in those silver eyes that fed the fire inside him too. He could certainly live better if he had a chance to wear those healing bracers. Maybe return them to Stormveil after, if he could convince Mal to let him have them as his share of their earnings.

Pulling Mal a little closer with his good arm, he turned his attention to his lover's dilemma. Curses weren't a magic Griff knew or understood any better than Mal despite his extensive studies in Stormveil's library. The elves' magic was that of healing the body, of nature, whistling to move the wind or stir up the tides, not altering the threads of fate.

True curses fell within the Shadow Queen's realm, a fact that rankled those who believed she was originally an elf—a being who couldn't wield such dark magic as necromancy. It would at least explain her very long life, though others suspected there had been several queens through the centuries, each taking up the same title and purpose. Still, no matter her origins, she didn't care who she cursed or who had to die for her cause.

"You spend a lot of time telling me I'm not allowed to die—what if I demand the same of you?" Griff said at last over the crackle of the flames and the crunch of Alys's boots as she picked up her pacing again, now in a more erratic line.

"Feels like the curse has changed lately. Now it seems to be that the gods want me to watch you almost die over and over," Mal lamented.

Griff didn't understand. "Why would that be your curse?"

But when Mal's only answer was to pull out his flask and take a liberal swig from it, he tried a different approach. "I was hoping to go first, you know. Supposing we get a say in such things. I don't much like the idea of living in a world without you—I've tried, and I was pretty shit at it." He rubbed Mal's arm, his broad hand warming the other man's shoulder.

Mal tipped the flask back again before answering. "You can't go first. Hell, I don't want you to go at all, that's the point of any of this. You, staying." Another drink, a shake of his head, and he pulled his knees up with a mild grimace. The motion must have tugged at his stitches. "Look, I've already made my peace with it. Sometimes knowledge is the best armor anyway."

In the distance, Alys stepped from the halo of firelight altogether, retreating to a twisted tree just outside it that offered several low-hanging branches.

Griff was relieved they could still see her. It seemed like someone ought to be keeping an eye on her in her current state.

Staring out into the dark, raising her blade hand slightly, she called to the shadows, "Come on, Mister No-Face. Mister Pretender. Do you want this treasure we're after so badly that you're trying to kill us for it? Want to tell me why you have all my papa's things? Well, here I am. Quit hiding and let's have a look at you. Unless you're a coward!"

The whiskey sloshed in the bottle as she spread her arms wide.

Closing his eyes and raising his voice, concern and frustration evident there, Mal called, "Alys, the last thing any of us needs right now is to interrogate any ghosts—least of all you, when you're the only one in fighting shape."

Alys half turned to face them, taking a long drink from the whiskey bottle and wiping the back of her mouth with her sword hand before saying innocently, "If it's not really Papa, I'm going to get rid of the shadow for us, just like Wynnie would, so no one else gets hurt. The night belongs to us, just like it always has, not to ghosts or shadows or any queen but me."

"Come on, let me have the watch," Mal pressed. Near his book lay his sword, along with the broken one he had been studying again before Griff woke earlier. "Get some sleep—you're not yourself right now."

"Alys," Griff tried. "I know you feel terrible about what happened with the mule, but nobody's mad at you. And—Mal and I are here, if you're tired of looking at the dark alone. If you want to remember the real Rhun together. I've found sometimes that helps."

But Alys turned to face the shadows again without another word.

Mal nearly raised his flask, but Griff's gentle, pleading touch on his arm stilled the motion. This, at least, was a place where Mal was willing to bend, even if he wouldn't consider putting a foot on the path toward home while there was still gold at stake. Like that still mattered more than this new thing between them.

"Right, then, now that we've talked curses . . ." Mal said a little gruffly, trying to keep his frustration at Alys from his voice. "What did you want to tell me earlier?"

Griff did his best to push his concern for Alys aside for now too. He knew firsthand that sometimes people didn't want to be helped.

There were several points over the last few days when he hadn't been sure he would survive the attack, and now here he was, sitting up and talking and sharing another night with Mal. No matter what else was wrong in the world, he still wanted to make the most of their time together, knowing too well that it could all be over at any moment.

"Just that I regret all the time I didn't get to spend with you over the years, because you enchant me far more than you exasperate me. You inspire me. Excite me. Challenge me. You even saved me. I love all of you, darling." He turned his head slightly to start kissing along Mal's jaw, moving up toward the curve of his ear, where he added in a whisper, "The good parts, and the hard parts . . . *and* the hard parts."

"You have a good memory for a man who nearly had the audacity to bleed out in front of someone who loves him—speaking of exasperating . . ." Mal murmured as Griff reached the end of his list, curling his fingers one by one into the other man's as he basked in the pretty words from the silver bard's tongue.

Griff trailed more kisses across his jaw, determined to melt away Mal's frustration, offering distractions from problems of curses and shadows and treasure still out of reach for now as he brushed his lips over Mal's ear next.

"There are plenty of hard parts . . ." Mal confessed on a quiet breath, a subtle twitch in his leg that Griff couldn't help but notice as the other man pressed himself closer. "So you're not allowed to die on me. Especially not while chasing the ghost of a man we already lost a long time ago, or anything pretending to be him."

"Wouldn't dream of it," Griff promised into the hot skin of Mal's neck. His next kiss there was hungrier, with a graze of teeth, as he slid his free hand down to Mal's thigh and began a confident exploration that wasted no time on teasing and got right down to the hard parts. "We've got years to make up for and so many fun things we haven't tried yet," he whispered against Mal's neck. "I still have to show you all the stars."

"You really fucking do. Turns out I've been looking in all the wrong places," Mal reflected on a heavy breath, sliding a hand into Griff's hair.

"If you ask nicely, maybe I'll draw you a map," he panted, raising his head so he could press his lips to Mal's in a return of the gentle kiss he'd received while hovering on the brink of consciousness some days ago. "And while we're telling each other things," he said through another brush of lips, "I should remind you that although my shoulder is completely fucked beyond hope of repair, the parts of me that know how to please you are still in working order . . ."

Searching those silver eyes that had become both familiar and uncharted territory all at once, Griff flicked his tongue across Mal's lower lip and added, "And I'll consider this night a terrible waste of not dying if you don't end up in my arms."

Mal's brows rose slightly at the softness and intention behind those kisses. He leaned his forehead against Griff's, answering quietly, "You nearly lost enough blood to make your own black pudding just days ago." The fresh reminder of it seemed to cool his own blood a little, even with Griff's hand still trying to stoke the flames between them. "You need rest, healer's orders." It was true, and Griff knew it—even if he wouldn't admit it—yet Mal hooked his fingers into Griff's belt loops and tugged all the same, evidently unable to leave the warmth and welcome of the green eyes gazing into his. "And *I'm* the healer right now, remember?"

Undaunted, with Mal's eyes still on him and the heat of their breath rising, Griff growled softly, "Well then, as my caretaker, you'll want to know that my many wounds are agony and I could really use a good distraction about now . . ."

With that, he pulled Mal into the depths of another kiss, and Mal drew himself into Griff's lap by the belt he clung to. Checking to make sure Alys was off in her own world on the other side of the camp, Mal started making quick work of the buckle and buttons beneath as his tongue made a couple of boasts to Griff of what was to come, no words needed as the metal of his belt clinked softly in the dimness.

"As your caretaker, I've decided that as long as you let me do the work, this still counts as rest," Mal declared, pressing a blazing kiss to the side of Griff's neck.

Then Alys screamed, effectively dousing their fire.

Chapter Twenty-Three

Mister No-Face

Mal scrambled to his feet even as he encouraged Griff to stay there against the tree, a hand clamped firmly on the foreman's good shoulder. He fumbled to grab his sword with his better hand as he narrowed his eyes across the screen of smoke from their fire and tried to make sense of what he was seeing outside the warm glow.

Alys, swept off her feet, hovering several inches above the ground.

Alys, gasping for breath.

Alys reaching desperately for her sword that had somehow fallen from her grasp, next to the whiskey bottle that had tipped over at the base of the tree.

Alys's pale hair blown back by a sudden strong wind that didn't quite seem to reach across the campfire, her braid gusting over her shoulder as she floated there and kicked fiercely at nothing.

Mal bolted across their campsite, grabbing the shard of broken sword so he could have the option to stab with both hands. He had been expecting something like this for days now, ever since the wyvern attack had forced another, longer halt to their progress, more revenants or trolls or worse—whatever "worse" might be.

There wasn't enough whiskey in the world to numb his nerves when there were so many of the Shadow Queen's green-eyed ghosts gathering at the edges of their camp each night since the attack, leering at him and counting down the precious days and hours he had remaining to reach the treasure before the other undead in the Mire had permission to kill him.

But he still had over a week left. Eleven days, to be exact. He'd kept careful count, pushing them to hurry as often as they could because he always expected the worst.

They could harass *him*, sure, but trying to kill Alys was completely out of bounds. Her Dreadful Majesty really needed to work on her idea of motivation.

As Mal hastily cleared the fire, he saw it: not one of the queen's servants after all but the damned shadow that most definitely wasn't Rhun, finally standing still enough as it lifted Alys off the ground, claws digging into her shoulders, for him to get a long look at its true face. He almost wished he hadn't. He wished it didn't have one after all.

It was even taller than it had appeared in shadow form; gaunt, nearly skeletal but for some ragged bits of flesh stretched thinly over its bones. It might have been human, once, or an elf; the circlet of what looked like long iron spikes on its head might have been a crown. It seemed to howl with rage through blackened teeth, though Mal couldn't hear anything but the faint rustling of wind moving the leaves on the trees.

He wouldn't let this thing have Alys.

He raised the blade—the broken one, using his dominant hand without thinking—and the transparent figure's lightless, hollow eyes locked on his.

No, not on his—even he might have frozen and forgotten how to fight for a second if he was fixed in the gaze of such a powerful spirit. It was staring at the blade.

It seemed to hiss at the shattered weapon, cracked lips pulled back as far as they could go to expose the many gaps in its teeth, like a snarling, feral dog.

And as Mal blinked against the cold wind rolling over him, the figure vanished. Sweeping his gaze around their camp, he realized that at some point in the moments since Alys had screamed, all the other ghosts that had gathered to nag him about his lack of progress had disappeared for the first time in days too.

Alys dropped at once, shaking where she landed in a puddle of spilled whiskey, and he tossed the blades aside to kneel and wrap her in his arms. His hands were bleeding again, leaving smears of crimson where he brushed a palm over her hair to try to smooth it, but he only cared that she was okay.

"Did you see it?" Alys tried to whisper, hiccupping at the end.

Mal nodded. It was now right up there with the list of things he never wanted to see again, like Griff bleeding out in his arms. "Did *you*?" he asked when he found the breath. "You stay put!" he added quickly and sternly to Griff, noticing the other man trying to climb to his feet. The last thing they needed was him falling apart now that they had no wonderful elf medicine to make anything okay when they were out of other options.

"No, I just saw—the Mire. But I felt it, and it's *not* Papa," Alys hiccupped, resting her chin on Mal's shoulder for a moment. "What was it? What made it let go?" Lower, so that Griff wouldn't hear, she added, "Was it—something else of *hers*? It has to be, right?"

"I don't know what the hell it was. Not human, though," Mal said, his mind still reeling. Usually ghosts looked like people or dwarves or elves; this spirit had been so much bigger, distorted from whatever it once was, that he couldn't be sure. It certainly seemed like something the Shadow Queen would create, but then why was it unaware of his deal when everything else out here seemed to know? "Think you could draw it for me, if I describe it?"

It might give them both something concrete to focus on, a chance to let their heartbeats slow while they tried to figure out what exactly their shadow was. If it wanted the treasure too, they were in for a hell of a fight to claim it when they got there. But who wanted easy? For Griff's safety, for his freedom, he would give everything he had until his last breath.

As Alys got to her feet, collecting her sword and the whiskey bottle, Mal tried not to look at how little of its contents were left—especially now that he needed a drink more than ever.

"This seemed to scare it off," he said as he studied Amaranth, the shard of a sword that had survived a long-ago troll attack. Wiping a thin trail of red from his palm on his pants, he wrapped the blade in the end of his shirt and walked with Alys to join Griff by the tree.

They watched together, Mal sipping liberally from his flask, as Alys took out fresh paper and charcoals and began to sketch what Mal described for her.

When she had finished, they all looked quietly at the drawing for a moment. Mal much preferred the noisy ravens, the hungry revenants, the usual mocking but ineffective ghosts, and even the troll to this new horror. He had no idea how he was going to keep Griff and Alys safe from this thing unless he was the one with the broken blade and always on watch, always keeping both of them within his sight until they had the treasure and had dumped it all into Kage's muscular, greedy arms. And that was assuming this gruesome spirit left them alone once this whole affair was settled—after all, Mal had first seen it back in Mayfair, at Griff's job site.

He was aware that he shouldn't be thinking that far ahead yet. Because the closer they got to the treasure, the closer he kept coming to losing the only man he could even halfway trust. Now it seemed like Alys wanted to leave him alone out here, too, and become a victim of her own recklessness.

Interrupting his thoughts, she hiccupped and said, "That's the ugliest ghost I've ever seen. Still think I could have fought it, though."

"Alys," Mal said in his calmest voice. "Whatever that thing is, whatever it wants, you're going to get us killed if you call it back here. You're going to die, and watch both of us die, and then we're going to hang around with you in this damned Mire for all eternity, telling you that we were right."

He didn't want to hear another word about spirits tonight. Still, they needed to figure out what they were dealing with, because they had to reach the treasure alive. Taking a breath to steady himself, pulling his eyes away from the black pits of the creature's eyes on the page, he asked Griff, "Have you ever seen anything like this in a library book?"

"I'm not sure," Griff admitted, his face tight with pain again; his shoulder must be bothering him. "But . . . can I see that, just for a minute?"

He motioned to the shard of sword beside Mal, who wouldn't be letting it out of his sight for the remainder of the trip, until the Mire was well at their backs, and Mal carefully held it out to him, not missing the way Griff winced as he took in the rough state of his hands.

Chapter Twenty-Four

Amaranth

The longer Griff looked at the blade, the more certain he was that he'd seen an illustration of it before, in Stormveil's library. Only then it had been whole, complete with the designs and gems on the hilt that would have made it easily identifiable, which had long since been lost in Rhun's battle with the troll.

"I think this blade is enchanted to cut spirits—if it's the one I'm thinking of," Griff said to the others, even though Alys was staring moodily at her drawing and Mal kept gazing uneasily into the trees as if searching for something. "Rhun might have known about the shadow too, since he brought this; maybe it was never meant for fighting the troll but happened to be the weapon he had at hand. The elves must have given it to him."

Rather than thanking Griff for remembering this kernel of potentially lifesaving knowledge while in an extreme amount of pain, Mal put his bandaged hand on Alys's shoulder and said, "You need to go to sleep. I know what the shadow looks like now, for all the good it does us. But I don't know what tomorrow's going to look like if you're too strung out to swing any kind of blade at all and summoning monsters right to our doorstep with your bullshit."

The distress showed plainly on his face as he rounded on Griff. "And *you*—I need you to rest too. Because I still fucking love you, which means living is nonnegotiable. I'm going to take the watch. Wynnie taught me how to handle plenty on my own too."

With that, Mal picked up the shard of Amaranth and slunk off toward the tree Alys had used earlier as a seat, stopping only to pick up the nearly empty whiskey bottle along the way and take a gulp of it, his chest heaving with every breath.

"Wynnie was always hardest on me," Alys said softly.

Griff, who was reaching for Mal's small book with the runes on the front—reading always calmed his nerves—realized she was talking to him. Her eyes were damp and her words harder to make out than usual. "I could fight drunker than this. On less sleep than this. Because she made me, time and again, half out of my mind, until I won. Until I won every single time. Maybe I don't like killing things, but I *can*. She made me so I'll never break. She made me so I'll always win. That shadow wasn't going to win, even if I couldn't see it."

Griff had no idea what to say to that—certainly now wasn't the time to appreciate all the damage he had escaped in avoiding most of those lessons—and so he was quiet for some time, just watching her. Eventually, he said, "I'm so sorry, Alys. I really am."

He rose slowly, with effort, and grabbed his cloak to wrap around her shoulders, pointing to the nearest of their bedrolls. But rather than urging her toward it, his hand lingered on her arm. He had failed to be there for her as much as he had Mal. Let her down, too, with his inability to stay through the hard things. "I should have done something. Protected you better."

Alys shook her head. "Maybe that line would work on Mal, but it's just us here, Griff. Let's be real. You couldn't have done anything. Maybe . . ." She hesitated, bit her lip a little too hard so that when she next spoke, it glistened with spit and blood. "Maybe

I should have learned to protect myself better from a lot of things." Gathering Griff's cloak tighter around herself, she stood and looked toward her bedroll. "I might sleep. Don't try fighting that shadow yourself while I'm out, all right? You're not Seimon, the bards won't sing about it, and I've had enough of watching you bleed out for one lifetime."

"I love you too, Alys," he sighed. Then he resettled at the base of the tree where not that long ago the night had seemed to belong to him and Mal, the pieces of that broken blade reflecting the starlight from across the clearing where Mal kept watch as Griff cracked the cover of the leather book and started at the beginning.

He wanted, more than anything, to better understand the frustrated man sitting by himself at the edge of their camp. To understand why going home now, together, wouldn't be enough for him. Sure, Mal would lose out on all the gold he could have made from selling the treasure, but Griff would be losing too, saddled with the pain from his stab wound for the rest of his life. Even then, didn't they have so much more to gain by staying together?

Mal still held the fragmented blade, but he had a long stick in his other hand now and was determinedly scratching something into the dirt.

Griff glanced away, toward the spot where Alys had been. Her sketch pad was still open to that gaunt, screaming drawing of the spirit, its bony face dark and yawning like it wanted to swallow him up. Something the Shadow Queen must have woven from a nightmare, if he had to guess. He reached for the sketch pad with his good arm and hastily turned the page.

And after reading a couple of long and thought-provoking passages of Mal's book, he picked up the pad again along with Alys's charcoal, an idea beginning to take shape that came from his own dreams.

When he had finished, he tucked a folded-up piece of paper into the pages of Mal's book and made his way toward the lone figure still holding his nighttime vigil, stopping just once along the way to pull Alys's braid out of her mouth and check her breathing.

He made no secret of his approach. His bandaged ankle dragging slightly with each step would have made that a challenge anyway. When he got near enough to Mal, he wrapped his good arm around the other man's shoulders for the second time that night and said softly, so as not to wake Alys, "I'm sorry tonight got so weird. And I'm sure Alys regrets calling out to the shadow. I'm sure we all regret a lot of things. But you're still not alone. I'm still with you unless you tell me to be gone, and even then, I'd have to be sure you truly meant it."

Mal stayed resolutely silent, even as Griff pressed his stubbled cheek softly into the wild nest of Mal's hair. But the blond also made no move to pull away.

"Thought you might like a little reading material while you're on watch," Griff said, undeterred, dropping the book gently down into Mal's lap. "You seem like you need your space tonight, and that's okay—we all have plenty to think about after what just happened—but you should know that I found page ten particularly interesting."

Mal's bandaged hand gripped the edge of the book. "Page ten," he repeated, though it was Griff, not the book, he was looking at. "Pretty sure I have that essay memorized. You know, Alys and Wynnie have always thought philosophy is just a bunch of—"

"Hopeless nonsense for people who love to be sad?" Griff supplied with a shake of his head, familiar with their views on the matter.

"That," Mal muttered darkly. "But I've had this book since I was in Thrallkeld, and I like rereading it once in a while. Always find something new to think about."

He relaxed slightly under Griff's arm, turning back in the direction in which he had been keeping watch, the toe of his boot nudging a symbol he must have carved into the dirt with the stick. But he made a little room on his branch seat as he did so, and seemed to struggle to fight off a shiver.

"Your cloak—" Griff began, but Mal shook his head, and Griff dimly remembered that it had soaked up a great deal of his own blood during The Incident, and probably needed a thorough washing.

Mal's better hand rose across his chest, reaching for Griff's where it rested at his shoulder and gently closing over it. "Would you still consider it a waste of not dying if you just stayed right here with me a little longer?"

Leaning in to the gentle air of teasing that always seemed to flow easily between them even when nothing else did, Griff muttered, "You know . . . I did have other plans tonight. I was going to go find this legendary treasure no one else ever could and make us all rich beyond our wildest imaginings, then come back a hero by breakfast . . . but I suppose my grand plans can wait another night."

Mal snorted softly. "It figures there's some big nasty trying to get the treasure too. With my luck, all that's at the X on this map is a pile of stones, or a list of everything I've ever stolen tucked inside an empty bottle."

"That actually doesn't sound as bad as some of the alternatives," Griff said with a slight shake of his head, thinking again of Alys's drawing and what it must have been like for Mal to see the real-life version looming before him. "We still keep on as planned, then?"

"Is that a serious question? We've got the spirit blade. Whatever the shadow can do, whatever game it's playing, we can handle it," Mal declared with his usual confidence. "Now that you're finally up and about, we need to leave by—"

"First light," Griff finished for him, unable to ignore the sinking feeling in his gut.

He lapsed into quiet after that, regretting having asked as he wrapped himself more thoroughly around Mal to help stave off the chill that had touched him now too. He shifted some of his weight to the branch as well, keeping his hold on Mal as he settled in, his gaze seeking upward for the swath of stars between gaps in the trees so that he could pick out familiar constellations, the sight of which always cheered him like greeting old friends.

The silence between him and Mal was easier than it had been in years, and it seemed to be some kind of balm for this bitter evening, loosening the tension in his shoulders the longer they sat together without the need for uttering a word, watching the stars and listening to the varied music of the Mire at nighttime.

But eventually, Mal picked up his book and untangled his fingers from Griff's, saying gently, "You should probably get some rest. Works wonders for not dying, so I've heard. I'll make sure nothing undead creeps too close, and maybe you can check on Alys again, make sure she's not choking on her own vomit or anything."

"I won't let her drown," Griff said as he slowly, painstakingly worked at unbuttoning his shirt. He pulled it off and wrapped it around Mal's shoulders in his absence, explaining, "So you don't get cold later."

Then he limped back into the halo of the fire and his waiting bedroll, pulling out a new shirt from his pack for himself and an extra one, which he slid carefully under Alys's head. She didn't stir. He finally lay down, settling on his back so he could watch the stars, mind too full of phantoms to drift right off to sleep no matter his intentions of staying on this earth.

Chapter Twenty-Five
The Quiet Game

When Griff had gone, Mal wrapped the shirt tightly around himself and smiled a little, because he liked the black. Black reminded him of Griff.

He didn't think that the shadow was the reason he was still cold enough to appreciate the bonus shirt, but he couldn't be sure. He hoped the mark he had scratched into the dirt would help take care of that, too, at least while they were resting. It was something that had popped into his head when he saw Alys's drawing. An old lesson from Vic, not Wynnie.

It was a ward against spirits, one she had learned from her people. Vic came from Asnan, an area of clannish, often-warring folk who frequently stabbed each other over contested land and resources. Hers was the kind of folk belief that Rhun would have looked down on, by all accounts, and deemed superstitious nonsense.

Seemed like the man might have gotten further out here if he'd been a little more superstitious, or listened to someone like Vic. Hopefully, the mark would at least be enough to keep the shadow out of the narrow circle of their camp; he hadn't thought to bother when it came to the dark queen's watchful spirits, because they didn't seem able or interested in hurting him and never came as close as the bolder shadow.

With the cool night pressing in around him once more, Mal tried to slide a little farther down in his seat to get comfortable, only to be met with a protest from his stitches again. With a frustrated sigh, he settled instead with his back against the trunk and rolled up the too-long sleeves of Griff's shirt.

The light of the fire had grown lower with no one tending it, so Mal had to search for a good angle by which to read. Yet on page ten, where he expected to find familiar words about ale and ethics, a neatly folded piece of paper greeted him instead.

Mal's eyes roamed over words written in the neatest penmanship he'd ever seen from a man wielding a piece of stubby charcoal. His brows arched in certain places and drew together in others. Grins sometimes played at the corners of his mouth as he read, while other times he frowned or his throat tightened.

Then he read it all again.

Three times over.

Mal,

It was beautiful and serene in Stormveil, and I hated it. Even seated among the most esteemed of our parents' friends, even in the concerned company of the princes and princess, my heart was only for you and my thoughts turned to despair the longer the silence stretched between us; that was worse than any distance.

You would have hated it: constant hushed voices, all the rules, the small niceties that felt like another language we had never learned how to speak. For years, your ghost was all I had, and most of the time I was content to be haunted by you forever rather than lose you entirely. Other times, I won't deny that I was resentful of the way I could never fully give myself to another, because even when you didn't know it, you had me. You always have me. From the first time I can remember looking into your eyes, you've had me.

. . . I set out to recreate for you here all the letters that were burned without my knowledge, bit by bit from memory, but then I realized they were all part of the same refrain, and you know the melody well enough by now. Maybe you don't need new letters about old wounds, anyway. Now that we're something more, something pulled right from my wildest dreams—you've ruined me for anyone else now, whether you intended it or not—it seems right to talk about what's next.

After all, you promised me a horse, and someone had better put that in writing so there's no question of ownership when I'm ready to collect.

And that got me thinking, I owe you a few promises, too: I promise that you'll never again know me only by the void my absence creates.

I promise I'll never again lash out at you in anger, with fists or words, so that one day the past will be like a fever dream and you'll question whether you ever knew anything but safe harbor when you turn to me.

I promise, too, to make a place for us, if you'd welcome it. For you and me, with my own hands. I know of some land outside town. I can plant good crops and put up walls to keep out the world, at least the parts of it that don't suit us, walls with far more space than the cottage and plenty of room to grow. Room for a horse or two, some good dogs, your weapons, that big bed and bigger stove you said you're going to buy. It wouldn't be the castle I know you dream about, but at least it would be ours. Just say the word—I'm at your command.

Before I go, have I told you lately—or perhaps, though I'm ashamed to write it, have I ever told you—how proud I am of who you've become? You're not like Wynnie or Rhun or Vic or anyone else. You're your own. And you're stronger for it. And I'm actually quite grateful I didn't die, because now I'll be around for whatever you do next. You continue to amaze me.

—Griff

With trembling fingers, Mal folded the paper back up and slid it into the book, giving the Mire—for once seemingly empty—one last warning glance. Then he pushed to his feet, tucking the book under one arm, and crept across the camp by the light of embers, leaving Vic's ward to guard them.

†

Mal found Griff's eyes just drifting closed when he stepped over the dark-haired man's bedroll, straddling him before dropping to his knees as gracefully as someone could with stitches tugging at their side. Then he placed the book just beside Griff's head with silent meaning before holding up a finger to his lips and laying it gently over Griff's mouth.

When he leaned in, he swiftly removed his finger and replaced it with his lips.

That letter was still running through his mind as Griff wrapped his good arm around him and pulled him in closer. Griff met his lips hungrily, with the intensity of someone who hadn't eaten in days, though his hands were much more cautious than his mouth as they gently sought beneath Mal's shirt, mindful of the tender places he had stitched.

Mal answered that rising hunger with a deepening of the kiss, trailing his fingers up Griff's chest and growling softly in the back of his throat.

They needed to be quiet. To not wake Alys, or attract anything that usually hunted by night. But there was still so much they could do while hardly making a sound.

This time around, Mal made faster work of Griff's buckle and buttons. There was so much heat between them they didn't even need to tend the fire. As he deepened their next kiss, his tongue sliding against Griff's, the foreman impatiently grabbed the hem of his shirt and started to peel it away with his good arm.

Mal tried to help by wiggling out of his shirt, wincing only once or twice at some unpleasant twinges in his side in the process. And though his skin was warm, even hot to the touch, a shiver ran through him as he was bared to the night.

"Fuck," Griff mouthed as they broke back from another breathless kiss. Whether it was a prayer, a curse, an invitation, or all things in one seemed to be left open to Mal's interpretation. Maybe there were some good curses, after all.

"Not just yet. But maybe, if you're good," Mal whispered teasingly, satisfying them both for now—or perhaps only stoking the fire—by rubbing himself slowly against Griff until he was sure they were both leaking from the friction, until Griff's panting became too loud and he had to force himself to stop because he realized his thigh was twitching and he was near to bursting from the pressure of Griff pressed against him like this.

Regaining focus after a few heavy breaths, he blazed a trail of hot kisses along Griff's body that started on his chest and moved with intentional slowness down toward his navel. "Good work gets rewarded. And you want to win the Quiet Game, don't you?"

Griff nodded, exhaling a little noisily, like he was fighting back a moan.

As Mal continued those kisses, he left one hand close to Griff's cheek, almost as if to stroke it—but really it was lying in wait, ready to muffle any unexpected sounds if Griff suddenly lost their game in the midst of an escalating stream of pleasures. His breathing was already growing increasingly ragged the farther south Mal's lips traveled.

"That's right," he whispered in encouragement as he licked and teased his way down the foreman's body. "Just like I thought. Good boy, Griff. So fucking good for me."

Gazing up from between Griff's legs with a sly grin, Mal made a few swipes with his tongue up the other man's thigh, deliberate brushes of his nose and lips sending Griff sprawling back against the bedroll. When Mal added the fingers of his better hand as well, dragging lightly over places where the skin was thinnest, Griff grabbed at handfuls of the grass, which Mal took as a sign that he was heading in the right direction. And went lower still.

Gently pushing Griff's cheeks apart, he flicked his tongue between them, soft licks and kisses given right against his entrance, an experiment—curious to see if Griff would open for him like this. And, just as he hoped, he did. Mal pushed the tip of his tongue inside, another new taste, sharper and wilder but still right somehow.

Griff tensed beneath him as he tried to hold in yet more noises, now using the hand of his good arm to stroke Mal's hair.

Mal thrust his tongue inside a few times in response to those fingers in his hair, but then—deeming the other man too close already, just from this—he retreated with a parting kiss. But not going far. He swallowed Griff as deep as he could, letting him nearly into the back of his throat without gagging this time, building up to a rhythm that had Griff watching the stars wheeling overhead in openmouthed wonder.

Mal lightly squeezed Griff's thigh with his good hand, drawing the leaf-green eyes he loved to watch back to his—and once their stares were locked, Mal managed to tilt his head back enough to take another inch in before he reached a new limit. Once there, he made a few strokes with his tongue that had Griff making the most delicious, delicate whimpers too soft to wake the undead.

When Mal used some of the spit already slicking the way to push a finger inside him too, soon working in a second, Griff whispered on a ragged breath, "I can't decide . . . if this is going to inspire . . . a poem . . . or a song."

Mal hoped all that time spelunking in the back of his throat might inspire a literary masterpiece.

It did, at least, draw a few more words from Griff on the faintest breath. "I'm gonna—Mal—" But then the light in his eyes shifted, a smile tugging at his lips as he asked just as softly, "Can I? Come? I need to come."

"Oh yeah?" It took only a second for Mal to guess the rules of this new game, grinning around his mouthful as he indulgently stroked the insides of Griff's thighs, enjoying the sounds of the soft pleas against his ears and all too willing to slip into the role made for him here. Griff must have to work so hard to always stay in control, watching himself around the bottle, trying his best to be a good worker and neighbor and friend—it must be a relief to leave everything in Mal's capable hands for a change. To let him call the shots the way he loved doing in this space that was just for the two of them.

"How bad?" Mal asked lowly, his voice full of understanding.

"*So* bad, gods, the mouth on you . . ." Griff whispered, running a hand through Mal's hair. "But you're going to have to swallow. So you don't choke." Then, more urgently, "Please, Mal, can I—?"

Mal squeezed Griff's thigh again, signaling his permission. Then Griff did cry out, the tensing of his body giving Mal at least a half second's warning to press that bandaged hand against his mouth and somewhat muffle the sound.

It was Mal's name he gasped as he briefly left his body, and Mal's name he repeated as he seemed to return to himself, using his good arm to draw Mal against his chest and share the warmth that was rolling off their flushed bodies.

He did it so sweetly, if loudly, that Mal decided to overlook the way he had momentarily forgotten the rules of their game.

But they worked out a new way to communicate without another word as Mal pressed his hardness against Griff's thigh, reminding him of what he wanted next: deeper kisses for *more* and *yes, I want you inside me* and lighter kisses for *not yet* or *go slower.*

The vial of oil Griff dug from his pack and held between his teeth like some kind of retriever—cooking oil, because no one had planned on getting any on this trip, but it would do—spoke for itself.

So did Mal's silent laughter as he eyed the glassware and mouthed, "Fancy." Then he slicked up his fingers and worked them into the man before him with deliberate slowness and care, stretching and stroking all the way up to three before Griff deepened their kisses again to signal what he wanted next.

Mal took his time pushing into him even then, struggling to find angles to move where he didn't feel the constant pull on his stitches—but once he was all the way inside Griff, kissing him with each slow rock of his hips deeper into him, he at least forgot the pain for a while, other parts of him burning with a fire more urgent than the one in his side.

When they moved together like this, Mal thought he was finally beginning to understand something about what it meant to be gentle. Gentle was soft kisses to Griff's cheeks, his neck, the corners of his mouth as he felt the clench of Griff all around him; it was sliding their palms together, learning the shapes of the scars there, feeling every contour of their joining and how right each one was.

Gentle was going slow enough to feel the length of Griff's hair sliding between his fingers.

Gentle was tracing a careful path along the scar below Griff's navel for the first time, like he had some right to be here, with this body, with this man. As if fighting so hard to earn Griff's safety somehow erased the stain of planning that attack.

Gentle was listening to every heated breath, drinking them in, and knowing Griff was taking him in with just as much intention.

Gentle was Griff kissing his nose as Mal hit the right spot to send them both tumbling through the stars all over again.

This night did belong to them, Mal decided once again as they lay tangled together and catching their breath on Griff's bedroll, Griff's fingers making a cautious sweep over Mal's stitches by starlight to make sure they had held.

And this time it was Griff who muttered as the sweat began to dry on their skin, "Stay."

Mal's eyes found his, gleaming with alertness, listening.

"Stay right here, with me, tonight." Griff delivered a hushed plea, draping his good arm again around Mal's waist with care to avoid his injured side. "You can sleep here; there's room for two in this bedroll. I want to hold you for as long as I can, just to be sure you're real, that this is all real. And then . . ." He took a breath, licked his lips, and added more softly, "Stop drinking yourself to death, and stay with me for as long as fate allows. You didn't like watching me bleed out—well, that would have at least been a quick death. I don't like watching you die slowly."

Mal stiffened for a moment. Then, rather than turning to rest his back against the hollow of Griff's chest, he rolled onto his good side so that they were face-to-face, his hands rising to cup Griff's cheeks, as available as he'd ever made himself to anyone.

As if he needed to answer further, he brushed his lips over Griff's in a long, deep kiss. *Yes, I want more of this.*

Then he let his head slump against the bedroll while he tangled his fingers comfortably in that dark hair, as if this could keep them anchored to each other even when they later passed into the dream world.

"I meant every word," Griff whispered, and Mal didn't have to search for the book in the dark to know exactly what he meant.

Mal kissed him gently again, and lapsed into a few minutes of thoughtful silence before he whispered to those emerald eyes still alert in the dark, "Listen, the part about a place for us—where do you live now?"

Griff hesitated. "Well, I was living with Liam. Before. But . . . I was planning to rent a room at the Wyvern & Wyrm when we returned. Figured I'd have the coin for it then."

Mal frowned at the slightest reminder of a man who looked a lot like him from certain angles, one whose name he could go the rest of his life without hearing again. He knew about Mayfair's Most Eligible and Griff's reputation. Still, Griff had said he wanted to stay. Maybe there was a chance Mal could finally be enough for him.

Drawing a breath to calm himself again, Mal said, "Why not come home instead? To the cottage, with me. I know it's crowded, but it would just be while you work on building us that castle you wrote about, Mister Foreman."

Griff grinned. "I love it when you call me that."

"Good," Mal breathed over his lips, his tongue darting out to taste Griff again. "Because I'm your client now. And just wait till you hear how I tip." But his teasing tone didn't linger. This was serious, and just like when Griff had been waiting to catch him the second he fell from the troll's grasp, Mal was hoping he could count on him again. "Will you—?"

"Of course I will," Griff said firmly. He smiled, deepening their next kiss. "I'm with you, Mal. I'll come home with you. It's time we made some new memories."

Mal ran a hand along his injured side, barely resisting the urge to scratch a sudden itch. "We can take trips out to the Wood like we used to," he said, trying to distract himself from the sensation. "I was thinking—I could get us a couple new hounds too. We could take Whiskey, even if we have to carry him. Someone will have to show the pups how to flush out the best coneys, and better him than us."

Griff laughed softly, muffling the sound against Mal's shoulder. "I'd like that," he agreed warmly. "Mostly I want to cook you dinner—on any size stove—and be the one you come home to."

Mal could almost see it as he lay there, breathing Griff in: a fresh pie cooling on the windowsill while Griff worked out back by the stream, chopping wood for the evening fire. Mal kicking off his boots carelessly in the entryway at dusk, sweeping off his cloak and exchanging it for the warmth of Griff's arms; eating together in the old armchair with Whiskey dozing at their feet; racing each other through the Wood on a sunlit afternoon until they were as tired as a couple of pups themselves, then sprawling in the meadow grass to read Mal's old book together. The pale light washing over them as they lay on the bedroll was silver, but in his mind it was golden, warm and rich and so real that they might as well have been there.

"I'd like that," he murmured, frowning at a cry from some beast that soared over the treetops. "But I'd like to travel some too. Linden is boring. Or rather, I get bored. Restless, sometimes."

"Where will we go?" Griff asked, his own eyes alight with interest as another beast, then a third, called back in answer to the first from another direction.

Mal tried to focus on the question at hand rather than the natural sounds of night. There was Cardraine, where Rhun was born, a kingdom of knowledge, good wine, and high culture; there were the southlands with their coffee too. The northern gnomish kingdoms, meanwhile, had never been of interest to Mal, as their flowers and cheeses paled in comparison to treasure hunts and lands where the castles had banners that seemed to scrape the sky.

"Anywhere," he said with a small grin. "I want to hunt for treasure where there aren't any mires. Who knows? Maybe we'll stumble onto a castle waiting for a new owner somewhere out there and you won't have to chop quite so much wood after all." His smile grew. "I'd like to travel far to the east and finally see the ocean. Swim with you in the salt water, mess up your hair." He paused, thinking some more. "I'd like to go south and see some of the more remote kingdoms—find out what they like to trade and come back richer than a dwarf. Richer than all the dusty old kings in your library books." His eyes glinted with visions of the precious metals and carved crystal statues he had admired in Mayfair's markets since he was small. "Maybe I could even show you Thrallkeld one day. It's not all just liars and thieves—or it won't be, once Wynnie cuts off Renaud's head for me."

Griff's fingers, which had been running up and down Mal's back, stilled between his shoulder blades. "That's how you asked her to do it? Why now, after all this time?"

"Guts—I guess she's . . . sort of a friend—heard that Renaud murdered my old friend Ella a few months back," he explained, the scar over his chest aching dully. "So I asked Wynnie to take care of him before everyone who ever helped me down there is dead."

Griff's eyes narrowed over the grisly scar on Mal's chest, the way the skin puckered and had never healed right, as he said, "Bet Wynnie will have a field day with that one."

"That's the idea," Mal murmured darkly. "As for cutting off his head, I thought we could have a party with it, with cake and confetti. Guess then old Leo will have some company . . ." Despite his burning desire for revenge, he yawned, finally spent. Ready to drift down into a deep sleep in Griff's arms, into a world where there were no mysterious shadows and no locksmiths who looked a little like him in the right light. One where Griff stayed long enough for Mal to show him how he felt by laying the promise of safety at his feet that only treasure could buy.

Instead, he sat bolt upright as his tattoo burned stronger than what he had grown used to out here, flames licking up his arm, the pain intense enough to dampen the discomfort in his side.

Another creature barked a question to the night—not a coyote; this came from a bigger, deeper chest—and when four or five more yowls answered, sounding much closer this time, Griff shot up beside him and reached for his maul.

Grabbing his knife, Mal turned to warn Alys and found that she was already awake, clutching Leo protectively to her chest and readying her sword.

"Wargs," she mouthed, her face in the starlight just as feral as their yelps and snarls as their hulking shadows appeared all around the edges of the camp.

Chapter Twenty-Six

Heat

The pack of six shambling wargs crossed Mal's protective symbol without hesitation and stalked into the boundaries of the camp with all the confidence of the born hunters they were. Which was impressive, seeing as they were merely the undead, rotting corpses of hunters, the stench rolling off them worse than Leo the Head after a day spent basking in the sun.

The ward must only work on actual spirits, then.

The wargs' presence was a message much louder and clearer than the shadow's: Mal was too far behind on the path to the treasure, and the Shadow Queen's patience was wearing thin.

He was grateful that the creatures' matted chunks of fur, their deep, exposed rib cages and stumpy tails, their gnashing yellowed teeth and flea-bitten pointed ears, didn't remind him of any dog he had ever known or loved. They were bigger than wolves, and smarter. Meaner.

It meant he wouldn't feel a shred of remorse about chopping off their heads and returning them to their graves.

Mal, Griff, and Alys all managed to get to their feet before the wargs advanced enough to show the broken-off stumps of their fangs, huge paws missing the occasional claw, the threads of sinew just holding a leg or neck together. Despite their advanced decay, their luminous eyes showed plenty of understanding and intention as they slowly shrank the ring they had made around the three humans, whose weapons didn't seem to trouble them in the slightest.

"Look, we're on our way. We're leaving right the fuck now to get this treasure, if you'll just let us through," Mal said through clenched teeth to the biggest of the wargs, a beast whose black pelt was flecked with white like fallen snow. "Won't stop till we've rowed across the lake and back with every last bit of shiny."

He didn't care that Griff might wonder why the hell he was trying to bargain with reanimated wargs. Getting them out of this was more important than worrying about what questions he might have to face later. He needed to make sure there *was* a later, and he wasn't sure they could hack their way through six of these beasts before the wargs devoured them.

Snarling, tails swishing, they continued their slow advance, apparently unimpressed with Mal's assurances.

Rather than reaching for the spirit blade, which was decidedly less useful against solid flesh in its current shattered state, he drew two knives. Now unable to scratch the relentless itch in his side, he could only hope his stitches would hold when these things pounced.

The wargs crept forward as one, slowly, taking their time in tightening the noose.

He hated that he couldn't see them all at once. He took a step back, trying to get a better look at what was happening around him, and was met with the solid warmth of Griff's and Alys's backs against his. For a moment, he could fully breathe.

Then the wargs sprang at them, Griff swinging his maul at the biggest of the bunch while a smaller, faster beast took both Mal's knives into its rib cage and still managed to pin him near his bedroll. Yet Mal grinned up at it through streaming eyes despite the claws cutting into his shoulders, because fighting dirty was his favorite.

"Your dreadful lady is gonna be pissed that you didn't just let us get on with it," Mal growled as he spat in the warg's eyes and pulled one of his knives free of the desiccated flesh.

As he tangled with the beast, other snarls and yelps and panted breaths filled the camp, but he didn't feel the need to take his eyes from his own fight for once.

Because between every heft of his lover's maul, every leap Griff made away from snapping jaws, and every kick of his boots into a brittle body, Griff called out to him, "Close one!" or "Hit it that time!" or "On your left!"

Mal was almost enjoying fighting like this, he realized as he sawed into the lean warg's neck with savage pleasure. Or at least, it was easier. Having two partners who could hold their own. Whom he could count on.

He hummed a little as he wiped thick ropes of the unmoving warg's drool from his cheek with his tattooed arm, but his expression changed as soon as he saw what Griff was doing with the biggest warg he still hadn't managed to put down.

He was feeding it, that beautiful idiot. Tossing whatever scraps he could reach from the pack slung over his good shoulder—strips of jerky, an extra boot, a leftover, crusty old cinnamon bun—as if he might charm the beast with his undeniably good cooking while he slowly edged toward Alys, who needed more help than Mal did right now.

One of the other wargs had already been reduced to a headless corpse, a pile of mottled gray fur gently stirring in the night wind, but there were still three on Alys near the fire, and she didn't seem to know where to aim her blade. Being drunk surely wasn't helping.

Mal clocked the distance, the breeze, and threw his knife, which flashed in the embers before burying itself into the thick ruff of fur on the neck of one of the three. The struck beast whirled around to confront him, snarling, just as Griff cried out in a way that wasn't meant to convey anything more than pain.

The big warg had gotten tired of the snacks and now had its jaws clamped around Griff's injured leg. His maul was several yards away, out of reach, as if he'd dropped it when the creature knocked him down. There was a gaping flap of skin in its underbelly, but of course that wasn't enough to stop it cold.

By the fire, Alys screamed too, and Mal didn't know where to look now that there was a pissed-off warg growling in his face and Griff was going to lose that fucking leg if he didn't do something to help.

He wasn't enjoying anything about this fight anymore.

With both his friends' shouts ringing in his ears, louder than the sounds of the undead, Mal only had a second to decide.

He made a gesture in the air to Alys as he lunged onto the broad back of the beast trying to make a meal of Griff, ignoring the pull of his stitches.

The warg with the knife in its back bounded after him, its teeth closing on his pant leg and shredding it as Mal crawled up the larger beast's body and settled between its hunched shoulders like he meant to ride it. "Okay down there?" he shouted to Griff over the creature's incensed cries as the foreman used his other leg to kick it in the face.

Griff actually managed a pained smile. "Now that you're here, I will be."

Mal was no stranger to dirty work, but gouging out the eyes of the giant warg until it stopped trying to chew off Griff's leg was one of the filthiest endeavors he had ever attempted. As Griff freed himself and started crawling over to grab his maul, Mal tore through the big warg's fur and rotting flesh with his bare hands, hoping to sever its brain stem as violently as possible. Extra punishment for trying to stain the ground with any more of Griff's blood.

But Griff wasn't badly hurt, Mal realized with a flood of relief as his fingers squished into something pulpy and the creature beneath him slumped forward, unseating him. His beautiful idiot was back on his feet, if a little unsteady, limping toward Alys.

The two wargs who had cornered her by the fire were both rolling in the damp grass while their pelts smoked and sizzled. She had seen Mal's frantic gesture and she had understood, lighting them up with blows from fiery kindling instead of her sword.

Griff chopped off their heads with what seemed to be a bit of unnecessary—but certainly understandable—force while Mal dusted himself off and glanced frantically around for the last warg standing, the one who had his knife in its neck. The one who had been following him when he tackled the largest beast, whom he had more or less forgotten about in his haste to help Griff.

It was gone.

No, not gone—it was somewhere nearby, sheltering in the trees, sending up a call to more of its companions who hadn't come with the first hunting party.

Several distant howls answered, and Mal could just imagine them splashing through muddy water as they bounded toward the camp.

"What now?" Alys asked breathlessly, bringing a few sooty fingertips to her sweaty temple like she had the beginnings of a terrible hangover already.

And although it went against everything he had ever been taught, Mal supposed there was a first time for everything as he bolted toward his friends, grabbing what supplies he could on the way and turning his back on the next fight. "Now we run."

They didn't so much as stop for a bathroom break all night, spurred on by the occasional call and answer somewhere at their backs. They didn't dare speak, though Griff took Mal's hand a few times and squeezed it with the reassurance that he wasn't dead yet, that he was coming home to the old cottage with him, even if he was limping worse than ever. Even Alys wasn't unscathed this time, her shirt tattered and bloody and a deep gouge under her eye that would need more of Griff's stitching when they finally stopped. If they dared stop again.

From either side of the path, green-eyed ghosts blinked at Mal and held up their filmy fingers to count the remaining days. Once they needed only one hand to do so, it would be too late, because those four weeks included bringing the treasure to the shop.

When he was sure Griff was looking elsewhere, Mal flipped a single finger at them.

"Hey, Prancer's back," Griff said suddenly, pointing at a shape standing very still in the bracken as if hoping to avoid notice.

"Fucking finally," Mal muttered, reluctantly accepting Leo the Head's pike as Alys raced ahead to grab the pack beast's dangling lead. The mule didn't try to skitter away from her despite her overenthusiastic approach, and Mal suspected it might even be glad to see them over the roaming wargs.

Sure enough, when Alys led Prancer over, he nuzzled Mal's pockets in search of treats. "Fresh out," he whispered apologetically. "Griff gave them all to the wargs."

But the mule, not understanding or perhaps hungry for a taste of whatever was on Mal's face—reanimated warg flesh, no doubt—raised its shaggy head, still sniffing, and whuffed a hot breath against Mal's cheek before nuzzling him right on the mouth.

"How about that," Alys laughed groggily as Mal jerked away, cursing under his breath. "Seems like everything that's ever been called Griff has a taste for you."

The claw marks in Mal's shoulders were still oozing by the time the sun was shining warmly through the trees and gnats were whining in his ear again. At least now the busy hum of bugs was accompanied by the sweet sound of saddlebags jingling with coins that belonged to no one but the three of them, and there were no more hunting howls.

"Mal," Alys groaned, shielding her eyes from the glare of the sun. "You make drinking look fun, but it really isn't. My head . . ."

"Here," Mal said, fishing a silver coin out of one of the mule's bags as it dutifully plodded along with Griff as its rider again. He studied it for a moment before handing it to Alys; he had never seen a star just like this stamped on another coin in all his trading ventures. "This will make you feel better. Money. Always cures what ails."

But that wasn't entirely true, because as a mild breeze moved the trees and they ventured into the shade, Mal couldn't stop shivering. That was odd, almost like he was coming down with a touch of something more than Alys's terrible hangover.

Griff reached into his pack and handed something down to Mal—a shirt, black. One of his own. "I like seeing you in my clothes," he admitted with a grin. Then he consulted the map, which was crumbling worse than ever after surviving the night. "Looks like we're only about a day's march or so from the lake and getting this treasure so we can get the hell out of here. My shoulder can make the journey if you're up to it. Crossing water with undead wargs on our trail and no boat sounds like just the kind of time I was promised out here anyway."

Mal groaned and shut his eyes briefly. Nothing about that sounded appealing in the slightest, even to him. He still had to fight not to see Griff covered in blood every time he closed his eyes, and now he was going to have to get him across a lake with his busted shoulder and leg. But they had made it this far without the shadow killing them, or them killing each other—they were so close to ending all this and walking out of here peacefully, weighed down with the means to secure their future.

Maybe Griff would even be willing to keep watch while he and Alys sailed out to the island and emptied the barrows, plucked crowns from the heads of long-dead kings, gathered swords and breastplates and mail coats from coffins. And, of course, those healing vambraces for Griff. That beautiful disaster didn't know the first thing about dirty work—his idea of risk-taking seemed to be staying at the library past closing hours—and he didn't need to start now.

After all, Griff came from a world of elven parties with porcelain bowls and the rules of Polite Society. He knew nothing of sheltering in cold stone and hewing muscle from bone, the feeling of his own heartbeat flickering out, and Mal would keep it that way once they got back to Mayfair too. He'd buy him a shiny horse and do all the dirty work so he could come home to that carefree laugh and those exuberant hugs just in time to watch Griff chop the wood for the evening fire. And he'd keep him well away from that locksmith who looked a little too much like him and clearly also had a taste for the finer things.

He wouldn't have felt remorse in the slightest for fucking someone else's boyfriend, but Griff was *his* now. Griff had chosen him, and he was more than just a boyfriend to Mal. He definitely wasn't Mayfair's Most Eligible anymore either.

While they marched and rode on, pushing aside branches and sloshing through filthy water to blaze their trail, Griff took the broken elf sword and used its cloth wrappings to try to fashion a hilt on one end that wouldn't cut anyone's hands the next time one of them needed to wield it. Though, thankfully, Mal hadn't seen the shadow since he'd charged at it with the broken blade.

"You really think that thing can cut a spirit?" he asked Griff. It was hard to even imagine what that might look like.

"Honestly . . . I'd rather not find out," Griff answered grimly. "I don't like that our best defense against something I can't see is a blade I *think* I remember reading about, but . . . we'll be out of here in no time, right?"

"That's the plan," Mal agreed, because it felt good to speak the truth, just before a light cough rattled in his chest.

Somewhere out of sight, a raven cawed lowly to one of its companions.

From astride the mule, Griff watched him with a little line of worry between his brows, toying with the ends of Mal's black scarf around his neck as if he meant to take it off and return it to its owner.

"You should keep it," Mal suggested, coughing lightly one more time to clear whatever it was from his lungs. "Looks better on you anyway."

Griff's smile was better than another trophy on his shelves.

"You two give me some kind of hope," Alys said, hanging back with them a moment to grab another silver from Prancer's saddlebag. She wedged the two coins into Leo's eyes to cover up his deadened stare, forever frozen in the state of half decay he'd been raised from the grave in, then surveyed her handiwork with a satisfied grin.

Even Mal could admit it was an improvement.

As the day wore on, the map led them to a place where the shadows grew longer and colder and the plants more colorful—and more likely to make them sick, if Alys got any notions about picking berries—as a greater quiet settled over the Mire. The chill made Mal shiver again. He even missed the birdsong and hearing Griff whistle back, though he really could have done without the rustling of wings as ravens flitted from branch to branch.

As he reached into his cloak for a drink, his eyes met Griff's, and he noted a wince in the other man's gaze. But Griff's brows swiftly rose in surprise as Mal pulled out a regular canteen instead of his usual flask.

"Leftovers of that tea you made yesterday," Mal told him with a little smile, the most he could muster when he still couldn't shake off this chill. "Guess I'm in the mood for something different."

Griff reached out with his working arm and took Mal's hand. "Proud of you," he said softly, pulling Mal right back to page ten.

Mal held on to that, just like he held Griff's hand until they broke for a bite of their remaining rations and to water the thirsty mule at a trickle that was too pitiful to be called a stream, but far more appealing and trustworthy than any of the stagnant green puddles they had passed so far today.

"Alys, I've got something for you," Mal called, holding out the canteen to her and accepting Prancer's lead for a while instead. He folded up the map, certain of their course until they reached the lake. "This tea might help your headache—better than anything the elves could have brewed, I bet."

The elven salve had to be the reason his side was so achy and hot, the reason the rest of him was cold by comparison. He never should have let Alys put that stuff on him or Griff. It likely wasn't going to kill them, but it didn't feel great either.

"What have you got against elves, anyway?" Alys asked curiously, still sounding a little hoarse from last night.

Griff grinned around a mouthful of jerky but quickly glanced at Prancer, like he didn't want Mal to notice how interested he was in the answer.

"They destroy lives and ruin friendships. They weren't letting Griff send letters to me," Mal said bluntly. "And if they were okay leaving me to die without my best friend, I don't really care what happens to them either. I'd say that's plenty fair."

Alys considered this as she took a sip of tea, then nodded. It relieved his shivers—at least for a moment—to know he had someone who was, rightly or wrongly, always on his side.

"I'd like you to consider meeting Rosemaris sometime, though, now that we're together," Griff told him, not quite meeting his eyes. "Maybe, if I write to her—and apologize profusely to her father for being the reason she snuck out of Stormveil in the first place—they might allow us to pay her a visit up there someday."

"She's their special princess, right?" Mal asked flatly, making his disinterest clearer.

But Griff smiled gently all the same, like the mere thought of her made him happy. "That's right. She saved me from drowning once," he explained. "Back when I didn't have very much hope for my future anymore, or any love to spare for myself."

Mal glanced pointedly at Griff's bloody, bandaged ankle, then up to his wounded shoulder. "Seems like that's still in short supply," he pointed out. But as they started walking again, Prancer trudging along with Griff on his back, Mal relented—because he wanted to make Griff happy, to be better than any locksmith named Liam, to make up for the stabbing he still couldn't bring himself to talk about. "I guess we could try it, though. Visiting the princess, if they'll even let the likes of me come there with you."

Griff nodded, seeming to consider the matter settled.

But Mal wasn't quite as ready to let go of the subject. A few minutes later, he added with a sideways glance, "What makes you so sure she's going to like me?"

At that, Griff flashed a smile that made Mal warm all over—at least for a moment, before the next shiver. "She loves what makes me happy."

Mal's answering look was far less carefree as he considered what this mysterious princess had done for Griff. How she had been around to save him when Mal hadn't, because it seemed Griff needed a lot of saving. "How many times did you do it?" he asked softly. "Try to drown when you were in Stormveil?"

The shadows were growing deeper still, like night at midday, and Alys fell into step with Mal, sticking closer to both her companions. She might have been ready to fight the shadow while bolstered by whiskey, but today she seemed chastened, just as haunted as any of them and less sure she had Wynnie's luck at surviving every battle.

"Just the once," Griff told him plainly, the passing of time seeming to have softened the difficult memories. "She jumped in with me. She helped me realize I wouldn't be showing you, or anyone else, the depth of my love and regret by leaving that way. After that, I wanted better for myself—and I suppose I became a bit of a project for Rosemaris. She got me involved in everything—sword practice, cooking, playing music, dancing; I think she was trying to show me there was so much I hadn't tried or learned yet."

"So what did she say to you?" Mal asked, his fingers tightening around Griff's. "That day. What was it that changed your mind?"

He hoped it was knowledge he would never need, but much like the broken blade they carried, he'd rather have it and not need it than try to go without.

Griff halted the mule's steps for a moment, his eyes on Mal's. "She told me I was going to miss the best parts of the story if I let it end there. She knew how much I love a good book." Nudging Prancer to resume the walk, he added lightly, "She said I shouldn't decide all was lost before I'd even found myself. And she was right, of course."

"I never needed help with not drowning, myself," Mal declared. "I've always known how to swim. Enough to help others stay afloat too." He took Griff's hand, drawing him closer and determined to keep him there.

Eventually, too exhausted to take another step after so much missed sleep, Mal realized they would have to make camp and call it a night, resigning himself to being stared at by more nagging ghosts while he slept. Only he hadn't seen any for an hour or so now, which was strange.

He supposed he should take the small victory. Tomorrow the lake should be within their sights as soon as they cleared the next stand of trees—already he could smell a hint of brine on the breeze—and then the ghosts and ravens could all fuck off back to his bosses and tell them he had done it with time to spare. Just like he had boasted he would.

Griff tethered Prancer while Alys picked a spot to stake Leo's head for the night.

Mal was supposed to be laying out their bedrolls; he planned to put his own right next to Griff's, to give them a bigger space to hold each other when they rested, but instead he wrapped one of the flat beds around his shoulders like an extra-thick cloak.

And as Griff stepped back from the mule, Mal saw it: an extra shadow, little more than a flicker at the corner of his eye as it darted behind the tree where the mule was tethered. Its real face was already burned into his memory.

He wasn't surprised that the broken blade hadn't scared it off for good, though he had dared to hope it might stay away a little longer.

"Alys," he called, reaching for a stick and starting to scratch Vic's ward into the ground again. He didn't know how much ground the symbol could protect at once, but Vic had used it on the cottage before to at least temporarily get rid of their ghost who kept coming back. If it could force the shadow to stay at the edge of their camp rather than slinking up behind any of them, maybe they could still get the sleep they badly needed.

He shivered again as Alys joined him, looking curiously at the lines and swirls in the dirt. "I think this kept us safe last night, or safe enough, so I want you to know how to draw it. Just in case there's some point soon where I can't."

Griff must have been listening in, as he stopped portioning out their dinner rations and followed Alys, kneeling beside Mal and pressing a hand to his forehead. It came away slick with Mal's sweat. "Pull up your shirt for me," he instructed, slipping into his role as healer for a change. "I need to look at your stitches."

"I feel fine," Mal insisted, but he did as he had been asked, lying sideways on Griff's bedroll so that Griff would have access to his stitched-up side. "I mean—mostly. I've been cold all day. And my side feels like I got hit with a flamethrower, but I thought that was just what wyvern scratches were like. That was my first time getting my ass kicked by one."

Griff nodded absently at this self-assessment as he inspected the wounds, Alys watching anxiously over his shoulder. "There's a spot here that's oozing fluid. Don't worry, I'm not going to touch it yet, but it's definitely infected."

And they were all out of the medicine that could have spared them any worry, all because Alys had drugged their mule without considering the consequences.

He knew she hadn't meant for something like this to happen, and couldn't have known that it would. Still, he understood the guilt shimmering in her gaze again as she hastily excused herself from his bedside, her hand pressed to her lips and her eyes damp.

Griff put a hand on his back for a moment as he explained, "I'm going to have to open up the stitches for a better look." And though he looked like the suggestion pained him, he gritted out, "You may want a sip from your flask before we get started."

Mal hardly made a sound as Griff worked, though he panted plenty, growing sweatier even as the air around them cooled.

The tenderness of his side had deepened over the past several days thanks to bits of dirt he must have pushed into the muscle when he'd picked at the wound before splashing whiskey in it. The infection would probably be hard for Griff to reach with only a salve.

Their resident healer was just opening up his kit to find the right tools when Mal laid a hand on his arm. "I'm going to stay," he muttered softly, too-bright eyes holding Griff's. "Trust me. I'll show you how it's done."

He would do it better than any locksmith too. Be more for Griff, do more, love him more, provide a safer home. He would be enough.

"I didn't think there was any question of that," Griff murmured, but the way his gaze swiftly fell suggested he feared otherwise.

Mal's head fell against Griff's shoulder, in need of someplace to lean just to stay partially upright. "I liked that letter you wrote me," he whispered, lacking the energy to speak louder anymore. "I was wrong when I told you I didn't need any new ones. I like when you say pretty words, even if I don't always say the right thing back. Words are hard for me, but—even being cursed doesn't feel so unbearable when you're around."

With that, he vomited all down Griff's back until there was nothing but bile coming up, then lapsed into a fitful fever sleep to the sounds of Alys sobbing.

Chapter Twenty-Seven

Funeral or Feast

They tended Mal tirelessly as they waited for the fever to break. Of course, Griff couldn't let himself look at Mal for too long, pale and sweating on that bedroll, or he knew he would break down himself. Couldn't let his hands or his mind idle, because they would lead him down the kinds of dark trails he knew he shouldn't wander.

Mal might not have known it, and surely would have argued to the contrary, but he was the light that made Griff want to be better, to be strong enough to fight to protect it and wise enough to know when to put his sword down and simply bask in its glow. There was so much good in the world, and all Griff had to do was look at Mal's willingness to challenge the dark to be reminded of why he'd wanted to be a hero in the first place.

Griff had never known anyone so beautiful. So confident, so defiant, so absurd, so determined to write his own rules for the world.

That was his man.

But he couldn't fight this battle for Mal, no matter how much he wanted to—not without the medicine he no longer had. He'd done what he could, cleaned and dressed the wound again and cradled Mal's burning head in his lap until he was so tired that he accidentally drifted off for a minute, but the rest was up to Mal. All he could do now was wait with him.

Mal would wake up, or he wouldn't.

Mal would stay, or he wouldn't.

Mal would finally agree to go home before they lost their lives over some stupid treasure, no matter what kind of artifacts it might hold, or they would have a serious problem.

Griff's hands were capable of so much. He could build a whole bakery or a home, but he couldn't pull a soul back from death, not in whatever way Mal's witch friend had done years ago.

Alys, who was plenty aware of why they didn't have the right medicine to offer Mal without Griff saying a word, seemed to need a purpose as much as he did. He tasked her with fetching water from the nearest clear-running stream while he used some of the herbs he'd found near the wyvern's lair to make a tea that could reduce fever. It was weak, but it was all they had.

She hauled buckets and rags to Mal's bedside and held the cool cloths against his forehead and neck, muttering things like, "If you die on us now, Griff and I will join the Wardens just so your ghost will be mad enough to come haunt us forever, and then the three of us will be together anyway, like I wanted."

Griff couldn't stand to listen to her any more than he could Mal's feverish mutterings and heart-wrenching whimpers, so he organized their camp despite having only one working arm, the other still in a sling and probably in need of rebinding. He kept a small fire burning despite Mal's earlier warning, counted bandages and rations and did several loads of laundry, hanging each piece to dry while singing tavern songs that had nothing to do with elves, something he thought might welcome Mal back to the world a little more pleasantly.

At one point in Mal's feverish babbling, as he writhed on his bedroll, he asked for a turtle. Alys went back to the stream where she'd gotten the water for Mal's rags and trapped one in their largest cookpot, placing it near Mal's head, as if this would be an incentive to shake off the fever and fully wake.

"Stay," Griff pleaded, his lips to Mal's ear, and he felt himself cracking open when Mal didn't so much as stir. "Stay, and take me home to the old cottage."

He strung a tarp he'd found at the bottom of his pack to make a shelter from wind and bugs.

He took inventory of each of their packs and recounted the silver in the mule's saddlebags.

He borrowed Alys's charcoals and made a blueprint he knew might well go up in smoke, or otherwise never materialize.

He cleaned and polished the mule's tack.

He stitched the cut on Alys's cheek carefully and gently.

He kept swimming, because he had learned how to stay afloat somewhere along the way, with Mal's hot fingers wound tightly around his.

Yet it struck him that Alys was the one who needed help treading water right now, as she started trying to drown herself with the rest of the whiskey bottle.

"Griff—if he doesn't wake up," she slurred miserably as she mopped Mal's forehead with one of many cool cloths they kept rotating through. She dribbled a little water into the turtle's cookpot, too, and offered it some grass clippings. "If he doesn't—what then?"

Griff came over to sit by her even though he didn't want to answer. He didn't want to think about that at all. Overhead, more ravens had gathered. So many rustling wings and the scraping of beaks between throaty conversations whispered through the trees above them. Beady eyes swiveled down, as if watching Mal's every shallow breath.

They seemed to be preparing for a funeral, perhaps—or a feast.

Overwhelmed by a sudden disgust for the creatures he knew Mal loathed, creatures that served the darkness his parents had fought against all their lives, Griff hurled a rock up into the trees and sent them wheeling skyward as they cried out at the indignity of it all. He threw another, and another, not stopping until every one of those dark shapes had scattered across the sky and they were little more than blurry blobs to his streaming eyes.

"If," he said, finally ready to try to answer Alys. "If . . . then I'll still move back to the cottage. Help you raise those kids of yours. You won't be alone, Alys. He wouldn't want that, and neither do I. You handle too much by yourself already, and that's not how it's supposed to be, no matter what lessons you took to heart."

She nodded tearfully, seeming not to trust herself to speak. She, too, was watching the birds. Already a few were returning to roost overhead, to continue their vigil at Mal's sickbed. Griff picked up a sharper, bigger rock, then set it down again, some of that disgust turning on himself when he knew better ways to fight than lashing out and there was still some blackened gore drying on the business edge of his maul.

"You made a mistake with the mule," he continued into the quiet, "but I've made too many of those to judge, and you couldn't have known we'd lose that medicine." He took her under his good arm and drew her close. "You were there for me when it mattered, even though I'd done nothing to deserve it, just like I'm going to be there for you."

"But that's just it—I should have known better," Alys whispered in the smallest voice. "Only, I was already high when I gave Prancer those mushrooms. And the buzz didn't even feel that good. There are so many things I think will feel good, be enough, but they never are. I wish I could take back what I did, never have packed them in the first place, anything so Mal would be awake and talking to us right now. I never mean to hurt him, or you, but it seems like that's all I'm good at anymore."

"I know plenty about that. Trust me," Griff muttered, his heart aching for them both.

Alys tore her gaze from the birds, her blue eyes glistening as she held Griff's instead. "I don't even know what I'm doing anymore, if I ever did," she confessed. "I hoped the Mire might help me figure it out, show me some other side of myself—but I don't like most of what I've seen, and I have no idea what to do about that."

He could only pull her closer and sit with her until the tears stopped. And the day after, helping her to tread water as they kept vigil along with the ravens, debating names for their new turtle rather than planning any funerals. Even if the shadow might be breathing down their necks all the while, with them unaware.

Chapter Twenty-Eight

Betrayal

The sight that greeted Mal when he finally stirred to consciousness was Alys and Griff huddled together by a fire under a pale-blue twilight. It was evening, the first stars just appearing, and he was parched like never before, a thirst he hadn't known even in Thrallkeld while he was in hiding.

There was a dull ache in his side, and he briefly considered chasing that dark oblivion again to escape it. But then he smelled something other than tea or broth on the wind—had Griff managed to make biscuits from their remaining rations?—and his stomach gave a growl that signaled he wouldn't be able to sleep again until he'd satisfied it.

Leaning up onto one elbow, he noticed that someone had left a mug of tea near his head. As he took a long drink, he stared down at a large spotted turtle in a cookpot prison and wondered just what Griff had been cooking to try to soothe his nerves while Mal was drifting between worlds.

"How long was I out?" he asked the others, drawing their weary gazes to him.

Alys answered first. Or at least, he could see that she was answering, though he didn't hear a word of it. By watching her lips and the distress on her face as she made her way over to his sweat-crusted bedroll, he could guess at some of the words, but they were muffled. Almost like his head was underwater.

Three days. He had been out for three precious, wasted days. The wards they had drawn must have been holding, or else surely the Shadow Queen's servants would have tried to drag his friends off to teach him a lesson. They must have been keeping the shadow at bay too.

Alys peeked into his mug, which was empty, and he supposed she was going to get him something to drink. Though if she said anything to that effect, it was just a low current rushing past his ear.

Hc shook his head, then glanced over at Griff, rubbing one of his ears with a growing line of concern cutting his brow.

"What did she say?" he asked. Even his own voice sounded far away, somehow muted, full of more buzzing than actual words. But he didn't even give Griff a chance to answer before he added, "Are you going to come here?"

Griff stared at him, drawn and pale, and didn't move.

"I won't tell anyone if you cry. I won't even complain about it," Mal offered lowly, and suddenly Griff's arms were around him, carefully holding him around the spot where his wound was restitched and finally healing while Griff sobbed rather quietly into his already hopelessly messy hair.

When the tears finally slowed, Griff repeated what Alys had said.

Mal couldn't hear him any better. He rubbed his ear some more. "You sound like you're underwater," he explained, growing increasingly annoyed. "I can hear you, but it's faint. Hell, I can hardly hear myself."

Griff frowned. "How about now?" he asked, clearly having raised his voice. It startled a few ravens from the surrounding trees.

Mal watched the little black shapes take flight but couldn't hear the rustle of their wings.

"That's better," he admitted, though it wasn't at all reassuring. "What's wrong with me?"

Griff scrubbed a hand over his face, looking pained, and Mal knew he wasn't going to like whatever he was about to learn. "You nearly died, Mal. That fever was cooking your brains, and none of the usual herbs I brought or found were enough to help you fight it." He touched his own ear and spoke slowly, giving Mal time to read his lips. "You must have lost some of your hearing to the fever—it was that bad."

Confident he had understood more than half of this, Mal nodded. "So how long until it comes back?" he asked. Leaning closer still, he added, "I did what I said I would in the end, didn't I? I stayed. I'm still with you."

Griff slid an arm around his waist in answer as Alys approached with tea and biscuits.

"Your hearing very likely isn't going to come back. That's not how cochlear damage works," he explained sadly, raising the hand of his uninjured arm and shaping signs near his mouth as he spoke. Sign language, Mal recalled, something they had learned together when they were younger so they could have private conversations in front of Wynnie and Vic. Griff had apparently kept up with it, and Mal still remembered enough that it made following the words easier.

"We're lucky we got as much of you back as we did," Griff added, eyes glistening again.

Mal kissed his cheek. "Thank you for looking after me," he said to them both, adding the appropriate signs with one of his hands. When Griff smiled in answer, he could almost trick himself into thinking they were simply using a secret language for old times' sake.

"Do you feel up to eating?" Griff asked, but the words were difficult to hear again. This time thanks to Alys's singing.

"Isn't that the chantey Rodric brought home from school a couple weeks ago?" Mal turned to her with a tired but appreciative grin. "The kind of sad one, with the mermaids and all the dirty words? Did he teach it to you too?"

Alys frowned around a biscuit. Her lips weren't moving, but the song continued. After a moment, she said loudly, "I'm not singing, Mal. I haven't really felt like it lately, for reasons I'm sure you already know."

Mal rubbed his ear again, and as the others watched silently, expectantly, he listened. While the voices of his friends were difficult to grasp, floating above his head like he was at the bottom of a pond and they were back on shore, whatever was singing sounded high and clear as the day. He didn't have to strain to hear the words, though he realized now that while the melody might be like the one Rodric loved, it wasn't in a language Mal knew.

It was older.

Old enough not to be dwarvish, even, or anything currently spoken, which meant the singer was also very dead.

"Great," Mal sighed. Here was more proof he was cursed; nothing ever went his way. "It wasn't enough that I could see the ghosts before. I must have been really close to death, because now I can hear them too. The gods sure have a sick sense of humor."

Griff put a hand on his shoulder while Alys reached for the broken blade, its new cloth-wrapped hilt making it easier to grab. "What do you hear?" he asked grimly.

"It's . . . something ancient, a song in another language, and it makes me feel cold all over. Colder than I felt when I was coming down with the fever, even," Mal explained as the singer went on, scanning the tree line until at last something flitted in and out of his view at the corner of his right eye.

The shadow. The gaunt, nearly skeletal spirit with blackened teeth and empty eyes that didn't like to be seen.

Griff squeezed his shoulder, drawing his attention again. "That's a wraith, Mal," he said urgently. "It has to be. Wraiths are some of the dark queen's oldest and most powerful servants. They sing songs that freeze the blood of those who can hear them. Usually, wraiths guard something in their afterlife—gold, a grave, a place—and when someone gets too near one without realizing . . . well, let's just say people don't see wraiths and live to tell about it when they get back to their cottages to finally rest their bum legs and shoulders."

"I have, though. I've seen more ghosts out here than I can count," Mal said. And what was one type of ghost versus another? "And I'm doing just fine, as you can see."

"Are you? Are we?" Griff countered, his eyes glistening with worry. "From what I remember, wraiths are most powerful near their bones. This one is probably buried with Rhun's treasure, or near it, since it followed us all the way here. Once we leave the safety of our warded camp and get closer to its resting place, it'll kill us for trying to steal from it, and no one will be cured of any pain or any the richer. Maybe that's why Rhun brought the spirit blade out here—he and his friends knew what they would be up against. And they still failed."

Of course the Shadow Queen would have a wraith out here to prevent a bunch of old Wardens from getting the valuables she wanted. What didn't make sense was why such a powerful spirit seemed to be trying to kill them when they were technically on the same team for now—unless Kage and Her Dreadful Majesty had set him up to fail from the start, knowing this thing would be the death of him. Maybe this was their sick way of entertaining themselves.

Another betrayal. Now it *was* making a certain sense. There was always betrayal, as sure and constant as the sunrise.

But then he thought again of the wraith's hollow eyes. Pits like voids, no glowing green light like what always shone from the gaze of any spirit under the queen's command. Which meant this wraith had broken free of her enchantment. It was—like Wynnie and Vic, like him and Alys and Griff—on its own side now. Capable of acting on its own whims, which currently seemed to include trying to kill them.

No wonder there weren't any green-eyed ghosts at the borders of their camp, silently counting down the days that were rapidly slipping through his fingers. They were probably just as afraid of the rogue wraith as he was, making themselves scarce while it was around so that they didn't end up injured by the more powerful spirit that was now in business for itself.

It seemed the Shadow Queen was the one who had been betrayed this time.

Before he could voice any of this out loud, Alys said suddenly within the bounds of his awareness, "I dreamed about Papa last night." Her voice was heavy as she met his searching gaze. "His last moments." Her eyes shifted to roam over Griff's face as she spoke, following the curve of his cheek, the angle of his jaw. "I was going to tell you sooner, but—I wanted to tell you together, if I could. You look so much like your father sometimes, Griff. Like Uncle Seimon," she continued softly. "Not just like him of course, but—like a Warden. The way you carry yourself. The wraith must see it too. Maybe that makes it angry."

"Speak up," Griff urged her, signing for Mal's benefit all the while. "Louder, for Mal."

"It was like when I dreamed about what happened to you in the Wood, Griff," Alys continued, louder. "It felt that real; I felt a burning—here." She touched a shaking hand to her throat, sliding her flattened palm down to the center of her chest. "The wraith must have drowned him. It tricked him. While his friends were sleeping, it made him see . . . me. Or what he thought was me, slipping into the lake, and he dove in after me and never came up. When he realized what was happening, an invisible hand held him down, and . . ." She shook her head, pausing to steady herself. "You both know how he was. It was probably easy to confuse him, since he didn't know real from his daydreams most of the time. But . . . that's not going to happen to us, is it? That's not what we signed up for."

Now she turned her gaze back to Mal, her eyes fully present and damp.

"Nope. No way," Mal said hotly. He filled them both in on what he had just realized about the wraith and its allegiance—or lack thereof—though only Alys would truly understand the significance. Then he raised his voice over the eerie singing, making sure every spirit and raven hiding out in the dusk could damn well hear him. "That wraith can try all it likes to get rid of us, but we have the spirit blade and we aren't afraid to use it, so we're going to succeed no matter what anyone else wants. We're going to show everyone what we're capable of, even if they're all fucking betting against us. We'll grab the treasure at dawn, and then we're out of here."

"Of course. You're right," Alys said, forever on his side.

But she and Griff both looked so worried that Mal had guilt burning his throat instead of whiskey as he tried to lighten the mood, to ease some of the lines from their troubled faces as he glanced at the cookpot near his bedroll. "What's with the turtle, by the way? Does turtle soup have some curative properties I don't know about?"

It was Alys who answered. "It's not for eating. You kept asking for it."

Mal pulled the pot a little closer, treating the creature with a fair amount of gentleness as he picked up it up by the shell with both hands to greet it eye to eye. "I don't know what that was about," he admitted, unable to remember much of the past few days. "But there was a turtle . . . a puppet . . . back in Thrallkeld that my friend Ella liked. Guess it was some weird dream."

"I named it Muffin," Alys said, sounding calmer. "An early birthday present, I suppose."

"What was that?" Mal asked, frustration with his hearing flaring anew as he scowled at the empty cookpot.

"Muffin," Alys shouted. "The turtle—is named—Muffin!" Apparently getting frustrated herself, she added, "You're going to need an ear horn!"

"I won't. I'm fine," Mal said in his usual dismissive way. But then he tried for teasing, hoping to reach some easier place between them tonight after how hard the past few days must have been for her. "You sure you don't want to name this thing Leo the Second? Looks a bit like him when you stare at it dead on."

Alys laughed, however reluctantly. Mal couldn't hear it, but he saw her smile and the slight shake of her shoulders.

Encouraged, he tried again with Griff, wrapping an arm around the other man's waist. "So, Mister Healer . . . going to look at these stitches for me after I eat?"

"I thought it was Mister Foreman," Griff murmured, the words decipherable only because he kept on using sign language. And though his upset still showed plainly on his face, he added, "I made something for you, by the way. While you were out of it."

He leaned away from Mal for a moment, grabbing something lying just a few feet away—Alys's sketch pad. He hesitated, then pulled off a scrap of paper and handed it to Mal, who recognized the words and markings right away as Griff's work. He studied it closely.

It was a blueprint. For a house.

Fit for a king.

"It would be a lot of work," Griff said as Mal held the paper to the firelight.

It was more than anyone had ever given him, and it hadn't cost a thing.

"I'm sure it's a long way off," Griff continued, the nerves evident in his voice, "but . . . I thought we could add to it, change it together when we have ideas. We've got plenty of time. Plenty of room to dream—if we're still *alive*." His eyes glistened as he added, "I could be back in Linden right now with Liam, planning a wedding. *He* wouldn't ask me to risk life and limb for some gold when we make plenty of money working our boring straight jobs."

Mal pulled himself from Griff's embrace, stung by the mention of Liam and weddings. Griff had been engaged to the locksmith and not bothered to breathe a word about it. Typical. Betrayal. Had he been thinking of going home on his own while Mal was out cold? It seemed just like the sort of thing Mayfair's Most Eligible would do, having a second option in his back pocket. Not fully choosing Mal, even now.

"The point isn't to get rich anyway," Griff went on, signing the words and then flexing his now-empty fingers as if they already missed Mal's warmth. "The point is to come home to each other. I don't give a damn about the money. That's why I've been training as a Warden—to make the world a little better and safer. To protect our future." He sighed. "Or at least I was until the stabbing forced me to take a step back. And look, I know you're not their biggest fan, but you'd be safer doing your, uh, *odd jobs* if I could throw the heat off you and keep the Wardens' focus on the things that really matter, like making sure Wills doesn't stab anyone else in the Wood."

Mal didn't voice any of the questions about Liam now running through his mind. Refused to have that name on his lips. Couldn't bear to know.

Instead, he asked, "You want to—what? Be a Warden while also being with *me*?" He didn't need any words repeated this time. He only questioned it because he didn't want to believe it any more than he wanted to think about Griff running back into Liam's waiting arms. "You seriously think that could work? The elves really have turned you daft, because I thought you were putting all that behind you when you chose me."

He was so different from Mal: the elegant, elf-loving, dragon-slayer's son. Too different. Griff was too good for the likes of him.

The eerie wailing reached an earsplitting crescendo and suddenly stopped.

Even Alys was silent and watchful, some fresh worry shining in her wide eyes by the glint of the firelight.

"Must be nice," Mal said, his eyes sliding away from Griff's and into the raven-crowded trees. "Never having to worry about where your money's going to come from or if you'll even make it back from the next job. I don't have your training, Griff, and I don't have your skills. My options are limited." He palmed at his stupid, useless ear as he narrowed his eyes at a stunted tree. "Your father was the biggest hero. You're the one with the big legacy. I'm just the sad orphan who's been trying to hold on to the only people I've known all my life, and even that doesn't seem to be working out for me. You want to be with me? The real me?"

Griff nodded without hesitating. He seemed sincere, and he *had* sketched out plans for a future with Mal, a space they could fill together. Space where Mal shouldn't be. Griff only loved him because he didn't have a clue what Mal had done. What bargain he had made to try to regain some sense of balance in his world.

His throat was tight, his insides white hot with anticipation of the hurt he knew was coming, but he managed to say hoarsely, "Well then, you'll have to say goodbye to those dreams of living up to your daddy's good deeds forever, or else end things with me now, because you can't be a Warden and have any kind of life with me."

Griff's gaze turned wary. "Why would that be such a problem? I know you don't like them, but—you like *me*."

"Well, let's see," Mal said, letting out a hot breath as he gently set those blueprints down. He hadn't earned the right to look at them. "Rhun was one of them, but did they ever bother to help Wynnie after he disappeared? Ever swing by the cottage to check on any of us? Didn't think so. And his friends must have known about this rogue wraith and didn't bother to warn anyone. If you think they're all really so perfect, then I have some property up by Deadman's Dike you'd love to purchase too, and it definitely wasn't built on top of any old graveyard."

Griff was silent, watching him.

Even so, Mal could hardly find the words to continue. He put a hand on the scrap of parchment with the blueprints, even though he didn't pick it up again.

"The world will never be safe, no matter how many heroes take up arms," he finally went on. "The job seems to have a pretty high mortality rate, too, from what we've seen. Your life would be a drop in the bucket, and for what? I figured out a long time ago that good intentions don't stay the blade. Power does. And if the best and bravest lose the fight . . . I'll crawl through the dark and make us a home in the shadows if it means we survive. That's a victory too."

"I don't disagree," Griff said, speaking more slowly this time, louder, and shaping signs with his hand. "I . . . I'd choose that too." He sounded as surprised to be speaking the words aloud as Mal was to receive them. But then, with more confidence, he added, "And I'd rather be yours than be a Warden. The training was always something I had to work at, but being with you? It feels as natural as . . . well, as being me."

That was all the encouragement Mal needed to continue. "Good, then, because Wardens are also deathly allergic to boundaries. The amount of times they turn up where I am, you'd think they were as interested in my private affairs as Old Man Corbyn—you know, the Linden Bedroom Creeper. Everyone has an agenda. We both know that," he went on, stalling. He had to tell Griff about his part in the attack now, before he had their whole life mapped out just to have to burn Mal off the page. "I don't care that Wardens like playing hero, because they're lying to themselves when they act like they're so much better than the rest of us. I doubt most folks would flinch at seeing me bleed. That's just how things are. But Wardens act like you ought to enjoy the stabbing if they tell you that it's for your own good."

He finally drew a breath and brought his eyes back to Griff's, tired of staring at restless raven's wings and searching for shadows. "If your heart is really set on this Warden shit, we'll figure it out. We just . . . won't be able to talk about work at all. Certain parts of our lives will have to stay really separate, more separate than I'd like, so I don't end up in prison or hanged or anything else that keeps us even further apart."

"Why is that?" Griff pressed, his features once again drawn with caution.

Alys rose abruptly and headed toward the teakettle—giving them space again, Mal guessed as Griff laid a hand on his leg.

"Why can't we talk about everything?" Griff went on, confusion and hurt in every line of his face. "If I wanted separate, I wouldn't have come all this way, and I wouldn't have felt my world collapsing when I thought we were about to lose you."

Mal's fingers crept toward Griff's. This might be the last time he got to hold his hand, and he wanted to remember what it felt like, even if he'd wish like hell later that he could just forget.

Out of the corner of his eye, he realized Alys hadn't grabbed the kettle after all. She was wielding her sword, watching the approach of something he hadn't been able to hear, a shambling creature that stopped at the edge of the ward marking their camp border. It was another dead orc, another revenant, bigger than the ones they had fought near the chest of silvers and missing an eye.

"Why?" he echoed Griff, his mouth still impossibly dry even after a sip of tea. Alys could handle the revenant for now, and if he didn't get the words out, he was afraid he would never find the courage again. He owed Griff this; the knowledge, and the freedom to choose him or turn away after. "Because I've still been working for—"

"Mal Pryce!" the pale orc thundered, a fetid stench wafting over them as it opened its mouth awkwardly, like some kind of puppet. The voice issuing from its desiccated vocal cords was too powerful to belong to such a lowly creature, and Mal knew immediately who was speaking to him, but he sure as hell wasn't about to bow as the orc's remaining greenish eye burned into his. "What's taking you so long? Bring me my treasure, wraith be damned, or your soul and Sayer's are mine, and I'll make you watch while I put more knives in him than your flimsy plan ever did."

Chapter Twenty-Nine
Dragon Heart

Down below his waistline, Griff's scar throbbed dully as he watched Alys hold her sword, ready to attack the orc's neck if it dared to put a toe over their wards the way the wargs had done.

Despite the growing pain in his old wound, he got to his feet and reached for his maul, because these things seemed to travel in packs. The motion of grabbing his weapon had become almost second nature, and besides, fighting dead things suddenly seemed far more appealing than thinking about what he had just heard.

Yet the hulking shape of the orc, slightly blurry to his gaze, didn't move a muscle. It stood there dumbly, watching as Mal hurried after him to the camp's border, trying to explain himself while Griff's heart and hopes sank deep into the Mire.

"I was going to tell you—" Mal started to say, but Griff cut him off.

"That you were working for the fucking Shadow Queen? That you—what, that you're the one who stabbed me? Or you had some part in it?" He could hardly get the words out, a wave of nausea swiftly rising in his throat as he pushed through. "When did you plan on mentioning it? After you had your fill of fucking with me?"

"Now! I know I should have done it sooner, a lot sooner, but can you blame me for not wanting to say a word when you're doing exactly what you always do, what I was afraid of? The thing you promised you wouldn't fucking do again?" Mal demanded hoarsely as both Alys and the undead orc watched them warily. He pulled out his flask and took a long drink.

"What's that?" Griff asked, no longer trying to walk away but rounding on him. He at least had enough presence of mind to lower the maul. "What do I always do?"

"Judge me, decide I'm less than you somehow, when you don't even know the whole story!" Mal said, brushing hatefully at the corner of his eye with the back of his hand before taking another sip like he knew how much it hurt Griff to watch him do it. "Yes, I've been working at Served With Love. Usually I help protect the transport of certain goods in and out of Mayfair when the dark queen's people need an extra hired sword. But they also had me plan an attack for them, a murder—yours." He swiped at his eyes again, then continued. "I didn't know. I wasn't holding the knife, I swear. I wasn't even with them when it happened. I had no idea they were after *you*."

Griff held up a hand for silence, too busy to listen and not really wanting to hear another word as he pieced things together in his mind that were starting to make terrible sense. The raven feathers newly tattooed on Mal's arm, the way he was so insistent that they keep moving to get to the treasure, never wanting to take the kind of break they all badly needed—he had assumed Mal had an interested buyer for some of the artifacts lined up back in Mayfair, but he'd had no idea that buyer was the Shadow Queen herself.

Why had he left a good thing, a good man, and come all this way with Mal, when he knew better than to ever trust a word out of the meanest mouth in the city? Why hadn't he wanted easy? He couldn't remember just now.

"If I'd had any idea it was you they wanted, Griff, I would have killed them all myself and buried them in their fucking cellar," Mal said into the tense and icy silence, sounding far more miserable than he had when he was lapsing into the fever. "They've made me kill people before. Wardens, usually. I've always had the sense that they'd kill me, too, if I refused. It's clear they hate the Wardens, but so do I, so that's never been a problem, and the pay is good. But they could never pay me to hurt you. No one could. I wouldn't. I—I love you. I love you, Griff, and I'm so fucking sorry. I'll be sorry for the rest of my life, however short it might be. That's why I made a deal with *her* to bring this treasure back, in exchange for your safety and the end of my contract with them. So neither of us will ever have to worry about stupid ravens and shadows after this is done."

Griff's head was spinning. The orc's remaining eye kept shifting back and forth between him and Mal like it was following the conversation, and he wasn't convinced it was just a trick of the firelight.

"You made a deal with the fucking Shadow Queen," he repeated slowly, at which the undead orc growled. "A deal. This is all about the money for you, isn't it? Still."

Mal blinked at him, disbelieving, and drank another long gulp. "Did you hear a word I said, or are you the one with the bad ear? I made this deal for *us*." He was practically shouting now, earning another grumble from the orc, and Griff winced as though struck.

These verbal blows somehow hurt worse than any of the times before, even though back then their fists had been landing right alongside the pointed words.

Alys half glanced at the creature, though she had lowered her sword, apparently deciding that whatever was happening between

Griff and Mal right now was far more of a threat to everyone's safety than a revenant, even one this size.

"You plotted to kill me for money, Mal—what the hell else am I supposed to think?" Griff demanded, too much blood rushing in his ears and too much pain in his old wound for him to properly take in what Mal was saying. He had too many words of his own to get out first. "And you were going to just give the Shadow Queen this treasure, knowing what it would mean for her side, without ever breathing a word of it to me? You were just going to let me be a part of that, after everything our parents fought for? Seriously? You couldn't trust me with this after I gave you absolutely everything?"

He had let Mal in, chosen him—not just the idea of him that he'd longed for back in Stormveil but the man himself, the real Mal, the thief with a temper who saw the world with a knife in its hand, ready to stab him in the back—and yet Mal was still only in business for himself.

He should have expected this, because the real Mal was also selfish. His eyes were always on the prize, and the prize wasn't Griff. Maybe this betrayal was even what he deserved, somehow, for letting Mal down all those years ago when he left. He wasn't worthy of Mal's love, he wasn't enough for him, no matter how he'd tried to be.

Most of all, he should have known Mal would always pick his other great love over him. Mal had a dragon's heart, strong and cold, and he would always go for the glittering riches, even if they were going to end up in someone else's pocket in the end.

A blast of icy wind shoved Griff in the back, cutting through his shirt and cloak. He pulled the old black scarf more tightly around himself, wishing he could use it to shut out everything he had just heard right along with the chill.

"I should have expected this," Mal said at last, quieter, as the wind shivered through his hair and rumpled clothes. "I should have known you would overreact. That you wouldn't listen no matter what I said, no matter my intentions. You were looking for any excuse not to stay, weren't you? So many empty, pretty words." He took a step toward Griff, who instinctively took a few steps back.

Old habits.

"You want to talk about trust?" Mal went on, his voice cold as the sudden wind. "Fine. Let's do it: I trusted that you could handle the truth tonight. I trusted that we were still going home together. But if you only ever trust one thing I say, let it be this: Trust that I'll get the treasure with or without you. Trust that I'm going to buy your safety no matter what you really think of me. You can run on home to Liam now and live a long, happy life, safe with the person you really want." Mal didn't wipe at his eyes again, though they were streaming harder. "Assuming he's enough for you. Or do you buy someone else's love on the side still? I've heard the rumors about how you two met."

As a tremor rocked the ground, Griff let his maul slip from his limp hands, aching and breathless and carved open by the calculated, cutting words that threw him off-balance far more effectively than the earth shaking beneath him. He had chosen Mal. He had intended to stay, at least until he learned who the treasure was really for and what Mal had done. But it seemed Mal had already decided for him how this was going to end. He had never trusted Griff to choose a future together.

Without bothering to look for the source of the crash, Griff took another step back, farther from their camp and Mal. Proving him right.

"Guys," Alys said suddenly, her voice high-pitched with alarm. She was pointing at the slumped form of the revenant now facedown on the ground. "It's dead. I mean, dead again." Emphasizing her point, she jabbed it in the back with her blade. No response. “That wind . . . I think that killed it somehow. It just shivered and dropped on the spot.”

Apparently, Griff wasn’t the only one not listening tonight, as Mal simply shook his head, then turned to him again to say coolly, “At least when we get home, I’ll have all those silvers to keep me warm in my big bed. Maybe I’ll even pay for a—”

His face changed as another gust of cold wind nearly blew Griff over with all the force of a charging steed.

Alys shouted something and tossed her sword aside, scrambling instead to grab the cloth hilt of the broken one.

“The shadow—the wraith—behind you!” Mal gasped, bolting toward Griff just as he began to realize that it was more than wind closing its icy fingers around him, digging into his injured shoulder hard enough to wring a gasp from him.

More than wind pressing on his throat, preventing him from crying out any last words.

In the heat of the argument, he had stepped outside the circle of Mal’s wards.

Tears slicked Griff’s face in the few seconds before the wraith started dragging him through the trees by his crude sling, dragging him toward his fate and oblivion, where at least he could start to erase Mal’s name from all of his songs.

Chapter Thirty
The Chill

"What about our deal?" Mal yelled to the night as Griff was swiftly dragged out of reach before his fingers could close around the ends of his old black scarf, his limbs stiff and clumsy with cold. "If you're so powerful, can't you do something about your monster that's broken free of its leash?"

But of course he didn't expect an answer from the Shadow Queen, especially not when the rogue wraith had just murdered the lackey she was using as her mouthpiece.

The wraith's music was also back, louder than before, mocking in his ears. As if he needed another reminder that he was losing Griff to this spirit—as if he couldn't have lost Griff all on his own.

It was a terrible song even in its softness, because beneath its outward beautiful sorrow was a dissonant drowning that reverberated painfully in Mal's teeth. The way the notes echoed in the curve of his ear, its message was plain: There was no hope here.

Even as the wraith pulled Griff toward the lake, the wind it seemed to have conjured continued to whip the leaves on the trees, earning several rebuking caws from the ravens who had stubbornly stuck around despite the threat. The gusts flung dirt and debris into Alys's eyes, making her recoil against the sting as she passed the broken blade to Mal. She drew Rhun's old sword again, then grabbed the raven-topped dagger from her belt as she ran alongside Mal in pursuit of Griff.

He shouldn't have hit the flask so hard; half his steps were stumbles that were costing him precious seconds. Seconds in which, from a distance, he watched the shadowy mist solidify into bone. Whereas before the wraith's eyes had been empty pits, a cold blue glow now illuminated the gaunt face from within, as if it possessed some magic of its own that crackled to life the closer it got to its resting place.

Still, his tattoo prickled as sharply as it had the day Kage gave it to him, because this spirit had been spun from the queen's magic in the first place.

The wraith pulled its cracked lips back in a snarl again as Mal staggered toward it, rushing past the bounds of the wards and even smudging one without care for his own safety, ignoring the burn in his side as his busted stitches throbbed in protest. "Hey!" he shouted, gripping the makeshift hilt of the spirit blade tighter. "I know you can hear me! Why don't you leave him the fuck alone and tell us what you're really after? You want the treasure? Fine! You can have it!" he lied.

He was stalling, because Alys was moving faster than him, and this was the best way he could think to help right now. To try to start making things up to Griff, if that was even possible. He would need Griff to let him know whether there was still a chance for them if they both made it out of this.

Alys certainly had things of her own to make up to the cinnamon-roll-loving foreman who would never agree to a deal with the darkness, because she had known about the deal from the start and kept it secret. He could guess some of what was on her mind as she aimed her father's raven-topped dagger at a spot several inches over Griff's head and threw it so that it spun neatly end over end, a trick Wynnie had taught them both.

The wraith smiled sharply, no skin on its lips, as it slid a hand up to Griff's throat and squeezed, dropping his limp form in the mud just in time to grasp the shiny raven-topped weapon that had sailed slightly to the left of the dark hole where its ear should have been.

It looked back up at Mal, winked at him, and disappeared, taking Rhun's dagger with it.

The wind that had been tearing through their camp stopped completely.

So did the sorrowful, teeth-aching music.

Alys ran the rest of the way to Griff, kneeling beside him and pressing her ear to his chest as if she was checking for breath. "Still alive!" he was relieved to read on her lips.

Mal finally reached her, passing the broken blade from his hands into her more capable ones without really looking at Griff. He couldn't let himself think about the man he loved right now, or how hurt he might be. He needed to focus on where the hell the wraith had run off to, so he could tell Alys where to aim their only useful weapon.

She shouted something to Mal, but he couldn't quite make out the words thanks to the sudden incensed screeches of the ravens. They were gathering at the base of the pike on which Alys had staked the shriveled orc's head, several yards away from the fire, hopping around as if greatly agitated.

He detected admonishment in their cries, giving him the sense that something was about to happen that their master didn't like.

Despite his dislike of the damn birds, Mal strode toward them, hurrying back over the broken wards that had marked their camp. He intended to shut them up somehow so he could listen for the wraith's ear-piercing song—but as he got closer, the silver coins fell from the orc's unseeing eyes, and he knew exactly what had upset the ravens.

Leo the Head blinked once, twice, freezing Mal to the spot where he stood as a cool bluish gleam of intelligence entered that long-dead gaze that moments ago had been gray, almost colorless, lost to the decay of time.

Leo's cracked lips twisted into something like a smile. "You want to talk?" it asked in a voice as old as the dirt, as brittle as the leaves in winter. "Talk, then. No one ever wants to talk with the likes of me, save for the Deathless Lady, and I'm afraid we are no longer on speaking terms. Haven't been for at least a century."

Mal could hardly find his own voice, shaking with cold as he was, but he squared his shoulders and stared into the glow in the orc's eyes. "What the hell do you want?" he demanded of the spirit inside the head, even if Wynnie had once told him that old line about flies and honey. The wraith had laid hands on both Alys and Griff now, and he didn't have any politeness left. "Let me guess: It's your treasure, not Her Dreadful Majesty's, and if we take another step toward that lake, you'll drown us and keep our weapons for your pile of pretty baubles?"

This thing was clearly powerful; Mal could feel magic radiating off the severed head like an invisible hand pushing against his chest, urging him to back away. But stubborn as he was, ever Wynnie's faithful student, he stood his ground and tried not to let his face betray any glimmer of fear.

"I want you three. Your souls. They're far more important than any armor or weapons, even enchanted ones. All those old things matter little to me these days." The head wheezed with laughter like the clack of bones. "The blood of heroes runs in you, no matter how you conduct yourselves to the contrary. You reek of it. Elf blood," the wraith continued through those long-decayed vocal cords, narrowing its eyes at Mal. "You'll make fine additions to my growing army of spirits; it's been well worth the wait, though I admit I'm surprised you made it this far. I almost had you on your own stupidity when you gave yourself an infection and nearly died from that fever. But I'm patient, and that always pays off . . . like when you angered your companion into stepping outside those wards."

At that, Mal darted another glance at Griff's seemingly unconscious form still slumped in the mud several yards away, his stomach writhing.

Then came movement at the corner of his eye. Beyond the agitated ravens, far in the distance, several filmy green-eyed ghosts had dared to peer around the trees. Watching, curious to see which way this battle would go, though they apparently still weren't going to risk getting too close.

"You'll be in good company here," the head rasped, as if trying to reassure him. "And when I've collected enough souls, we'll move against the Shadow Queen together. That should make your dark-haired friend very happy."

Mal took a step back, darting a quick glance over at Alys. Like him, she was staring at the head, seemingly able to hear every word now that it was speaking through a mouth of flesh and bone.

"They'll be delicious too," the wraith crooned, clearly trying to rile him.

Mal didn't answer. He was trying to make sense of what he could now see just behind his friends, the army of ghosts that the rogue wraith had boasted about, trapped souls of elves and humans and all sorts gathered around to watch the proceedings. At their forefront, near Griff's unmoving body, a few pale forms knelt—no, had been shoved to their knees, Mal realized upon closer inspection, weighed down by ephemeral chains that must be heavy on their shoulders and ankles.

One of them was vaguely familiar, and before he even glanced up and into Mal's eyes, Mal knew who he was. Rhun.

He had been here all this time. He'd never left. Never chosen another life for himself but the one he'd had with them and Wynnie. And now he was being held an arm's length away from Alys, close enough to reach out to his daughter if his hands hadn't been bound.

The sight made Mal so angry that he ran at the pike and punched his fist right into Leo's nose, breaking off what crumbling shards of bone were left there to begin with. "I don't care if the queen is scared of you—I'm not, and I'm going to fucking end you!" he shouted at the head as splinters of bone cut his much-abused hand.

"You would if you could, I'm sure," the wraith murmured almost sympathetically. "I was an enemy of the elves in life, so they killed me and bound me here. Then I became a servant of the Shadow Queen, a lieutenant in her fight. I was charged with keeping souls that threatened her here in my domain, but once I had gathered enough, once I learned how to feed on their energy, I grew stronger," the wraith continued, as if Mal bashing its borrowed face in was of no consequence. "I shouldn't have to bow to anyone, not even the Deathless Lady, with a power like mine. The one who raised you has been *so* unhappy you're here, by the way, but he's a little too tied up to greet you at the moment."

Mal only glared. He wasn't going to give this thing the satisfaction of goading him into further destroying his hand. He stepped back again, eyes still on the wraith, though he kept watching the luminous gathering of spirits near his friends out of the corner of his eye too.

No wonder Rhun's companions had never breathed a word of what they had experienced out here. The wraith would have wanted this same fate for them, to keep their souls trapped here, and it had already demonstrated how far it could travel, even if its powers were greatly muted in Linden.

"I've almost had the tall one a few times now too. He looks a bit like the other Warden among my ranks," the wraith went on, clearly meaning Rhun. "He has the most elf blood of any of you; he's going to taste the best when I grind his bones to dust and wrap him in my chains."

The chains.

It was the mention of them that finally got Mal moving his numbed feet again, slowly and subtly inching him toward Alys and Griff and the broken blade. He needed to use it. He had an idea.

"But the girl . . . the girl is going to make the sweetest screams when I bind her soul to my service." The wraith leered, once again bidding for his attention.

Mal's jaw tightened, and he swallowed a retort that would do nothing but anger the spirit more. Still, he couldn't help shaking his head the slightest bit. As if anything, man or demon or wizard or wraith, could ever take from Alys without her consent, even if she didn't fully understand yet that she could be even stronger if she didn't fight all her battles alone.

"You all have done a better job of avoiding all the Mire's little misfortunes than I would have expected," the wraith went on as Mal stepped closer yet to his friends. The soft glow of the spirits gleamed silver white along the shard of blade he was stealthily creeping toward.

"The wyvern attacking in daylight—that was you," Mal said, hoping to keep the wraith distracted. "And you were waiting by the silver chest, hoping to trap our souls after the Shadow Queen's revenants ripped us apart. All this time, you've been using Rhun's things to bring us closer to where your bones are, where you're strongest, so you could claim our spirits before your ex-lady had the chance."

The orc's eyes glinted as if pleased at all this understanding.

"I'll enjoy passing the long years with you," the wraith laughed. "With a mind and a mouth like that, I might even put you on the front lines. The hero of my collection. My champion. So clever. *Too* clever, I'd say; I've been watching you since the moment you were handed my map."

The map. Of course. Kage had to have known the baggage it came with, which meant there was no way his boss had expected him to return. Kage hadn't wanted to risk sending anyone of actual importance to try to retrieve what his queen felt was still rightfully hers.

Alys's shaking, chilled hand grasped Mal's ankle, but he didn't look at her. Not yet. His scowl deepened as he locked gazes with the wraith again, the cloth hilt of the broken blade now snug in his cold fingers. Out of the corner of his eye, he saw the slight rise and fall of Griff's chest, and that was all he needed to keep going and do something truly risky.

"Well *you're* not very clever, you stupid bag of bones, because I have no interest in being anyone's hero or doing a damn thing with my life that anyone wants me to," Mal snarled, bolting toward the spot where Rhun's spirit watched helplessly as the wraith prepared to kill his daughter and his best friends' sons.

Mal's eyes met his for the briefest moment before he used the broken blade to cut the chains on Rhun's ankles and wrists.

Somewhere behind him, the wraith howled, and the ravens answered with their own angry chorus.

Mal turned and shouted over it all, "Alys—I'm sorry about Leo. I know how much you liked him."

He was counting on the long years of understanding between them.

And with that, he tossed the broken blade back in her direction, into her waiting hands.

"Seize them!" the wraith shrieked at someone—all the chained ghosts, Mal realized.

The long-dead entity must have power to command and compel those it held bound, just like the queen he once served. It must have forced Rhun's spirit to wander near the wyvern's nest that day, almost leading Griff to his death.

Mal threw himself over top of Griff's prone form, trying his best to shield him as he felt sharp, icy fingers start to tug at his clothes and hair.

The ravens beat their wings and swarmed overhead, sounding as unhappy with this turn of events as he was, making it hard for Mal to see where Alys was now. If she was able to do what he had suggested.

He caught the flash of the blade raised above her head, and two large chunks of Leo went rolling off the pike before the wraith had a chance to slither out of there. It moaned, a death knell that made Mal's stomach writhe, and then they were left alone in the aftershocks of a suddenly quiet night.

The icy fingers had stopped tugging at him and Griff. Even the ravens settled, no longer making a racket. Mal turned to hazard a look behind him, and there were no more gaunt, chained ghosts forced to follow orders. No spirits around them at all anymore that he could see, and definitely no shadow.

There was no more sad song in some other language echoing in the curve of his ear. No more biting, unnatural cold. The wraith was gone from this place for good, struck by the spirit blade in the hand best suited to wielding it, banished back to the shadow realm, where it would have to answer to its maker.

Mal finally rolled off of Griff to get a better look at the other man's face and found that he was awake again despite nearly having the life squeezed out of him. As he did so, a heavy hand gripped his shoulder. Not Griff's. It was too cold to be Griff's, broader and callused from gripping a sword for so many years.

"Rhun?" Mal asked quietly over his shoulder on a soft exhale.

The smallest breeze stirred his hair. "You shouldn't have come here."

It was him; Mal would never forget the rasp of that broken voice, and every word seemed to punch right through him with the bittersweet ache of things lost and found. He glanced quickly at Griff again, but the other man didn't seem to hear a thing.

"But I'm glad you did," Rhun went on, his words coming slowly, as if at a great cost. "Thank you. Consider any debt between us more than repaid. You're never as alone as you think, Mal. Nor as damaged, nor as designed to damage others. You could just live, and live well—all three of you—and that would make all our sacrifices matter. Look after Alys for me. I know you and Griff will look after each other, as it always should have been." The hand gave a gentle squeeze, followed by a pat on Mal's back, and then it was gone.

Rhun was gone.

Griff's pale face became a blur as Mal tried to catch his breath, the words still echoing down into the heart of him that he had convinced himself was so unreachable. Alys rejoined them some hazy moments later, a hand rubbing her shoulder as if she, too, had felt that phantom touch. One last goodbye.

"I thought," Griff said groggily, raising a hand to his good shoulder. "I could have sworn I felt—"

"It was him. Even if I couldn't see him—I'll never forget the feeling." Alys broke first as she finished choking the words out, the floodgates opening. Griff must have been alert enough to put things together, because he was quick to follow, tears streaking his grimy face as he lay there not quite ready to move.

Even Mal didn't have enough energy left to fight the burn at the back of his eyes.

The trio held each other as night deepened around them. As the ravens began to depart in droves, no doubt to bring word of the battle to their master. As a few green-eyed ghosts dared to come close enough to offer Mal their solemn, silent bows of thanks rather than hold up their fingers in warning. The three old friends kept their arms around each other until their tears were mostly dry, until it was time for words again. Time to figure out if what was between Griff and Mal could be saved too.

Chapter Thirty-One

Real

Griff was still half out of it, but he was very much aware that Mal was holding fistfuls of his shirt and gazing at him like he thought he would never see him again.

That had been so close. Too close. He had caught some of what the wraith said, enough to understand that they had all narrowly escaped eternal servitude. A fate worse than mere death.

Reaching up with a shaking hand, Griff touched his tender throat, sure that bruises were already blooming where the wraith had grabbed him. His wyvern-ravaged shoulder, however, remained too numb to feel much of anything.

"I'm going to talk for a minute," Mal said hoarsely, while in the distance behind him, Alys finally busied herself with the kettle. If ever there was a time they all needed a hot cup of tea, it was now. "And you're going to really listen this time. Because I've worked too hard at getting you back into my life to give up on us this easily. Say what you want about me, but I'm no quitter. I'm a damn good swimmer, and I've kept my head above water through the worst life has thrown at me so far." Softer, wrapping one of

Griff's curls around his finger, he added, "I would have jumped into a fucking elf pond for you any day."

When Alys brought over two steaming tin mugs of tea, Mal cut her a glance, his eyes shimmering with exhaustion and thanks as she quickly went on her way again. Then he met Griff's patiently waiting gaze and continued, "There's no version of my existence without you in it, even when I tried to pretend otherwise. And if I'd known, I wouldn't have left you to die, not ever, not for a king's ransom. The last thing I ever wanted to be was the death of you, and the whole point of this trip was me trying to make it right, even when I still thought you hated me."

He paused, swallowing with a wince like there was a bitter taste in his mouth, then took a sip of scalding tea. "No matter what you think, this wasn't about money," he insisted. "I don't get to keep a single coin beyond those silvers we found, since they're not part of it. The only thing I asked for in exchange for bringing back the treasure was that you'd be safe from them for the rest of your life, and I wouldn't have to work there anymore. That was the deal even before I knew how you felt. Before I knew how *I* really felt. But now, if you still want it too, I want to make this something that's good for both of us. Something real, so it lasts."

Griff had plenty that he wanted to say, but Mal had asked to talk first, so he simply squeezed the other man's forearm—the one without the angry-looking tattoo—to encourage him to keep going.

"Look, maybe making a bargain with the Shadow Queen was the stupidest thing I could have done, but there didn't seem to be any other way to get what I needed—which was you no longer being a target. How would you feel if you'd been responsible for *my* near death without realizing it until later?" Mal asked, frowning into his tea.

Now that Griff sat and really thought about it, it made sense that Mal would be working where the good money was. It also made sense that he didn't care what he was being asked to do, to a point. Mal had grown up listening to Wynnie, after all, and wanting to impress her. But what made the most sense of all was Mal having no idea what his boss's motives were, not wanting to know more than he had to, and not knowing he was helping with something that had nearly cost Griff his life.

Not knowing was the worst.

Griff hadn't known Mal was in so much trouble in Thrallkeld. He'd been too busy being above it all with the elves, and Mal had died, alone and friendless and without the person who claimed to love him.

He couldn't hold what Mal hadn't known against him, not if he wanted Mal to forgive him for not coming to Thrallkeld back when. "I'd feel like shit. I *do* feel like shit, because I already know exactly what that's like. It's how I've felt since I found out you were alone and eating rats in a tunnel somewhere without me." He reminded himself then to speak more slowly, using his other hand to sign now that half of Mal's hearing was gone. "One thing I'm sure of is that you wouldn't hurt me on purpose. I know your heart, so I know you don't support the dark queen, but—being in business with *her* people?"

"I'm in business with business," Mal insisted, still clutching Griff's shirt with one hand like it was giving him strength. "Look, there are plenty of other things we didn't know about each other before this trip, yet here we are, together and in love. Or at least, I think we are." Before Griff had a chance to offer any kind of assurance, he added quickly, "I have to make a living somehow. Pants don't last very long, nor are they cheap. But I'm done with Her Dreadful Majesty once we bring this treasure in. For good. Fuck her agenda and her gold."

"Horses aren't cheap either, and you still owe me one," Griff reminded him, making a little galloping motion with his fingers to get the point across. There were so many signs he could improvise for them. He was going to have fun with that, if they survived the rest of their time in the Mire. Because even if it wasn't easy, he still wanted this thing with Mal.

The thief grinned and slowly leaned closer, as if assessing his welcome back in Griff's presence. "I'm going to have to buy you a fancy cane too, for that ankle," he murmured, finally letting go of the shirt to run his hand over the top of the bandages on Griff's lower leg. "You'll never want for anything with me, even if that means working overtime for life."

"I already don't," Griff insisted, reaching for that hand. "You say you want something real, Mal? Well, I'm real. You're real. How much I love you—that's real too. If it wasn't, if I was choosing someone else, I would have gone home well before now. Liam or not."

Mal frowned at the name, just as he had done earlier when he was shouting it at Griff. "I love you too. But I don't need any more apologies or pretty words. No promises, just proof." He held Griff's gaze a moment before continuing, "You know that person you loved all those years after you left for Stormveil? He wasn't real. That was just you, conjuring a phantom of me."

"I did love imaginary you," Griff said, taking his first generous gulp of tea even as he kept his eyes on Mal's. "But I love this you too, the more I've come to know you. And I want to figure this thing out just like you do. Build it so it lasts."

"Well then. More than anything, I need to know that I'm enough for you, just like this," Mal admitted quietly. "And maybe, as much as I want that, I need to show you that you're enough for me too. The part where I want more with you than I ever have with anyone else? That's real too." Tears slid down his dirty cheeks, and he didn't glance away or try to wipe them. "I may have kissed a lot of girls, but you—you're my best ever, and you always will be. And all those big plans of mine? The travel, the castle, spending all those silvers? I chased them so hard because I'm the only one who's never let me down, but that's not giving you a real chance to show up for me. And lately I don't give a damn about any of those plans if you're not in them, if that wasn't clear. Without you, they're no good, and I'm done dreaming.

You're my biggest dream. My castle. My world. None of it matters without you at the center."

Griff's lips parted, but for once, no sound came out. He had to hope there was plenty of love in his eyes to light the way. To trust that that was enough.

"I've been thinking a lot about curses lately too," Mal continued in the silence that was rapidly thawing between them. "Mostly mine. When we fought, when you left for Stormveil, you told me I wasn't anything to you and said I should leave too. And I just . . . went. All the way to my death. I held a knife to my own throat time and again. Just like you, only in different ways."

His fingers trailed over the flask in the pocket of his jerkin, and Griff tensed, anticipating the scent of whiskey. But instead, Mal only said, "Doesn't feel like there's much room for this thing in here anymore. Not with your letter and those blueprints to carry too. It's starting to feel like . . . maybe I've outgrown it."

Griff reached for Mal's fingers, drawing them away from the flask and toward himself. "I never planned to tell you how I felt about you," he said after a little while, using his free hand to sign again. "Thought I'd take it to the grave. When we came out here, before it slipped out, I was afraid to look at you sometimes. I thought you'd be able to sense it somehow—that I loved you—and I was so sure you wouldn't feel the same, that you'd use it against me as one more way to mock me to my face, or behind my back. But that was deciding for you, wasn't it? Not even giving you the chance to really choose me, not letting you try to show up either."

He drew a long breath, his eyes never leaving Mal's. He had thought, for a few horrible moments as unseen hands tore at their hair and clothes, that he would never get to look into those silver-gray eyes again. And that would have been a shame, because there was so much he had missed there before. "Of course, you haven't exactly made it easy to tell you things. Like yes, Liam was going to propose, but no, I didn't accept—when I left him to come on this trip, it was over. And then there's the issue of *you* not telling *me* certain important things about whose mission we're on, even when your intentions were actually quite—"

"I know," Mal cut in, his face grim in the low light cast by the fire Alys had rekindled after the wraith's wind extinguished it. "You're right. I've pushed you away so many times, and I've made it all harder than it needs to be—and I'm sorry too. I can't ask you to stay and not show you that I mean it by not letting you in all the way, even if I think you won't like the pile of skeletons and assorted weaponry in my closet. That's yours to decide."

"And from now on," Griff said, drawing them closer by their joined hands now that they were coming together instead of unraveling, "when something feels too much or too hard, I'll tell you—even if it scares me worse than any unhinged spirit to say things I think you don't want to hear. Like how I want to be your boyfriend. I want the title, and all those things you think are foolish. And how you're the only one I want to hold me when the nightmares get bad."

Mal reached into the pocket of his jerkin and pulled out the folded pieces of parchment there. "I hear you, and I want this," he said, pointing to a list of promises and some pretty impressive blueprints. "I want us to do this right, and I want you to hold me through it all, only now your arm can't even feel things to hold."

"My shoulder might be numb, but I can still hold you in every way that counts," Griff insisted, spreading his good arm wide. "Do you want me to? Could I be . . . enough?" As he waited for an answer, he wiped his damp face on his shirt.

Slowly, Mal scooted in, fitting himself into a spot that hadn't been frequented in many years. He buried his face into the shaggy black hair at Griff's neck, wrapped his arms around a chest grown broader over their years apart, and only then did he give a muffled answer. "Of course I fucking want you to. All my world has ever been missing is you."

Maybe he and Mal hadn't been listening to each other during that horrible fight, but he was sure the other man would hear him now. Sure that Mal was holding what he wanted most in this life as he snuggled closer, and it wasn't cold steel and gems. And there was one thing he really wanted to tell him in that moment.

"I love you so much," Griff told him, his voice thick with tears just threatening to fall. Who said they couldn't have easy sometimes too? "I love you, Mal," he repeated as he kissed the tangled blond hair pressed close to his face and rubbed a little stress from the shoulders of the tensest body he'd ever clutched against his own.

Eventually, when they drew back for breath, Mal picked up one end of Griff's scarf and used it to wipe the tears from his face. "You're a fucking mess," he accused as his fingers traced some of the wyvern claw marks on Griff's shoulder that weren't quite covered by his bandages. "But I love you too. A lot."

Griff started to smile as Mal leaned his forehead against his own.

"I know you're not having a nightmare right now, but—" Mal peered deep into his eyes. "Do you want me to hold you too? Because I want that."

For the second time that night, Griff was rendered speechless, if only for a moment. "There aren't even words for how I feel about you," he said, despite the evidence of the letter that had already been returned to its safe, snug place against Mal's chest, despite the ones he'd already spoken. Running a finger over Mal's lower lip, he added, "And yes. I really fucking do want you to hold me. That would be more than enough for me."

Mal answered that finger tracing across his lip with a brush of his mouth against Griff's, trailing a hand up the side of his face and into his dark curls. Then he shifted, offering his arm and his chest as a place for Griff to lay his head and his cares for as long as he liked.

Griff couldn't think of sleeping just yet, though.

Not even when he had finally found the most comfortable pillow this side of the Teeth—the place where his face was cradled just so against Mal's chest—no matter the claims Mal might make about the bed he planned to buy.

"I haven't ever really figured out how to love myself, not in Stormveil or anywhere else," Griff admitted into the inviting quiet. "But you make me want to try. You make me think I'm worth it, like maybe I can finally get it right if I put in the work."

Mal's fingers stroked softly through Griff's hair for a long time before he said, "Hey. I thought of something. Can I have the map back? I need to look at it for a second."

A slight tension returned to Griff's spine and his good shoulder. Yet now that he understood why they had to see this through, now that Mal had let him in, he pulled the old parchment from under his leg and handed it over.

Without another word, Mal tore the map into little pieces and tossed them into the air.

"We can find some other way to get Her Deadly Majesty off both our asses if it's that important to you that she doesn't get the treasure. Though we should at least look for those bracers for you, since we've made it this far and the lake is so close," Mal declared as bits of yellowed paper fell around them like confetti, a few nesting in his hair and Griff's. Mal leaned in for a deeper kiss, waking Griff's stunned lips. "I used to think I'd made my peace with being cursed, or whatever hell the gods have in store for me. But now that I have you, the real you—I just want to live again. Really live. Good thing I'm no quitter."

Those whiskey-soaked kisses reminded Griff of all the work Mal would have to do, too, to make that happen. But for now, Griff pulled Mal more snugly into his arms, blowing the pieces of paper out of his hair.

"That was incredibly brave and awfully noble for a . . . businessman, and more than I would have ever expected," Griff praised him, now flooded with warmth after the coldest night of his life. "But since we're really in no shape to fight all the creatures the dark queen will send our way if we don't keep up your end of the bargain, we should probably just go get her treasure once the sun's up. And not just the vambraces, as I can't think of any other way to get you out of her service for good. We need to finish this. Unless—"

He cast a glance over at Alys, who was still dutifully tending the fire and putting on a fresh kettle while giving them their space. "Hey, Alys, do you think we should go get the treasure in the morning before we hightail it out of here, rather than fight our way out?"

"Yeah, Alys, what do you think?" Mal echoed, giving Griff's good shoulder a grateful squeeze. "You still in, knowing the risks and the reward, now that there's no rogue wraith on our trail?"

"You two not getting killed is the only treasure I need out of this ordeal. I'm in," Alys called, her voice alert and certain despite the late hour. Muffin the turtle was in her lap, apparently still alive after the wraith's attack, and he was blinking sleepily up at her as she stroked her fingers over his brown-and-gold-patterned shell.

"And we *do* have all that silver," Mal murmured quietly to Griff, the beginnings of more big dreams evident in his gleaming eyes. "So I'm going to buy you all the horses you can build a stable for, you fuck. I love you."

"Horses?" Griff laughed as tiny bits of the old map swirled across the grass, blown by a gentler breeze. He leaned in, letting himself be fully held and knowing he was safe with Mal. Safe at home after too long away.

"Don't act like you don't know that you've got enough ass for two of them, at least," Mal teased softly.

Griff grinned, though only briefly. Now that he was seeing more clearly, he was realizing how generous Mal really was with him. Not just focused on his own riches after all. "Not sure I'll need any horses at all, though, now that I'm never going to finish my Warden training even if I'm fully healed."

He wasn't Seimon Sayer, after all. He really liked being Griff, playing his lute and building places where people could make memories, in the light or dark. Maybe he wasn't destined to hear ballads about his own heroics someday, but he would bet all his savings that in another twenty or thirty years, he would still be making a damn good egg. And he would still know how to make Mal laugh, the best music he had ever heard. Things that were all his own.

"Thank fuck," Mal breathed. "Thank you. And you're welcome."

"I want the freedom to travel with you," Griff said as more of the tension left Mal's body and he melted into him. "I want to make our own destiny. I want to find out what that is. I want to make history with you. The kind that, when we look back on it, matters to us alone."

"Thank you," Mal said again, softer this time. "Because back when you left me to be the next dragon-slayer, or whatever the hell you were after in Stormveil, it left a mark worse than my scar." Fingers trailed up Griff's chest as Mal continued. "I can find other treasures, but I could search the world over and never meet another you." He lowered his hand as it started to tremble, but Griff caught it in his own and curled his fingers around Mal's.

Mal leaned in and kissed him slowly, without teeth or anything to prove for once.

Griff rather liked the taste of it.

But while he would have been content to linger there a while, Mal still had more to say. "Speaking of which—from now on, your enemies will have me to answer to." He pressed a kiss to Griff's temple. "You won't have to fight if you don't want to, not while I'm around. But," he added, a hint of his usual scowl reappearing, "that doesn't mean I'm about to go making friends with any elves either, even if they do let me into their special city someday."

Griff drew Mal tighter against him, accepting it all gratefully as they stood together on this new side—their own.

"And while I'm no longer working for the Shadow Queen, I'm going to need to keep up all my other businesses," Mal warned lowly. "So if that bothers you, I'd rather know now." Before Griff could ask, he elaborated, ticking them off on his fingers. "The wolf business. The orchard business. The crystal business. Property acquisitions. Protection for other merchants. Whatever I come up with next—I'm thinking enchanted elixirs."

"I'll have dinner on the table and a fire going when you come home," Griff assured him through a tired grin, glad to see that trudging through the swamp hadn't dampened the ambition he had admired for so long. "Not having to worry whether you'll come home at all—that's the part I like, no matter what kind of business you call it."

"Okay," Mal agreed, tucking a dark curl behind Griff's ear ever so gently. "But if anything starts to bother you—I want you to tell me right away, even if it's hard. Give me a real chance not to lose you, to show you that you're enough just like this."

Griff leaned into that soft touch and nodded. "Understood. I don't want to lose you either." His hands made a suggestion then, guiding Mal toward his lap, pressing lightly against the other man's back to see if he was willing. "Are there any of *her* ghosts watching us right now? Any new shadows?" he couldn't help but ask before taking this any further.

"None."

Mal climbed onto Griff with seemingly little effort despite his still-healing side, settling in and sliding his palms along the span of Griff's back. They kissed for a while in the quiet, having a wordless conversation that gave Griff a great many answers until he was too tired to keep his eyes open any longer.

There in the dark with Mal, he was living, and it was everything. More than enough. Their own sort of light.

Chapter Thirty-Two

Prizes

In the morning, when Mal woke at sunup despite his exhaustion, he turned in Griff's arms to brush a soft kiss over the pale forehead of the man sleeping soundly beside him. Then he disentangled himself as gently and quietly as he could, wrapping his own cloak around Griff so that he might not notice his absence for a while yet.

As he prowled around the smoldering remains of the fireside in search of the silver flask he had discarded sometime last night before bed to prove a point, Alys's eyes fluttered open. She blinked a question at him, and when Mal put a finger to his lips, she nodded. One hand crept out of her bedroll to grip the cloth hilt of the broken sword—just in case any green-eyed ghosts were still lurking around and their queen got any funny ideas before they went to retrieve the treasure in an hour or two.

She kept up her silent guard as he tucked the flask into the inner pocket of his jerkin, close to his heart, beside Griff's letters. With a golden dawn threading streaks of light through his hopelessly knotted hair, he slipped away to the nearby creek.

Picking a flat rock just wide enough to perch on, Mal sat with his bare feet touching the water, mud squishing between his toes, just him and his shadow—no extra one to speak of anymore. No burning in the lines of ink feathering his forearm. No eerie singing, just the booming call of an ordinary bittern.

There wasn't even the flutter of a raven's wing in the branches above. At least, none that he could see, and hearing was beyond him at this point. It was time he faced it.

Past time he faced a lot of things he'd rather not.

His usual headache was pounding between his eyes, begging for him to take a sip from his flask or at least pour a generous splash into some tea and make himself a breakfast toddy. Out of habit, he unscrewed the cap. But remembering all the things he and Griff had agreed would be different from now on, he didn't take his usual first sip.

Instead, he turned the flask upside down and fed it to the creek as he stared at his reflection in the water's dark, slow-moving surface. The slightly crooked nose, the sneer that seemed permanently stuck some days, silver eyes narrowed in dislike or distrust.

He sat there until the sun began to warm him enough for him to lose his shirt, continuing to wear the same hard look as he studied himself in the water. Eventually, he threw a rock at his own face, shattering that reflection, and started to remember.

Dark holes. Lice. Living like a rat while he sucked the flesh from their bones. Dreams of running Thrallkeld himself going up in flames. The carving of his own flesh, the foreign sound of his screams echoing in his ears, the witch's small, strong hands pulling him out of the tent where they had planned to carry out his execution.

Oblivion. One, two, three failed attempts at breathing, three sharp presses of those hands against his chest, and finally, the gasp as air rushed back into his lungs and his heart shuddered back to life in time for him to catch an echo of a few whispered words, a magic older than that of most of the elves who now lived in their airy sanctuary, as the witch brought him back from death.

Salve packing his grisly wound as Tansy, the witch, fought the infection there. Knife flashing in the late afternoon sun, scraping down to his scalp as she cut off his long gold hair that was full of bugs and itching relentlessly until he hardly recognized himself—battered face, shaved head, nasty scar. For his own good. All for his own good.

He had walked the long road down to Thrallkeld alone. Challenged Renaud alone. Spent months healing in the witch's hut alone. Traveled back to Linden to reclaim what was left of his life alone.

Maybe Griff hadn't been there for him in Thrallkeld. No one had. But he had always been able to rely on himself. And he needed himself now more than ever, needed to choose himself again if he was going to keep choosing Griff too.

He didn't hear the flask as it splashed into the water like a leaping fish.

But it came right back up again. He had unthinkingly screwed the cap back on after draining it, and now it was too light for the dramatic drowning he had envisioned for his faithful companion. With a frustrated sigh, he stood and shed the rest of his clothes before diving into the creek. The cold sent a shiver rushing over his skin as he swam a few strokes out to where the flask now bobbed tauntingly, gleaming more gold than silver in the morning light. He tried to grab it, but it slipped right out of his bandaged hands a few times. He muttered curses at it until he grasped it again.

He didn't tip it to his tongue for a farewell taste. He unscrewed the cap and plunged it under the surface until there was nothing left to keep it afloat.

As bubbles rose and the flask grew heavy, he remembered some more.

Rhun, his stiff gait and his whispers, the odd times he would play music or help with dinner or take the boys on walks. The promises of safety and a love that would never leave—promises

Mal never trusted after that, because love of such a kind was something he could only give to himself.

Kage, cloaked and hooded as he stood outside Mal's window late one night, recruiting him into service at the not-really-a-tea-shop.

The nasty scar on Griff's stomach.

What didn't stay had never really belonged to him, he reflected as the flask finally dropped out of his hands and buried itself in the dark silt of the creek bottom, all his old hurts and mistakes swept over by the sea of memory.

Back on his rock, hunched over and hugging his knees, Mal thought about curses. Some were real, woven by magic. But he had only been cursing himself. Been doing it for years. His curse was little more than a feeling, one he'd conjured for himself while being haunted by too many wounds from the past.

Which made it his to break too.

It belonged at the bottom of the creek with the flask.

Rising up onto his knees, he drew his hunting knife and bent over the water.

And just as Tansy had once done for him, he cut his hair close to the scalp, hacking away until all his tangled problems and unbreakable knots were nothing more than a flurry of gold flakes on the creek's surface. He watched as the mess was swept along in the slow current, sometimes swirling in little eddies, while he felt the smooth, warm fuzz left on top of his head.

It wasn't as even as he'd hoped; it would grow back choppy and unruly. But his. And fresh. Plenty of room for new growth.

He stood, pulling on his pants and shirt, and headed back to camp, where the others were picking through their dwindling rations for a quick breakfast, ready to press on to the lake that was glimmering through the trees to the east.

Griff's eyes widened a touch as he took in Mal's new look, a smile breaking over his face a moment later as he declared, "Change looks good on you."

Mal, who hadn't needed anyone's approval of his new hair anyway, didn't realize he was smiling until after he had slipped comfortably into the spot made for him at Griff's side, leaning against the other man while he grabbed his share of jerky.

"Any tea left before we get going?" Mal asked hopefully, his expression catlike and contented as Griff rubbed his fingers over his fuzzy head.

The request wasn't so unusual as to raise any eyebrows.

But when the flask didn't emerge from Mal's inner pocket to pour a healthy serving into the mug he was handed, Griff's gaze lingered on him curiously.

"Alys," Mal said with some effort, "would you do me—*us*," he amended, thinking of how Griff never took him up on his offers to hit the flask and finally realizing what that must mean, "a favor, and go dump the rest of that bottle in the creek?" He pointed to the large amber bottle he had brought with them. "I'm done with all that. Who wants easy, anyway? Might as well dry out while we're hauling this treasure back and my side is all fucked up."

"Can I hug you?" Alys asked, her voice thick.

He nodded, and she threw her arms around him for a moment before heading off to dispose of the bottle. Muffin, tucked into the top of her shirt, gazed warily at Mal and then out at the wider world.

As the two men watched the proceedings, Griff drew Mal in against his side and said for the third time in nearly as many days, like a deluge of rain after a drought, "I'm so proud of you." But a line of worry creased his brow all the same as he added, "But you'll be more than thirsty soon. It's going to be hell. You're going to sweat out what feels like that whole bottle and then some. It'll feel like you have the bad fever all over again by tomorrow, and probably for a couple days after that, speaking from experience. It might mean an extra night or two of camping out here, so I hope that fits in your deadline."

Mal's eyes glinted with his usual determination as he stood and then helped Griff to his feet, keeping the other man's hand in his as he declared, "Well, let's go make the most of today, and whatever happens after that will be tomorrow's problem."

And with a sore side and curious green-eyed ghosts watching from between the trees, counting down his remaining time again, Mal did things the hard way and started sweating out the whiskey as they found an old rowboat at the lake's edge and cleared it for use.

The water was dark, flat, and still, no skeletal hands reaching up from the depths as they rowed out to the small island dotted with scrub and thorns and the long-neglected barrows of the ancients. Mal had insisted on the three of them going together, him and Alys paddling across with Griff sitting in the middle, which meant that ferrying each load of crusty old armor and gold and gem-studded weaponry took longer than it should have.

Yet no ghosts appeared to admonish him; those who watched from a distance as the trio rowed the last load to shore merely raised a filmy hand in acknowledgment, or bowed, or gave a nod. It seemed Mal was finally getting a little respect from his audience—that, or after killing the wraith, at least a silent truce from the Shadow Queen, since he had put her enemy to rest. He wondered if it would hold all the way home.

Feet firmly on solid ground again, Griff dug through the piles and pulled out the intricate silver vambraces of lore as Alys cheered. They toasted with cold tea while Griff fitted them on his forearms to heal his stab wound for good, though Prancer the mule didn't seem to feel much like celebrating with them this morning—no doubt realizing that most of this would be his burden to carry out of the Mire on top of the heavy silvers.

The part of Mal that loved shiny things hated knowing that none of this was his to keep as he started stuffing gold and dusty baubles into a mostly empty pack, but the gleam of the sun on Griff's borrowed bracers struck him with sudden inspiration. Pulling a few pieces of the treasure back out, he called Griff and Alys to his side.

As he held up a delicate silver crown and nestled it into Alys's hair, the serpent diadem at its center somehow untarnished, he told her, "Wear this until we're out of here. So you never forget who the fuck you are."

Next, he placed a crown of sculpted marigolds and lupines—clearly an elven design—gently onto Griff's dark curls, and couldn't help but think it seemed to have been made for him.

Last, he picked up a sturdier silver crown, its practical and proud design suggesting dwarven origins, and crowned himself too. "We've earned these, at least until it's time to hand them over," he declared with the authority of a king. "Like Wynnie always says, there are no prizes for suffering—only winning."

And something in his face must have shown just how much he enjoyed seeing Griff in that crown—and in those legendary vambraces, and the handsome silver breastplate he was going to have to wear because it wouldn't fit in any of Prancer's saddlebags—because the next thing he knew, the dark-haired man was leaning in for a slow kiss with plenty of tongue.

They'd fucking done it. They'd killed a wraith. They had the treasure. Making a life together now seemed easily within their reach too.

Still kissing Griff, Mal put an arm around Alys, pulling her into a tight hug at the same time. They couldn't have done this without her, mistakes and all. Noticing Mal's shift in posture, Griff slipped an arm around Alys's shoulders, and despite the many miles ahead on the road to home, they stayed just like that for a few minutes. Crowned in their victory. Together.

What did Mal really know about curses?

He was more fortunate than most. In fact, he had everything; a sister who always stuck by him and his hero, his knight, ready to stay through the battle ahead.

†

All day they followed the creek's meander back into a darker, denser area of the Mire where poisonous flowers gave off the sweetest perfumes.

By the time they reached a slope with an adequate break in the trees, a wildflower-dotted embankment colored with splashes of fireweed and a running bramble of what looked like ordinary blackberries, a faint layer of sweat coated Mal's face. He was finally starting to feel the way the hours without a drink stretched on.

Still, for now it was nothing he couldn't ignore as Griff settled in the dry grass and rolled up his pant leg so that Mal could have a turn as healer, replacing his bandages again.

"You might as well look at my shoulder, too, while you're at it," Griff said, signing with his hand as he spoke and bringing a pleased grin back to Mal's face despite his fatigue. It was a shame the elven bracers only worked on magical poisons and not on mauling wounds. "Two-for-one special, right?"

"Prizes, remember . . ." Mal murmured into the curve of his ear. A promise for later, when he had shaken off the worst of the withdrawals and they could put on those crowns again to properly enjoy them. Costumes really did something for him. For now, he glanced at Alys tending the mule and the turtle and waved her over.

"Ready to be home?" Griff asked Alys as she settled in beside him, Muffin poking his head out from her cupped hands.

"I'm ready to see Rodric and Mags and Derry," she answered after some thought. There was something raw in her voice, an uncertain note that had replaced her usual airy detachment. "But . . . beyond that, I don't know yet. I know I don't want to be the Warg of the West anymore. She's officially retiring."

"No more sword practice?" Mal asked, surprised, because while the Warg of the West wasn't really her, neither was putting her blade down for good.

"Oh, I wouldn't go that far," Alys assured him, her blue eyes clear and present as they met his. "Griff still needs someone to show him a few things, and who better than me? But I've decided I want to move out of the cottage, me and the kids. Out of Wynnie's shadow. If being out here has shown me one thing besides a lot of undead, it's that I've got to learn to do things my own way—and accept a little help when I need it. And then, maybe . . . well, I like drawing and painting a lot. I like that perhaps more than anything. I think I'm good—"

"You're amazing, Alys," Mal interrupted before she could even finish. "Always have been. Nobody else can draw like you, and you always get the little details just right."

Her cheeks flushed scarlet.

"He's right," Griff added confidently. "I've seen the elven painters at work, and some of your landscapes rival theirs. You should start charging for your art."

His words brought even more heat to her face. Her lips parted as if to acknowledge the compliment, but no sound came out for a moment. "All right," she agreed at last, still pink. "I bet I could do some portraits to start. And as for the rest . . . I suppose I've got my whole life ahead of me to figure out what I'm going to make of myself. At least now my feet are on the path."

She stood again as they prepared to trek on, running a hand down her braid. And for the first time since they'd set off from Linden, she seemed to stretch up toward the sun like a flower finally unburdened of rain.

"Who knows?" she continued, blue eyes full of the afternoon sky, not gazing toward any far-off horizon or castles in the clouds today but at her oldest friends. "Maybe one day I'll be the kind of friend you both deserve, the much-less-selfish kind. Maybe I'll even become the knight Rhun never had the chance to be for me—the one I needed."

Mal's throat tightened, but he still managed to say, "That's your best idea yet."

Maybe Alys was in for some prizes of her own. But as for the ones he had promised Griff, he realized they would have to wait even longer as his body began to turn on him throughout the rest of the evening.

Through sheer stubbornness and knowledge of his looming deadline—just under a week remaining to make it all the way home—he managed to travel through most of the next day before finally surrendering to the vomiting and shakes, at which point they made camp on the driest ground they could find.

Griff put Mal up on his bedroll, which smelled far more pleasant than the one on which he had sweated out his last fever. Then the foreman went off in search of a deep pool where he could wash Mal's old bedding while Alys stayed to mop his flushed, sweaty face.

Later, they traded places, and it was Griff who held out Muffin's cookpot for him each time a little bile threatened to come up. Putting a clammy hand over Griff's, he confessed, "I think . . . we'll be here a little while, like you warned me. You rest that leg, I'll sweat out my weight in whiskey, and there's a chance we can still make it back just in time. Then we'll have our victory dance."

That must have been a pretty good prize, because Griff finally cracked a smile.

And though the next day was spent mostly tossing and turning and accidentally hurting his still-healing side as he waited for the worst of the withdrawals to release their grip on him; though he knew little but Griff's cool hands on his forehead and the water dripped carefully into his mouth whenever it got too dry; by the second day, when he finally kept down a few pieces of damn good egg someone had found somewhere, Mal still believed what he had told Griff that first day: Victory would soon be theirs.

Mostly because Griff had stayed with him through it all. The sweating, the vomiting, the surly and sullen moods that had gripped Mal unexpectedly.

Griff was so getting a horse when they got back. The biggest, friendliest horse Mal could afford with their restamped silvers.

Despite the necessity of immediately resuming their travels while he was still weak, as night dropped its shadowed cloak over them and he began to feel more like himself at last, Alys announced with more cheer than she had shown since setting foot in the Mire, "I'm going to go give Prancer and Muffin a bath now, so they're not filthy when we get back. No sense making extra work for Vic." As she added the broken sword to her belt, her gaze roamed over her friends as she smiled, and Mal understood—no words needed.

She would be a while.

Mal turned to Griff as the foreman banked up the fire and noticed for the first time that he was once again wearing kohl around his eyes, which somehow made them an even richer shade of emerald and added an illusion of length to his already-long lashes.

"It's a good night to wear that crown again," Mal suggested, unable to keep a bit of breathiness from his voice. It had been several days since their last time together, and Mal was more than ready for any excuse to dress up and then take Griff's shirt off.

"Probably one of our last chances," Griff agreed, biting his lip as Mal nestled the carved metal flowers into his hair and began undoing the buttons of his wrinkled black shirt.

As he worked, he said playfully, "You know, I'm sick of this fucking Mire. Even though we'll be out of here soon . . . tonight,

I was thinking we could visit our old tree house." Scooting closer, he pressed himself slowly against Griff's thigh, evidence of just how much he liked seeing Griff properly adorned with the finest things. "Remember, the one we built together, where you kept your practice sword?"

He slipped a hand into Griff's back pocket while his other pressed right up against the front of him, a combination that had Griff staring at Mal like he was the one who had hung all the stars above them. "And while we're there, I might steal all the silvers out of your pocket before you even know what's happened."

The hand that had briefly sought to provide some friction for Griff now dipped down into his front pocket, Mal's fingers reaching as deep as the fabric allowed and grabbing far more than a handful of coins in his search of the premises.

"Oh, you bad fucking bandit," Griff managed to groan as Mal started handling and stroking the riches he had found.

"You'd better chase me up to the top of the ladder, then, before I get away with all your money," Mal teased, breath gusting over Griff's neck before he started kissing the place where his good shoulder and his neck joined, noting the way the graze of his teeth made Griff leak a little in his pants.

Grabbing Griff's belt loops from the back, he started to pull the other man closer as their eyes finally met again and he ran his other hand up into Griff's hair, displacing the crown slightly and already past caring.

"I'll have to be careful on the third step," Griff panted, his eyes glowing brighter than the fireflies that had emerged in the humid night around them. "You know how it shakes. And I don't suppose my flimsy sword is going to be enough to barter to spare my life—but perhaps . . ."

He paused, sliding his way down between Mal's legs and starting to undo the fastenings of his pants in the way only Griff could—with just his teeth—starting to undo Mal in the process too. "I could be of some other use to you?" Griff continued finally, a grin crossing his face just before he ran his tongue slowly along the underside of him. "Perhaps if I please you well enough, you'll let me stay here in your bandit's lair?"

It took a moment for Mal's muffled hearing to make sense of what had just passed by his ears, but when he did, he laughed, as this was both somehow expected and utterly surprising. Soon after, the flash of a firefly illuminated Griff's knowing smile as Mal gasped and arched his back, offering himself more freely to Griff's skilled mouth.

"That's right, um, you know your options," Mal managed to say as Griff worked his mouth around the dripping tip of him and reached out to add a hand into the mix. His breath hitched again as Griff did something wonderful with his tongue, something that made Mal whine in the back of his throat. "Go on, then. Prove your worth."

Of course, Mal didn't leave Griff to question his fate as a victim of a ruthless bandit for long with the way he snared his fingers in Griff's curls and panted, "Oh, you're so fucking good at that." And rather than pushing himself forward to take more of what was being offered, he leaned back on his elbows to watch and enjoy the show as Griff demonstrated just what sort of performance was worth his life.

He even unbuttoned his shirt to give Griff a little show of his own, grinning down at the dark-haired man's eagerness until the heat rising between his legs became so much that he could focus on nothing else.

Then he reached out to lay a hand on Griff's good shoulder as the other man sucked him down, a dragon holding tightly to the biggest thief's ransom of all, the only prize he cared about bringing home from the Mire or anywhere. As soon as he came, he was going to give to Griff until he redefined the word *generous* altogether.

Much later, as the clouds over the moon broke apart and he was resting his head in a spot on Griff's chest he'd never realized until now was made just for him—like a cave on a map whose entrance is revealed only in moonlight—he said softly, "I've been thinking . . . would you like to call me your boyfriend from now on?"

Griff's breath caught, and after a moment, he said, "Of course. I'd love that."

Reaching up to run his fingers through Griff's hair, Mal decided, "I'd like you to call me that too. Of course, you'll always be Griff to me at the end of the day. Like all the black: That's you. Hot breakfast and eyeliner and songs: That's you. Mine: That's you too."

"What about marriage being a scam and titles being for the insecure?" Griff asked in a voice of awe and gentle teasing, one hand poised near their faces to help convey his meaning with sign language rather than raising his voice.

Mal's eyes crinkled at the corners. "Guess I was waiting for the right person to commit to. *Boyfriend* has a certain ring to it, after all."

"You already know I would have stayed without it," Griff assured him.

Mal's only answer was to use the hand behind Griff's head to draw him closer and kiss him breathless, even though they had already done plenty of that tonight. Even though the road to home promised much more of the same for one dragon and his knight.

And when, much later still, Griff woke him from a dead sleep, shaking and slick with tears and sweat after one of his nightmares, Mal roused himself enough to murmur, "Oh darling, you're all wet." And he wrapped himself around Griff, holding him even after the shaking had stopped, his shield against the dark.

Chapter Thirty-Three

Business as Usual

Late one summer afternoon, three road-weary figures in want of a real bath and a mule in want of some new handlers rounded a bend in the wide dirt path that cut through Linden, coming within sight of a particular slightly crooked cottage—its roof in need of patching—and its sprawling garden—in need of some thoughtful weeding—in time to catch a show from the setting sun, yellow orange as the egg yolks they had enjoyed for breakfast thanks to Mal helping himself to someone's coop.

After all, what didn't stay had never really belonged to them in the first place.

Just like the treasure he had delivered to his former employers before daybreak on the last day of his deadline while his sleep-deprived companions hid around the corner outside, weary from the breakneck journey home. Kage's grin was sharper and toothier than Mal's own as he inventoried the spoils in the cellar—down to the gleaming silver vambraces and the crown of lupines and marigolds.

Mal sure was going to miss the crowns, but he wouldn't miss smelling the inside of Served With Love or working for his enemies. And he wouldn't miss worrying about someone plotting another attack on Griff. On his sweet boyfriend with the kohl-lined green eyes that haunted him in the best way.

He wiped sweat from his brow with the back of his sleeve, grateful for his choppy new haircut as Griff glanced over at him from atop the mule, that black scarf still tied around his neck despite the rising warmth of the day.

This was it. Just like he had promised, Griff had come home with him.

From the porch, a very old gray-brown dog who might have once had some red in his fur cracked open a lazy eye to watch their approach and bellowed a greeting, long and low.

Before they could close the remaining distance, the door burst open.

Out ran a girl of about four in a pink summer dress, gold hair falling into her dark eyes, dirty bare feet slapping the worn boards. Mags, his niece. She put a hand on Whiskey's back—the dog was now standing, with some effort—and then bared her teeth in a wide wargish smile, growling louder than the hound as she raced down the steps. She leaped neatly over the darting shape of a white cat that yowled at her as her foot grazed its tail, finally reaching the bottom and turning to call back into the house, "They're home!"

This brought the sound of a window creaking open—not from the cottage itself but rather from the house across the lane. The people who lived there had always been curious about the goings-on at Wynnie's cottage. The kind of curious that meant they frequently called Liam to come change their locks.

Mal would make sure they used a different locksmith from now on.

After a quick dinner, Alys tucked her kids into bed while Vic did the dishes. In their absence, Wynnie had left for Thrallkeld on Mal's errand of revenge—a birthday present was how she'd described it to Vic—so she wasn't around to hear the impressive tale of how he had left the Shadow Queen's service just as she once did. With the rest of the cottage suitably occupied for the evening, Mal helped Griff to his feet and led him to his old room, to his narrow bed. The same one he'd had since childhood.

"I already have the best pillows in Mayfair, and now they're yours too," he boasted, warm and familiar, hoping to put Griff at ease after so long away from this place.

"I'm all for a good pillow, but I don't think we need the biggest bed this side of the mountains when I'd rather be right next to you anyway," Griff observed slyly, sounding plenty comfortable already as Mal's hand worked at undoing all his buttons. "This one is plenty cozy. Structurally sound too," he teased, rapping on the underside of the bed frame, "if you want my professional opinion."

"A free consultation from Mister Foreman? Must be my lucky day." Mal chuckled as he popped open the last of Griff's buttons and pulled his pants off, tossing them into a far corner of the room where a pile of laundry from the Mire waited to be tackled by some enterprising soul that wasn't him.

Tracing his fingers lightly over Mal's bare shoulder, Griff asked, "Can you still see that stupid griffin statue from your room? You know the one."

Mal cracked a sharp-toothed grin. "Sure can. Still close enough to piss on, if you're motivated enough. I never did like that thing."

Griff seemed to know a dare when he heard one, a good sign for their future.

Laughing at their own juvenile plan, they let the blankets fall away and climbed to their knees, which gave them just enough height to gaze fully out the window that overlooked the scraggly weeds and grasses of the backyard, currently blanketed in velvety night.

Taking himself in hand, Griff aimed at the stone head, whose perked ears were just visible peeking through a tangle of small yellow flowers.

But he'd barely started trying when Mal slipped a hand around him from behind too, guiding his stream closer to the griffin's head until he found his mark, fingers teasing all the while. "Remember," Mal whispered against his neck, his breath hot and eager as he ran his thumb along Griff's slit, "Rewards are for winners."

And his boyfriend certainly seemed to feel like a winner as Mal began to stroke him to full hardness. They fell back into the blankets together as Mal kissed him, running a hand through his hair just the way he liked and praising, "You got that old thing so good."

With that, he reached under the bed for the vial of oil he'd stashed there earlier when putting their packs in the room. Then Griff rolled on top of him and kissed him, pulling a pillow over their heads to blot out the starry night and everything but the sounds of their breathing and the scent of each other so close in the dark.

"These *are* the best pillows, you're right," Griff said—far too loud to be romantic, and probably entertaining any curious ears within these thin walls, but sparing Mal from having to strain to hear as he kissed the other man's throat and ground their hips together. "But we'll both sleep better if we test the structural integrity of this bed with two, just to be safe."

Mal groaned as Griff reached down between them to palm his hardening groin, but kept something of his usual boastful air as he reminded him, "You should know by now that I give the biggest tips."

It's possible Griff thought he meant the slick fingers that stroked their way gently between his cheeks and spent longer than usual preparing him, pushing past that ring of muscle with tender focus again and again until Griff begged for something bigger.

But later, when the whole bed was knocking rhythmically into the wall in time with Mal's thrusts as he buried himself balls deep in Griff—apparently, doing such a good job that Griff was unabashedly drooling onto one of the best pillows in Mayfair—he tossed something into the air seconds before his own climax.

The silvers from the Mire.

They glittered in the air for a moment before raining down all around them amid groans and curses and laughter.

There was no need for blankets after that, with flushed skin kept warm by the tangle of their limbs.

Brushing a few coins off the bed, Griff leaned in to kiss the scar over Mal's heart. It gave a strong kick in answer.

"You're so good at . . . everything," Mal murmured as he lazily trailed his fingers down Griff's stomach until they came to rest between his legs, cupping him with a gentle familiarity. "I love you. And I love this too."

"You're going to get me going again," Griff warned with an ambitious smile of his own. But after all they had demanded of their bodies over the past few days, it was apparently a dare for later.

"Welcome home, Griff," Mal whispered as his eyelids grew heavy.

And he was pretty sure he heard Griff answer loud and sure as he drifted off, "Been there for a while now. No more bad dreams."

The weeks of a long, golden summer tumbled one into another like frogs hopping along the banks of the creek, becoming a sweltering blur of days spent working or tadpole catching with Alys's children and firefly-bright nights with Griff where they made plenty of their own heat, the kind a window flung fully open couldn't even touch.

True to his word, Mal continued with his other businesses as usual, though now sans any late nights at the tea shop—only the occasional overlong call at the widow's place. Griff was on leave from his construction job yet again as he rested his leg and shoulder and picked at his surviving lute, sometimes doing odd repairs around the cottage that Wynnie and Vic had neglected. The lute wasn't even that annoying. At least, not in Griff's hands. Sometimes Mal even sang along despite his own dubious ability to carry a tune, forgetting himself and remembering how to have fun. He was still more talented than those damned Yule carolers who dared climb the cottage porch each winter anyway.

As Alys started restamping their silver coins to look like the crescent-marked half-dollars that circulated in Mayfair, Mal set aside some of his hard-earned pay from each job. He told Griff that the money would be going toward the new, bigger bed he wanted (they were, in fairness, putting the old one through its paces)—that is, until he came home early one day, holding the reins of a handsome black horse for Griff.

He still reached for the flask on occasion, only to find his inner pocket full of little notes from Griff instead, which he now collected like the treasures they were. Griff left them everywhere for him to find, since his world had gone so quiet with the loss of his hearing. He'd spot them slipped under a plate of egg-in-a-hole at breakfast; in the mirror; under his pillow; curled into a boot. Some were silly drawings of things that had happened recently, like the mule kissing Mal on the mouth, while others were words of encouragement and love, or even stories of things that had happened in their long years apart.

They still had plenty of catching up to do.

And they did. Over breakfast in bed on the weekends, when they would crack open his dwarvish book of philosophy and pick a page to discuss for hours as they nibbled their bacon and toast and sipped the flavorful tea that Griff made to help with Mal's occasional cravings for something stronger.

It was helpful enough that he stayed sober, and so did Griff along with him.

Griff held him through plenty of those cravings, just like Mal held him through his nightmares, though they seemed far less frequent by the time summer was nearing its end.

By then, Griff was even helping Mal with his wolf business, such as it was, howling outside the homes of various marks to convince them that they needed Mal's hunting services in order to keep their livestock safe. Griff seemed to take particular pleasure in spooking Leo Raintree this way to pay him back for years of childhood transgressions. While perhaps his howls weren't very realistic, the moonlight threading through his hair—grown longer and lovelier as summer had passed—combined with the kohl around his luminous eyes, made him look like some kind of mysterious, otherworldly creature at times as he'd turn, breathless, to look at Mal before darting off into the cover of the trees.

Mal didn't mind that he had to work harder than ever in the absence of his paychecks from the tea shop. What mattered was that they had made it back alive from the Mire, all of them. All his treasures and loves were right where he wanted them, safe at home to admire.

And then one day, when the air turned crisp again, Mal came home to smoke rising from the cottage chimney and the familiar rhythmic sound of a splitting maul echoing from the backyard. From the kitchen window, a glass of water in hand, he watched as Griff swung that maul, as wood fell off the stump, never having imagined he would see this particular figure performing this chore in this very spot again outside of his wildest dreams.

Just like that, he was the wealthiest man this side of the Teeth.

He drank the water in a long, slow gulp, watching for quite some time—long enough that Mags, who was playing nearby, came over and started chatting at him. Long enough for her to grow frustrated when she realized he wasn't listening at all and demand to be picked up.

From the circle of his arms, she watched with him for a while, sometimes looking at Griff doing yard work and sometimes simply studying her uncle's oddly relaxed face as if she had never seen him smile quite so gently.

But then Vic threw a towel at Griff and told him to wash up at the creek, and Mags poked Mal in the cheek extra hard just to see what would happen. At the same time, the two new sort-of-dogs Mal had brought home from a dodgy connection earlier that week—long-nosed, pointy-eared, whip-thin beasts with sleek coats and nubby wings that allowed their feet to skim above the ground in pursuit of prey, no ordinary rabbit hounds as advertised—decided to chase each other through the house, knocking over swords and boots and a coatrack, and it was back to business as usual.

Chapter Thirty-Four
Good Castles

When the leaves on the trees began to turn and the village ran with color like the time Mags upended one of Alys's paint palettes onto the worn floorboards, Griff and Mal stole away from the cottage and headed to the Wyrmwood for a week.

It was strange for Griff to consider how much had happened since they had come home. Alys and her children had moved into a small house in Linden not far from Liam's, bought with some of their silvers. Dove was in and out of town, keeping a close eye on the tea shop and Wills from Griff's construction crew—that traitor—among other things, like who was running a counterfeiting scam in Mayfair. And who had murdered three travelers and stolen their mule somewhere east of Mayfair, leaving only their disoriented cook to tell the tale about a couple of masked madmen in red and black scarves.

Griff himself was finally back at work, back to swinging his maul and putting up new homes and businesses around Mayfair with his crew (even Wills, still alive but subdued after his encounter with Wynnie, from whom he now kept a wary distance despite his efforts to make it seem like nothing had changed. Mal thought it was safest this way). The numbness in his shoulder hadn't gone away, which meant the damage there was likely permanent. But at least he didn't have random pains from his stab wound anymore.

Business as usual.

What wasn't usual was the scuffle Mal had gotten into with Liam, right in the middle of the main thoroughfare through Linden; Mal claimed Liam started it, and Liam didn't exactly deny it, or say anything about it at all to Griff. Mal had ended up with yet another broken nose, while Liam had taken a dagger to the leg and was now as hobbled as Griff had been after an arrow to the leg. Alys and Dove had both witnessed the whole ordeal and nearly gotten into a scrap themselves, which was all anyone in town was talking about as Griff and Mal packed their bags and headed on their getaway to hunt coneys in the Wood like old times.

The swelling in Mal's nose had finally returned to normal, although there was a touch of darkness to one eye where Liam had landed a blow, and some cuts on his face still healing that Griff would put salve on when they decided to camp later that night.

"Wynnie should be back by the time we get home," Mal panted to Griff as he staggered through shafts of sunlight beaming through the trees on a crisp but golden afternoon, the bulk of their old dog Whiskey slung across his shoulders.

Nothing was wrong with the dog, technically, but his joints were stiff and creaky and he liked to be carried like a princess sometimes.

Griff slipped up beside Mal to take a turn carrying the old boy, calling to the other two not-quite-dogs who were bounding just out of sight, leaves crunching under their enormous paws: "Rooster! Wally! Not too far now!" Then he turned to Mal, pulling Whiskey up onto his own shoulders as he thought about Wynnie.

Thrallkeld was just over a week's ride away on a fast horse. Not distant enough to explain the time this errand was taking her, even if Renaud was as dangerous as Mal said and making a move on him would have required some months of careful observation. "And if she's not?" he asked, louder than usual, since he didn't have a hand free to sign.

Mal leaned against a tree for a moment, catching his breath and sipping some of the tea Griff had made from his canteen. "Then we'll go after her," he said without hesitation. "Because she's Wynnie."

Just then, the younger dogs decided to circle back and see what was keeping their humans.

Calling them dogs was, perhaps, a generous term, but it had been generous of Mal to try to buy them in the first place, and Griff knew what they were meant to be. The excitable, stubby-winged, knockoff rabbit hounds were huge, and more like cats than dogs in that they didn't seem to particularly heed either Griff or Mal or care about pleasing them in the slightest.

At least they seemed to enjoy catching coneys.

And eating Mal's belt.

They were, like Griff and Mal, a work in progress.

By the time the two men were covered in sweat and practically swimming in their clothes anyway, Griff called a halt to the hunting for the day with five plump rabbits to fix for supper, a feast for themselves and the dogs. They made camp near a pond where they could bathe and then see to the cooking.

As the pups splashed and Whiskey took a nap while pretending to guard their packs, having thoroughly overexerted himself while being carried all day, Griff pulled out a couple of small wooden sailboats he'd made and they raced them across the cool, dark water.

Mal won, of course, because Mal always cheated at boats, but Griff pulled the thief's body fully against his own in the chill and kissed him until he was sure he was winning too.

And when Griff swept Mal off his feet and carried him back to camp, there was no protest at all from the younger man at such treatment. Only laughter, arms thrown carelessly around Griff's neck, and hands tangled in his long hair, Mal's body relaxing as Griff carried the weight of him.

As the light began to rapidly fade, Griff banked up a fire, and all three dogs gathered to watch as Mal sliced up the meat and Griff got it roasting over the flames. While they waited for it to cook, Mal leaned back against him, dagger still in hand, and showed Griff how he could balance the point of it perfectly on the tip of his index finger.

"Show-off," Griff growled against his ear.

Mal's lips parted as he made a telltale noise in answer, and then he smiled. And did the trick again.

Despite the cooler air, a few fireflies appeared in the dimness, diving and doing tricks of their own as the men ate, talking about their week and the dogs' antics, and then set up their tent. Given the deepening chill of the nights lately, it would help to have the weatherproofed, oil-slicked canvas blocking out the cold.

After supper, Griff made hot herbal tea, and they lingered at the fireside for a while with Whiskey and the two near-pups, one of which had gotten ahold of a pair of pants stuffed in the top of a pack and was shredding them without a hint of shame.

The men joked and laughed and howled at the moon, the dogs joining in like a pack of wild things, until something in the distance howled back. Coyote, probably. Though Griff's maul was within reach, just in case.

"Seems like our new pups could be good for business," Griff teased, though his mind was elsewhere. He was thinking of the way the murky water of the Mire seemed to sparkle whenever Mal smiled or laughed, and wishing he had bottled some.

"Business? What's that again?" Mal breathed as he adjusted the black scarf around Griff's neck, using it to tug him toward the inviting warmth of their tent at last. "The moon is out, we're the only two for miles around, and all I can think of are all the things I want to do with you tonight."

If there was one thing Griff had learned since setting out for the Mire, it was how to listen to Mal like Mal was learning to listen to him—his words and looks and silences, like the way he held Griff's eyes as Griff went to light the candle in the glass jar they used as a lantern.

Abandoning the task, he gathered Mal into his arms instead, knowing what Mal was going to say before he even said it, because he had read it so plainly on his face and in the light pressure of the fingers stroking along his cheek.

"Griff, will you . . . fuck me tonight?" Mal asked softly, eyes on his prize. "I'm ready. I want you to have me, any way you want."

The words themselves didn't have to be delicate to carry so much more than their simplest meaning. Mal was holding open a heavy door just for him, no knives or armor to defend this most vulnerable of positions. Offering himself almost like a proposal, or as close as someone who despised the institution of marriage was likely to get.

For Mal, this was everything, given freely to the one he trusted most.

Griff pulled him closer, and as he pressed his lips to the other man's in answer, he was suddenly sixteen again and in a too-small sweater. But instead of crying over the emptiness, he reveled in how the sweater was hugging him back tight.

Mal's hand slid into Griff's hair.

Now Griff was nineteen again, and instead of drinking himself to death to conjure visions of Mal to his cold, empty room in Stormveil, he was saddling up a horse to go after the Mal he already had. One who was brash and flawed and perfectly meant for him.

He was here in the Wyrmwood, and maybe he couldn't undo those old mistakes, as Mal had said with surety many times—but he wasn't who he used to be, and neither was Mal. They were two saplings still growing, but now growing together, limbs stretching toward each other like they were the sun.

He tugged Mal into his lap with care, smiling at the changes in the other man's breathing as he slid his hands under Mal's shirt and started to kiss his neck with growing enthusiasm for what was to come.

Mal tipped Griff's face back up toward his own, and his answering kiss was deep and inviting in so many new ways. An open door. And a warm hearth beyond it, one where the fire had never fully died, and now was blazing brightly.

Griff had built many walls, put up solid doors and roofs, learned how to make a place safe and sound far more effectively than he had ever learned how to cure a fever; he had been building things for so many years now that he was practically an expert. But with Mal's eyes gazing into his, he somehow found he was just as adept at kicking open doors to invite Mal all the way in, as safe with this man he chose as he had ever been on his own. More than ready to let that solid roof and those sturdy walls shelter two against the shadows as capably as one. In his professional opinion, with the foundation they had here, they were well on their way to building a good castle already—even if the Widow Isabel's land wasn't theirs yet.

He kissed Mal until their lips were swollen and they were both breathless, teasing Mal's tongue with his own to remind him of all the things his mouth could do, running his hands over the short, rough ends of Mal's hair to show him the kind of care he could expect all night.

Pants joined shirts in the tent corner, along with a belt that Griff didn't really care if the dogs ate or not. Inside the close, hot world of their tent, there was no armor, no knives, no treasure. It was clear as Mal climbed into Griff's lap that what he was offering, for once, wasn't his skills or a lie but simply himself. Nothing mattered to Griff but the man in his arms. He had never known a love like this before, one he wouldn't run from but toward, for the rest of his days. After so many long and bitter years away, he was home.

And they stayed the rest of the night in each other's arms.

And the night after that. And again.

Because it was real.

Acknowledgments

These characters have been part of my life for a very long time. This means there are quite a few people I'd like to recognize who played a role in shaping this book's narrative or simply guiding me somewhere along the way—be it only as a side quest or be it in following me all the way from a safe and cozy home to this journey's end.

To my editor, Melissa Rechter, I have to say again: Thank you for seeing me as much as you see Griff, Mal, and Alys. Thank you for all the love and creativity you've poured into this world and its characters; there's no going back, you're now part of Wynnie's family and in on all the jokes too. Thank you for tirelessly slogging into the Mire with us, even knowing it was going to be messy every time. I'm glad you're on my side.

Katelyn Detweiler, I quite literally couldn't have done this without you. Thank you for loving me and these rogues through so many drafts, so many dreams and almosts and triumphs. Your endless kindness and patience will never cease to amaze me. You're a true advocate and I'm lucky to know you as an agent, fellow mom, and friend. Excited for so many more adventures together!

I am so grateful to every member of the Alcove team who had a hand in shaping this book, be it through design, production, or getting the word out: my deepest thanks to Rebecca Nelson, Eve Keith-Henningsen, Thai Fantauzzi Pérez, Dulce Botello, Mikaela Bender, Bethany Pullen, Lexi Baker, Julia Abbott, Megan Matti, and Stephanie Manova.

Olivia Hintz, thank you for giving me the book cover of my dreams! I'm honored to have your beautiful work be the first thing people associate with me and the story of my heart, and I'll remember the thought and care that went into this stunning piece every time I look at it.

Jemma at The Little Wilderness, thank you for bringing the rogues' world to life with a breathtaking map that has more detail than my brain or hands could possibly conjure! You must be magic, which means you'll fit right into Mayfair—you're a part of this now too, and I am so glad to have gotten to know you throughout this process.

So many artists have lent their unique and incredible talents to illustrations of Griff, Mal, Alys, and the friends, foes, and beasties that make up their world. All my love and gratitude to Rayne (RayneCreates), Jacque (JacqueIllustrates), Hannah (hannahelatham), Han (Hansoeii), Rez (4Resna), Allie (Allieeecakes), Powder (Powder_Cat14), Kat (Calicoture), Rosario (musetheart), MisterSealy, Chase (Chaseru), Koti (KotiKomori), Alice Blake, and Nikolai Espera (nikespera)—for your enthusiasm, kindness, and vision. Also, many thanks to Kat from Sanctum Flames (SanctumFlames) for making beautiful scents inspired by this world. I've included these amazing creators' social media handles where possible so that you can look them up and commission them yourselves or just admire their other work!

My dear friends, whether you've been along for the adventure for years or joined somewhere along the winding path, I'm so proud to have you all in my fellowship. For all the laughs and rants and late-night memes we've shared along the way, my gratitude is endless. You know what "because it was real" means to me on some level, because you really get me: Sparks, Lenore, KT, Gwen, Amber, Jen, Erin, Allie, Deathwitch, Fiona, Fox, Ellie, Tegan, Evan, Christina, Jordan, Tiffany, Hanna and Kuzco, Sierra, Lindsey and, of course, my extended family at CACGA pottery. Then there's the one and only Dee—my bestie on the other side of the world—and Kira; I'm so thankful to have gotten to know you both over the past few years, even if my Russian needs so much work still.

All my love and thanks to my friends at the Get Shit Done Club for keeping me on track and inspiring me; the 2026 Debut Discord for all the advice, commiseration, and encouragement; and my local foodie friends for giving me fun dinner breaks to look forward to! Shout-out to Emma (TheStarlitNook and The Indie Project) and to the incredible Lydia (books.before.bed), who really care about helping authors as well as about building a book community! Thank you to Jake Honor for your friendship and a great assist. Thank you to my street team for sticking by me and my questionable movie night choices—love to Laurel, Alex, Shannon, Ari, Ash, Nicole, Ally, Rachel, Meg, Jordy, Abby, Tonya, Arty, Jenna, Madison, Andrew S.M., Hannah, Brittany, and more not mentioned here!

Then there's the one and only Seán Astin, John-Rhys Davies, and Farris Gerard. It's one thing to admire your heroes from a distance, quite another to meet them. And, yet another still to get to know them on some level and, after having supported them since you were a child, receive support from them in return (my mom approves, by the way). I will forever be your biggest fan.

And, of course, my family. Chris, just like steadfast Sam Gamgee, you've been there from the start (and, let's be real, to always carry my heavy shit without complaint). So, I'd say we made this climb together. Dawn, I hope that seeing me live out this dream inspires you to reach for all of yours. I'll lift you as high as I can, always.

As for my readers, thank you so much for being here. Thank you for taking this journey with me. It's such an intimate thing to connect through art and stories that move us in some way. And if "because it was real" made you feel anything, hit me up and let's chat. Wherever you are on your own adventures, whether you're snuggled up at home or ankle-deep in mire muck and mosquitos, you matter to me. Remember, survival is resistance too, even if we sometimes have to live in the dark. Love you.

Want more from Sarah Glenn Marsh?
Enjoy a novella set in the world of Rogues.